"Why don't you and I sit down and get to know each other before I get Tommy?" Daisy suggested.

She said it in a way that set off a whole lot of wicked images Walker was sure she hadn't intended.

"Ms. Spencer, as much as I would love to get to know you better," he said, giving her a thorough once-over that brought a blush to her peaches-and-cream complexion, "I'm here to meet my nephew. You and I can go a few rounds another time. Which way's the kitchen? Through here?"

He was already heading in that direction when she caught up with him, snagging his arm with a surprisingly firm grip. He glanced down at the pale fingers with their neat, unpolished nails against his thick, tanned forearm and felt an unexpected slam of desire. He swallowed hard and stepped away, but without making any further move toward the kitchen.

"Detective, perhaps you can bully suspects in Washington, but around here, we have ways of conducting ourselves that meet a higher standard."

Walker stared down into those flashing eyes, admiring again that startling shade of amethyst and the fringe of dark lashes. A man could forget himself and his intentions pondering the mysteries of eyes like that....

"With skillful dialog and great situations, this is a joy."
                    —*Romantic Times* on *Angel Mine*

Dear Reader,

I hope you enjoy your first visit to Trinity Harbor and the chance to get to know the Spencers. Any time I get an opportunity to write about the part of Virginia where I spent so many happy childhood summers, it feels like going home to those lazy, sultry days again.

As for Daisy, Bobby, Tucker and, of course, King, there is nothing I love more as an author than writing about families and about small towns. I think in this day and age, when so many of us have scattered around the country far from our own families, books about families and tightly knit towns remind us of the way things used to be. They give us a sense of the kind of connectedness we long for.

I hope you will come to think of the Spencers and all the residents of Trinity Harbor as family and that you'll find that Anna-Louise provides a moral compass in today's increasingly complex world.

After you've read Daisy's story, I hope you'll watch for Bobby's story in *Ask Anyone*, scheduled for release in March 2002. I can guarantee that there's an incredible woman waiting in the wings to spice up his life and that there will be yet another test of wills between him and his father over just about everything. Just thinking about it puts a smile on my face.

Until then, all good wishes,

Sherryl Woods

Sherryl Woods

About that Man

MIRA

ISBN 1-55166-815-7

ABOUT THAT MAN

Copyright © 2001 by Sherryl Woods.

All rights reserved. Except for use in any review, the reproduction or utilization of this work in whole or in part in any form by any electronic, mechanical or other means, now known or hereafter invented, including xerography, photocopying and recording, or in any information storage or retrieval system, is forbidden without the written permission of the publisher, MIRA Books, 225 Duncan Mill Road, Don Mills, Ontario, Canada M3B 3K9.

All characters in this book have no existence outside the imagination of the author and have no relation whatsoever to anyone bearing the same name or names. They are not even distantly inspired by any individual known or unknown to the author, and all incidents are pure invention.

MIRA and the Star Colophon are trademarks used under license and registered in Australia, New Zealand, Philippines, United States Patent and Trademark Office and in other countries.

Visit us at www.mirabooks.com

Printed in U.S.A.

For Relda and Kyle,
with thanks for all the boating background,
and for the friends—old and new—in the "real"
Trinity Harbor (aka Colonial Beach, Virginia).
You all keep me inspired.

Prologue

The whole town of Trinity Harbor—probably the whole state of Virginia—was buzzing like a swarm of bees, and whose fault was it? His daughter's. Robert King Spencer slammed down the phone for what had to be the fifteenth time that morning and rued the day he'd ever bred such an ungrateful lot of kids.

Daisy, of all people, his beautiful, headstrong, but previously sensible thirty-year-old daughter, was stirring up gossip like a rebellious teenager. It was exasperating. No, King thought, it went beyond that. It was humiliating.

He had half a mind to go charging over to her place and put a stop to things before she tarnished the Spencer name with her shenanigans, but he'd learned his lesson on that score. A father interfered in his children's lives at his own peril. Better to handle things from the sidelines, subtly.

King could all but hear the laughter of his family and friends at that. It was true, subtlety wasn't exactly his style. Never had been, but for once he could see the value in using other people to do his dirty work. His sons, for instance.

Tucker and Bobby ought to be able to straighten out this mess. Tucker was the sheriff, for goodness' sakes.

Maybe he could wave that badge of his around and get Daisy to see reason.

King sighed. Not likely. Tucker took his duties seriously. He wasn't likely to use his office to carry out his daddy's personal wishes. And Bobby...well, Bobby was an enigma to him. No telling what he would do—probably the exact opposite of what King wanted.

That was the way it had been lately. Not one of his children paid a bit of attention to him, or to their Southern heritage. What kind of respect could a man expect in his golden years if his own children went around stirring up the kind of trouble Daisy had gotten herself into?

Respect was important to a man. King had always liked being a mover and shaker in Trinity Harbor. He figured he deserved it, since his very own ancestors had wandered over from Jamestown to start the town. That pretty much gave him the right to have his say about everything that went on, from raising Black Angus cattle or growing soybeans to politics. Most people actually listened. Being a Spencer in this town still meant something. Or it had until a few hours ago.

Nope, it was clear that Daisy didn't give two hoots for tradition or bloodlines or any of the other things that made the South great. She was just hell-bent on getting her own way, no matter what it did to her daddy, her brothers or the family reputation.

It was her mother's fault, of course. Mary Margaret—God rest her soul—was the one with the modern ideas. Let her shoulder the blame for Daisy's behavior, even if she had been dead for twenty years. She should have done something—though he couldn't say what—before she went and abandoned them all.

Since Mary Margaret wasn't around to fix things,

though, it was up to King to save Daisy from herself. He prided himself on being clever when clever was called for, and today certainly seemed to be one of those days. He had the headache to prove it.

1

Daisy Spencer had always wanted children. She just hadn't expected to wind up stealing one.

Okay, that was a slight exaggeration. She hadn't exactly stolen Tommy Flanagan. The way she saw it, nobody wanted the boy. His father was long gone and his pitiful, frail mother had had the misfortune to die in the recent flu epidemic. The story was the talk of Trinity Harbor and had been for weeks now.

While they searched for relatives, Social Services had placed Tommy with three different foster families in as many weeks, but Tommy wouldn't stay put. He was scared and angry and about as receptive to love as that vicious old rooster Daisy's father insisted on keeping over at Cedar Hill.

Despite all that, Daisy's heart just about broke when she thought of all the pain that ten-year-old had gone through. She figured she had more than enough love to spare for the little boy who'd been one of her brightest Sunday school students, a boy who was suddenly all alone in the world, a boy who'd lost his faith in God on the day his mother died.

Daisy's own faith had been tested half a dozen years ago when she'd been told she would never have children of her own. The news had almost destroyed her.

It *had* destroyed her relationship with Billy Inscoe, the only man she'd ever loved.

All Daisy had cared about was having children she could shower with love. Adoption would have suited her just fine.

But Billy hadn't been able to see beyond the fact that his fiancée was barren. Billy had wanted sons and daughters of his own. He'd wanted his blood running through their veins, proof of his manhood running through the streets. He'd wanted to start a dynasty as proud as the Spencers'. When Daisy couldn't give him that, he'd taken back his ring and gone looking for someone who could.

With the exception of Daisy's minister, nobody knew the truth about what had happened between her and Billy. Daisy kept quiet because she'd been so humiliated by the discovery that she wasn't woman enough to give Billy what he thought he needed from a wife. Billy had been discreet for his own reasons.

Her own father thought the broken engagement was the result of some whim on her part, as if she'd turned her back on marriage because she thought someone better might be waiting around the next corner. He couldn't conceive of the possibility that his handpicked choice for her had been the one to walk out, and Daisy had let him have his illusions.

And so, until this morning Daisy had pretty much considered her dream of a family dead and buried, right along with every bit of respect and love she'd ever felt for Billy Inscoe.

The last few years she'd thrown herself into her job teaching history at the local high school. She was advisor for the yearbook, the drama club and the 4-H. She taught Sunday school classes. She took her friends' children fishing on the banks of the Potomac River and on outings to Stratford Hall, the birthplace of Robert E. Lee, or Wakefield, the birthplace of George Washington, both of which were nearby. She gardened, nurturing flowers and vegetables the way she'd always wanted to nurture her own babies.

Heaven help her, she'd even brought home a cat for company, though the independent Molly spent precious little time with her mistress unless she was hungry. And as if to mock Daisy, she'd just had her second litter of kittens.

In another era, Daisy would have been labeled a boring spinster, even though she'd barely turned thirty. Frankly, there were times when that was exactly what she felt like: a dull, dried-up old lady. The role she'd always envisioned herself playing—wife and mother—seemed totally beyond her grasp. She was on the verge of resigning herself to living on the fringes of other people's lives, to being Aunt Daisy once her brothers married and had families of their own.

Today, though, everything had changed. Early this morning she'd gone to the garage and found Tommy, cold and shivering in the spring chill. He'd been wearing a pair of filthy jeans, a sweater that had been claimed from the church thrift shop even though it was two sizes too big and a pair of sneakers that were clearly too small for his growing feet. His blond hair was matted beneath a Baltimore Orioles baseball cap, and his freckles seemed to stand out even more than usual against his pale complexion.

Despite the sorry state he was in, the boy had been scared and defiant and distrustful. But eventually she'd been able to talk him into coming inside, where she'd fixed him a breakfast of eggs, bacon, hash browns, grits and toast. He'd devoured it all as if he were half-starved, all the while watching her warily. Only in the last few minutes had Tommy slowed down. He was pushing the last of his eggs around on his plate as if fearful of what might happen once he was done.

Studying him, for the first time in years Daisy felt a stirring of excitement. Her prayers had been answered. She felt alive, as if she finally had a mission. Mothering this boy was something she'd been meant to do. And she intended to cling to that sensation with everything in her. Even Molly seemed to agree. She'd been purring and rubbing against Tommy since he'd arrived.

"I ain't going to another foster home," Tommy declared, allowing his fork to clatter against his plate in emphasis.

"Okay."

He regarded her suspiciously. "You ain't gonna make me?"

"No."

"How come?"

"Because I intend to let you stay right here, at least until things settle down." Even as she said the words, she realized she'd made the decision the minute she'd seen him.

His gaze narrowed. "Settle down how?"

Daisy wasn't sure of that herself. Her heart had opened up the instant she discovered Tommy in her garage, but she was smart enough to know that she couldn't just decide to keep him. Frances Jackson over at Social Services was looking for relatives, and there were probably a thousand other legalities to consider. All Daisy knew was that if she had anything at all to say about it, this boy had run away for the last time. Maybe for once, being a Spencer would be a blessing.

People might like to gossip about the family, but they tended to bow to their wishes.

"You'll just have to trust me," she said eventually.

He scowled at that. "Don't know why I should."

She hid a grin, wondering what made her think this smart-mouthed kid was a gift from above.

She gave him a stern look. "Because I have been your Sunday school teacher since you were a toddler, Tommy Flanagan, and I don't lie."

"Never said you did," he mumbled. "Just don't know why I should think you're any different than all those other people who promised I'd get to stay, then kicked me out."

"Nobody kicked you out. You keep running away," she reminded him. "Isn't that right?"

He shrugged off the distinction. "I suppose."

"Why did you do that?"

"They just took me in because they had to. I know when I'm not wanted. I just made it easy for 'em."

"Okay, then, for however long it takes to find your family—or forever, if it comes to that—you are going to have a home right here with me. And I'm going to see to it that you don't have any reason to want to run away. Don't take that to mean I'm going to be a push-over, though."

She said it emphatically and without the slightest hesitation. Her gaze locked with his. "Do we have an understanding?"

"I guess," he said, apparently satisfied for the moment that she meant what she said.

Relief washed through her. This was going to work out. She could feel it. Daisy didn't even consider the fact that she'd caught him trying to hot-wire her car as a bad omen. Hopefully Tommy wouldn't mention that little detail to anyone. She certainly didn't intend to.

She did worry ever so slightly about the repercussions once word got back to her father, but she was convinced she could handle that, too. She just hoped it would take the grapevine a little longer than usual to reach Cedar Hill. King wasn't as easily won over as a scared kid.

In the meantime, she knew she did have to call Frances Jackson. Frances took her job at Social Services very seriously. Tommy's disappearances were wearing on her nerves. Daisy reached for the portable phone.

"Who're you calling?" Tommy demanded, scowling.

"Mrs. Jackson. She needs to know that you're with me and that you're okay."

"Don't see why." He gave her a pleading look. "Couldn't we just keep this between us? You tell her, and the next thing we know she'll have the sheriff over here hauling my butt away."

"The sheriff won't lay a hand on you," Daisy reassured him fiercely, but she put the phone back on the table.

"How come?"

"Because the sheriff is my brother and he'll do what I tell him to do." At least she hoped he would.

Tommy still looked skeptical. "Have you got something on him?"

Daisy chuckled. "Not the way you mean. Just leave handling Tucker to me. It won't be a problem. Besides, when you go back to school on Monday, people are going to want to know where you're staying. We might as well be up-front about it."

"I thought maybe I wouldn't go back," he said, looking hopeful. "It's almost summer, anyway."

"Not a chance," Daisy said firmly. "Education is too important—you can't take it lightly. And there are weeks to go before summer, not days. You will go to school and that's that. Now go on upstairs, Tommy, take a bath and then get a little rest. I'm sure you didn't sleep much last night. There are clean towels in the closet, and you can have the guest room at the end of the hall. If you need anything, just ask. We'll talk some more later."

Tommy nodded and started out of the kitchen, then paused. "How come you're being so nice to me?"

For an instant he allowed her to see the vulnerable, lost little boy behind the defiant facade. "Because you're worth being nice to, Tommy Flanagan," she told him.

He seemed a bit startled by that, but he gave a little bob of his head and took off, thundering up the stairs, Molly trailing after him.

"And because I need you as much as you need me," she whispered when he was out of earshot.

Once again she reached for the phone and made the call to Frances.

"Oh, Daisy," the social worker murmured when she'd heard what Daisy had to say. "Are you sure you want to do this? Tommy's a real troublemaker. Not that it's not understandable, given what he's been through, but he needs a firm hand."

"He needs love," Daisy retorted. "And I intend to see that he gets it."

"But—"

"Is there some reason I'm not a fit foster mother for him?" Daisy demanded.

"Of course not," Frances said, as if the very idea that someone would consider a Spencer unfit was ludicrous.

"Then that's that. Tommy stays here."

"Until I find a relative," the social worker reminded her.

"Or not," Daisy said. "You'll take care of the paperwork, then?"

Frances sighed. "I will. I'll drop it by later for you to sign, though I can't imagine what King is going to say when he hears about this."

"Then you be real sure not to tell him," Daisy retorted. "Or I'll make him think this was all your idea."

Frances was still sputtering over the threat when Daisy hung up. A little grin of satisfaction spread across her face. It was about time she gave the residents of Trinity Harbor something to talk about besides her long-ago broken engagement and her pecan pie.

"Sis, you are out of your ever-loving mind," her brother Tucker, the local sheriff, told Daisy when he arrived within an hour of her conversation with Frances.

Obviously the instant he'd heard what she was up to—probably straight from the social worker—Tucker had hightailed it over to lecture her as if she were sixteen instead of thirty. Hands on hips, he was scowling at her as if she'd committed some sort of crime, instead of simply seizing the opportunity that had been presented to her.

"That boy's going to land in juvenile detention," he declared in his best doom-and-gloom tone. "You mark my words. Doc's caught him stealing comic books. He broke Mrs. Thomas's window. And he rode his bike through Mr. Lindsey's bean patch and mowed down most of his plants. Something tells me that's just the things we know about. There could be more. He's headed for trouble, Daisy.''

Daisy stared right straight back into Tucker's eyes, ignored his stony expression, and countered, ''Well, of course he is…unless someone steps in and does something.''

''And that has to be you?''

''Do you see anybody else who's willing?'' she demanded. ''He's already run through half the foster families in the area. As for those pranks of his, you and Bobby did worse and nobody did more than call Daddy to complain.''

''That was different.''

''How?''

Tucker squirmed uneasily. ''It just was, that's all.'' He tried another tack. ''When Dad hears about this, he is going to go ballistic.''

She shrugged off her brother's assessment as if it was of no consequence. ''Dad is always going ballistic about one thing or another. Usually it's you or Bobby who gets him all worked up. It's about time I took a turn. Being King Spencer's dutiful daughter is starting to wear thin.''

''You'll get your heart broken,'' Tucker predicted, his expression worried. ''You can't just take in some stray kid and decide to keep him. That's no way to get what you want, Sis.''

Her big brother knew better than anyone how desperately she wanted a family. He had been the one to console her when Billy had walked out, leaving her convinced she would never marry. Even without knowing anything more than the fact that Billy was the one to break the engagement, Tucker had wanted to throttle the man. Daisy had persuaded him not to, assuring him that Billy Inscoe wasn't worth another second of their time, much less the risk of an assault charge that could ruin Tucker's career in law enforcement.

"Sooner or later, they'll find Tommy's family," Tucker warned, regarding her protectively.

"I don't know what makes you so certain of that," she said. "There's been no sign of anyone so far, and you know how dogged Frances is when she's working a case."

"That's exactly what makes me believe she'll eventually get results. When she does, you'll have to let him go."

"And until then, he'll have me," she insisted stubbornly, not wanting to consider what she would do when that day came.

"Where is he now?" Tucker asked.

"Upstairs."

"Cleaning out your jewelry box, no doubt."

She scowled. "Sleeping," she contradicted.

"Wanna bet? If I prove otherwise, will you forget about this?"

Without responding one way or the other, Daisy marched to the stairs, then waved Tucker up ahead of her. "See for yourself, smarty-pants."

Unfortunately, just as they reached the top of the stairs, Tommy bolted out of her bedroom, pockets bulging, Molly trailing along behind him in a way she never did with Daisy. Tucker snagged Tommy by the scruff of the neck but kept his gaze on her. He plucked a favorite antique necklace out of the boy's pocket and dangled it in front of her. Great-grandmother's diamonds sparkled mockingly.

"I rest my case," he said.

Daisy refused to let her brother see that she was even remotely shaken by the discovery. "Tommy," she said sternly, "you know perfectly well that doesn't belong to you."

"No, ma'am," he said, his expression defiant. "But I was taking it anyway."

Avoiding a lecture on the Golden Rule and the Ten Commandments, all of which they had studied thoroughly in Sunday school, she instead asked, "Why?"

"To buy me some food."

Molly meowed plaintively, as if to lend her support to Tommy.

"There's plenty of food downstairs in the kitchen, if you're hungry," Daisy said.

"That's now. Sooner or later you'll send me packing. I need to have the money for backup supplies. I figured I could pawn this stuff over in Colonial Beach or maybe even down in Richmond. Then I could head someplace brand-new where nobody would be on my case all the time or tell me how sorry they are that my mom is dead."

She brushed aside Tucker's restraining hands and rested her own against the boy's cheek. "We've been over this. I will not send you packing," she said very firmly. "However, nor will I tolerate you stealing from me. You're grounded until we can discuss this further. Go to your room."

She wasn't sure who was most surprised by her pronouncement, Tommy or her brother. But Tucker had known her longer. He heaved a resigned sigh and stared at Tommy. "I'd get a move on, if I were you, son. My sister generally means what she says. Take it from someone who knows, don't mess with her."

Relief washed over Tommy's face, though he was quick to duck his head to hide it. He started to scoot down the hall, but Tucker halted him with a sharp command.

"Aren't you forgetting something, son?"

Tommy's gaze rose to clash with his. "What?"

"Empty those pockets."

Tommy dug his hands into his pockets with obvious reluctance, producing more of her jewelry. Most of the rest had more sentimental than monetary value, but its glitter clearly had appealed to Tommy.

Tucker took the baubles and handed them to Daisy. "Costume jewelry or not, I'd get this stuff into your safety deposit box if you ever expect to wear it again."

Daisy met Tommy's gaze. "I don't think that will be necessary, do you, Tommy?"

He looked for a moment as if he might make some sort of defiant retort, but Daisy's gaze never wavered, and he finally wilted under the stern scrutiny. "No, ma'am."

When he had gone, the cat on his heels, she turned a smile on her brother. "Satisfied?"

"Far from it, but I can see you're not going to listen to a word I say."

She patted his cheek. "Smart man. And don't try sending Dad over here to raise the roof, either."

"I won't have to send him. Once he hears about this, you'll have to bar the door to keep him out."

"Well, he can rant and rave all he wants, but it won't work. For once in my life I am going to do exactly what I want to do, what I know is right."

Not that her declaration would stop her father from trying to interfere when he finally found out what she was up to. Despite the precautions she'd taken by warning Frances off, Daisy predicted it wouldn't take long.

Trinity Harbor was a small town. Cedar Hill, the Spencer family home for generations, was the biggest Black Angus cattle operation in the entire Northern Neck of Virginia. Her neighbors would probably fight for the chance to be the first to tell Robert ''King'' Spencer that his sensible spinster daughter had just taken in a stray troublemaker.

The story would be even juicier if anyone found out Tommy had already tried to steal her jewelry and her car. She was pretty sure she could keep a lid on the attempted car theft, but Tucker might not be so discreet about the jewelry. In fact, since that necklace had been in her father's family for generations, he might feel obliged to tell their father that it had come very close to heading for a pawnshop.

And then, she concluded with a resigned sigh, this little squabble with Tucker was going to seem like a romp in the park.

2

Washington, D.C., detective Walker Ames had just finished investigating his fifth drive-by shooting in a month. This had been worse than most—a five-year-old girl who'd done nothing more than sit on her front stoop playing with her doll on a pleasant spring evening. She'd caught a stray bullet meant for a gang member who'd been walking past her run-down apartment building in southeast Washington. The intended victim hadn't even stopped to see if he could help.

This kind of incident was not the reason Walker had become a policeman. He'd wanted to make a difference in people's lives, not just clean up after the tragedies. Innocent babies dying, grandmothers shot without a second glance, kids on school buses killed over a pair of sneakers...there was something seriously wrong with the world when a cop had to spend his days working crimes like that. His stomach churned with acid just thinking about it.

He'd been at it for fifteen frustrating years now, and not a day went by anymore when he didn't wish he'd chosen another profession. Unfortunately, law enforcement was the only one he cared about, and he happened to be good at it. His arrest-conviction ratio was the best in the department, because he refused to give up until he had the right suspect in custody. Few of his cases were ever relegated to some cold case file left for others to solve years from now.

"You get a line on those punks that did it?" his boss asked when he spotted Walker crossing the squad room and heading straight for the industrial strength coffee.

"Half a dozen people on the street at the time of the incident," Walker told Andy Thorensen, the caring, compassionate chief of detectives who'd also been his best friend since he'd joined the department. Andy was fifteen years older and going gray, but pushing papers hadn't dimmed his street smarts or his indignation over crime.

"Four people claim they never saw a thing," Walker added as he poured a cup of coffee and took a sip. "The two who admit they did aren't talking. The girl's mother is too upset to question. I'll go back when things have settled down and try again. Maybe when it sinks in that it was a five-year-old who got caught in the cross fire, their vision will improve."

His boss gestured toward his office, then waited till Walker was seated before asking, "What about the guy the bullet was meant for?"

"Vanished. He has to live in the neighborhood, though. We'll find him. I'm not letting go of this one, Andy." He rubbed a hand over his eyes, battling exhaustion and the sting of tears. He tried not to let these things get to him, but that was impossible. He had kids of his own, boys he thought about every single time he had to handle a case like this. He might not be raising them since his divorce, but they were never far from his thoughts.

To buy himself a minute, he gazed out the window and finished his coffee, then said, "You should have seen the kid, Andy. She was just a baby, still clutching her doll. Somebody's going down for this, if I have to drag every gang member in D.C. in here for questioning."

Andy Thorensen nodded, his expression sympathetic. "Stay objective. That's one of the first things they teach you in the police academy. I'd like to see one of those classroom cops stay objective when they find a kid's blood splattered all over the sidewalk in front of her own house. It never gets any easier, does it?"

"I don't think it's supposed to," Walker said. "If we get used to it, we're as bad as they are."

"Let me know if you need any help. We're short-staffed, but I'll see what I can do to free up some additional units," Andy promised. "There's going to be a hue and cry all over town until we close this one."

Walker didn't care about the headlines or the calls from the mayor's office. He'd stay on it because that little girl deserved justice. He didn't envy Andy's need to balance justice with politics. He just respected his friend's ability to take the heat while letting his men do the job they were paid to do.

"I'll try not to leave you on the hot seat too long," he promised.

"You can't know how much I appreciate that," Andy said wryly. "By the way, before I forget, you had a call earlier, some woman by the name of Jackson. When she heard you were out, she demanded to speak to me." He grinned. "Tough lady. Seems to have something on her mind."

Walker shook his head. "Don't know her."

Andy fished the message out of a pile of papers on

his desk. "Says she's with Social Services down in Trinity Harbor, Virginia."

"Never heard of it."

"I've been there. It's a great little town on the Potomac a couple of hours from here. The sweetest crabs you'll ever taste. Victorian houses. A bunch of little froufrou shops. You know, the kind women love. Antiques, crafts, all that artsy crap. Gail was in heaven. She wants me to buy a place down there so we can spend weekends and summers away from D.C. Says she could support us by opening a shop of her own." He sighed. "To tell you the truth, after a day like today, it's beginning to sound real good to me."

"You'd be bored to tears in a week," Walker predicted.

Andy grinned. "Maybe less, but I'm willing to give it a try. Give the woman a call. She said it was important."

"Whatever," Walker said, tucking the message into his pocket. Strangers took a back seat to the immediacy of this investigation.

Two hours later, the message was still in his pocket, untouched, when the phone on his desk rang.

"Ames."

"Walker Ames?" an unfamiliar voice asked.

"That's me."

"This is Frances Jackson. I left you a message several hours ago," she said, a note of censure in her voice.

Andy might have found her tough attitude amusing, but prissy women like this always got Walker's back up. "So you did," he agreed, tilting his chair back on two legs as he prepared to enjoy himself a little. On a day like this, any amusement, however slight, was welcome.

"Then you did get the message?" she asked.

"I did."

"I believe I mentioned it was important. Didn't your boss explain that?"

"He did."

"Then why haven't you returned the call?" she asked impatiently.

"I've had some important things of my own to deal with."

"Such as?"

"A dead five-year-old, shot right through the chest."

Her dismayed gasp gave him a certain measure of satisfaction. "Okay, then," he said, ready to end his little diversion and get back to work. He wanted to hit the streets again before dark. It was destined to be another fourteen-hour day. "You've got me now. What's on your mind?"

"Are you related to Elizabeth Jean Flanagan?"

Oh, hell, he thought, as the front legs of the chair hit the floor with a thud. What had Beth gone and done now? His baby sister had always been troubled. She had taken off at sixteen with a worthless piece of trash named Ryan Flanagan, who'd eventually gotten around to marrying her, gotten her pregnant two years later, then dumped her on a highway somewhere outside of Vegas when he concluded the responsibility for a kid was more than he'd bargained for.

That was the last Walker had heard from her, ten, maybe twelve years ago. She'd called him in tears, saying she couldn't live without that jerk. Walker had badly wanted to tell her she was better off without him, but he'd managed to keep his opinion to himself.

Instead, he had overnighted her some money for a ticket back to D.C., but she'd never shown up. Nor had she ever called again. He'd tried every way he knew how to trace her, but if she was working, it was for cash. There wasn't a Social Security number in the system, probably thanks to the gypsy lifestyle she'd led with Flanagan. The man had thought the government was evil and that the less it knew about him, the better. Some of that must have rubbed off on Beth. She didn't own a car and hadn't registered for a driver's license. There was no trail of credit card debt he could follow. He'd been stymied. He didn't even know if she'd had the baby or gotten an abortion the way she'd been talking about doing.

"Detective Ames?"

The woman's testy voice snapped him back to the present. "What about my sister?"

"Then she *is* your sister?"

"You wouldn't be calling unless you knew that," he said tightly.

"Not with certainty," she said. "I discovered the names of Beth's parents through her birth certificate. Then I ran into a dead end finding them."

"They died several years ago."

"That explains it, then. At any rate, I checked at the hospital where Beth was born and discovered that an older brother had been born to the same parents, one Walker David Ames."

"Maybe you should be the detective, Ms. Jackson."

"I'm just persistent," she said. "Besides, once I finally had your name, you were much easier to locate."

No one went to that much trouble without a really good reason. Walker was beginning to get the uneasy sense that he should have taken a page out of Flanagan's book and maintained a lower profile.

"And now you've found me," he congratulated her. "Why?"

"When was the last time you heard from your sister?"

"Years ago."

"Are you her closest relative?"

"Yes. Why?"

"I'm sorry," she said, sounding suddenly sympathetic. "I really am."

"Sorry about what? What the hell is going on?"

"Your sister is dead."

Once the blunt words were spoken, he realized he should have expected it. He'd been on the other end of enough calls like this to know exactly how they went, but Beth? Dead? It just didn't compute. For all of her reckless ways, he couldn't imagine her dead. She'd been beautiful and full of life before she'd gotten mixed up with Flanagan.

"How?" he asked in a choked voice, fearing the worst. In his line of work, homicide and drug overdoses came to mind quicker than anything else.

"She caught the flu a few weeks ago. She didn't get to a hospital until it was too late. It turned into pneumonia, and the antibiotics didn't work. There was nothing else the doctors could do. We've been trying to locate her family ever since." She paused, then corrected herself. "I mean the rest of her family."

The implications of her remark made his blood run cold. "Don't tell me she was still with that scum Flanagan."

"No, he died before she ever came to Trinity Harbor. A motorcycle crash, I believe. But there is the boy. Her son. Your *nephew*," she stressed in a way that suggested she had specific expectations.

"What are you telling me, Ms. Jackson?"

"I think you'd better come to Trinity Harbor, Detective. You and I need to talk."

"About what?" he asked, though he already knew the answer.

"There's a little boy here who is desperately in need of a family. Unless there's someone you haven't mentioned, it appears you're all he's got."

Walker's heart thudded dully as he considered that. If it was true—and there was little question that it was—then the kid was in one sorry mess. According to his ex-wife, he was a lousy father and a worse husband. He had no reason to dispute her. He was a workaholic, always had been. His family had taken a back seat. He regretted it now, but he doubted if he could do things any differently.

"Ms. Jackson, there must be—"

"What? Another solution? Do you have one in mind?"

Walker's spirits sank. He was it. Heaven help the kid. "I'll be there," he said without enthusiasm.

"When?"

"When I can get there, Ms. Jackson. I'm in the middle of a homicide investigation."

"And given the state of things in Washington, I'm sure there will be another one after that and one after that," she said, her tone wry. "Meantime, your nephew needs you now."

Walker sighed at the accuracy of her assessment. "I hear you. I'm off on Thursday. Is that soon enough to suit you?"

"I imagine it will have to be, Detective Ames."

"Damn straight," Walker muttered in one last display of defiance as he hung up.

Why did he have this sinking sensation in the pit of his stomach that solving a few homicides was going to be a piece of cake compared to the turn his life was about to take?

Daisy had fully expected to be confronted by her father before that first day was out, but when that day passed and the one after without a visit, she thought maybe he was going to keep his nose out of her plan to keep Tommy. Not for a single minute did she believe he might not know what was going on.

Not only did her father stay away, so did everyone else, aside from Tucker, who'd been poking his nose in on a regular basis, most likely to count the silver behind her back.

At any rate, after the better part of a week she was beginning to believe that everything was going to work out just as she'd intended. Tommy was settling in. He was back in school and behaving himself, according to his teacher. He was still eating her out of house and home, but she assumed that was to be expected from a growing boy who'd gotten it into his head that his next meal might be in doubt. Daisy hadn't cooked so much in years. Nor had she ever enjoyed it more.

Even now, the kitchen was filled with the scent of chocolate chip cookies baking. Tommy had already grabbed a handful and headed outside, swearing that his homework was done as he grabbed his cap and let the screen door slam behind him. Molly meowed indignantly at the disruptive sound, but Daisy just smiled. One of these days she'd get around to breaking him of the habit, but for now she liked the way he was filling her too-quiet house with noise.

When the doorbell rang, she froze. For a second, she consoled herself with the fact that her brothers or her father would have knocked once and walked right in. So would most of the neighbors, for that matter. Unfortunately, that left one possibility, and it wasn't a good one. The chiming of the bell meant someone was paying a formal visit and that usually meant trouble.

"Please don't let it be Frances," she whispered with a quick heavenward glance. She didn't want anything to rock this new life she was creating for herself and Tommy.

Wiping her hands on her apron, she took her time going to the door. When she found her minister, Anna-Louise Walton, on her doorstep, a welcoming smile spread across her face. The redheaded pastor had already made a huge difference in town with her blunt talk and warm compassion. Daisy had liked her from the instant they'd met. She also liked her husband, a former foreign correspondent who had taken over the town's weekly newspaper. With his liberal editorials, Richard had already become a thorn in King's side, which had endeared him even further to Daisy.

Now, however, when Anna-Louise returned her smile with a somber look, the likely implication of this unexpected visit sank in. Apparently King, who'd been among those on the committee to select a new pastor, was even sneakier than Daisy had imagined. He'd evidently sent Anna-Louise to do his dirty work for him. No doubt his backing of a woman for the job made him feel entitled to use Anna-Louise as his personal representative in what should have been a family matter.

"Here on a mission?" she inquired tartly as she and Anna-Louise settled at the kitchen table with a pot of tea and a plate of the freshly baked chocolate chip cookies still warm from the oven.

"Why would you think that?" Anna-Louise asked, her expression suddenly as innocent as a lamb's.

"Am I wrong? Are you just here to pay a call on one of your flock?"

"Absolutely," Anna-Louise said.

"A preacher shouldn't fib."

A grin spread across the other woman's face. "Okay, I did get a call from your father a few days ago. He seemed to think you required counsel."

"I imagine what he said was that I needed to have my head examined."

Anna-Louise chuckled. "Words to that effect."

"And you agree with him?"

"Actually, I'm on your side on this one," Anna-Louise said. "Which is why I didn't rush right over. Naturally I neglected to mention my opinion to your father. No point in making his blood pressure shoot up any higher. Richard's last editorial about the need for a riverfront development plan has already sent it into dangerous territory. King spent an hour after church last Sunday trying to convince me that I needed to look closer to home when it came to saving souls. He apparently feels Richard's is in danger."

"You're right. He wouldn't have appreciated your opinion a bit, if it disagreed with his own," Daisy told her. "You can see that I had no choice, can't you? Tommy needs to have someone in his life that he can count on."

"No question about that."

"And I can give him a good home."

"Of course you can," Anna-Louise agreed.

Daisy's gaze narrowed at all the ready agreement. Despite what she'd said, Anna-Louise wouldn't be here now if Daisy's actions had her full blessing. "But?"

"What happens to you when he leaves?" Anna-Louise asked, her expression filled with genuine concern.

"Who says he's going to? His mother is dead. So is his father. None of the foster families worked out. Where would he go?"

"Frances found his uncle today," the minister said quietly.

Daisy felt a cry of dismay sneaking up the back of her throat, but she managed to keep it from escaping. She forced a smile. "That's wonderful! Is he coming here?"

"Next Thursday."

"Has he agreed to take Tommy?"

"Not exactly."

Relief flooded through her. She was willing to seize any reprieve, however temporary. "Well, then, we'll just have to wait and see what happens, won't we?"

Anna-Louise put her hand on Daisy's. "I know how much you love children. That was evident to me from the minute I got here. And you've told me about the doctor's opinion that you'll never have children of your own. You're the best Sunday school teacher we have, as well as the best history teacher at the high school. The kids adore you. You'd be a terrific mother to Tommy, and you deserve this, Daisy, you really do, but it might not work out. I just want you to be prepared to let go."

"God would not bring Tommy into my life and then snatch him away," Daisy countered.

"We don't always know or understand what He plans for us," the minister reminded her. "We just have to accept that He has our best interests at heart."

How could losing Tommy be in her best interests? Daisy felt the sting of unshed tears at the back of her eyes. "What do you know about this uncle? He and Tommy's mother can't have been close. He didn't come for the funeral."

"He's a cop in D.C. Beyond that, I don't know much. Frances was fairly stingy with what she considers to be confidential information. She just wanted me to prepare you."

"Is he married?"

"I don't think so."

"Then why would he be any better suited to care for Tommy than I am?"

"It isn't a matter of 'better.' It's a question of family. He and Tommy are related."

Daisy wanted to argue that a loving stranger might be better for Tommy than a bad relative, but until she met this man and knew the whole story, she had no cause to stand in judgment of him. Anna-Louise was likely to tell her she didn't have the right even then. Judgment was God's business.

And so it was, Daisy thought. But just in case He had other things on His mind besides Tommy Flanagan, she intended to look this uncle over very carefully before she relinquished Tommy to his care.

3

Driving into Trinity Harbor, Walker shuddered. It was exactly the way his boss had described it. Quaint. Picturesque. Charming. Slightly faded, like a fancy dress left hanging in the closet too long, but with a hint of past glories. Lawns were well-tended. There were churches every few blocks, some of them clearly quite old. And every now and again there was a glimpse of the Potomac, shimmering in the bright sunlight.

He hated places like this. Give him a little grit and grime any day. Give him bustling sidewalks and clogged highways. Give him skyscrapers and run-down neighborhoods. He knew the rules of survival in a city like D.C. He liked the anonymity. He didn't know beans about getting along in a town where everybody knew your name and your business.

He followed the directions Frances Jackson had given him, drove on through the town of Trinity Harbor, then past open farmland just sprouting green, through the county seat in Montross until he came to what looked more like a remodeled school building than a government agency. The discreet sign on the front door proved otherwise. Westmoreland County Social Services, the sign stated in neat letters.

Once he'd turned off the engine, he sat perfectly still, unsure whether he could go through with this. It wasn't just the thought of having Beth's death confirmed in black and white in the form of a death certificate. It was all the rest—his nephew, the expectations, and the regrets that he hadn't found his sister before any of this had happened.

Because of all that, Walker had taken his own sweet time leaving home this morning. He'd stopped by the station, had a chat with Andy, looked through some paperwork, then, finally, when he could delay no longer, he'd hit the road. He'd managed to delay his arrival till midafternoon—much later, no doubt, than the imperious Mrs. Jackson had been expecting him. He braced himself for her displeasure along with everything else, took a deep breath and headed for the door.

Inside, he discovered that Frances Jackson was nothing at all like some of the social workers he'd come across in D.C., dedicated, but wearied by their caseloads. Nor did she fit the image he'd conjured up on the phone—a starchy woman, mid-fifties with a perpetually down-turned mouth. No, indeed, Frances Jackson was nothing like that.

Sixty if she was a day, she had unrepentantly white hair, round cheeks and rounder hips, and eyes that twinkled behind rimless glasses. She reminded him of picture book illustrations of Mrs. Claus. He smiled despite himself, felt himself finally beginning to relax. He could get around a woman like this. He'd be out of here and back to D.C. in no time. Alone.

"You're late," she said briskly, but without censure. "Let's go." She grabbed her purse and headed for the door.

Once again, Walker was forced to reassess the woman. He'd allowed himself to forget for just an instant that appearances could be deceiving. Right now he had a panicky feeling that she intended to take him straight to wherever this nephew of his was, introduce them, then abandon them to fend for themselves, her duty done. He was nowhere near ready for that. He would *never* be ready for that.

"Whoa," he said, standing stock-still in the middle of the corridor. "Where's the fire?"

"It's almost dinnertime in these parts and I'm starved, Detective. I missed lunch waiting for you. We can talk over food." She gave him a thorough once-over. "Besides, next to music, I hear it's the best thing for soothing a savage beast."

He chuckled, caught off-guard by the display of humor. "And that would be me?"

"You do pride yourself on it, don't you? I could tell that when we talked on the phone."

"In my line of work, it's helpful," he said, feeling defensive about his initial display of rudeness when she'd called.

"I'm sure it is," she agreed. "But down here we like to think we're more civilized."

Outside, she gestured toward her car, a brand-new Mustang convertible that surprised him yet again. "I'll drive," she said.

He regarded the car with envy. "I'll be even more agreeable if you'll let me."

"Because you don't trust a woman behind the wheel?"

He heard the unmistakable challenge in her voice, but he didn't need to lie. "Because I've been dying to test-drive one of these babies and haven't had the chance," he countered with absolute honesty.

She tossed him the keys. "In that case, it's all yours, Detective."

She directed him back onto the highway and into town, then down a side street past the stately old courthouse with its square of grass in front to the Inn at Montross. Tucker regarded the historic facade and little flower-lined brick patio doubtfully. Places like this gave him hives.

"Isn't there someplace we can get a basic burger and some fries?"

"I'll refrain from commenting on your deplorable eating habits," Mrs. Jackson said. "I'm relatively certain you'll find something on the menu here that will do. And they've done me a favor by keeping the kitchen open past their usual lunch hour."

Walker remained skeptical as they climbed the brick steps into the white building that dated back to the 1600s, according to a sign by the front door. He stepped into the wide foyer, glanced around at the antiques and the open, airy rooms and began to revise his opinion. The place had big-city class, he'd give it that.

Without waiting for a hostess, Mrs. Jackson led the way onto a closed-in front porch and settled at a table by an open window. "Sit down, Detective. I promise you the chef can offer more than tea sandwiches."

Duly chastised, Walker sat. The social worker regarded him with amusement.

"I'm sorry I couldn't offer you a fast-food place. The nearest one is miles away, and I got the distinct impression that you're in a hurry."

"Always am."

"Well, then, as soon as we order, we'll get right to it."

Ten minutes later, Walker had a beer in front of him

and the promise of a blackened chicken wrap sandwich that would bring tears to his eyes. When it came, Mrs. Jackson watched with amusement as it did just that.

"Too spicy for you, Detective?"

"No," he insisted, gulping half his beer to tame the taste. "Best sandwich I ever had." He nodded toward the piping hot potatoes accompanying it. "Best fries, too."

"Better than a fast-food restaurant?" she inquired, eyes twinkling.

"Are you teasing me, Mrs. Jackson?"

"Just trying to make a point."

"Which is?"

"The big city doesn't have all the advantages over us country folks."

"No," he agreed. "I can see that."

She paused in eating her own sea bass bisque. "You know, Detective Ames, it hasn't escaped my notice that we've been together for a half hour or more now and you still haven't asked about Tommy."

Walker sighed and put his sandwich down. "To tell you the truth, I'm not sure what to ask. Until you called, I didn't even know he existed."

"You and your sister weren't close?"

Walker recalled a time when they had been. Beth had trailed him around adoringly, pleading to be allowed to play with him and his friends. He had tolerated his younger sister because no one knew better than he that they received little or no attention at home.

"She was a beautiful little girl," he said, recalling her huge blue eyes and halo of strawberry blond curls that had later darkened to a golden hue. "She was always laughing. Then she got involved with Ryan Flanagan, and the laughter died."

The social worker regarded him sympathetically. "How old was she?"

"Sixteen, still a girl, really, but we couldn't stop her. My parents tried in a halfhearted way. I tried, but I was away at college and Beth was starved for attention. When Ryan asked her to run away with him, it was too much for her to resist, I guess. When our parents died, I couldn't even locate her. I had to tell her about their deaths the next time she checked in, which was three or four months later, around the time she and Flanagan got married. She called to give me the big news."

The anger and dismay he'd felt back then was still alive in him today. "I wanted to grab her and shake some sense into her, but it was too late."

"Was that the last time you heard from her?"

"No, she called again after he'd abandoned her. She was all alone, scared and pregnant. I wired her some money and begged her to come home. I was married by then. I told her she could stay with us until she had her baby." He shrugged. "She said she might not even have the baby, and she never did show up. And *that* was the last time I heard from her. She was somewhere outside of Las Vegas."

"I'm sorry," Mrs. Jackson said. "That must have been very difficult for you."

"It drove me nuts," he said honestly. "Here I was, this big city cop with all sorts of investigative skills and a lot of high-tech resources at my disposal, and I couldn't even find my own sister. Turned out she was a couple of hours away and I didn't even know it."

"You should know better than anyone that a person who wants to drop out of sight can pull it off if they're clever enough. Maybe she was making her way back to you when she ended up here. Maybe she just wanted to be back on her feet by the time she saw you. She and Tommy had been here a few years. They were doing well. She worked a variety of jobs, since much of the work around here is seasonal. She cleaned houses from time to time, waited tables, helped out in several of the shops.''

''Why not just one job?''

For an instant Mrs. Jackson looked uneasy. ''I suppose it's of no consequence now, but she seemed to have this fear of getting 'caught up in the system,' as she put it. Several people offered her full-time work, but when it came time to fill out the paperwork she balked.''

Walker uttered a curse. ''That was Flanagan's paranoia at work. No Social Security number, no taxes, nobody tracking his every move. The man liked living on the fringes of society, picking up odd jobs whenever he could, always for cash. I thought Beth was smarter than that.''

''I'm sure she was. In fact, she'd been offered work right here at the Inn, and I think she'd almost convinced herself to take it. Anna-Louise—she's a minister here in town—said Beth had been talking a lot about taking that final step so she could get back in touch with her family. She must have been talking about you. It was the only clue we had that she had anyone in her life other than Tommy.''

''She didn't have to prove anything to me,'' he said, though he was relieved if she'd done all of that for her own sake. And for her son's.

''Maybe she thought she did. I'm sure she knew she let you down.''

''That didn't matter,'' Walker insisted. ''I just wanted my baby sister to be okay.'' He looked at her.

"And now she's dead," he said bitterly. "What kind of brother does that make me?"

"One who did the best he could, I suspect."

He frowned at being let off the hook so easily. "No lectures?"

"Not my job," she assured him. "We can't change the past, much as we might like to. I prefer to deal with the here and now."

"Meaning Tommy?" he guessed.

She nodded. "Meaning Tommy." She slid a snapshot across the table. "I thought you might like to see this."

Walker hesitated before picking it up. His hand shook as he lifted it off the table. He sucked in his breath as Beth's blue eyes stared back at him. The boy had her crooked, mischievous grin, too.

"I'll bet he's a handful," he said finally.

"Oh, he is," Mrs. Jackson said fervently. "Not that it's much of a surprise. A boy all alone in the world has to find some way to deal with the fear. He's been better since he's been living with Daisy."

"Daisy?"

"Daisy Spencer. The Spencers were founders of Trinity Harbor—not Daisy, of course, but her ancestors. Her daddy, King, is still the most respected man in town. The richest, too, by all accounts, though my own father disputed that with his dying breath."

"Bad blood between the Spencers and your family?"

"More like an unending rivalry. King Spencer is the kind of man who doesn't like anybody challenging his supremacy."

"Is his daughter the same way?"

"Not at all. Daisy is a wonderful person."

"And she's a foster parent?"

"Not usually, no."

"How does her husband feel about this?"

"Daisy isn't married."

Walker was beginning to get a clear picture of the woman. A society do-gooder looking to gain a few more points.

"How exactly did Tommy end up with her?"

"She found him in her garage the other morning after he'd run away from another foster home. He's been acting out a lot since Beth died...mostly mischief, but clearly cries for help."

"And despite that, this Daisy just decided to let him stay?"

"Daisy is a remarkable woman, as I'm sure you'll see. She knew your sister and Tommy from church. She never hesitated about taking him in."

"Maybe we should leave things the way they are," Walker said, trying not to flinch under Mrs. Jackson's immediate frown of disapproval. "If Tommy's been behaving since he moved in with her, maybe she's just the person to keep him on the straight and narrow, to give him whatever he needs."

"You would turn around and leave here without even seeing the boy?" she asked. "Is that what you're saying?"

"It could be for the best," he insisted.

"Perhaps so," she agreed stiffly. "But I thought you were made of tougher stuff than that, Detective."

"I'm just saying that this woman sounds like a good role model for Tommy."

"You're his *uncle,*" she reminded him. "The only family he has left. You would deny him that sense of identity, that sense of connection, because it's inconvenient?''

He could feel the heat climbing into his cheeks. "I didn't say—"

"You didn't have to. You're a coward, Detective Ames."

The blunt assessment hit its mark. What had ever made him think that he could get around this woman? She was one tough customer. He met her gaze evenly. "Maybe I am, Mrs. Jackson. You don't know much about me."

"I know that you're willing to turn your back on a little boy without even meeting him."

"It wouldn't be the first time," Walker muttered, thinking of the accusations his ex-wife liked to throw at him about his treatment of his own kids.

"What was that?"

He sighed. "I have two children of my own, Mrs. Jackson. Two boys."

"Yes, you mentioned being married."

"Divorced, actually. My ex-wife has moved to North Carolina. I see my kids for two weeks in the summer. My ex claims that's still more than I saw them when we were living under the same roof."

She surveyed him with that penetrating look that disconcerted him.

"Is she right about that?" she asked.

"Probably. I'm a dedicated cop. It's never been a nine-to-five job for me."

"Which is to your credit. I'm sure it's not easy. Based on our phone conversation, I'm sure you've seen things that the rest of us would prefer to pretend don't happen. That must take a terrible toll. The work must consume you at times. I know mine does, and it can't be nearly as difficult as what you face.''

"That's still no excuse for neglecting my family," he said. "I was a lousy husband and not much of a father."

"Your words or hers?"

He smiled at her indignant expression. "Hers, but she pretty much nailed it. I don't deny it."

"Owning up to your mistakes," she said with a little nod of satisfaction. "I think maybe you have potential, after all, Detective."

"I haven't changed," he insisted.

"But you can, with the right incentive." She pushed the picture of Tommy back in his direction. "At least meet him. Tommy needs to know that he still has family out there. You owe him that. You surely owe your sister that."

Walker couldn't debate that point. He owed Beth for not being there for her, for not trying harder to keep her away from Flanagan, for not finding her years ago.

"Okay, you win. I'll meet Tommy, but I'm not making any promises, Mrs. Jackson."

"Fair enough." She reached across and patted his hand. "I'm sure you'll decide to do the right thing when the time comes."

Walker wished he shared her faith. There was one more thing he had to do while he was here, though. He needed to go by the cemetery, see where his sister was buried.

"Before we go to see Tommy, there's something I'd like to do," he began.

"Stop by the cemetery," she guessed. "It's five now. I'll call Daisy and let her know we'll be there about six. And if you'd like to take flowers to your sister's grave, I know where we can get some lovely ones.''

He hadn't thought of flowers, but she was right. He needed to make a gesture, leave something behind. Maybe wherever Beth was she would know and would understand that she'd always been in his heart.

King waved his latest housekeeper out of the dining room. Never could trust the help not to pass along every word that was spoken in his house. Finally satisfied that she wasn't lurking at the keyhole, he regarded his sons intently and asked, "Okay, now, what are we going to do about your sister?"

"I should have known you didn't just invite us over here for a nice dinner," Tucker grumbled.

"He never does," Bobby agreed. "Steak always comes with a price. Daddy inevitably has something up his sleeve."

King scowled at the pair of them. "Don't smartmouth me. Your sister's in trouble and I want to know what you're going to do to fix it."

"Last I heard, Daisy was a grown woman who knew her own mind," Bobby said. "What's she done that so all-fired wrong? She saw a kid who needed someone and she took him in. Isn't that what you've always taught us? That we have an obligation to look out for other people?" He lowered his voice and intoned, "'Spencers do their duty for the less fortunate.'"

King frowned at the mockery, but decided to ignore it. "Not when she's going to wind up getting her heart broken," he countered.

"I've warned her," Tucker said. "She says she knows what she's doing."

"And Anna-Louise has warned her, too," Bobby

pointed out, then grinned at his brother's startled expression. "Daddy's covering all the bases. I gather we're the second string, which must mean Anna-Louise struck out."

The truth was, Anna-Louise hadn't reported back to him yet, which galled King no end. He'd deal with her later. In the meantime, he needed someone else on the case.

"Somebody's got to look out for your sister." He scowled at Tucker. "I don't know why you didn't take that boy out of there when you had the chance."

"You wanted me to arrest him?"

"He was stealing her jewelry, wasn't he? You told me that yourself."

"He tried. He didn't succeed. I doubt Daisy would have approved of my slapping handcuffs on him and hauling him off to jail. She'd have demanded to be in the cell right next to him, and she'd have had Anna-Louise's husband down there snapping pictures for next week's front page."

King didn't doubt it. Richard Walton was a troublemaker, and a Yankee to boot. Actually, he was from Virginia, but he'd worked for one of the Washington papers, which was just as bad as being a Yankee by birth. Tucker was right. Walton would have stirred up a ruckus.

"Besides," Bobby said. "I don't think we're going to have to do anything. I hear Frances found the boy's uncle. He's due here today."

"They're over at the Inn as we speak. I saw Frances's car there when I left the courthouse to come on out here," Tucker added.

"This uncle, is he taking Tommy with him?" King asked, feeling hopeful for the first time in days.

"No word on that," Bobby admitted.

"Well, why the heck wouldn't he?" King demanded. "The boy's his responsibility. Dammit, Frances isn't going soft, is she? Do I need to call and tell her how to do her job?"

"I'd like to see you try," Tucker muttered.

"I heard that," King said, scowling at his oldest son. "The day hasn't come when I can't take on the likes of Frances Jackson. One word to the Board of Supervisors and she'd be out on her tush."

"I think you're underestimating the respect people around here have for her," Tucker said. "And don't forget, her ancestors are every bit as blue-blooded as ours."

King chafed at the reminder. It was a fact Frances liked to throw in his face every year when Founders' Day rolled around. In fact, the blasted woman prided herself on being a thorn in his side. She had been ever since grade school, when she'd publicly trounced him in a spelling bee. His daddy had never let him forget that he'd been beaten by a girl.

"I don't want to talk about Frances," King grumbled.

His sons exchanged amused glances. The spelling bee incident was one of their favorites.

"You know, I could disown both of you," he declared. "Neither one of you shows me an ounce of respect."

"I thought you did that last week," Bobby said.

"No, it was last month," Tucker countered. "I remember distinctly that he said he was going to disinherit us because we told him at Sunday dinner that we didn't care about the price of cattle."

"Well, dammit, what kind of sons don't give a fig

for the business that their daddy is in, and their grand-daddy before him?'' King demanded, thumping his fist on the table so hard it rattled the china and brought the housekeeper scurrying out of the kitchen. He waved her off. ''Get back in there. I'll call you when we're ready for dessert.''

Bobby shot a sympathetic look toward the woman, who'd only been on the job for a few weeks. ''You're going to run off another housekeeper if you're not careful,'' he warned his father.

''So what if I do? It's my house.''

''We'll remind you of that when you start grumbling about having to do the dusting,'' Tucker said, grinning.

King wondered what he'd ever done to deserve such disrespectful sons. If he didn't need their help with Daisy, he'd have thrown them out and gone through with his threat to disinherit them.

''We're getting off-track,'' he said instead. ''I expect you to do something about this situation with your sister. Make sure that boy leaves here with his uncle, preferably tonight. Am I making myself clear?''

''If you feel so strongly about this, why aren't you over there telling Daisy what you think?''

''Because she doesn't listen to me any better than the rest of you. If I show up, it'll only make her dig in her heels.''

''True enough,'' Bobby said. ''Daisy got her stubbornness from you.''

''She got it from your mother,'' King contradicted. ''I'm a perfectly reasonable man.''

Tucker and Bobby hooted so loudly at that it brought the housekeeper peeking through the kitchen door. King gave up. He'd either made his point or he hadn't. Tucker and Bobby would do what they wanted to do, the way they always did. So would Daisy, for that matter, even if it ruined her life. He could console himself that he'd tried to fix things.

He frowned at the eavesdropping housekeeper. "You might as well get on in here and clear the supper dishes, Mrs. Wingate."

"Will you be wanting your pie and coffee now?" she asked as she eased into the room, giving him a wide berth as she loaded a tray with the dinner plates and serving dishes.

"I'll take mine in the study," he said. "These two can take theirs wherever they want."

"I'm thinking I'll take a couple of extra slices and head on over to Daisy's to see what's what," Tucker said, glancing toward his younger brother. "What about you?"

"Sounds like a plan," Bobby agreed.

King regarded them both with satisfaction. Maybe their skulls weren't quite as thick as he'd been thinking, after all.

"You'll let me know what you find out," he ordered them as Mrs. Wingate delivered his piece of apple pie and coffee and set a covered pie plate in front of Tucker.

"You could come along," Tucker suggested.

"Not on your life," King retorted.

"Scared of the heat," Bobby observed.

"Probably so," Tucker concurred.

"No, just saving the big guns for later, in case you two mess this up," King told them. He scowled. "Which I am counting on you not to do."

"Daddy, we will do our best, but this is Daisy we're talking about," Tucker reminded him. "I haven't won an argument with her since she was old enough to talk.''

"Then it's high time you figured out why that is and changed it," King told him, shaking his head at the pitiful admission. "What kind of sheriff lets a little slip of a woman walk all over him?''

"One who's smart enough to know when to cut his losses," Bobby suggested.

"Exactly," Tucker agreed.

King threw up his hands. "I swear to God I am calling my lawyer right this minute and changing my will. I'm leaving everything to a bunch of blasted bird-watchers. They're bound to have more gumption than you two."

"Glad to see we've made you proud yet again," Tucker said, giving him an unrepentant grin as he headed for the door with the pie plate in hand.

Bobby gave his shoulder a squeeze as he passed. "See you, old man."

"I'm not old," King bellowed after them, then sighed. He might not be old at fifty-nine, but his children were going to send him to an early grave. Every one of them seemed to be flat-out dedicated to it.

4

Daisy had spent the past few hours preparing Tommy for meeting his uncle. She had really tried to put the best possible spin on things for his sake, but he wasn't any more thrilled by the prospect than she was. She had no answer for all of his questions about why he'd never even known of the man's existence. Frances hadn't been willing to share a single detail when Daisy had tried to pry a few out of her.

"I'm telling you I ain't going nowhere with no cop," he said flatly as he spooned soup noisily into his mouth late Thursday afternoon as they awaited the arrival of Walker Ames. Molly meowed plaintively, as if she understood his distress.

She had allowed Tommy to stay home from school, and she had taken the day off as well. It had probably been a mistake, since they'd spent the entire time sitting around the house brooding about whatever was to come. And when Frances had called midafternoon to report that Walker hadn't even shown up yet, Daisy had been ready to take Tommy and vanish. What sort of man was late to a first meeting with his own nephew?

But he was in Trinity Harbor now. Frances had called from the Inn a few minutes ago and said they'd be by around six. Daisy had fixed Tommy a bowl of soup and a sandwich to distract him, but she hadn't been able to touch a bite of food herself.

Tommy's declaration hung in the air, adding to her stomach's queasiness. How could she in good conscience send him away with a man he didn't know? How could she not, when that man was his only living relative?

Finally she met Tommy's belligerent gaze. "Tommy, do you trust me?"

"Some," he conceded grudgingly.

"Then believe me when I tell you that you won't go anywhere unless it's for the best."

He eyed her warily, his blue eyes far too skeptical for a boy his age. "Who gets to decide what's best?"

The question made her pause. The truth was, she supposed that Social Services or the court would have to make the call. But Tommy was ten. He ought to have some say. And she intended to have quite a lot to say herself once she'd seen this Walker Ames with her own eyes. She considered herself to be a very good judge of character, although there was the matter of Billy Inscoe to contradict that fact.

"All of us," she said finally. "You, me, a judge, the social worker and, of course, your uncle."

When the doorbell rang, Daisy froze. Tommy dropped his spoon, sending splatters of soup every which way. For once, Daisy ignored the mess. For one wild moment, she considered grabbing Tommy by the hand and hightailing it out the back door, but that would only postpone the inevitable. She reminded herself that her students—rambunctious teens, at that—considered her quite formidable. A mere policeman would be no match for her at all.

"You can stay in here and finish your soup," she

said, then gave Tommy's hand a reassuring squeeze. "It's going to be okay. I promise."

"Whatever," he said, his doubt plain.

With Tommy's skepticism ringing in her ears, she went to do battle with the man she was already inclined to think of as the enemy.

Walker wasn't sure what he'd expected in terms of age or appearance when Frances Jackson had told him that his nephew was being cared for by the daughter of one of the town's leading citizens. He'd simply dismissed her as some small-town society do-gooder without giving her another thought.

And maybe that was precisely what Daisy Spencer was, but she also happened to be years younger than he'd anticipated—no more than thirty, he guessed—and so beautiful it took him a full sixty seconds to catch his breath and accept her outstretched hand. She had the kind of beauty that came from incredible genes and a classy upbringing. Walker was rarely left speechless, nor did he tend to get poetic...but she inspired both. Her skin was flawless, her eyes the color of spring violets.

"Detective," she said oh-so-politely, then acknowledged the woman with him with a curt nod and an unmistakable hint of betrayal in her voice. "Frances."

Walker had the feeling it was more good manners than Southern hospitality that had her inviting them in. Daisy Spencer was studying him warily, as if she feared he might rob the place if she turned her back. He was used to being regarded with distrust, but that was usually by the bad guys, not by an upstanding citizen. The woman was uptight as hell about something, but darned if he could figure out what it was.

Shouldn't she be relieved that he was coming to see his nephew, that she'd most likely be off the hook if Frances Jackson had her way? Surely all these small-town do-gooders were of the same mind—foist Tommy off on him and end their involvement.

"Would you care for a cup of tea?" Ms. Spencer asked. Again, her voice was measured, with just a teasing hint of a drawl.

"That would be lovely," the social worker said.

Frances might be content to follow some sort of local protocol, but Walker was impatient to get the reason for the visit out of the way. He had reluctantly agreed to meet Tommy today, see how they did together. Beyond that he'd remained neutral, refusing to commit to anything, despite Mrs. Jackson's evident expectations. Now that he was here, he just wanted to get the awkward moment over with. He was still shaken by that visit to the cemetery and the finality of seeing a headstone with Beth's name on it.

"Where is he?" he asked bluntly, ignoring the offer of tea.

The question drew a disapproving frown from the woman currently caring for his nephew. Which, in turn, drew attention to a mouth so kissable it made him forget for an instant why he was here. His gaze traveled from that tempting mouth to curves that were barely disguised by a prim white cotton blouse and linen slacks. Discreet gold jewelry flashed at her wrists, and a delicate diamond and sapphire ring winked on one slender finger. Not an engagement ring, he noted with an odd sense of relief. Wrong hand.

"If you're referring to Tommy, he's in the kitchen finishing his supper," she told him, gesturing vaguely to another part of the small but tastefully furnished house.

The house hadn't been exactly what he'd expected, either, given her reported status in town. It was little more than a cottage, really, painted a cheerful yellow, with old-fashioned white Victorian trim. It came complete with a white picket fence, all of it the epitome of a young girl's dream. Hell, it was on Primrose Lane— how quaint could you get? The tiny front yard was a riot of flowers, even though it was still early spring. Neighboring houses were bigger, more imposing, but none had been cared for more lovingly.

The inside was tended with just as much care. Walker couldn't help wondering how long some of Daisy's expensive porcelain knickknacks would last with a rambunctious boy around. Apparently she wasn't all that concerned, because she hadn't hidden them. That raised her a notch in his estimation.

"Why don't you and I sit down and get to know each other before I get Tommy?" she suggested.

She said it in a way that set off a whole lot of wicked images Walker was sure she hadn't intended. Even so, he frowned. No wonder Frances had kept her questions to a minimum. Apparently she intended to let this woman do her job for her. Walker had other ideas.

"Ms. Spencer, as much as I would love to get to know you better," he said, giving her a thorough once-over that brought a blush to her peaches-and-cream complexion, "I'm here to meet my nephew. You and I can go a few rounds another time. Which way's the kitchen? Through here?"

He was already heading in that direction when she caught up with him, snagging his arm with a surprisingly firm grip. He glanced down at the pale fingers with their neat, unpolished nails against his thick, tanned forearm and felt an unexpected slam of desire. He swallowed hard and stepped away, but without making any further move toward the kitchen.

"Detective, perhaps you can bully suspects in Washington, but around here, we have ways of conducting ourselves that meet a higher standard."

Walker stared down into those flashing eyes, admiring again that startling shade of amethyst and the fringe of dark lashes. A man could forget himself and his intentions pondering the mysteries of eyes like that. He sincerely regretted that he didn't have the time to spare. It was getting late, and he wanted to hit the road before dark.

"Ms. Spencer, you are the second person today to suggest that I'm uncivilized." He leveled a hard look at her that usually worked quite well during an interrogation. "I'm beginning to take offense."

Not so much as an eyelash flickered. "Then prove me wrong."

"How?"

"Talk to me. Tell me about yourself and the life you're prepared to offer Tommy."

He shook his head. "You're not going to be satisfied till we play Twenty Questions, are you?"

"Not a chance," she agreed cheerfully.

"Then by all means, let's talk."

He followed her into the living room, settled back in a chintz-covered easy chair and kept his gaze pinned to hers. She perched on the edge of the sofa, kept her own gaze perfectly level with his, and began a litany of questions that suggested she'd made a list before his arrival. She started by asking about his parents, where he'd gone to elementary school, what his favorite subjects had been, whether he'd liked sports.

He grinned at her. "Ms. Spencer, at this rate, it'll be midnight and we won't even get to my college years."

Her expression brightened. "You went to college, then?"

"I didn't think to bring along a copy of my diploma, but yes, I graduated from the University of Virginia."

"A fine school," she said approvingly.

"Are we finished now?"

"Not quite. Are you married, Detective Ames?"

"Not anymore."

"I see." Her mouth pursed ever so slightly. "Any children?"

"Two boys."

"And they live with you?"

"No, they live with their mother in North Carolina."

"I see."

There was no question about the disapproval in her eyes now. She flashed a quick look at the social worker, whose expression was carefully neutral.

"Anything else?" he asked. "Are you interested in my favorite colors? Maybe whether I wear jockey shorts or boxers?"

Color flamed in her cheeks. "Of course not."

"Then I'd like to see my nephew."

Unfortunately, Walker was soon to discover, while they'd been wasting time on all those ridiculous questions, Tommy had vanished into thin air. When Daisy at last led them to the kitchen, they found it empty, and there was no sign of Tommy anywhere else in the house or yard.

Walker cursed his own stupidity. He should have guessed that the woman was stalling so his nephew could make a break for it, though why she should do that was beyond him. It was a diversionary tactic that he'd seen used often enough in his career. Still, he was surprised that Daisy Spencer would flat-out try to thwart this reunion that Frances Jackson was so dead-set on bringing about. Maybe they'd gotten their signals crossed.

It seemed Frances' thoughts were running parallel to his own. "Oh, Daisy, what have you gone and done?" she asked, dismay written all over her face.

"Me?" Daisy said, regarding her incredulously. "You think I hid him?"

"I know you want him to stay here, but this is not the way," the social worker said.

Walker regarded the two women intently. "Are you saying she is deliberately keeping the boy from me?" he asked, surprised to have his own suspicions confirmed so openly.

Frances looked flustered, but Daisy was quick to respond. "That is exactly what she's saying and, to tell you the truth, I'm insulted." She frowned at the social worker. "We've known each other for years. I would have expected better of you, Frances."

"And I, you," Frances retorted tartly.

Patches of color once again flamed on Daisy's cheeks, spurred no doubt by the indignation Walker could see flashing in her eyes.

"Blast it all, I'm as shocked as you are that he's not where I left him," she snapped. Quickly she amended, "No, I take that back. I'm not shocked at all. The boy's life has been a shambles since his mother died. He hasn't felt as if he truly belonged anywhere. It's little wonder that he doesn't trust a single adult to keep a promise, not even me."

"Exactly what did you promise him?" Walker asked.

"That no one would take him away from here unless we all decided it was for the best, him included."

"Daisy, he's just a boy," Frances said with a dismayed sigh. "Why would you make him a promise you knew you couldn't possibly keep?"

"I intended to keep it," Ms. Spencer shot back.

"Maybe we should just focus on finding him," Walker suggested. "We can work out the rest of this later."

"I agree," the social worker said at once. "I think we'd better get Tucker over here."

"Who's Tucker?" Walker asked, grasping at last that there was a whole lot more going on here than he could begin to fathom. Unfortunately there was no time to ask the right questions or to try to sort out the clues.

"My brother," Daisy answered, just as Frances said, "The sheriff."

"Then, by all means, let's get him over here," Walker agreed, just as two men came strolling around the corner of the house, one of them carrying what looked to be a foil-covered pie.

"Tucker, Tommy's vanished," Daisy said, automatically taking the dish from his hands. "You have to do something."

"What do you mean, he's vanished?"

"While your sister kept me occupied in her living room with an endless barrage of questions, my nephew bolted," Walker explained succinctly. "I'm Walker Ames, by the way. Detective Walker Ames."

"He's a D.C. policeman," Daisy said derisively. "One who apparently likes to make unfounded accusations. I did not deliberately try to assist Tommy in making a getaway. Not that I blame him. He's had far too much disruption in his life lately. He's just beginning to feel secure again.''

"In a few days with you?" Walker asked.

She gave him a defiant look. "Exactly. Because he knows I care about him. He doesn't even know who you are. Why would you expect him to choose you over me?"

"I guess the gloves are off," the other newcomer observed with a sigh. "Sis, you're not helping matters."

Walker grinned as she whirled on the other man.

"Bobby Spencer, you're supposed to be on my side," she said indignantly.

"I am, always," he insisted. "And right now you need to keep your mouth shut."

Fury danced in her eyes. "I most certainly will not."

Walker grinned. "Don't shut her up. I'm finding her comments enlightening."

"Enough," Tucker said firmly. "Let's all settle down and establish what we know. Daisy, when was the last time you saw Tommy?"

"He was finishing his supper when his uncle and Frances arrived. I left him in the kitchen. That was around six."

"And it's nearly seven now. Why the delay?"

"I had a few questions," Daisy said defensively.

Bobby rolled his eyes and shot a sympathetic look at Walker.

"How did Tommy feel about meeting his uncle?" the sheriff asked.

"I've already told you. He wasn't happy about it," she said.

"And I'm sure you did everything you could to see that he felt that way," Walker said, surprised by the depth of his anger that someone who didn't even know him would try to turn his own nephew against him.

"I did not. I told him he had to give you a chance, that I was sure there was an explanation for why he'd never even heard of you or why you'd never been to visit."

"Phrased like that, I can see why he'd be anxious to meet me," Walker snapped.

Daisy Spencer looked exactly the way he imagined a mother tiger would look right before it took on a predator threatening her young. Despite his exasperation with the woman, he couldn't help admiring her fierce protectiveness when it came to Tommy. A part of him was glad that his nephew had someone like that in his corner.

"Shouldn't we stop wasting time hurling accusations and look for Tommy?" Frances suggested mildly. "It'll be dark soon, and I don't like the idea of him being outside all alone once the temperature starts to drop. It gets cold along the river this time of year. And there are the cliffs…" Her voice trailed off, leaving the dire implication unspoken.

"Absolutely," Tucker agreed. "Frances, you stay right here in case Tommy shows up. Bobby, you go search along the river. I'll go door-to-door here in town. Walker, you and Daisy can drive up and down the streets and along the highway."

"Together?" Daisy asked as if she'd rather eat worms.

"Yes," Tucker said in a tone that didn't permit an argument. "Walker doesn't know his way around the area."

"Fine," she said. "But I'm driving."

"Whatever," Walker agreed, following her to a nice,

sedate little sedan that suited her perfectly. No flash and dazzle for this woman. She probably never drove the car over the speed limit.

Her agitation was plain as she started the car, grinding the engine in the process. She threw it into reverse and shot out of her driveway in a way that had even a veteran of high-speed chases clinging to the armrest with a white-knuckled grip. It was the second time today he'd misjudged a woman in this town.

"Don't take out your frustration with me on the car," he suggested quietly as she skidded around the corner onto another tree-lined street. "Getting us killed won't help anyone, least of all Tommy."

"Oh, go to hell," she snapped. "This is all your fault."

"You'll have to explain that one to me."

"It just is."

Walker bit back a grin. "Now there's a rational bit of logic. How very female."

She slammed on the brakes so hard, he almost banged his head on the windshield. When he'd recovered, he turned to find her staring straight ahead with what might have been tears glistening on her cheeks.

"I'm sorry," she said so softly he almost didn't hear her.

"What? I thought I heard you apologizing."

"Don't let it go to your head," she retorted.

"Maybe we ought to start over. I don't think we understand each other's point of view here."

"Probably not," she conceded with a sigh. "It's just that Tommy means a lot to me. I don't want to see him hurt."

"Believe it or not, Ms. Spencer, neither do I."

She finally turned to face him. "Since it looks like

it's going to be a long night, maybe you ought to call me Daisy.''

Walker chuckled. "I always prefer to be on a first-name basis when I'm spending the night with a woman."

"Yes, I imagine you do."

He was pretty sure he saw a smile tugging at the corner of her lips. It wouldn't do to focus on that, though. He had the feeling that thinking about those lips could get him into a whole lot of trouble.

"How well do you know Tommy?" he asked instead.

"Better the last few days, but even before that, he and I had a certain rapport. He was in my Sunday school class. He has an irreverent attitude that reminds me of the way I always longed to be when I was his age. Because of that I let him get away with quite a lot." A full-fledged smile spread across her face. "I suppose this is payback for that leniency."

Walker seized on the hint of wistfulness in her voice when she talked about yearning to rebel. "Somehow I can't envision you ever having a rebellious streak."

"You'd have to talk to my brothers and my father, then. They could tell you. Especially Tucker. He knows exactly how many times I came really, really close to trying to break free of my father."

"But you never did it?"

"Not until now," she confessed with obvious regret. "Well, my moving into town put his nerves on edge, but he got over that."

"And what have you done recently?"

"I took in Tommy. Believe me, it has my father in an uproar, though he hasn't shown his face around here himself. He's sent everybody else to do his dirty work.

I'm sure Tucker and Bobby showing up tonight was no accident. That pie they were carrying came straight from my father's kitchen. They were probably here with yet another lecture on how I'm trying to ruin my life.''

"By taking in a little boy?''

"A little boy who tried to steal my jewelry,'' she said.

This was the first Walker had heard about any jewelry being taken. His gut clenched at the thought. "Tommy tried to steal your jewelry?''

Her expression fell. "Damn, me and my big mouth. Yes, he tried to take it. He intended to sell it to get money for food in case I wouldn't let him stay.''

"But you caught him?''

"Actually, Tucker caught him. It was incredibly inconvenient since it only added fuel to the fire, but I managed to assure them both that it would not, under any circumstances, happen again. I think Tommy got the message.''

Walker sighed. "I hope you're right,'' he said, envisioning his nephew well on his way to a life of crime.

"Tommy is not a thief,'' Daisy said, as if she'd read his mind.

"What would you call it?''

"He's scared and he's acting out.''

"Stealing is stealing, no matter the reason. Don't make excuses for him.''

"Spoken like a true cop.''

"I *am* a cop.''

"That doesn't mean you can't make allowances for circumstances.''

"Making allowances is the reason petty thieves turn into career criminals.''

"Tommy doesn't need a hard-liner in his life. He needs someone with a little compassion."

Walker shook his head. Daisy's soft-hearted, do-gooder nature had just come out into the open. The woman was too naive for her own good. He'd met a hundred others just like her, always eager to defend the juvenile offender as being "just a kid."

He was tempted to enlighten her with a few stories of kids who'd been let off too easy by the courts, only to turn right around and commit the kind of serious crimes that gave the justice system a bad name. She wouldn't get it, though. She wouldn't give a hoot about *those* kids, when they were talking about Tommy.

"Maybe we should just concentrate on finding my nephew," he said finally. "And agree to disagree about the rest of it."

"Maybe we should," she concurred, though she looked oddly disappointed.

He studied her speculatively. "Unless you'd rather argue about it some more."

She grinned. "And waste my breath? I don't think so."

"So, where do you think Tommy might be hiding?"

"Could be anywhere," she said with a shrug. "Just about every house in this area has some kind of garage or toolshed in back. And a lot of them have docks on the river with boats tied up. Tommy's fascinated with boats."

"Would he steal one?"

She looked taken aback, but she considered the question before shaking her head. "I don't think so. Not with night coming on, anyway."

"Okay, then, what about those cliffs Mrs. Jackson mentioned? Are they dangerous?"

"They're clay and they're slippery, but I doubt Tommy would be anywhere near them. Frances just said that to get all of us moving."

"Why don't you think he's headed in that direction?"

"Because the cliffs are at the state park miles away from here. Trinity Harbor has nice sandy beaches. The only danger to Tommy there would be catching a chill if he were foolish enough to go in the river."

"You're not really worried about him, are you?" he guessed.

"Not especially. Trinity Harbor is a safe place. Tucker sees to it."

"Then why the ruckus back at your house?"

"I think my brothers and Frances just wanted to get us out from underfoot so they could decide what's best for Tommy without our input."

"And we're supposed to live with whatever they decide?" Walker asked incredulously.

"Not me," Daisy said at once. "I'm rebelling, remember?"

Walker chuckled. "And doing a darn fine job of it, I might add."

"Thank you." She slanted a look his way. "I really do love Tommy, you know."

"I know," Walker said. "And I just want the chance to get to know my sister's son. I don't have any idea what's best or how this is going to work out."

"You'll keep an open mind, then?" she asked.

Her eyes were shining with what he guessed to be hope, though he couldn't begin to interpret exactly what she was wishing for or why. "If you will," he agreed.

She nodded slowly. "I can do that."

Walker held out his hand. "Then we have a deal."

But Daisy evidently wasn't satisfied with a hand-shake. She stopped the car and, before he realized what she intended, slid across the seat and gave him a fierce hug.

Walker froze at the feel of her soft curves pressing into him, at the whisper of her breath against his cheek. The latter meant those incredibly tempting lips of hers were too close to be ignored. He turned and without taking the time to think about what was smart or right or anything else, he kissed her.

And realized belatedly that he'd just slammed smack into more danger than he ever had on the streets of D.C.

5

"Maybe we'd better go back," Daisy whispered, when she could finally unscramble her thoughts after Walker had ended that totally unexpected, mind-boggling kiss. Nobody had ever kissed sensible Daisy Spencer with such total abandon, such wicked hunger. She was too stunned to even contemplate lecturing him on the inappropriateness of his behavior. In fact, she was wondering if she could get him to kiss her again.

Bad idea, her remaining functioning brain cell announced. "We definitely need to go back," she said more emphatically. "Besides, we've been driving around for two solid hours, and there hasn't been a sign of Tommy. Maybe the others are having better luck."

"Yeah, good idea," he said, barely sparing her a glance.

To Daisy he sounded a little too eager. She found it vaguely insulting. Not that she intended to let him see it. She wasn't going to let him think for a second that she was some inexperienced country girl who could be shaken by a simple kiss.

"Well?" he prodded when she still hadn't started the engine. "Are we going back or not? My gut's starting to tell me that if Tommy felt safe with you, then he didn't wander that far off. He's probably hiding close by."

"Probably."

She was very proud that she managed to get the response out without sounding breathless. Obviously they weren't going to talk about the kiss, she concluded with a sigh. She certainly didn't want to focus on it. At least he hadn't apologized and listed a litany of regrets, even if his expression indicated he wasn't at all pleased with the turn of events between them. She could leave it alone, too. She could pretend that nothing out of the ordinary had happened.

Or at least she thought she could. The fact that she hadn't risked touching the keys for fear he'd see how badly her hands were shaking indicated she wasn't as cool and calm as she wanted Walker to believe. And the longer they sat there, the worse it got. Darkness had fallen, making the atmosphere in the car just a little too cozy, a little too intimate. The tension sizzling between them wasn't going to go away, which meant it needed to be addressed.

She took a deep breath, then blurted out, "Look, you don't have to be embarrassed. I mean, it was just a kiss. No big deal, right?"

"Right," he said flatly.

Clearing the air apparently wasn't going to be the snap she'd hoped. Her nerves were still jumpy; his expression was still insultingly grim. She plunged in one more time. "I've been kissed before. I'm sure you have been, too. And I suppose I started it with that hug. I was just so relieved that you were willing to meet me halfway on this."

He turned then and scowled at her. "Daisy, will you please let it drop? Maybe it shouldn't have, but it happened. It's over. Forget about it."

She blinked rapidly at the irritation in his voice. "Of

course, yes, I can do that," she said. With a great deal of concentration, she managed to keep her hand steady as she started the car.

In fact, she even kept her mouth shut until they turned the corner to her block. Then she decided that she couldn't go the rest of the way home without trying one more time to address the ridiculous tension between them. If they walked into the house like this, her brothers would know in an instant that something had happened. For men, they were way more intuitive than they should have been. She'd learned early never to hint by so much as a down-turned mouth that a date had gone badly. Otherwise Tucker and Bobby would threaten to take on the boy who'd hurt her. Billy Inscoe was practically the only boy she'd known that they hadn't scared off. Maybe that was why she'd thought herself in love with him, because he hadn't been intimidated by her brothers.

At any rate, fearing Tucker and Bobby might not have outgrown the habit, she slammed to a stop and cut the lights and the engine, then turned and glowered at Walker.

"That kiss was an impulse, Detective. Nothing more. I'm sure you regret it. So do I. It won't happen again."

"I know that," he said emphatically, frowning right back at her. He gestured toward her house. "Why don't we just get back there and see if anyone else has had any luck finding Tommy?"

"You don't deal well with your emotions, do you?" she asked irritably. "I noticed that earlier when we were talking about your sister. You got all stiff and uncomfortable, just the way you are now."

"Maybe because you were beating the subject to death, just the way *you* are now."

"It's an interrogation technique," she said. "Tucker told me. Surely you're familiar with it."

His lips twitched ever so slightly. "I am, which is why it doesn't work well on me. I get annoyed."

"I'll try to remember that. I just didn't want Tucker or Bobby to get the idea that you and I have been..." She hesitated, then said, "Arguing. They're very protective."

Walker's lips twitched. "Your brothers don't scare me. I think I can take care of myself."

"Okay, then," she said, forcing herself to let the subject drop. An instant later she faced him as another worrisome issue occurred to her. "You're not going to yell at Tommy for running off, are you?"

His level gaze met hers. "Are you?"

"Of course not."

"Then why would you assume I might? I do understand what it's like to be a kid and to be scared."

Daisy was surprised by the admission. "I can't imagine you being scared of anything."

"Because you don't know me. I wish you'd try to remember that."

Daisy doubted she could forget it if she wanted to. The kiss might have been a rare display of intimacy, but he hadn't let her into his head or into his heart, not for one single second since they'd met.

Sighing, she put the car into gear and drove the rest of the way down the block, pulling into the driveway next to Tucker's sports-utility vehicle.

"Not much sign of activity," Walker observed as they left the car.

Just then they heard laughter from the backyard.

"It sounds more like a party," Daisy said, leading the way around the side of the house. She stopped abruptly at the sight that greeted her.

Her brothers, Frances and Tommy were all sprawled in lawn chairs on the deck facing the river, empty pie plates beside them. Tucker was pointing out some of the constellations visible in the velvet-black sky. Their not-a-care-in-the-world demeanor irked her as much as anything that had happened all day, which was saying something.

"Having fun?" she inquired tartly.

Four pairs of guilty eyes turned her way.

"You might have let us know that Tommy was safe," she said peevishly.

"You didn't take your cell phone," Bobby pointed out mildly. "We had no way to get in touch with you."

"Somebody could have gotten in a car and come after us," she said, regarding Tucker accusingly. "I'm sure someone could have spotted us since the streets around here are practically deserted at this time of night."

"The point is that Tommy is back," Tucker responded quietly, refusing to rise to the bait. He turned to Tommy. "Son, this is your uncle, Walker Ames."

The introduction brought on a heavy silence. Daisy watched as the boy warily eyed Walker. Neither of them budged an inch. In fact, Walker looked a little shell-shocked. Finally, after a firm nudge by her elbow, he crossed the deck and hunkered down beside Tommy.

"You look just like your mother," he said softly, a hint of wonder and sorrow in his voice. "Same eyes, same hair, same smile. I noticed that in the picture Mrs. Jackson showed me earlier."

Tommy's expression remained sullen. "So?"

"It's just that it makes me realize how very much I missed her," Walker said.

"Then how come you never came to see us?" Tommy demanded.

"Because she didn't tell me where she was and I couldn't find her."

"Like you really tried," Tommy scoffed.

"One day, if you like, I'll show you a file with every single thing I did, every place I searched," Walker offered. "Your mom was my baby sister. I never wanted anything bad to happen to her."

"Well, something bad did happen," Tommy shouted, jumping up. "She died! Just like my dad, only I never even knew him. My mom was all I had and she's dead. Now I got nobody."

"That's not true," Daisy protested, taking a step toward him.

Before she could reach him, he scrambled away from Walker, skirted around her and ran into the house, letting the screen door slam closed behind him.

"I'll go after him," she said at once, heartbroken for both of them.

"No," Bobby said. "Let me. You stay here with Frances and Walker and work things out. You all have a lot of tough decisions to make."

Daisy reluctantly agreed. Her younger brother had a way with kids. Maybe it would be best to let an unbiased third party try to calm Tommy down.

As Bobby went inside, Tucker stood and gave Walker's shoulder a squeeze. "How about a beer?"

His expression numb, Walker nodded. "Sounds great. I'll come with you."

That left Daisy alone with Frances.

"I'm sorry about accusing you of trying to hide Tommy," Frances said eventually. "You know how fond I am of you, but I have a job to do."

"It doesn't matter. We were all upset. We all said some things we shouldn't have," Daisy conceded. "Where did you find him, by the way?"

"Tucker found him hiding in Madge Jessup's toolshed. She said she'd heard noises out there earlier, but thought it was a raccoon. Tommy was sitting on the riding mower eating a peanut butter sandwich when Tucker checked it out. He swore he'd planned to come back as soon as he knew his uncle and I were gone."

Daisy sighed. "What a mess. What do we do now?"

"I'm going to try to convince Walker to stay here for a few more days so that he and Tommy can get to know each other. Then we'll see. It's obvious that they can't be united overnight. Neither of them is ready for that."

A few more days might be the reprieve they all needed. "Do you think he'll agree?" Daisy asked.

"I don't know. And I don't know what to make of the man. What do *you* think?"

An hour ago Daisy would have guessed that Walker Ames would tear out of Trinity Harbor at the first opportunity, but that was before she'd seen the look on his face when he got his first glimpse of his nephew. "I think he'll agree," she said at last. "He might not be happy about it, but he knows in his heart he owes it to his sister."

"Agree to what?" Walker asked as he and Tucker came back outside.

"To stay a few more days," Frances said. "And don't tell me about your job. I'm sure under the circumstances, they could spare you through the weekend. The crime will still be there when you get back."

"Exactly what my boss said when I spoke to him not five minutes ago," Walker said. "It seems I'm not indispensable after all."

Daisy didn't like the way her pulse kicked up at his announcement. She was pretty sure the reaction didn't have a thing to do with Tommy's best interests.

"You're welcome to stay here," she said impulsively.

His gaze clashed with hers, and for a moment the air sizzled with more of that astonishing electricity. Then he shook his head. "Bad idea."

"I agree," Frances said.

"But you're the one who said he and Tommy need time to get to know one another," Daisy protested. "What better way than if they're under the same roof?"

"Yes, but they'll also need some space. And frankly it won't help if half the town is gossiping about you having a stranger living with you. Somebody will want to make something of it, and you'll be left to live it down."

"He could stay at Cedar Hill," Tucker suggested slyly. "There are plenty of rooms to spare over there."

"Absolutely not," Daisy said fiercely, scowling at her brother. She knew exactly what he was up to. She could just imagine Walker being subjected to an endless diatribe from her father, probably followed by an attempt to bribe him into taking Tommy away from her.

"What's Cedar Hill?" Walker asked, regarding her curiously.

"My family's home, still ruled by the indomitable

King Spencer,'' she explained. ''Trust me, you do not want to go there.''

He grinned. ''I don't know. You're making it sound like a challenge.''

''My father is a trial, not a challenge.''

Tucker's eyes flashed with amusement. ''Trying to keep them apart, Daisy? What are you afraid of?''

''You know perfectly well that Daddy will try to stick his nose in and manipulate this so it works out the way he wants it to.''

''You're not giving me much credit,'' Walker said.

''You are no match for my father,'' she insisted. ''I don't want you anywhere near him.''

''He doesn't matchmake, does he?'' Walker asked with a deliberately exaggerated shudder.

''With a Yankee? Heaven forbid,'' Daisy said.

''Then I don't see the problem.''

''She's afraid our father will have you and Tommy reunited and out of town before daybreak,'' Tucker explained. ''No matter how he has to accomplish it.''

A teasing glint appeared in Walker's eyes. ''Which one of us are you most afraid of losing?'' he inquired.

Daisy could feel heat climbing into her cheeks. She hadn't blushed this much in years, if ever. She avoided glancing at her brother or Frances before she said quite firmly, ''Tommy, of course.''

A grin spread across Walker's face. ''Of course.''

''Am I missing something here?'' Tucker inquired, his brotherly antennae clearly on full-alert.

''Nothing,'' Daisy said sharply. ''Not one damn thing. You all settle this however you want to. Walker can sleep on the ground for all I care. I'm going to say good-night to Tommy, and then I am going to bed.

Breakfast's at eight, Detective. If you're still in town then.''

A low chuckle followed her inside, but she couldn't tell if it was Walker's or her brother's. At this point, it didn't much matter. She held the same low opinion of both of them.

Upstairs she found Bobby and Tommy engaged in a cutthroat round of a Monopoly game.

"Watch him, Tommy. My brother really, really likes to acquire real estate. He's already bought up half the waterfront in Trinity Harbor."

Tommy's eyes widened. "For real? You own the beach?"

"Not the beach," Bobby said. "Just the land nearby."

"What are you going to do with it?"

"He's already built a marina," Daisy said.

"The one with all the boats and the neat restaurant?"

Bobby nodded. "That's mine."

"Wow. My mom took me to eat there once. It was last year on my birthday. We got all dressed up and everything."

Bobby grinned. "Did you like the food?" he asked casually.

Now there was a loaded question if ever Daisy had heard one. "Careful how you answer, Tommy. Bobby's also the chef."

Tommy looked puzzled. "You mean like a cook?"

"Yep," Daisy confirmed. "That's just a fancy name for it."

"I didn't study at Cordon Bleu just so you could call me a cook," Bobby grumbled, clearly offended. "Isn't it bad enough that I have to put up with Daddy saying that?"

"He's just ticked because you refuse to take over the cattle operation."

"I've been telling him since I turned ten that I was not interested in raising Black Angus. I'm twenty-eight now—wouldn't you think he'd be over it?"

"Daddy?" Daisy said skeptically. "The man who still hasn't forgiven his brother for buying a prize bull out from under his nose thirty years ago?"

"I see your point," Bobby said with a sigh.

Daisy leaned down and kissed him. "He loves you, though. You do know that, don't you?"

Bobby grinned. "Being loved by King Spencer is not necessarily a blessing."

She laughed. "You may be right about that. It just means there's more pressure to do things his way." She gave Tommy a hug. "Want me to stick around and tuck you in?"

"I don't need to be tucked in," he said with an embarrassed glance at Bobby.

Her brother winked at him. Daisy let it pass. She'd slip in later after the lights were out and make sure Tommy was okay. "All right, then. Good night, you two."

"Daisy?" Tommy called after her, his voice hesitant.

"What, sweetheart?"

"Is my uncle…is he still here?"

She tried to read his expression and couldn't. "He's going to stay through the weekend."

"Here?"

"No. They're downstairs deciding that now. Probably at the hotel by the river."

Tommy's shoulders seemed to ease then, and she realized that, despite his outburst earlier, he didn't really want his uncle to disappear from his life. Family relationships might be complex and frustrating, but they were still the most powerful ties a person had. As terrified as she was that Walker might take Tommy away from her, she couldn't bear to deny them this time together.

"Maybe when he comes over in the morning, he'll tell you all about what your mom was like when she was a little girl," she suggested.

Tommy's eyes lit up for the first time since he'd learned that Walker was coming. "That would be cool. She never said much about when she was a kid."

"Then you ask him," she said softly, fighting back the sting of tears.

Bobby followed her from the room and gave her a hug. "You did good in there," he told her.

"I hope so." She stared at her brother wistfully. "What if I lose him, though?"

"Then his staying wasn't meant to be. You'll survive."

Daisy envisioned an empty future and wished she shared Bobby's confidence.

Later, alone in her too-quiet, too-lonely room, Daisy could admit that the meeting with Walker had been a disaster, start to finish. But as she thought back over the evening—from Tommy's disappearance to the awkward reunion a few hours later—what stuck in her mind was that unexpected kiss she and Walker had shared.

Why couldn't she shake the memory? Was she so desperate for a little attention that any man's kiss would have thrown her off-kilter like this? Maybe so.

In fact, that had to be it. It had nothing at all to do with Walker Ames.

Yeah, right. She touched her fingers to her lips. Even now she could almost feel the whisper-soft caress. It hadn't lasted more than a few seconds, but it had felt like an eternity. He had seemed almost as shocked by it as she had been.

It was definitely a good thing that he had declined her invitation. Hopefully he'd also declined the suggestion that he stay at Cedar Hill. He'd be just fine at Trinity Harbor's one fancy hotel. Near enough to drop in, but far enough away to avoid temptation.

She sighed. She had a feeling that kiss was going to keep her up all night as it was. Having Walker Ames right down the hall would have been more than she could bear.

His concession to stay in Trinity Harbor through the weekend was a blessing for Tommy, but it was going to be tough on her. In one single gesture, Walker had reminded her that she was a woman, that she had needs and desires that had been ignored for far too long. He'd be lucky if she didn't drag him off somewhere and try to ravish him.

She blushed at the thought. What had come over her? She never thought like that, much less behaved in such a wanton manner. Not once in all of her thirty years had she felt such an intense need to have a man's tongue intimately invade her mouth, to have his hands on her breasts or to feel his body inside hers. Not even Billy had aroused this kind of desperate yearning. Their lovemaking had been sweetly satisfying, but she'd never seen stars, never felt as if the earth were tumbling out from under her feet the way she had tonight. These days, on those rare occasions when she passed Billy on the street, she felt nothing at all. Yet even now, she couldn't imagine a time when the sight of Walker might not affect her.

Which just proved that it was way past time for her body to wake up and come alive again. Once again she tried to reassure herself that the physical response was just that—physical. It did not have anything whatsoever to do with Walker Ames specifically.

She needed to keep reminding herself that his decision to stay simply gave her three more days with Tommy, three more days to convince everyone that he was better off with her in Trinity Harbor than he would be in a city like Washington.

Her father, who had more prejudices than Daisy would ordinarily condone, had it just right when it came to the nation's capital. The city's level of crime was a disgrace. It was no place to raise a small boy. Surely a man who dealt with that crime every day of his life would be able to see that. She just had to sit down and reason with him.

Unfortunately, she had discovered tonight that Walker Ames had the ability to rob her of the power to speak coherently, much less forcefully. He knew it, too, more's the pity.

But Daisy hadn't been raised by a man like King Spencer without learning a little about ignoring her fears to get the job done. If Walker Ames thought he could use his masculinity to fluster her, then she could just as easily use a few feminine wiles to turn the tables on him. The more she considered the prospect, the more anxious she was to see him in the morning and put her plan into action.

In the meantime, it might be wise to say a little prayer that she wasn't deliberately throwing herself to the wolves…or to one wolf in particular.

6

Walker had a lot of excess tension to work off. He woke up at dawn after a restless night on a hard hotel mattress, feeling every one of his thirty-five years. His shoulders ached. His knees were stiff, the result of too many years of hard physical activity from football in high school to the jogging he now did daily to keep in shape.

More troublesome than the aches and pains were the mental cobwebs. As if dealing with his first face-to-face meeting with Tommy weren't stressful enough, there was Daisy Spencer and her far too tempting mouth to consider. She'd played a prominent role in his dreams. No wonder he'd awakened thoroughly aroused and totally exasperated with himself.

The last thing he needed in his life was a woman who looked at him with moist lips half-parted by unmistakable lust and eyes shining with innocence and vulnerability. There was a contradiction there that he didn't want to get mixed up in. No way.

He hadn't wanted to belabor the discussion of the kiss they'd shared because he'd been very much afraid he'd be tempted to kiss her again just to shut her up. She had that exasperating effect on him, an effect no woman had had for a very long time.

Bottom line, he needed to get her out of his system

before he saw her this morning and did something that would only add to the regrets he already had. A good workout ought to accomplish that. Luckily he kept his gym bag in the trunk of the car. He changed into shorts and a sweatshirt, tugged on his running shoes and hit the road.

For the first few blocks, he was barely aware of his surroundings beyond the lack of traffic and the faint tang of salt in the air. His concentration was totally focused on getting into his rhythm, getting his breathing to match his relaxed, easy strides in a way that would bring the optimum results.

Eventually he began to take note of the tidy lawns with their picket fences and abundant splashes of spring flowers, the wide porches and old-fashioned swings, the cheerful flags that adorned most houses. The few people who were outside at this hour glanced up at him and waved, their friendly smiles a stark contrast to the hostile suspicion he was used to receiving back home.

Only after he'd turned a corner and set off along the wide, tree-lined street bordering the river did he realize that he no longer had the pleasantly cool morning to himself. He heard the slap of other sneakers on the pavement, the ragged breathing of a beginning runner and the steadier sounds of someone more experienced. He glanced over his shoulder and spotted a couple half a block behind. The woman waved, then nearly stumbled. The man caught her arm.

"Are you okay?" the man asked, gazing worriedly at her flushed face. "It's only your second week. I can slow down."

"No, no," she said between gasps. "I can keep up."

The man grinned at Walker, who jogged in place waiting for them.

"Stubborn as a mule," the man observed when they were closer.

Walker winked at her, then admonished the man, "Hey, give her credit for trying."

"That's what I've been telling him," she said, bent over at the waist as she tried to catch her breath. When she could finally speak without gasping, she added, "I think he's just afraid I'll collapse in a heap and he'll have to carry me all the way home." She held out her hand. "I'm Anna-Louise Walton, by the way. And you're Walker Ames." She chuckled at his surprise. "It's a small town. I've gotten a full description from half the people in Trinity Harbor. Your arrival was big news."

He regarded her with bemusement. "Why?"

It was the man who spoke up. "Speaking as a journalist, I can say it's because the story has all the makings of a real tearjerker. Long-lost uncle comes to claim his orphaned nephew, pitting himself against the daughter of the town's leading citizen." He grinned. "By the way, I'm Richard Walton. I own the paper here. Anna-Louise is my wife, and before you mutter that curse that's obviously on your lips, you should know she's a minister."

For the third time in less than 24 hours, Walker was shocked into silence by a woman in this town. Obviously the females in Trinity Harbor were a breed apart.

"Don't worry," Anna-Louise said to cover his apparent discomfort. "People say whatever they want in front of me. If I feel the need, I'll pray for your soul later."

"Good to know," Walker said.

"So, how did it go yesterday with Tommy?" she asked. "And with Daisy?"

He wasn't going to touch the topic of Daisy with this woman or anybody else. As for Tommy, he wasn't sure what to say. "I wish I knew," he said eventually. "Tommy has a lot of understandable resentment where I'm concerned."

Anna-Louise nodded sympathetically. "Look, since I'm obviously winded and pathetically out of shape anyway, why don't we go get some coffee? Maybe I can help."

"Or we could just leave the man alone and let him handle his own life," Richard countered, regarding his wife with amused tolerance. "Anna-Louise likes to meddle."

"It's not meddling. It's my job," she chided.

"Only when a member of your congregation actually asks for help," Richard reminded her. "Walker's barely been in town for a full day, he's never set foot in your church and I haven't heard him ask for any advice."

She laughed. "Okay, so sometimes I anticipate a need before it's expressed. Sue me." She regarded Walker hopefully. "How about that coffee?"

Because he was willing to listen to advice from any quarter, Walker nodded. "Lead the way."

"Earlene's is the only place open for breakfast," she said. "The coffee is strong and the country ham and eggs are worth trying if you don't give a hang about your cholesterol. At this time of the morning we should have a shot at getting a booth. The regulars don't start coming in for another half hour or so, and Fridays don't bring out the tourists this time of the year. Tomorrow's another story." She turned to her husband. "Coming with us?"

"Nope. I might be too tempted to put something you say in confidence on the front page of next week's paper."

She rolled her eyes. "Don't listen to a word he says," she told Walker. "Richard is the most ethical man I know. He just wants to gloat later that he finished his run and I pooped out."

Richard leaned down and pressed a firm kiss to her lips, then grinned. "That too," he said. "Nice meeting you, Walker. If you stick around, maybe we can get together and talk about D.C. I used to work there myself."

"Really?"

"Well, for the paper, anyway. I was a foreign correspondent, so I never spent all that much time in Washington, but I certainly kept up with the politics."

Walker nodded as recognition dawned. "You're *that* Richard Walton. You wrote some damn fine pieces from some pretty awful war zones. Won quite a few awards, too, as I recall. I thought your byline had been missing for a while now."

"Fours years. I took a leave of absence when my grandmother got sick. Then Anna-Louise and I got married and I bought the paper in my hometown. When she got the transfer here, I bought this one and brought an old buddy in as editor of the one over there."

"Now he's a media mogul," Anna-Louise teased.

"Two weeklies do not an empire make," Richard retorted. "Besides, I like it here." He gave his wife another kiss. "Don't lose this job. I don't want another paper to worry about."

She laughed. "I didn't lose the last job. I just got an

irresistible offer. King Spencer can be very persuasive.''

"So I've heard," Walker said.

"Oh, good, then we can talk about him, too," she said. "See you later, honey."

"Should I be bothered by the fact that you're suddenly so eager to be rid of me and spend time with another man?" Richard teased. "Is the honeymoon finally over?"

"You'll have to decide that for yourself," she said, then led Walker off in the opposite direction.

On the walk to the small riverside restaurant, which sat next to a weeping willow just beginning to get its pale green leaves, silence fell. At first Walker felt the need to fill it, but he realized very quickly that Anna-Louise was one of those rare women who didn't expect conversation. She seemed perfectly content with the quiet.

The restaurant's windows were shaded by blue and white awnings. Pots of just watered flowers sat beneath. Bicycles were propped against the building.

Inside Earlene's, there was indeed a last booth available. The gray-haired waitress had their coffee cups filled practically before they'd slid into their seats. She gave Walker a thorough once-over, but didn't ask any questions. Either she'd already guessed who he was, or she was the only person in town who kept her curiosity in check.

Instead of asking about him, she turned to Anna-Louise. "Honey, you look plumb worn-out. Has Richard been making you run again?"

The minister grinned. "He doesn't *make* me. I'm trying to get healthy."

"If you ask me, there is nothing healthy about working up a sweat on a day God just meant to be enjoyed."

Anna-Louise's expression grew thoughtful. "You know, Earlene, you could be right. Maybe there's a sermon in that."

Earlene patted her hand. "Honey, that's why you're so popular. You find sermons in all the everyday things people can relate to."

When the woman had taken their orders and moved on to other new arrivals, Walker studied the woman opposite him. Funny, now that he knew what she did for a living, he thought he could detect an unusual serenity in her eyes that should have tipped him off. He'd seen the same thing in the eyes of police chaplains and other clergy he dealt with after a crime had taken a terrible toll on a family. He always wished he could grasp what it was they knew that lesser mortals didn't. Even the other faithful didn't seem to have it to the same degree. Men like him didn't have it at all. And he couldn't help wondering if a man like Richard Walton, who'd seen some of the worst the world had to offer, still believed in anything whatsoever.

"I can see your mind's working overtime," Anna-Louise said, cutting into his thoughts. "What are you grappling with? What to do about Tommy?"

"Actually, I was wondering what it takes to be a minister, especially a woman minister."

"The same thing it takes a man," she said at once. "Just a little more of it. Dedication. Faith. Compassion. And in my case, a healthy supply of grit and determination."

"Something tells me it's not as simple as you make it sound. Otherwise more people would answer the calling."

"Okay, for a woman, maybe it takes the ability to withstand a few shocked looks, a lot of doubting remarks and occasionally an organized campaign to have us banished."

"There," he said. "That sounds more like it. Did anybody ever try to banish you?"

Her expression clouded over. "All the time at first."

"But you were tough enough to take it," he said approvingly.

"I had a strong backer," she replied.

"Richard?"

"God."

Walker was taken aback by the quick retort, but then a smile spread across his face. "Yes, He would be a help, wouldn't He?"

"He usually is, if we listen."

"I'm not sure I can hear what He's saying about me and Tommy," Walker confided.

She gave him a serene smile. "Oh, I think you can. Maybe you're just not ready to listen."

"You're telling me I should pack Tommy up and take him with me," he said, a sinking sensation in the pit of his stomach. He almost regretted asking her opinion, because she was right. He wasn't ready to hear it.

"No," she said at once. "I'm not telling you anything. It's for you to decide."

"Do you think he'd be better off here with Daisy?" he asked, trying to get a clear-cut answer from her one way or the other.

"I know she loves him," Anna-Louise conceded, clearly choosing her words carefully.

"I thought I heard a *but* in there."

"Did you?"

He shook his head at the deliberate evasiveness. "I could find you extremely annoying, Mrs. Walton."

"Anna-Louise will do. And you only find me annoying because I won't make your decision for you."

"I thought your job was to point people along the path to righteousness."

"That puts them in good standing with God. This decision is about you and your family. A private matter."

"What if I ask for your advice?"

She laughed. "I'll answer with a question. What do you think is right and best for Tommy?"

He dragged a hand through his damp hair. "I wish to hell I knew," he said without thinking, then immediately apologized. "Sorry."

"No problem. I will give you this much advice. Give it time, Walker. You don't have to decide today or even tomorrow."

"Tell Frances Jackson that. She's chomping at the bit to get Tommy off her plate and onto mine."

"No, she's just trying to make sure he's with someone who loves him. Every child deserves that, especially one who's just been through the trauma of losing the only parent he's ever known."

"Yes," Walker said slowly. "Yes, they do."

But was he in any position to give Tommy the kind of love he needed? Did he even have any love left to give? The three people who'd been closest to him in his life certainly didn't think so.

Daisy's gaze kept straying toward the back door. She'd expected Walker to show up by now. It was after eight, and there was still no sign of him. Fortunately

Tommy didn't seem to care one way or another. He hadn't glanced at the door once.

Still, she was disappointed. It wasn't that she'd expected him, exactly. After all, wasn't she the one who'd anticipated that he might bolt straight back to Washington? She'd merely hoped that he would keep his promise and be here this morning—for Tommy's sake.

"How come you keep looking out the door?" Tommy asked eventually. "You've already burned one waffle because you weren't paying attention. Looks to me like the next one is going to go any second now."

She whirled around just in time to see the steam coming from the waffle iron turn to something that looked suspiciously like smoke. "Blast it," she said, yanking it open to reveal a waffle almost beyond edible.

"It's okay. I'll take it," Tommy said, holding out his plate. "Looks like it's the best I'm going to get this morning."

"Very funny, young man," she said as she tossed it into the trash instead. "The next one will be perfect. You'll see."

"I hope so," Tommy told her, "'Cause I'm about starved to death."

Daisy carefully spooned more batter onto the waffle iron and closed it, then faced Tommy. "Now that you've had some time to sleep on everything that happened yesterday, what did you think of your uncle?"

Tommy's face scrunched up. He shrugged. "He was okay, I guess."

"You weren't very nice to him."

Tommy frowned. "Why should I be? I just said what

you were thinking. We talked about it, remember? You don't know why he abandoned my mom either.''

''Maybe I didn't understand it before he and I talked, but I do now,'' Daisy told the boy. ''He deserves a chance to explain it so you'll understand it, too. He told you yesterday that he tried really, really hard to find her.''

''And you bought that?'' Tommy said scathingly.

She nodded slowly. ''He sounded sincere. And it is true that your mom didn't have a lot of the identification papers that most adults have, like a driver's license and car registration. She always rode a bike.''

''Because she liked the exercise,'' Tommy said defensively.

''True, but she didn't have a Social Security number, either.''

''I don't even know what that is,'' Tommy said. ''But if she didn't have it, it was 'cause she didn't want it.''

Daisy grinned. ''I know that, but most grown-ups do have one. Some kids, too, if they want to get jobs. All of those things would have helped your uncle to find her.''

''He should have tried harder. He must be a really lousy cop,'' Tommy said stubbornly.

Daisy sighed. She knew better than to push too hard. Even in just a few days, she had seen that Tommy didn't respond well to pressure. He had a definite mind of his own, and she was a big believer in a child's right to his own opinions. She could only try to shape them a little at a time. Besides, how much of her faith in Walker's sincerity was because she wanted to believe he was a good man for her own reasons? If she lost

Tommy, she needed to believe he was with someone who could love him the way he deserved to be loved.

Well, the proof would come soon enough. If Walker didn't show up this morning, it would pretty much confirm Tommy's low opinion of him. She sighed again and opened the waffle iron just in the nick of time, finally managing one that was golden brown and steaming hot.

She put it on Tommy's plate, then sat across from him.

"You ain't gonna have one?" he asked as he slathered butter into every little nook, then poured maple syrup over it.

"Not yet."

"How come?"

"I thought I'd wait."

"Wait for what?"

Because she didn't want to bring up Walker's name again, she said, "Until I've had another cup of coffee. I'm still half-asleep."

The answer seemed to satisfy him. "Yeah, Mom used to say the same thing, except sometimes I thought it was because she knew we only had enough for one person and she wanted me to have it."

Daisy felt her eyes sting for this little boy who saw too much, and for the mother who'd tried so hard to give him a better life. Beth Flanagan had worn clothes until they were practically threadbare, but she'd brought Tommy to church every Sunday in slacks that had been neatly pressed and a white shirt and tie. His shoes had been polished and his hair combed. She would have been horrified to see him dressed the way Daisy had found him.

"Your mom was very special," she told Tommy.

He nodded. "She was the best. I just wish she hadn't had to work so much. That's why she got sick, 'cause she was so tired all the time." His expression turned serious. "Can I ask you something?"

"Anything."

"Where do you think she is now?" he asked, his lip quivering. "Is she really in heaven like Anna-Louise says? Am I ever gonna get to see her again?" As if a dam had burst, his tears began to flow unchecked.

Daisy opened her arms and Tommy scrambled into them. "Oh, sweetheart, I know that's where she is, and she's up there looking out for you every single second. It's like having your own private angel."

"That's good, isn't it?" Tommy asked, swiping impatiently at his face with a napkin.

"Very good."

A sigh shuddered through him. "I just wish I could see her."

"You will someday," Daisy told him.

"But I mean now. What if I forget what she looked like?"

"You won't, I promise you. And you have pictures, don't you?"

He shook his head. "She took lots and lots of pictures of me, but we never took any of her."

Daisy heard a sound at the back door and looked up to see Walker standing there, his expression unreadable.

"I have some photos you could have," he said to Tommy as he came inside. "Of course, they were taken when Beth was just a girl."

Excitement and wariness warred on Tommy's face. "You mean I could have 'em, like, forever?"

"Absolutely," Walker said, still standing just inside the door as if he were uncertain of his welcome.

"When?"

"The minute I go home I'll find them for you."

Tommy hung back, still tucked against Daisy's side. "Am I gonna have to go away with you?"

Walker cast a desperate look toward Daisy, then said, "That's something we'll have to talk about."

"I don't want to," Tommy said, his expression belligerent.

"I can understand that," Walker said.

Tommy's expression faltered. "You can?"

"Sure. You don't really know me. And I don't know you. That makes it a pretty scary prospect for both of us."

"I ain't scared," Tommy insisted.

Walker barely managed to hide a smile. Daisy caught the quick twitch of his lips and admired the fact that he didn't want Tommy to detect his amusement.

"Then we'll just leave it that I am," he told Tommy.

"Do you got any kids?"

"Two," Walker told him, his expression sad. "They don't live with me, though. They live with their mother in North Carolina."

"You live by yourself?" Tommy asked. "Or do you have a girlfriend?"

This time Walker did grin. "No girlfriend."

"How come? You're not too bad-looking."

Daisy chuckled at the massive understatement, then blushed when she caught Walker's speculative gaze on her.

"No time," Walker said. "That's why my wife took the kids and moved away, because my job took up too much of my time."

Tommy seemed to be trying to absorb this, his expression intense. "Then you wouldn't really have any time for a kid like me, either, would you?"

Walker looked startled by his insight. "I'd make time, if that's what we decide is best," he promised.

"Would you take me to a baseball game sometimes?" Tommy asked. "I like the Orioles a lot, but I've never been to see a game."

"We could do that," Walker said. "I like baseball, too."

"How about fishing? Do you like to fish?"

Walker nodded. "Do you?"

"A whole lot," Tommy said. "Mom didn't. She thought the worms were disgusting. Sometimes she'd go with me, though, as long as I put the bait on her hook."

Walker nodded. "Sounds like a fair arrangement."

"I've got a boat," Tommy announced. "It's not much to look at. It's just an old rowboat I found washed up on the beach, you know, before..."

"Before what?"

"Before my mom died. I haven't had much time to work on it yet, but it don't sink or nothing. I'm saving up to buy some paint for it."

He inched away from Daisy and approached Walker with caution. "I could take you to see it," he said hesitantly. "If you wanted. Daisy and her brothers helped me bring it over here a couple of days ago. It's down by the river."

"I'd like that," Walker said.

Tommy nodded solemnly, then turned to Daisy. "You want to come, too?" His expression brightened. "Maybe we could have a picnic. I'll make the sandwiches, so it won't be too much work for you."

Daisy chuckled at his enthusiasm. "Why don't you and Walker go on ahead? I'll make the sandwiches and bring everything with me in a little while."

"Are you sure?" Tommy asked. "I don't mind helping."

"I'm sure," she said, and sent them on their way.

She wanted time to compose herself. Seeing the fragile bond blossoming between Tommy and his uncle had shaken her. So had seeing Walker, for that matter. He was entirely too appealing, entirely too masculine. She liked the way his sun-streaked brown hair curled a little at the nape of his neck, the lines that fanned out from the corners of his eyes.

And his cautious, sensitive handling of Tommy had unsettled her. Daisy wanted desperately to hate him, wanted to believe he was unfit to take Tommy away from her, but he was destroying all of her illusions about that.

He might not want Tommy yet. He might be uncertain how he was going to fit a ten-year-old into his bachelor life, but suitable? Oh, yes, he was father material. He might doubt it, but she didn't. It had become very clear to her in the last few minutes.

Once he realized it, too, then what? She hated the empty feeling that settled inside her as she thought about letting Tommy go. She was pretty sure the sensation had a lot to do with her heart breaking.

7

Tommy was a chatterbox. Somehow that surprised Walker. After the boy's distance the night before and his caution earlier, Walker had expected a lot of uncomfortable silence when they went to look at this rowboat Tommy had rescued from the beach.

Instead, it was as if something inside of Tommy had been unleashed. Not that Walker thought the boy had decided to trust him. He suspected Tommy had just been longing for a male to talk to about all the things he didn't feel he could share with his mom. He'd been glad to learn that Tommy had never gotten to know his father. Maybe it was stubbornness or selfishness on his part, but he didn't think Ryan Flanagan could possibly have given anything positive to this boy beyond the donation of his sperm to give him life.

"What should I call you?" Tommy asked eventually.

"Uncle Walker or just plain Walker. It's up to you."

"Okay. I guess I'll call you Uncle Walker. I never had a real uncle before."

Walker refrained from pointing out that he'd had one all along. He had no idea why Beth had kept that fact from her son. Maybe, as Frances had suggested, she'd simply had too much pride to turn to her brother or even acknowledge his existence until she felt she had her life under control. Maybe she'd grown tired of having Walker judge the decisions she'd made. Whatever the reason, Walker couldn't help feeling that he'd let her down badly even though he'd been little more than a teenager himself when she'd run off. That she'd come so close to having her life on track, maybe even to making that fateful call that would have reunited them, broke his heart.

When he and Tommy reached the narrow stretch of sandy beach down a sloping hill from Daisy's house, Tommy left Walker's side and raced ahead.

"It's right over here," he called excitedly. "Wait till you see. We should have brought fishing poles. We could have taken her out."

By the time Walker neared, Tommy was sitting on the pale golden sand, tugging off his shoes and rolling up his pant legs. He scrambled up and grabbed Walker's hand to half drag him toward the most pitiful specimen of seaworthiness Walker had ever seen. Whoever had abandoned the boat had obviously known what they were doing.

"You haven't taken this out on the river, have you?" he asked, trying to keep a note of panic from his voice.

"Not yet. I've been scraping off the paint and stuff, getting it ready. My buddy Gary—he's older than me, but really, really cool—anyway, he's been helping me, when he's got the time. See how smooth it is?" he demanded, pride shining in his eyes.

The weathered wood was smooth, all right, and probably rotted straight through, Walker concluded after closer examination. He was fairly certain he could see daylight between some of the planks. He knew better than to criticize it, though, or to warn Tommy away from it. He had to figure out another approach that would retain the boy's enthusiasm, while still keeping him from capsizing.

"You've done a lot of work," he said, choosing his words carefully.

"Every day. Mom said it looked like a pile of junk, but I could see right off that it had potential. I mean, how else is a kid like me gonna get a boat? This one was free. It just needs a little attention."

Sort of like Tommy himself, Walker guessed. "What does Daisy think of it?" He imagined she would be even more horrified than he was.

A little of Tommy's excitement died. "She just told me never, never to take it out in the water unless she was right here on shore where she could watch me." He stared at Walker, radiating disbelief. "Like I'm some kind of a baby or something."

"No, she's just being smart. A good boater always tests his craft to make sure it's seaworthy before taking it out to sea. After all, her brother probably knows a whole lot about boats. He's bound to have taught her a few things."

"I guess," Tommy said.

"Listen to her," Walker advised. "And maybe Bobby and I can help you with some of this work so it'll get done faster."

Tommy's eyes widened. "Really?"

"I don't see why not." He reached in his pocket for his ever-present notebook and pen. Fortunately this one didn't yet have notes on an ongoing investigation. "Let's sit here and make a list of what we'll need. Then you and I can go to the hardware store or the marina after lunch."

"Okay," Tommy said eagerly, plopping onto the

sand at Walker's side. "Maybe Gary can come over, too."

"Sure," Walker agreed. "Now what should I put on this list?"

"First of all, I think we need blue paint. And maybe white for the trim." He gazed at Walker. "What do you think?"

"I think those would be terrific colors for a boat. Now how about some caulk to make sure those planks are sealed nice and tight?"

Tommy nodded. "Oh, yeah, I forgot about that." He snuck a hopeful glance at Walker. "And it doesn't have any oars."

Walker made a note. "Then we'll definitely buy some oars."

"And more sandpaper. I've about used up all I could find in Daisy's garage." He blushed a fiery red. "She gave it to me when we brought the boat over last week after she said I could stay. I didn't steal it or nothing."

"Good. Daisy strikes me as the kind of person who'd let you have just about anything as long as you ask first."

Tommy nodded. "Daisy's the best. Sometimes she can be pretty strict and stuff, but I think that's just because she never had any kids of her own. She worries a lot that I'm gonna break something."

Walker frowned. He didn't want Daisy turning his nephew into some sort of sissy who had to worry about the breakables in her house. "You mean like those little porcelain things in her living room?"

"No, you know, bones and stuff."

Walker's brief flare of indignation died at once. Laughter bubbled up inside him, which he repressed for the sake of Tommy's dignity. "Yeah, I can see where she might worry about that."

"I guess it's a girl thing, huh? Mom used to get crazy about stuff like that, too."

Walker nodded, wondering if he would ever share a moment like this with his own sons, regretting that he'd lost so much time with them. He tousled Tommy's hair.

"Definitely a girl thing," he agreed. "Not that I think you should be testing your luck by climbing onto the roof or anything."

"Nah," Tommy said. "There's nothing up there, anyway."

A niggling sense of dismay crept through Walker. "How do you know that?"

"I looked out the bedroom window," Tommy said reasonably.

Walker breathed a sigh of relief. For a minute he'd wondered how Daisy had kept her sanity with Tommy around even for the week or so he'd been here, but apparently under that adventurous streak, the kid had been imbued with a healthy dose of common sense. Since he'd only been with Daisy briefly, that had to be Beth's doing. Obviously, for Tommy to turn out this well, Walker's little sister had to have gotten her act together. If only...

He sighed. Thinking about what could have—or should have—been was a waste of energy.

He glanced up just then and spotted Daisy scrambling awkwardly across the deep sand, lugging a picnic hamper that must have weighed a ton, and with a blanket tucked under her arm. She was barefooted and wearing khaki shorts that displayed very attractive legs. Her T-shirt was neatly tucked in, a prim touch that at the same time managed to emphasize just how tiny her waist was.

Walker started to rise to go and help her, but she waved him off.

"I've got it. It's not as heavy as it looks. Tommy, you could take this blanket, though."

As she neared, Walker didn't miss the dismayed glance Daisy gave to the rowboat before she set the hamper down and began spreading out the blanket.

"The sand's still damp and cold," she told him. "You shouldn't be sitting on it."

Tommy groaned. "See, I told you she worries about everything."

Daisy looked embarrassed. "I do not. I just try to be sensible."

"Then, by all means, let me join you on the blanket," Walker said, deliberately crowding her when he sat down. He stretched out his long legs until he was virtually thigh to thigh with her. "You're right. This is definitely warmer."

She shot him a knowing look. "Very amusing."

"My goal is to entertain."

Tommy stood stock-still in front of them, a frown puckering his brow. "You two look kinda funny. You like each other, don't you?"

"We hardly know each other," Daisy protested defensively.

"I think he's concerned about whether or not we are capable of getting along," Walker said, his voice threaded with amusement. Her quick denial had been way too telling. She was definitely still thinking about that kiss the night before.

Of course, to his consternation, so was he. And despite his attempt to clear his head earlier, he was a very long way from knowing what he intended to do about it.

Daisy wanted to shrivel up and die. How could she have imagined that Tommy was asking if the two of them were becoming a couple? Why would a ten-year-old even imagine such a thing about two people who'd just met?

Of course, a case could be made that a thirty-year-old woman ought to know better, too. And hadn't she been imagining that very thing herself more than once in the last 24 hours?

Focus on the food, she instructed herself firmly. She couldn't get into trouble if she was dutifully playing the proper hostess role she'd been taught to perform all her life. In a houseful of men, it had been up to her to see that social events ran smoothly, that their guests' needs were met.

"Is anyone hungry?" she asked, aware that her voice sounded a little too determinedly cheerful.

"I am," Tommy said at once.

"Why do I suspect that you always are?" Walker teased. "Wasn't that breakfast you were eating when I got here? And that was when, an hour ago?"

"Yes, but I'm a growing boy," Tommy retorted, accepting the chicken sandwich Daisy handed to him along with a bag of chips. "Anything to drink?"

"Sodas and lemonade," she said.

"I'll have a cola."

She found one in the small cooler she'd put in the picnic hamper, popped the top and handed it to him. She risked a glance at Walker. "How about you?"

"Not just yet. I had a big breakfast not that long ago."

"Oh?"

"I ran into some friends of yours earlier, Richard and Anna-Louise Walton."

Daisy froze. Anna-Louise was capable of great discretion...most of the time. When she wanted certain things to come about, she had a way of bending her own rules. "Oh? How did that happen?"

"I went out for an early morning run. They caught up with me."

Daisy knew all about Anna-Louise's determination to get healthy. She was surprised that she was still at it two weeks after announcing her intention to join her husband on his morning runs.

"Anna-Louise actually caught up with you?" she asked skeptically.

Walker grinned. "I was jogging in place at the time."

She chuckled. "That sounds more like it. If you ask me, she's going to kill herself, especially with summer coming on and the temperatures climbing."

"It was barely sixty this morning, and Anna-Louise looks as if she's pretty healthy, even if she is a little out of shape. Maybe you should join her."

Daisy regarded him intently, trying to determine if he'd deliberately meant to be insulting. His expression was totally innocent.

"I was brought up to believe that proper Southern women didn't do anything to work up a sweat," she told him.

He gave her a puzzled look. "What do they do?"

"If they have to exert themselves at all, they glow." She shrugged. "Same difference, if you really want to know, but it's the one thing about which my father and I are in total agreement. I'm not going out and making a public spectacle of myself running around the streets of Trinity Harbor.''

''Daisy, Daisy, Daisy, I thought you were more of an enlightened woman than that. Physical fitness is essential for men and women. Unless, of course, you want to die young.''

The words were no sooner out of his mouth than a look of dismay passed over his face. He turned in Tommy's direction, but fortunately the boy had grown tired of their company and was down by the river's edge skipping stones.

''Oh, God, what was I thinking?'' he murmured. ''What if he had heard me?''

''He didn't.''

''But he could have. He would have thought I was criticizing his mother. I'm sure of it.''

''Then you would have explained.''

''How?''

''By telling him that it was just an offhand remark, that it had nothing to do with what happened to his mother, though the sad truth is, she might not have died if she'd taken better care of herself. She worked too hard. She was physically exhausted. And when she caught the flu, she didn't see a doctor right away.''

''Why not?'' Walker asked. ''Didn't she have insurance?''

Daisy rested her hand on his forearm, felt the muscle tense. ''Any doctor around here would have seen her whether she had insurance or not. She didn't go because she didn't realize how sick she was. How many people do you know who just assume they have to weather the flu, let it run its course? I'm sure that was what Beth thought, too. When one of her bosses came by to check on her, she realized how bad things were and insisted Beth go to the hospital, but it was already too late.''

Walker looked tormented by the image she had painted. ''It's not your fault,'' she told him gently. ''You couldn't do anything if she wouldn't turn to you. None of us could.''

''And you can live with that?'' he asked bitterly.

''I have to. So do you.'' She touched his cheek until he turned to face her. ''We have to for Tommy's sake, because if we don't, he could start to blame himself. He was the one with her day and night, the one struggling to nurse her. He did the best he could, because she didn't tell him that she needed more help than he could give.''

''He must have been terrified.''

Daisy shook her head. ''I don't think he really understood, not even when the ambulance came to take her to the hospital. Anna-Louise stayed with him. She was the one who told him when it was over. She took him home and kept him with her until after the funeral. Then Frances stepped in.''

''Why didn't he stay on with Anna-Louise?''

''Oh, I think she would have let him stay in a heartbeat. So would Richard. But Frances made them take a good long look at the precedent they'd be setting. Anna-Louise has a good heart. If there's trouble, she's the first one there. People will take advantage of that as it is. Frances warned her that unless she was prepared to be a foster parent to every child in trouble, she needed to take a step back.''

Walker regarded her intently. ''And what did Frances tell you?''

Daisy shrugged. ''Nothing I wanted to hear.''

He grinned. "Yes, I imagine you march to your own drummer."

"I haven't always," she admitted. "When you grow up with King Spencer for a daddy, you march to his, at least until you decide to take charge of your own life."

"How old were you when you made that decision?"

Daisy debated lying, then decided it couldn't possibly make any difference. He might as well hear the truth now. "Thirty," she admitted.

She almost enjoyed Walker's shocked expression. "Yes, that's right. As I told you yesterday, my first significant rebellion was the day I moved out, and that was earlier this year. The second came the day I found Tommy in my garage and decided to let him stay. I wasn't kidding about any of that. I knew my father would be scandalized and I did it anyway."

"I see," he said, his expression thoughtful. "Then Tommy's just part of some battle you're having with your father?"

"Absolutely not!" Daisy said indignantly. "Tommy is not a means to an end. He's a little boy who needed someone to love him. No one else was available, so I decided to step in."

"How noble of you."

"There was nothing noble about it." She scowled at Walker, resentful of his deliberate misunderstanding of her intentions. "This isn't about duty or obligation or rebellion. It's about Tommy needing a home and someone to love him. You might keep that in mind while you're deciding what you intend to do, Detective. If you're not prepared to be a real father figure to that boy, then leave him with someone who's committed to providing him with love and stability."

"In other words, you."

Her gaze clashed with his. "That's exactly right."
She stood up and brushed the sand from her clothes.
"You and Tommy can bring these things back to the
house when you come," she said stiffly before stalking
away.

She felt Walker's puzzled gaze on her as she crossed
the beach and went back up the hill. His suggestion
that she'd only taken on Tommy to make some sort of
a point with her father was outrageous. She resented
the implication.

And she could have proved him wrong if she'd just
told him the real reason she had taken Tommy in, but
what woman wanted to admit that she was so desperate
for a child that she had eagerly latched on to the opportunity that had been presented to her? She did not
intend to have Walker Ames thinking of her as some
sort of pathetic spinster, even if that was the way she
sometimes saw herself.

Besides, with every day that passed, she was coming
to love Tommy for himself and not just because he
fulfilled a need in her. With every minute they spent
together, she realized that she did have it in her to
nurture a child, to provide a loving home.

When no one had come along after Billy broke their
engagement, she had begun doubting herself, wondering if maybe he hadn't been right to leave her, if she
wasn't emotionally as well as physically barren. Ra-
tionally, she had known how absurd that was, but her
aching heart had been filled with questions about God's
purpose in taking away her ability to have a child.

She had asked Anna-Louise about that at one point,
in a rare moment of vulnerability. It had been a difficult
moment for both of them, because Anna-Louise, for all

her wisdom, had had no answers for her. And the explanation that God's reasons would become clear in His time had done nothing to ease her sorrow.

Now, at last, she knew. God had intended for her to be there for Tommy, a little boy who was desperately in need of someone to fill in for the mother he'd lost.

Still disgruntled by her conversation with Walker, she spent the rest of the afternoon working around the house, muttering about Walker's assumption and her own failure to make her point more forcefully. She cleaned and dusted and did laundry. She had just yanked out the silver and started to polish it just to work out her frustrations, when Bobby showed up. He took one look at the silver spread out on the kitchen table and started to back right out the door.

"Get back in here," she ordered her brother.

"Not when you're in one of those moods."

"What moods?"

"When the silver polish comes out, it only means one thing."

She stared at him blankly. "I don't know what you're talking about."

"It means you're fed up with one of us. Who is it this time? Has Daddy been over here bugging you?"

Daisy honestly had no idea what he was talking about. "I haven't seen Daddy since Tommy moved in."

"Tucker, then?"

She shook her head.

"Well, it can't be me. I just got here." Suddenly his expression changed. "Uh-oh. Not Walker? You barely know the man. What's he done to get you in a dither?"

"I am not in a dither," she insisted.

"Sis, you're polishing the silver. It's a dead give-away."

She impatiently sorted the knives, forks and spoons back into their tidy, lined box. "It is not. I was just..."

Words failed her. She'd had no idea that she resorted to polishing the things in times of stress. No wonder her silverware was never tarnished. There was a lot of stress associated with growing up at Cedar Hill, even with growing up in a tranquil place like Trinity Harbor where Spencer behavior was always in the spotlight.

"Where's Walker?" Bobby asked, wisely letting the topic of her mood drop.

"Down by the river with Tommy."

"They're getting along?"

"Well enough. I think they're making big plans for that pitiful boat Tommy found."

"Does that bother you?"

"The boat? Or the fact that they're getting along?"

"Either one."

"I'd prefer that the boat got washed out to sea in the dead of night."

"And their relationship? Does that upset you?"

"Don't be ridiculous. Why should it?"

"Don't fib, Daisy," her brother scolded. "I know you too well. You were hoping they'd hate each other on sight."

"I was not!" she said, aghast that he would accuse her of such a thing.

Bobby grinned. "Were, too."

"I am not going to engage in such childish bickering."

His expression sobered. "Okay, no bickering. But, Sis, maybe it's for the best."

"What?"

"Walker and Tommy getting along. They do belong together. They're family. We were brought up to understand what that means."

Daisy sank down heavily and sighed. "I know that." She met her brother's worried gaze. "But Walker hasn't said a thing about taking Tommy with him. They're getting along okay, yes, but that's as far as it's gone. I don't want him raising Tommy's hopes and then breaking his heart."

"What about yours?"

"This isn't about me."

"Of course it is. Don't you think I know how badly that idiot Inscoe hurt you when he broke your engagement? Tucker's not the only sensitive one in the family. I can read between the lines as well as anyone. Oh, you put on a brave front, told everyone it was for the best, but I saw the haunted look in your eyes."

"Bobby, I don't want to talk about Billy. That was over with a million years ago. If he didn't live right here in town, I'd never think about him at all."

"Okay, forget Billy. Let's talk about the real issue."

"Which is?"

"Kids. Babies. Nobody deserves to be a mother more than you do. As little as you were when Mama died, you did your best to replace her for Tucker and me. I'll never forget the way you'd scold us when you bandaged our cuts or spend your Saturdays in the kitchen baking cookies because you didn't think the housekeeper did it the way Mama did."

Tears stung Daisy's eyes. She hadn't realized that either of her brothers had really noticed her efforts. She thought they'd taken them for granted. "I did that as much for me as I did for you," she told him. "I wanted things to be like they were before she died. When I smelled those cookies baking, if I closed my eyes I could pretend she was in the kitchen.''

"Me, too," Bobby said, squeezing her hand. "But the point I was trying to make was, that if you want to have children, you don't need a man to do it.''

Daisy might have laughed if his expression hadn't been so serious. "Oh, really?"

He frowned. "I don't mean that. You can always adopt, even as a single woman. Tucker and I would back you, and we'd be there as father figures for any child you had.''

"Will you back me if I fight for Tommy?"

He glanced outside before replying, and whatever he saw made him pause. He beckoned her over. "Before I answer, take a look.''

Daisy saw Walker and Tommy coming up from the river, dragging that pathetic rowboat with them. Whatever Walker was saying, Tommy was hanging on every word, his expression rapt. Daisy felt her heart shatter into a million pieces.

"Walker hasn't said he wanted him," she said, clinging to one last shred of hope.

"Oh, Daisy," Bobby murmured, his arm around her shoulders. "Don't wait until he does before preparing yourself to let Tommy go.''

8

For a boat that was falling apart, the blasted thing weighed a ton, Walker thought as he and Tommy struggled to drag it up the sloping lawn. He'd concluded that they could get more work done if they weren't constantly dragging tools back and forth to the beach. He probably should have asked Daisy how she felt about that, but he was still smarting from the way she'd told him off in that prim little way of hers before stalking off and leaving him with the uncomfortable task of trying to explain to his nephew why she'd run off.

"You didn't make her mad, did you?" Tommy had asked worriedly.

"Maybe a little," he'd admitted, figuring the tension once they returned to the house was bound to be thick enough that even a kid would discern it.

"How come?"

"We just disagreed about something," Walker said. "She'll get over it."

Tommy had regarded him doubtfully. "I don't know. I heard that Mrs. Jackson say that Daisy's like a dog with a bone once she gets an idea in her head."

"She'll get over it," Walker had repeated emphatically. "Have you ever known her to stay mad at you for long?"

"I guess not."

"Of course not," Walker said firmly. "Now let's get this boat up closer to the house."

Fortunately that task had pretty much prevented any further conversation. When they'd maneuvered the boat close to the garage, Walker sank gratefully onto the edge of it, only to look up and see Bobby Spencer regarding him with a great deal of mirth.

"Fine time you picked to show up," Walker grumbled.

"Actually, I've been here awhile."

"I don't suppose you saw us struggling with this sucker, did you?"

"As a matter of fact, I did. I figured you two were bonding."

Walker scowled at him.

"What's bonding?" Tommy wanted to know.

"Getting to know each other," Bobby explained.

"Oh, yeah," Tommy said, losing interest. "I gotta have something to drink. You want something, Uncle Walker?"

"Water, beer, cola—anything that's cold and wet."

"Okay. I'll be back." The door slammed behind him.

"Looks as if things have improved between you two since last night," Bobby said.

"I suppose."

"Do you have a plan?"

Walker's gaze narrowed. He had a feeling he was about to get more of the advice the people in this town liked to dole out indiscriminately. "What sort of a plan?"

"For the future. You know, where Tommy's concerned."

A shudder washed through him. He was making it

through the weekend one minute at a time. He wasn't ready to grapple with the future. "No, no plan."

"Don't you think you should start considering one?"

"Hey, give me a break. This is all new to me. I found out about Tommy less than a week ago. I met him for the first time yesterday."

Bobby sat down beside him. "I can understand that, but you can't leave the boy dangling forever."

"Is it Tommy you're worried about, or your sister?"

Bobby regarded him with approval. "Both of them, as a matter of fact."

"If everybody would cut me a little slack, maybe I could think this through," Walker said. "Instead, I get a call out of the blue telling me my sister is dead, that I need to get down here and talk about her son's future. I get here and I've got people telling me I need to bond with a boy I knew nothing about, and other people..." He glanced toward the house. "Other people who would just as soon I vanish and never show my face around here again."

"Yeah, it's a tough call, all right," Bobby said, though there was little evidence of sympathy in his tone. "But dragging it out isn't going to make it any easier on anybody, even you." He slanted a look toward Walker. "The way I see it, it's kinda like a splinter, you know? You can take your time and wiggle it out, or you can get some tweezers and just yank. In the long run the fastest way is best. Know what I mean?"

Walker was tempted to chuckle, but Bobby's expression was too serious. "I know what you mean."

"So?"

"Sorry, but I think this is one time when we all need

to take our time and figure out what's best. There's no point in uprooting Tommy only to find out there's no way in hell I can make it work. Then what would happen to him?''

Bobby released a heartfelt sigh. ''Much as I hate to admit it, you have a point. Being a cop is not exactly a nine-to-five job, not even for Tucker, and it must be even crazier for you in D.C.''

''You got that right.''

They sat there side by side in silence for quite a while, before Bobby finally turned his attention to the rowboat.

''Where the devil did Tommy get this thing?'' he asked. ''It looks even worse than I thought the night I helped him haul it over to the beach in front of Daisy's.''

''Apparently it washed ashore. Tommy claimed it.''

''Too bad,'' Bobby said.

''Isn't it?'' Walker agreed. ''Don't worry. I volunteered you to help us fix it up.''

''Me?''

''You run a marina, don't you?''

''I own it. I don't exactly get out and scrape the hulls when the boats are in dry dock.''

''Doesn't matter,'' Walker said, determined to have backup. He figured if Bobby was going to meddle, then he could darn well provide a little assistance, too. ''You know people who do.''

''It's not worth hiring people to fix this boat up. It ought to be chopped up for firewood.''

''You want to tell Tommy that?''

''Not me,'' Bobby said fervently.

''Okay, then, here's the plan I do have. You get the

advice from the experts at the marina. We'll do the work.''

''We, as in you and Tommy?'' Bobby asked hopefully.

''No, as in all three of us. And some kid named Gary.''

Bobby sighed again. ''I was afraid of that.''

Just then the sound of a speedboat shattered the afternoon quiet. Tommy came racing outside, his gaze locked on the river even as he handed Walker a can of cola.

''Wow, will you look at that?'' he said in an awed voice as the boat shot down the river toward the bay.

''Some kid's going entirely too fast,'' Walker observed, but when he glanced at Bobby he thought he saw something more than disapproval in the other man's eyes. ''What?''

Bobby shook his head, shooting a warning look in Tommy's direction.

''You know who that boat belongs to?'' Walker asked.

''I've seen it around a few times.''

''And something about it makes you uneasy?''

Bobby shrugged. ''I'm probably imagining things. Just because a boat can go fast doesn't mean it's anything more than a pleasure craft, right?''

Walker let the matter drop because that was obviously what Bobby wanted, but he couldn't stop thinking about it. Bobby Spencer didn't strike him as a man prone to imagining fires when he hadn't seen *and* smelled the smoke. If something about that boat bothered him, then it was probably worth looking into.

Of course, Bobby's brother was the sheriff. If Bobby really suspected trouble, he could turn to Tucker. It wasn't any of Walker's business. He had more than enough trouble on his hands as it was.

Daisy stared out the kitchen window at her brother, Tommy and Walker. Her breath caught at the sight of Tommy's uncle, who'd stripped off his shirt sometime since she'd left him on the beach. Had he done that just to make her crazy? Surely it hadn't gotten that hot since she'd come inside. Of course, right now, the kitchen felt as if the temperature had shot up twenty degrees in the last five minutes.

"Don't look at him," she warned herself, but it was easier said than done. Her gaze kept straying back to him as the three of them stood side by side, examining that pathetic excuse for a rowboat as carefully as if it were the *QE2*. Tommy's expression was downright reverent.

That the men were willing to indulge Tommy's fantasy—and to assure that he didn't drown—touched her in ways she didn't care to examine too closely. She was beginning to have a hard time remembering that the end result of all this closeness could be losing Tommy.

"Daisy!"

The shout from the yard drew her attention. With a great deal of reluctance given the way her last contact with Walker had ended, she stepped outside and immediately felt his intense gaze searing her. She forced herself to look at her brother.

"What's up?"

"You know all about this boat deal, right?"

"Pretty much."

"And you've given it your blessing?"

She caught a glimpse of Tommy's worried expression and pushed aside her own doubts. "As long as Tommy follows the rules. That boat doesn't go anywhere near the river until he's been given the go-ahead by one of you. And a grown-up has to be around."

"Fair enough," Walker said. He looked at Tommy. "Is it a deal?"

"I guess," Tommy said, sounding sullen. But a sharp glance from his uncle had him adding, "Yes, sir."

"Okay, then," Bobby said. "Tommy, you and I will take a ride over to the marina and see if we can get some advice on what supplies we need."

"Isn't Uncle Walker coming?"

"No, I think he and Daisy have some things to discuss."

"We do?" Walker and Daisy asked simultaneously.

Bobby grinned. "Seems that way to me."

He headed for his car, with Tommy skipping ahead of him, before Daisy could think of a single argument to either stop them from leaving her alone with Walker or get him to leave with them.

"Can I get you something to drink?" she asked, trying to keep her gaze away from the way his well-muscled chest gleamed in the sunlight. This was one policeman who definitely did not exist on coffee and doughnuts, not with that body.

Walker lifted his can of cola. "I have something." A grin tugged at his mouth. "Are you nervous for some reason?"

"Nervous? Why would I be nervous?"

"I don't know. I'm no threat to you."

She sighed at that. He was wrong, in more ways than one. She walked to the far end of the rowboat and sat on the edge of the bow. "You and Tommy seem to be doing better."

"He's a good kid. I have a hard time believing that he was raised by my sister."

"Why on earth would you say that?"

"Because Beth did a lot of stuff when she was a kid. She got mixed up with Ryan Flanagan, who was nobody's idea of a decent human being. He was one of those paranoid, antigovernment, anti-everything guys. I know he had her into drugs for a while, and who knows what else. Then he got her pregnant and dumped her."

"That was hardly her fault. And how old was she when she got mixed up with him?"

"Sixteen."

"A lot of us make bad choices when we're sixteen."

Walker met her gaze. "I'll bet you didn't."

Daisy smiled at his confident tone. "You'd be wrong."

"What did you do? Throw toilet paper streamers in a neighbor's tree? Climb the water tower and paint the class year on it?"

"Nothing like that," she conceded. "But I did fall for a man who turned out not to have much character." She saw no point in acknowledging the role her father had played in planting Billy Inscoe in her path as often as possible.

Walker's hand stilled midway to his lips. The condensation on the can of cola dripped onto his chest. Daisy watched in fascination as that single drop of moisture slid slowly down toward the waistband of his jeans.

"Did you marry him?" he asked eventually.

"No, but only because he broke the engagement."

"Why?"

Daisy didn't want to share this particular part of her life with a man she barely knew. She wasn't entirely comfortable with being barren herself. How could a man possibly understand? And if she told him, would he see too much about her motivation in wanting Tommy? More than likely.

"It's complicated," she said eventually.

"Broken relationships usually are."

"Do you have much contact with your ex-wife?" she asked, relieved to be able to shift the attention away from her and onto him.

"Not if I can help it."

"Not even for the sake of your children?"

"Believe me, that is not a concept that holds any relevance for Laurie."

"How terribly sad."

He regarded her with a penetrating look. "You really mean that, don't you?"

"Of course."

"Why? What could my relationship with my kids possibly matter to you?"

"It just seems to me that in any acrimonious divorce it's the kids who wind up suffering, and none of what happened is their fault."

"To hear their mother tell it, I wasn't much of a father before the divorce. She doesn't think anything's changed." He shrugged. "I probably shouldn't tell you that. You'll probably race right on over to share it with Frances Jackson, but I can save you the trouble. I told her myself."

Daisy was shocked by his accusation. "Why would I do that?"

"You don't want me to take Tommy, do you?"

"Honestly?"

"Of course."

"No. I love having him here. But I also know he needs to know he has family out there."

Walker shot her a rueful grin. "Out there? Not front and center?"

"You know what I meant."

"Do I? Are you really that selfless, Daisy Spencer?"

"Why do you ask that as if it's some sort of crime?"

He shrugged. "Not a crime, just unusual. Frankly, it bugs the daylights out of me."

She tried not to let the comment hurt, but it did. She fought to keep him from realizing it, though. "I can see where it might," she said lightly. "Since you're so obviously unfamiliar with the concept. Feeling a little guilty, perhaps?"

"Maybe," he admitted.

His candor surprised her. "Good for you. Maybe there's hope for you, after all."

"I wouldn't place any bets on it."

"Can I ask you something personal, Detective?"

"Isn't that what you've been doing all along?" He grinned. "This must be a doozy, if you're asking permission."

She frowned at his teasing. "I'm serious."

"Then, by all means, ask away."

"Do you love your children?"

"Of course," he said without hesitation.

"Miss them?"

He leveled a look into her eyes. "You cut straight through the garbage, don't you?"

"I try."

"Okay, yes, I miss them. Having them with me for

the occasional holiday and two weeks in the summer breaks my heart, but it's the way it had to be."

"Why? Because it was easier than fighting for more?"

He stood up and began to pace, avoiding her gaze.

"Walker?" she prodded.

"No," he said finally, his expression anguished. "Because that was all I deserved."

"According to whom? The court?"

"My ex-wife."

"Under the circumstances, I imagine she was fairly biased."

"Justifiably so." He met her gaze then. "Look, Daisy, I'm not going to try to put a pretty spin on things. My marriage fell apart within four years. I spent too much time on the job. And when I wasn't at work, I was thinking about it. Being a cop in D.C. can become an all-consuming mission. Laurie warned me time and again, she wanted more from me. More time. More attention. More fun. I constantly felt like I was being torn in two."

"And in the end she concluded that you loved your work more than you did her," Daisy guessed.

"Exactly."

"Was she right?"

"In a way, I suppose she was. I just know I was tired of all the fighting, tired of putting the kids through it. There was no way I was ever going to be able to give her what she wanted, so I agreed to a divorce. I agreed to let her move home to North Carolina with the kids. I thought maybe once she was there she'd be happy, and that could only be good for the kids, right?"

"And *is* she happy?"

"Not that I've noticed."

"And your children?"

"They're doing okay."

"Just okay?"

He scowled at her. "Look, what do you want me to say? They've got aunts, uncles and cousins around. They have a yard to play in and good schools. They have a grandmother who bakes them cookies and a grandfather who will play checkers with them."

"They don't have their dad," Daisy pointed out quietly.

"Dammit, Daisy, I've made peace with this. What business is it of yours, anyway?"

"None," she conceded. "Except that it says a lot about the kind of life Tommy could expect to have with you."

"There's no comparison. This situation is entirely different," he said defensively.

"Yes," she agreed. "Tommy doesn't even belong to you. How much can he possibly expect, given the way you've abandoned your responsibilities with your own sons?"

"Leave it alone," he said, glowering at her. "Just leave it the hell alone."

With that, he whirled around, grabbed his shirt and took off around the side of the house.

She followed him. "Walker!"

His pace never even slowed.

"What should I tell Tommy when he gets back?" she shouted after him.

He turned then, and Daisy was almost certain she caught the sheen of tears in his eyes, but the moisture could have been caused by the sun's glare rather than emotion.

He hesitated, then said gruffly, "Tell him I'll see him in the morning before I go back to D.C."

Though his decision to leave a day early wasn't unexpected, her heart fell. She'd pushed too hard, and now Tommy would pay the price.

"Come back for dinner," she pleaded.

"I can't."

"Other plans?" she mocked.

"As a matter of fact, yes."

She regarded him doubtfully. "What plans?"

He stared hard at her, radiating a mix of indignation and defiance. "Not that it's any of your business, Ms. Spencer, but I plan to spend the evening getting stinking drunk."

He hammered the words at her, then watched for her reaction. Daisy knew he expected shock or disgust, but she refused to show either one.

"Suit yourself," she said mildly.

"That's it? Just 'suit yourself'?" He mimicked her prim tone in a way clearly intended to goad her.

"Did you expect a lecture?" she asked, not rising to the bait. "You're a grown man, Walker. You'll do whatever you want to do, whether I approve of it or not."

"You've got that right," he said belligerently.

Daisy hid a smile. He sounded just like Tommy, trying to be tough when he already knew he was in the wrong.

Deliberately ignoring him, she stood, brushed imaginary lint from her slacks, then headed for the backyard. She paused one last time before turning the corner.

Walker stood as if he'd been rooted to the same spot in the sidewalk.

As Daisy was about to go inside, she finally spared him one last glance. ''Dinner's at seven if you change your mind.''

''I won't.''

She smiled. ''Whatever.''

She allowed the door to swing shut behind her, then leaned against the jamb. Only when she heard his muttered curse did she allow herself a full-fledged grin.

And then she began to set three places at the table. Walker might be furious with her. He might be genuinely convinced he was a lousy father. He might be thoroughly confused about whether he wanted Tommy in his life. But he would be back. He would never willingly hurt his nephew by staying away. She was as sure of that as she was that the sun would streak through the sky in the east in the morning and set the river ablaze.

9

Walker flatly refused to go waltzing back to Daisy's for dinner, tail tucked between his legs. He knew that's what she expected. The woman thought she had him all figured out.

Maybe she did. Maybe she didn't. Either way, he didn't intend to let her get the idea that she could manipulate him, and that was exactly what she was trying to do. *Whatever,* indeed. She was about as indifferent to his decision as he was to those delectable curves of hers.

Which, he reminded himself, was another extremely good reason to stay away. What did he need with a prissy, impossible woman who lived eighty miles from D.C.?

There was just one problem with his plan. He was starving. He didn't feel like dressing up and heading for the Inn where he'd eaten with Frances Jackson. There were bound to be other places around, but none where he could guarantee he wouldn't run into somebody who'd feel inclined to share an opinion about what he ought to do. He'd passed the marina, considered the bar there, but dismissed it. Bobby would no doubt be back from running his errands with Tommy and, if he was anything like a certain other Spencer, he'd feel inclined to dispense yet more advice with any booze he served.

Other than Earlene's, Walker hadn't spotted any restaurants along the beachfront. Earlene's was open only for breakfast and lunch. And once he'd driven past the town limits, the only thing between Trinity Harbor and Montross were fields and pastures. Rural living might be quiet and serene, but it was damned inconvenient when a man wanted a burger and a plate piled high with French fries. Maybe he'd drive on over to Colonial Beach. There were seafood restaurants over there. He could order a dozen crabs and relieve some tension by hammering them into oblivion and getting a decent meal in the process.

As he considered that option, Walker showered and changed his clothes. He wasn't prepared for the soft little knock on his door. Nor was he prepared to find his nephew standing in the hallway, shifting uncomfortably from foot to foot.

"Hi," Tommy said, his expression brightening when he saw Walker.

"What are you doing here?" Walker said, unable to hide the hint of exasperation in his voice. When Tommy's face fell, he felt like a jerk. "Sorry. I just wasn't expecting you."

"I know. Daisy told me not to come, but I had to."

So Daisy knew he was here. Terrific. Now she'd have something else to hold over Walker's head. "Why did you have to come?"

"Because of the boat. Bobby and me got all sorts of neat stuff, but he had to go back to work and Gary can't come over tonight and I don't know what to do with it." He regarded Walker seriously. "I was thinking maybe you could show me after dinner. I mean, you might not have time tomorrow, if you're leaving, right? Daisy said you might go back a day early.''

Big blue eyes, just like Beth's, stared up at him hopefully. Walker held back a sigh. Guilt, an emotion with which he was becoming all too familiar this weekend, reared its ugly head once again.

"Come on in," he said finally. "Let me shave and I'll come with you."

"You don't have to shave," Tommy said, following him inside. "Daisy won't care."

"A word to the wise, kiddo—women always mind stuff like that. They hate having anyone coming to the dinner table looking disreputable."

Tommy looked unconvinced. "You think so? I know she makes me wash my face and hands, but she never says much if my clothes are all dirty from playing."

"Trust me."

"Then I'm glad I'm not a grown-up," Tommy said fervently. He watched Walker in the bathroom mirror as he scraped the razor over his cheek. "Doesn't that hurt?"

Walker realized then that Tommy had probably never even seen a man shave before. "No, not if you're careful."

"But the razor's sharp, right?"

"Very sharp."

"And Mama said the nicks sting like the dickens."

Walker grinned. He'd heard Beth say exactly those words when she'd cut her legs shaving them for the first time. "That's why you try really hard not to nick yourself."

"Well, I'm never gonna shave," Tommy vowed. "I'm gonna let my beard grown down to here." He gestured to his knees.

"Then you'll probably never have a girlfriend," Walker suggested.

"Who cares? I don't like girls anyway."

"That'll change."

"I don't think so."

"Trust me," Walker said for the second time. This time, as the words left his mouth, he realized that he wasn't just saying them. He really wanted this boy to trust him. He wanted to do things right with his sister's child, as he hadn't been able to do with her, as he hadn't been able to with his own kids.

Daisy's nagging words about the way he'd let his boys slip from his life without a fight came back to haunt him. Was that what he'd done? Had he just taken the easy way out when he'd let Laurie have full custody and settled for an occasional visit with the boys as his due? Probably, he admitted reluctantly. It had been easier than fighting, easier than trying to come up with an alternative.

It wasn't going to be that easy to figure out what to do about Tommy, though. Tommy didn't have a mother to take responsibility for him. There was Daisy, of course, but did Walker have the right to foist his obligation off on her, no matter how willing she might be?

Or did doing the right thing mean taking Tommy with him to D.C.? What kind of life could a bachelor cop give to a ten-year-old boy in a city with every sort of peril? Could he make all of the adjustments entailed, logistically or emotionally? And how could he possibly decide any of that by tomorrow or even Sunday, if he decided to stick around that long? He was already dreading the moment when he had to face all those expectant faces—Daisy's, Frances Jackson's, Anna-

Louise's, maybe even Tommy's—and give them his answer.

Right now, in fact, he wasn't even sure exactly how he was going to get through the next couple of hours with temptation staring him straight in the face.

Daisy had no illusions. Walker wasn't sitting at her dining room table because he wanted to be there. In fact, he looked as if he wanted to be anywhere else on earth. Clearly his arrival was Tommy's doing. The fact that he'd come at his nephew's behest was heartening. At least, she thought it was.

The sorry truth was that she had no idea what was right or wrong in this situation anymore. And she was pathetically grateful that Walker was there. As impossible as he was, she felt more alive around him. Of course, some of that was the urge she had to throttle him for trying to make himself out to be such a hard-hearted jerk when it was increasingly plain to her that he was anything but that.

She was relieved, though, when he and Tommy bolted the instant the meal was finished. Walker made a dutiful offer to help with the dishes, but she waved him outside. His thorough once-over on his way out suggested he knew precisely why she didn't want to be left alone with him.

That was another thing that threw her about the man. Despite his obvious anger earlier, despite the fact that it hadn't seemed to fade, he still couldn't seem to keep himself from flirting with her. He did it outrageously, too, with those deliberately lingering looks, an occasional wink, even a casual caress as he passed by on his way outside. All of it left her feeling completely off-kilter and out of her depth. She liked the sensation, probably a little too much.

With the dishes washed and put away, she stood in the doorway for the second time that day and watched as Walker bent over, patiently showing Tommy how to use the plane on the wood, smoothing patches that had been misshapen by time and weather.

"You could come out and help," Walker said without looking up.

Daisy hadn't even realized he was aware of her. "I don't know what I could do," she said, deliberately making herself sound like the helpless female he most likely thought her to be. The truth was, she was anything but that. Catching him off-guard promised to liven up the evening.

"You could sweep up all this gunk," Tommy suggested, falling neatly into her trap.

Walker chuckled. "Uh-oh, you've put your foot in it now."

Tommy stared at him in confusion. "How come?"

Daisy came over and tugged on his cowlick. "Because you automatically assumed that I was only suited for sweeping up your mess."

"But you sweep all the time," Tommy protested, then shook his head. "I don't get it."

"Sweeping is sometimes thought to be women's work," Walker explained. "By suggesting that's all she could do, you offended her and implied she wasn't capable of doing the guy stuff we're doing."

"But she's the one who said she didn't know anything about fixing a boat," Tommy grumbled. "I figured sweeping was something she knew about."

Walker sighed dramatically. "I know. I know. Trying to understand women is a full-time job. You'll get the hang of it one of these days."

"Who's going to teach him?" Daisy asked. "You or me?"

"That's a lesson best passed on man to man," Walker said.

"Oh, really?" She bumped her hip into his. "Move over. Hand me that plane."

Walker looked startled, but he shifted out of her way. "By all means," he said, handing over the tool.

"Now watch and learn," Daisy said, and went to work.

Tommy opened his mouth to protest, but Walker wisely silenced him. When she'd finished the section of the boat they'd been working on in half the time it had been taking them, she dusted the wood shavings off her clothes and stood up.

"Not bad," Walker said.

"Not *bad?*" she repeated indignantly. "It's perfect. Who do you think made all those cabinets in my kitchen?"

"You?" Both Walker and Tommy sounded stunned.

"You got it, my male friends. I made them."

"But you said—" Tommy began, only to be cut off by Walker, his expression amused.

"She hustled us," Walker said. "I'm surprised she didn't try to get us to put money on it."

"This time was just fair warning," she said, her gaze locked with his. "Never underestimate me."

"Not a chance," he said softly. "Not a chance."

Daisy was still gloating over her victory two days later, but she had to concede that it hadn't gotten them any closer to reaching a decision about Tommy's future. When she found Frances waiting on her doorstep right after church on Sunday, she sighed.

"What's wrong? Aren't you glad to see me?" the social worker asked with a grin.

"Of course she is," Anna-Louise said, coming up the walk right behind Daisy. "Coffee ready?"

"It will be in five minutes," Daisy said, relieved that Anna-Louise had accepted her invitation to join them. She'd hoped the levelheaded minister might be able to keep her from saying things she had no business saying, either to Frances or Walker. "I just have to plug the coffeepot in."

"Is Walker coming over?" Frances asked as she followed Daisy into the kitchen and began taking a mountain of legal-looking papers out of her briefcase.

"When he left here last night, he promised to be here by noon," Daisy told them as she got the coffee started. She had to keep her gaze averted from those papers. They sent a chill down her spine.

"And Tommy?"

She gestured outside. "He was chomping at the bit to get to work on his boat. He's probably still wearing his best pants, but I didn't have the heart to force him to come inside and change. I'll take his lunch out to him in a minute. He shouldn't be interrupting us."

Silence fell as Daisy busied herself setting out plates and the coffee cake she'd baked that morning. She put a peanut butter and jelly sandwich and potato chips on a plate, grabbed a can of cola, then carried it out to Tommy.

When she came back, the coffee was ready. Anna-Louise had already poured cups for herself and Frances. Daisy made herself a cup of herbal tea. She was afraid her stomach would revolt if she drank anything stronger. She felt as if her entire life was hanging in the balance. Putting her fate into the hands of a man she barely knew terrified her, but there was no choice. Walker had undeniable rights where Tommy was concerned. She didn't have to like it, but facts were facts.

"How are Tommy and Walker getting along?" Frances asked as she dumped two scoops of sugar and plenty of cream into her half cup of coffee.

"Well enough," Daisy said.

Daisy knew the precise instant when Walker stepped into the room. The hair on the back of her neck stood up and goose bumps danced over her arms.

"Shouldn't you be asking me that question?" he asked.

"Well, of course," Frances said. "I didn't hear you come in. How do you think it's going?"

"He's a good kid."

"I think we can all agree on that point," Frances said impatiently. "But what are we going to do about his living arrangements?"

Daisy stared straight into Walker's eyes, but she couldn't get a fix on how he felt or what he really wanted. She could only speak for herself.

"Tommy can stay on with me," she said in an attempt to seize what little control of the situation she could. "He's happy here and I love having him. And there's school to consider. It's the middle of the year, not the best time to uproot him."

"But Walker is his uncle," Frances pointed out needlessly. "In a custody case…"

"It's only a custody case *if* Walker wants him. Otherwise, it will be up to you and the court to decide where he's better off, isn't that right?" Anna-Louise said.

Frances scowled. "Yes, but—"

"Is there any reason we have to rush into a decision right now?" the minister persisted. "What about a compromise for the time being?" She glanced at Walker. "Unless you've already decided what you want to do?"

Walker's shoulders visibly sagged with relief. "Not yet," he admitted.

Daisy's heart thudded. "What sort of compromise?"

"As you've already pointed out, school won't be out for a few weeks. Why not keep Tommy here with you until he finishes the school year? Detective Ames can continue to visit on the weekends and get to know his nephew. He can take a closer look at the adjustments he'd have to make to his life to accommodate having Tommy with him. Then all of this can be resolved during the summer." She glanced at Frances. "What do you think?"

"I had hoped..." she began, then shrugged, her expression resigned. "If Detective Ames and Daisy agree, I suppose it could work. We want this to be a smooth transition for the boy."

Holding her breath, Daisy waited for his answer. Walker looked like one of those deer that got caught in the headlights during hunting season around here. He was clearly torn between obligation and his desire not to complicate his life with a boy he barely knew.

"I think it's a wonderful solution," Daisy said finally, hoping to force the issue.

He frowned at her. "How often would I have to come down here?"

"Weekly, I should think," Frances said.

"Impossible," he replied at once. "Not with the kind of job I have. Half the time I don't even know my days off until the last minute. And if I'm caught up in a case, I might not take time off at all.''

"Then you'll have to work on changing that," Frances retorted with a touch of exasperation. "After all, the whole idea is for you and Tommy to get to know one another. It's not as if there are travel expenses to consider. It's an easy drive, two or three hours at most. If necessary, I could speak to your boss about making sure you have the time off. He seemed like a reasonable man.''

"Forget that," Walker said fiercely. "*I'll* tell Andy whatever he needs to know.''

"You can stay here at the house," Daisy offered again, ignoring Anna-Louise's warning look. "It'll be easier for you and Tommy to bond if you're under the same roof. And you won't have any extra expenses.''

"It's not the money," Walker protested. "It's the time.''

"I guess you're the only one who can decide what your priorities are," Frances told him.

With three expectant faces turned his way, Walker sighed heavily. "Okay, fine. We'll give it a try. I'm not promising I'll be here every weekend, though.''

"As long as you intend to do the best you can to be here as often as possible," the social worker told him.

Walker frowned at her. "Whatever made me think you'd be a pushover?''

For the first time, Frances grinned. "I'll take that as a compliment." She gathered her papers together and stood up. "I'll see all of you next weekend, then. We'll plan to get together every Sunday to assess how things are going.''

"I never said—" Walker began, then muttered a curse under his breath. "Okay, whatever.''

His lack of enthusiasm didn't bother Daisy. All that mattered was the fact that he intended to come back. And he hadn't said no to staying here with them, either. That little shiver of anticipation that washed over her had nothing at all to do with winning a first-round victory for Tommy's sake. Oh, no, she suspected it had everything to do with the prospect of having Walker right where she could keep an eye on him.

"What do you mean the boy is still with Daisy?" King blustered at Anna-Louise on Tuesday morning. He'd summoned her out to Cedar Hill the minute he heard about the big powwow at Daisy's Sunday morning. To his indignation, she'd taken her own sweet time about coming. The woman had had the audacity to tell him she was off on Mondays. He was still smarting over that one.

Frowning at her, he said, "I thought I told you to take care of this. Can't anybody do what they're supposed to these days? Do I have to do *everything* myself?"

"Your daughter knows exactly what she's doing," Anna-Louise retorted.

"Don't be absurd. Daisy's got a soft heart. She needs to be protected from herself."

"If you ask me, the only person Daisy needs to be protected from is *you*," she shot right back. "You want to control her."

"Don't you get uppity with me, young woman. I think I know my own daughter."

"Then why don't *you* handle her, instead of asking me to do your dirty work for you?"

King frowned at her. "Isn't that what I'm paying you for?"

"You're not paying me," Anna-Louise said mildly. "The church board is. And nobody's paying me to tell people how to live their lives. I lay out God's recommendations, but He pretty much gave us free will."

"His mistake," King grumbled.

Anna-Louise looked highly amused. "You want to tell Him that?"

"I might," he declared. "As for who's in charge, me or the board, who do you think tells them what to do?"

She dared to grin at him. "I know you think you do."

"I do, dammit!" He caught himself as soon as the words were out of his mouth. "No disrespect intended."

"I'm sure," she said, lips twitching.

King's gaze narrowed. "You don't take me seriously, do you?"

"Of course, I do."

"Then fix this."

"How?"

"If I knew that, would I be asking you?"

"Probably. You enjoy delegating. You get your way without having to catch any of the flak. In fact, I suspect your biggest frustration these days is that you're running out of people you can delegate to. Bobby's got his own jam-packed life to manage with the marina and his restaurant. Tucker's worrying about the safety of the whole county. And, most galling of all, I'm sure, now Daisy's paying more attention to Tommy than she is to you."

King frowned at the accuracy of her assessment. Granted he had a whole cattle operation to run, but he was beginning to feel useless and out of control where his own family was concerned. There had been a time when all of them jumped to do his bidding, Daisy especially.

When her mama had died, Daisy had done her best to step into the void, even though she was only an itty-bitty thing herself. She'd kept King's life comfortable and running smoothly, at least until she'd gotten the ridiculous notion to move into town. Now this.

"Those three will still do what I tell 'em." *More or less and in their own good time,* he added to himself.

"Will they?" Anna-Louise challenged mildly.

King sighed heavily. He'd liked the way the pastor had stood up to him when they'd been interviewing her for the job. Now he was finding it damned inconvenient.

"Letting them grow up and make their own mistakes isn't a bad thing," Anna-Louise told him when he remained silent. "That's what every parent has to do sooner or later. You've kept them under your thumb long enough, taught them some invaluable lessons in the process, I'm sure. Now it's time you had a little faith that they'll wind up doing what's best."

"Best for whom, I ask you?"

"I think I'll let you work that one out for yourself," she said. "See you in church next Sunday."

"Oh, I'll be there," King told her. He regarded her with a dire expression. "You might give a thought to whether or not *you* will be."

To his astonishment, instead of quaking in her boots, she planted a kiss on his cheek.

"You don't scare me, King Spencer," she informed him.

"Well, damn," he murmured after she'd gone. Seemed like he didn't scare anybody these days. He was going to have to do something about that.

10

The boy seated on the brick step next to Walker reminded him of another kid he'd just spent a lot of time with. Small and wiry, his face innocent, he had the same distrustful attitude that Tommy had had when Walker first arrived in Trinity Harbor.

Of course, that was where the resemblance ended. This child's huge, chocolate-brown eyes had already seen too many horrors, including the death of a five-year-old neighbor the week before. Walker was trying to get the kid to open up about what he'd seen, but so far he'd had no luck. Rodney Carmichael wasn't talking.

He tried again. "You know, Rodney, what happened to Keisha is a bad thing."

"Shit happens," the boy said with a disinterested shrug and far too much cynicism for a child his age.

Walker wanted to shake him, to tell him that accepting the shooting of a playmate as normal was wrong. Instead, he forced himself to temper his response.

"Next time it could be you."

"No way," Rodney protested. "I ain't no fool. I know how to stay out of the way."

"A bullet doesn't give you a lot of time to duck."

"Yeah, but I know who's who around here. Nobody's comin' after *me*."

"They didn't come after Keisha either. She just got in the way. She was practically a baby, and now she's dead. Do you think that's right?"

"Ain't none of my business."

"Rodney, I know you saw who did this. I know you know who that shot was really meant for. Give me something to work with, okay?"

"No way."

Walker felt like screaming in frustration. He got to his feet and pulled Rodney up with him. "Okay, let's go."

At long last a reaction. Alarm flared in Rodney's eyes. His gaze darted around as he looked for help.

"Go where?" he demanded, though he was losing a little of his belligerence.

"Down to the precinct."

"You can't arrest me," the boy said with one last display of smug defiance.

"Watch me," Walker said, all but lifting the boy off his feet.

Rodney struggled to break free, but Walker kept him dangling in midair, though Rodney was in grave danger of losing the baggy pants that were barely clinging to his narrow hips. Walker had already spoken to Rodney's mother, who had authorized him, in writing, to question the boy, at the police station if need be. Mrs. Carmichael said she'd done her best to get an answer from her son about what had happened that night, but Rodney had clammed up with her, too. Keisha's mom was her best friend, and she was beside herself at not being able to help, at not being able to convince her boy to do the right thing.

"I want that murderer caught," she'd told Walker. "Killing babies ain't right. And if Rodney knows something, you make him tell you."

Then she had called her son and told him to answer Walker's questions. Her advice hadn't swayed Rodney a bit.

"This is police harassment, man," he shouted now. "It's brutality. I want a lawyer."

"Yeah, yeah, yeah," Walker said, unimpressed. "Report me."

"You think I won't? Wait'll my brothers hear about this. You ain't gonna be safe in the 'hood."

"They aren't here protecting you now, are they?" Walker had seen them scatter when he'd arrived in the neighborhood. These so-called brothers of Rodney's—most of them older and doubly street-smart—wouldn't give two hoots about this ten-year-old unless he snitched. Walker was going to have to be very careful to be sure they never found out...assuming he could actually persuade Rodney to talk.

"But they'll come when they find out," the boy said, fighting tears as well as the truth—that he had been abandoned by older teenagers he wrongly idolized. "They will, and you'll be sorry."

"What I'm sorry about is that Keisha is dead. That's the crime, Rodney, that and the fact that you won't help me find the killer. You know what that's called? It's called obstruction of justice."

"I ain't obstructing nothing. I'm telling you I didn't see nothing."

Walker carried the still wriggling boy to his unmarked car, put him into the back and locked the doors. Rodney refused to be intimidated. He was still mouthing off when they got to headquarters a few blocks away. Walker saw a lot of officers hiding a grin when he crossed the squad room with the belligerent boy in tow.

"Sit," Walker ordered, gesturing toward a chair beside his desk.

Rodney remained defiantly standing.

"You want something to drink? A soda maybe? There's a vending machine with candy, too."

He watched as Rodney struggled against temptation. "There's nobody here to see if you accept something," Walker said more gently. "Come on. Let's go see if there's something you like in there."

He led the way to the cluster of vending machines in a small break room. He handed Rodney enough change to buy whatever he wanted. The kid surveyed the candy machine first, then the drinks, then the cigarettes.

"No way," Walker said when he realized what had captured the boy's attention. "Something to drink or eat. That's it."

"What are you, my mother?"

"I'm the guy who's trying to teach you to do the right thing."

"Well, who asked you to?"

"Nobody. I'm just a nice guy."

Rodney rolled his eyes, but he finally popped the change into the machine and retrieved a soft drink, then added a candy bar and chips.

"Okay, over here," Walker said, pointing to a table in the corner. He waited until Rodney had wolfed down the chips and started on the candy bar before he reminded him why they were there. "Nobody can see you in here. Nobody's going to know you said a word."

Rodney stared at him as if he'd lost his mind. "Everybody saw you haul me off. If you go rushing out and pick somebody up, who do you think they're gonna blame?"

To Walker's deep regret, Rodney had a point. "I'll talk to a lot of people before we go after anybody," he promised. "Rodney, you have a chance to do the right thing. Maybe you'll be saving another kid's life."

"A lot of good that'll do me, if *I'm* the one who's dead."

"Nobody's going to kill you. I'll see to it you have protection. You and your mom."

"And if I don't help you? Are you gonna put me in jail?"

Walker sighed heavily. Jail was not an option for a ten-year-old. Not when Walker couldn't prove the boy had seen something when he swore he hadn't. He suspected Rodney knew it, too. These children had the wisdom of adults when it came to knowing their rights. It was bred into them by their older, tougher heroes with a little help from the cop shows on television.

"No jail," he admitted. "You'll just have to live with your conscience."

Rodney seemed totally comfortable with that. A swagger in his step, he headed for the door. "Then I'm outta here."

When Walker started to rise, Rodney waved him off. "I can walk, man. That's better than being seen with you twice in one day."

Resigned to failure, Walker watched him go, then got himself a cup of coffee. He sat back down and tried to figure out where to go next. Andy wandered in, grabbed a soda and sat across from him.

"Any luck?"

"The kid figures his chances are better with the bad guys than with us."

"He could be right."

Walker rubbed his eyes. "God, I hate this. Interrogating kids who ought to be riding their bikes or playing ball makes me sick."

"Did you show Rodney a picture of Keisha's body lying in a pool of blood on the sidewalk?"

Walker had debated with himself long and hard over that one. "He's ten years old. He shouldn't have to live with that image for the rest of his life. It's hard enough for me."

"Maybe he needs to live with it," Andy suggested. "Maybe all of them do. Maybe if they were forced to face the reality of what they've done, it would finally sink in that this isn't some damned macho game, that innocent kids are dying. It's not like TV where the actors get up, dust themselves off and go out for a beer. Maybe we should take the pictures of Keisha and all the others into the schools. Maybe that would shock some sense into these kids. They don't value life, not the way you and I do. Damned if I know how to fix that."

Andy's voice shook with frustration and anger. That was one of the things that Walker most admired in his boss. The man cared deeply.

"I think the ones we need most to reach are already lost," Walker said. "They've dropped out of school."

"Then we'll start with the younger ones. Find some way to make them care about themselves and each other. Maybe those pictures would get through to them."

"And you know what the reaction from the parents will be. They'll be in front of the school board hollering that their babies don't need to see that kind of thing," Walker said. "Doesn't matter that it's happening right in front of their eyes as it is."

Andy closed his eyes. "Yeah, I know you're right. How do we stop it, though? What's the magic way to put an end to this?"

Walker sighed heavily. "I wish to God I knew."

They sat there, the silence between them filled with shared dismay. Finally, Andy said, "Let's get out of here. I need some lunch, the greasier the better."

Walker's expression brightened. "I know just the place."

They headed for a barbecue joint where the shredded pork was doused in spicy sauce and the fries were crisp and plentiful. Andy didn't say much while they ate, but as soon as he'd finished, he studied Walker.

"Okay, you want to tell me what went on down in Trinity Harbor?"

"Not especially."

"You going back down there to see your nephew?"

"I promised that I would."

When he thought of that promise, it wasn't Frances Jackson's face or even Daisy's that he thought of. It was Tommy's. The boy had stared up at him, fear and hope warring on his face, his voice trembling as he asked if his uncle was coming back. Walker had known right then that whatever his trepidation, whatever his misgivings, he had to go back.

He just couldn't bring himself to think beyond that.

Daisy was beginning to settle into a comfortable routine with Tommy. They ate breakfast together and then she dropped him at his school on her way to the high school a few blocks away. In the afternoon, he walked over and met her in her classroom and they drove home together.

Usually Tommy chattered nonstop about his day, about the progress he was making on his boat and his anticipation of his uncle's next visit. It was clear that Walker had already become something of a hero to him.

On Friday afternoon, though, Tommy was unusually quiet. Nothing Daisy asked could draw him out.

"Did something happen at school today?"

"Nah."

"Do you have a lot of homework for the weekend?"

"Same old stuff."

"Is there anything special you'd like to do?"

When he didn't respond, she slanted a quick look at him and saw a tear spill down his cheek. Suddenly she understood.

"Tommy, Walker will be back. He promised."

Tommy's shattered face turned toward her. "But when? He hasn't even called," he said angrily. "Not once."

"I'm sure he's very busy. He has a very difficult job."

"I suppose."

At that moment she could have cheerfully strangled Walker. She bore some of the blame. Why hadn't they even discussed his calling Tommy, especially if Walker couldn't make it down for the weekend?

"You could call *him*," she suggested.

A glimmer of hope flared in Tommy's eyes. "Really?" Then his expression fell. "It's long distance. That costs a lot."

"Not that much—and even if it did, it wouldn't matter. It's worth it. I'll call Frances and get the number the minute we get home."

"All right," Tommy said excitedly.

The minute they reached the house, Tommy dismissed her offer of cookies and milk. "Just call, okay?"

Daisy went to the phone and dialed.

"Tommy hasn't heard from him all week?" Frances asked, immediately indignant. "I thought that man had more sense. Maybe *I* should call him."

"I'll do it," Daisy said. She had a few things she'd like to say to him herself, once Tommy had talked to him.

As soon as she'd hung up, she handed Tommy the number and the phone. "You can call him. Just remember, I'd like to speak to him when you're done."

Tommy was so eager, he punched the numbers too fast and made several mistakes, winding up with a wrong number. Disappointment spread across his face. "This number's not right."

Daisy guessed what had happened. "Try again, but do it slowly."

Tommy punched in the numbers with exaggerated care. Suddenly his face brightened. "Uncle Walker, it's me, Tommy."

Suddenly the room was filled with familiar, excited chatter. Daisy listened, a smile tugging at her lips from time to time. Her nerves tingled with anticipation as she waited for her own turn.

"This won't do," she muttered under her breath. She was supposed to be working up to give Walker a piece of her mind, not getting all jittery like a schoolgirl waiting to talk to the boy she was crazy about.

She looked up and realized Tommy was regarding her with a puzzled expression.

"Did you say something, Daisy?"

"Nothing, sweetie. You finish talking to your uncle."

A minute later he turned and handed her the phone. "He says he's coming tomorrow," he said happily. "He didn't forget."

"Good," Daisy said. "Now you get your cookies and milk and run along while I talk to him. You can call your friend Gary when I finish talking to your uncle. Maybe Gary would like to work on your boat with you."

"Can he stay for dinner, too?"

"Of course." She wanted to spend a little more time with the older boy, anyway. He was new in town, and she knew barely anything about him or his family.

His good mood restored, Tommy pumped his fist in the air. "All right!"

Daisy waited until Tommy had dashed from the kitchen before she spoke into the phone.

"I was beginning to wonder if you'd forgotten I was on here," Walker said.

"Well, some of us were beginning to wonder if you'd forgotten all about your promise."

"Is that so?"

His amused reaction wasn't at all what she'd expected. "Boys depend on adults keeping their word," she said, fully aware that she sounded exactly like some prissy old maid schoolteacher. Which, of course, was what she was. Except around Walker she didn't feel so much like that anymore.

"I know they do," Walker said. "What about you? Were you depending on me, too?"

"Well, of course I was."

"Is that so?"

She heard that same disconcerting mirth in his voice again. "For Tommy's sake," she snapped.

"Of course."

"You are a very maddening man, Walker Ames."

"If I'd been able to convince your friend Frances of that, maybe we wouldn't be in this predicament."

Dismayed, Daisy sucked in her breath. "Are you saying the only reason you're coming back here is because Frances pressed you to do it?"

Walker sighed. "She wasn't the only one," he admitted. "I didn't want to see that look of disappointment in Tommy's eyes."

"That's good, then. Apparently you do have a conscience."

"And if I didn't, I suppose you'd try to reform me."

"I'm not sure that would be a good use of my time. I think I'd be better advised to see that Tommy has a loving home right here in Trinity Harbor."

"With you?"

"Of course with me. Who else?"

"Some would say he needs two parents."

"Well, certainly," she said at once. "I'm not denying that. All children deserve two parents who love them and each other, but that's not always possible. Tommy would certainly have male role models if he were with me. Bobby and Tucker would be here for him. So would my father, once he accepts that he's not going to change my mind."

She suddenly realized she was trying to sell Walker on her qualifications to raise Tommy. "I'm sorry. I'm not trying to persuade you to stay away. I just want you to know that Tommy would have a good life with me, if that's the way things work out."

"Daisy, I never doubted that your heart's in the right place," he said quietly. "And you could be right about what's best for Tommy. It's just too soon for me to know."

This time she was the one who sighed. "I know that."

"Isn't this something we can talk about and decide together when the time comes?" Walker asked.

She was surprised he was willing to take her opinion into account. "Absolutely," she said at once.

"I'll see you in the morning, then."

"Yes," she said. "In the morning." As she hung up, she realized her own expression was very likely every bit as excited as Tommy's had been.

"You're pitiful, Daisy Spencer. Totally pitiful."

That said, she still decided the house could use a thorough cleaning before Walker's arrival on Saturday. As soon as they'd had dinner and Tommy's too-reticent friend had left, she went to work with a vengeance. She would worry another day about Tommy's friendship with the thirteen-year-old who gave off signals that made Daisy a bit uneasy.

She reassured herself that any woman would want the house to sparkle when guests were anticipated. Dusted furniture and polished floors were nothing more than what was expected in a gracious home. It was just good manners, a demonstration of Southern hospitality. Dusting and polishing certainly weren't the way to a man's heart.

Which was probably why she was up till midnight baking two pecan pies, a double batch of oatmeal raisin cookies and a chocolate cake with fudge frosting.

* * *

King decided that this nonsense about his daughter taking in a stray boy had gone on long enough. He'd been up half the night thinking about it, worrying himself sick about what was to become of Daisy when this thing ended badly. If nobody else could talk sense into her, it was up to him. He'd obviously left the task to a bunch of incompetents. If a man wanted something done right, he had to do it himself.

Besides, he was worn out from trying to explain her actions to all the busybodies in town. The men were as bad as the women, pestering him about this latest news that Daisy intended to let the boy's uncle move in with her. That had been the last straw. King wasn't going to hear of some damn Yankee ruining his girl's reputation.

He arrived on her doorstep at the crack of dawn on Saturday, figuring he could get a decent breakfast while he was at it. Daisy's pancakes were a whole lot better than his housekeeper's.

Before he could knock, the sound of hammering drew his attention. He walked around the side of the house, then stopped stock-still at the sight of his daughter and a towheaded kid bent over what presumably had once been a boat. Now it was a disaster waiting to happen.

"What the dickens are you doing, woman?" he demanded before he could stop himself. He knew better than to get her dander up first thing.

Daisy's head shot up. She stared at him in dismay. "Daddy, I wasn't expecting you."

"No, I imagine not." His gaze shifted to Tommy. "This is the boy?"

She shot him a warning look. "Yes. This is Tommy

Flanagan. Tommy, this grouchy old man is my father, King Spencer. Don't pay a bit of attention to his temper. I've learned not to.''

King frowned at her. "Is that anything to say to a child?''

"It's the truth. Haven't you always been a big proponent of the truth?''

King's gaze narrowed. "What's happened to you? You never used to be this contrary.''

"I've grown up," she suggested. "You don't scare me anymore.''

King regarded her indignantly. "When did I ever scare you?''

She shrugged. "Okay, maybe that's the wrong word. Maybe I just allowed you to intimidate me, just the way you try to do with everybody else in this town.''

"I never did any such thing," he retorted.

Daisy chuckled. "Oh, for goodness' sakes, Daddy, be honest. You know you did, and you loved every minute of it. Of course, your best friends are the ones who don't let you get away with it.''

He chuckled despite himself. "Okay, maybe I did. Somebody has to keep this town on track. The fool politicians certainly aren't going to do it.''

"And this family?" she suggested.

"That, too," he conceded. "What's a man have to do to get some breakfast around here?''

"Go in the kitchen and fix it," she responded, then grinned at him. "Never mind. I was about to fix ours anyway. You can join us.''

"What a gracious invitation," he grumbled. "You sure it won't be any trouble to set an extra place?''

She came over and gave him a fierce hug then. "No

trouble, but I think you'd better come inside with me while I cook.''

King hadn't intended to do any such thing. He'd planned to stay right here and talk to this boy she was making such a fuss over. He was about to voice his intentions, when she tucked her arm through his and started to the house.

"You afraid of something?" he demanded, when she'd successfully steered him inside.

"Just cautious," she said. "I don't want you hounding Tommy with a lot of questions that might make him feel unwelcome."

"Getting to know the boy is not hounding him, as you put it."

"I'd say that depends on how it's done," she said. "Let's face it—you're not known for your tact. How about a cup of coffee?"

King resigned himself to staying put. He settled down at the kitchen table. "Don't mind if I do."

She poured the coffee and set it in front of him.

"Surprised you have a pot made," he said. "You usually prefer tea."

"Walker likes coffee," she said, then looked away hurriedly.

"Walker? That's the Yankee? That boy's uncle?"

"Exactly."

"So, you're expecting him again?" he asked in a gloomy tone.

"I am," she said.

She faced him with a defiant tilt to her chin that reminded King of her mama, God rest her soul. There were times when his heart still ached for Mary Margaret. Seeing signs of her in Daisy usually gave him comfort.

"Where's he staying this time?" he asked, hoping that the rumors had been wrong for once.

"Here."

King lost his struggle with his temper. He thumped his fist on the table. "No way, young lady. You will not have that man living under your roof."

"Of course I will."

"You'll ruin your reputation."

"I think maybe you've forgotten what century we're living in."

"Dammit, a woman's reputation is a delicate thing. People will talk, and you know it."

"Let them. I'm sure you will be the first to set them straight." She regarded him with a level look. "Won't you?"

"Well, of…of course I will," he sputtered, indignant at the suggestion that he would ever do less than defend his daughter's honor. "When is the boy's uncle due?"

"Sometime this morning. I'm sure you'll be long gone by the time he gets here."

King regarded her stubbornly. "Wishful thinking," he muttered.

He was prepared to settle in for a long siege, if need be. He intended to meet this Walker Ames and have a thorough, man-to-man talk with him. It seemed to him they had a lot to discuss, beginning with a warning to Walker that if he did anything to hurt Daisy, he was going to have King Spencer to answer to. If his daughter thought he'd been intimidating everyone all these years, she hadn't seen anything yet. King Spencer was going to personally ensure that he left this hotshot Yankee detective quaking in his boots.

11

Walker was in a somber mood when he finally got away from Washington on Saturday morning. He'd just been to Keisha's funeral, which had been delayed for the arrival of her paternal grandparents, who'd insisted on driving up from Mississippi.

"Don't know why they want to come now," Keisha's mother had told him. "Didn't want nothing to do with us when Keisha was alive. They thought I'd used that child to trap their precious son. As if that man would ever let himself be caught in a trap. He took off the day I told him I was having his baby. Hasn't been seen since."

"Why did you tell them, then?" Walker had asked her.

"Wasn't me who called them. It was Devon's no-good brother, Jermaine. He said his mama and daddy had a right to know. What right, I ask you? Ain't none I can think of. They ain't never even sent that child a birthday card."

"Maybe they regret that now," Walker suggested.

"What good is regrets gonna do my baby?"

Walker hadn't had an answer for that. But he had noticed the elderly couple at the funeral, the man's shoulders stooped, the woman's eyes red from crying. He had concluded that they would struggle for a long time with what their hardhearted attitude had cost them: the chance to know a beautiful grandchild.

He'd also seen Rodney at the church, clutching his mother's hand as she determinedly led him past the tiny open casket. Later at the cemetery she had made it a point to come up to Walker just before he left to say that she was going to get through to her boy.

"You see if I don't," she said, tears in her eyes.

Walker patted her arm. "Thanks. I know you're trying. And I understand that he's in a tough spot. He doesn't want to betray his friends."

"What kind of friends would put him in a spot like this in the first place?" she demanded indignantly.

"Now there's the million-dollar question," Walker told her.

As he drove toward Trinity Harbor, to his surprise he felt his tension beginning to slip away. His shoulders eased. Maybe spending time with Tommy was just what he needed. He needed to be reminded that there were other kids in the world who were growing up in a safe environment. Kids who could laugh and play outside and ride their bikes without worrying about violence snatching away the rest of their lives.

Walker actually caught himself noticing the blooming pink and white dogwood that splashed the landscape with color. It was such a sunny, warm day that he rolled down the windows. The sky was a peaceful shade of blue with pillows of white clouds. The soft spring breeze brought with it the scent of plowed earth, recently cut grass, and salt air the closer he got to Trinity Harbor. Soon there would be pale green cornstalks poking through the ground and an endless green sea of soybeans surrounding the white farmhouses perched in groves of ancient oaks and cedars. It was hard to believe that such serenity could be had less than two hours away from D.C.

An image of Daisy crept into his mind, as it had repeatedly during the last week, always at the most unexpected moments. He'd enjoyed her acerbic tongue almost as much as that memorable kiss he'd stolen that had left her flustered and him unbearably aroused. Their brief conversation the night before had filled him with an odd sort of anticipation, a sensation he hadn't experienced for a long, long time. Serenity gave way to an edgy, purely male neediness.

That must have been why he was filled with disappointment when he saw another car in the driveway and heard the sound of a man's booming laughter. Probably one of her brothers, he told himself, then wondered why he jumped to such a conclusion. He had no idea if Daisy had a man in her life. Nothing had led him to believe there had been anybody special since her fiancé, but he knew better than to make assumptions. Cops were supposed to rely on hard evidence before reaching conclusions.

Only one way to find out, he told himself as he headed for the backyard.

But the man out back wasn't either Bobby or Tucker. Judging from the gray threaded through his hair, the neatly trimmed moustache, the already tanned skin and the straw hat perched on his head, this was the indomitable King Spencer, gentleman farmer and—if Daisy was to be believed—all-around pain in the neck.

Tommy spotted Walker before the others. He started to break into a run, then held back as if afraid of how Walker might react. "Hi, Uncle Walker," he said shyly.

Daisy's head snapped around at his greeting, and

something that might have been alarm flared in her eyes. She glanced worriedly at the man who had stilled beside her.

"Hey, kid," Walker said, trying to gauge the reason for Daisy's suddenly wary mood. "I see you've lured somebody else into supervising the work on your boat."

Tommy nodded. "This is Daisy's father. He knows lots of stuff about boats."

"Is that so?" Walker said, not sure why the news left him feeling vaguely disgruntled.

When King Spencer finally turned around, Walker noted blue eyes that snapped with intelligence. They had narrowed with suspicion and unmistakable disapproval.

"Nice to meet you, Mr. Spencer," Walker said. "I've heard a lot about you."

"Mr. Ames," King said, greeting him with a nod and ignoring Walker's outstretched hand.

"Daddy," Daisy said sharply. "Don't be rude. And you know perfectly well, it's Detective Ames."

"Walker will do," Walker told them both.

King's gaze shot to the overnight bag at Walker's feet. "You intending to stay here?"

"If the invitation's still open, yes."

"Of course it's open," Daisy said, frowning at her father. "I'll show you to your room, Walker. Maybe by the time we get back, Daddy will recall his manners."

"That's no way to speak to your father, young lady."

"Just following your example," she said tartly and led Walker inside.

In the kitchen she turned to Walker. "I'm really sorry."

"I gather your father's not happy about me staying here."

She grinned. "Another damned Yankee invasion to hear him tell it. Don't worry about it."

"Didn't that particular war end a long time ago?" he asked, amused despite himself that he was being blamed for something he'd had no part in, especially not the part King was attributing to him.

"Long before his time," Daisy agreed. "The results still grate on him, though."

He hadn't considered the impact his presence might have on Daisy's reputation in a small town where strangers—especially male Yankee strangers—were regarded with suspicion. "If my staying here is going to cause problems, I can go to the hotel."

"Absolutely not," she said fiercely.

Walker studied her flushed cheeks. "Because my being under your roof is best for Tommy, right?" he suggested lightly.

His teasing remark clearly left her more flustered than ever. When was the last time he'd met a woman who blushed so readily?

"Of course," she said. "Why else would I want you here?"

He deliberately allowed his gaze to lock with hers. "Why else, indeed?" His glance shifted to the kitchen counter, where pies, a cake and clear glass jar filled with cookies sat. "Had a sudden urge to bake, did you?"

"Last night," she said. "I always bake when I can't sleep."

Walker found himself stepping closer, crowding her. "And why couldn't you sleep, Daisy?"

She swallowed hard. "I...I had a lot to think about."

He slowly trailed a finger across her lush, moist lips. "So did I," he murmured, filled once more with that strange sense of restless anticipation. "From the minute I hung up the phone after we talked, all I could think about was kissing you again."

Her eyes widened. Her lips parted. And Walker found the temptation far too powerful to be ignored. He bent down and slanted his mouth over hers. A part of him wanted to discover that memory had failed him, that tasting her wasn't nearly as exciting as he'd recalled.

But that notion was dispelled in an instant as she swayed into him, clinging to his shoulders, tentatively opening her mouth to him. Her reaction was unpracticed but instinctive, and far more enticing than a bolder response might have been. Desire slammed through him. Only the knowledge that her father—her disapproving father—was right outside kept him from taking full advantage of the moment. Of course, the fear of discovery added an undeniable element of excitement, as well.

That was it, he told himself as he pulled away. It was the knowledge that King Spencer disapproved of him that made him want Daisy so badly.

Of course, that didn't explain why he'd wanted her a week ago, before he'd ever met the man and experienced that scowling disapproval firsthand.

Daisy touched her fingers to her lips and regarded him with confusion. "Why did you do that?"

"Just testing my memory."

Understanding flared in her eyes, and a smile tugged at her lips. "And?"

"Right on target," he admitted with reluctance.

She nodded. "I thought so, too."

Walker was surprised by her ready acknowledgment. "You know this is a bad idea, though, don't you? We can't keep kissing."

A grin spread across her face. "I'm not the one starting it."

"True, but you need to put an end to it."

"Why? Because you can't be trusted to ignore your baser instincts?"

"Exactly."

"Hogwash."

He stared at her. "You don't believe me?"

"If ever a man had a tight rein on his emotions, it's you. Something tells me you don't do anything you haven't thought over and weighed very carefully."

She was right, but Walker couldn't imagine how she had pegged him so cleverly. For years he'd honed his ability to reveal nothing of what he was feeling, to do nothing without thinking of the consequences. It wasn't just a professional necessity. He considered it smart self-preservation after the way he'd misjudged everything about his marriage.

Then again, these kisses he'd been stealing from Daisy were pure impulse. He doubted he could have stopped himself if he'd tried. That was something he needed to sit down and think long and hard about, preferably when her innocent lily-of-the-valley scent wasn't wafting around him.

"You were going to show me to my room," he said, deliberately changing the subject and injecting a flat, even tone into his voice.

"I was," she agreed, her gaze searching his. "But I think I'll just tell you where it is, instead." That penetrating look never wavered. "In case I'm wrong and you can't control those baser instincts, after all."

Walker caught the hint of amusement in her voice and the flicker of something in her eyes—a dare, maybe? Apparently Daisy intended to be more of a handful than he'd imagined.

She gave him very precise directions to his room, but when she turned to go, he snagged her hand. She froze in place, as if she found that contact more intimate, more disturbing than the kiss.

"What?" she asked in a voice that held a telltale quiver.

"I don't know what's going on here, Daisy, but it can't get in the way of me getting to know my nephew. We have to put Tommy first."

"Well, of course, we do," she retorted. Exasperation darkened her eyes to an even deeper, more intriguing shade of violet. "I'm not an idiot, Walker. I know the only reason you're here is because of the debt you feel you owe to your sister and her son."

"That's right," he said forcefully.

But he was beginning to wonder.

"Foolish man," Daisy muttered as she went back outside to deal with her father. She had to stop him from trying to make Walker feel unwelcome.

Unfortunately, King had left.

"He said he had business to take care of," Tommy told her. He regarded her worriedly. "How come he doesn't like Uncle Walker?"

"He doesn't dislike him," Daisy said. "He doesn't even know him."

"But he's mad 'cause he's here, isn't he?"

Daisy gave the boy an impulsive hug. "It's nothing for you to worry about, sweetie. He's not going to drive your uncle away, not if I have anything to say about it."

Tommy, who'd generally held himself aloof when she'd tried to hug him in the past, suddenly hugged her back. The gesture brought tears to her eyes. Naturally Tommy spotted them at once.

"How come you're crying? What did I say?"

"You didn't say anything," she reassured him. "And these are happy tears."

Tommy looked perplexed. "I don't get it. You're crying 'cause you're happy, not sad?"

Daisy nodded. "It's something women tend to do. And, trust me, men never get it."

"You've got that right," Walker chimed in, joining them.

Daisy wondered how long he'd been standing just inside the screen door eavesdropping.

"Women are an enigma," he added.

"What's that?" Tommy asked.

"It means men can't figure us out," Daisy explained. "Their brains can't grasp the workings of a superior mind."

Walker grinned. "Careful, Daisy. You're outnumbered here."

"You seem to forget I was raised in a houseful of pigheaded men. You can't intimidate me."

Tommy looked from Daisy to his uncle and back again. "So, are we gonna work on my boat or what?"

Daisy chuckled. "You two go to it. I'm going for a walk on the beach." She needed the exercise, but more than that, she needed to put some distance between herself and Walker.

"Want us to tag along?" Walker asked.

She wanted exactly that, more than she should. She forced herself to shake her head. "No. That boat's going to take a lot of time. You shouldn't waste a second. I'll probably end up in town, though, if you'd like to meet me at Earlene's for lunch around twelve."

"How about it, Tommy? Does a burger sound good?" Walker asked.

"Can I have a milk shake, too?"

"Anything you want," Walker told him.

"Within reason," Daisy amended.

"Spoilsport," Walker accused.

She met his twinkling eyes. "Someone around here has to do what's sensible."

"And you've designated yourself for that role?"

Though her every instinct was to give Tommy anything and everything he wanted, yes, that was precisely what she had done. She nodded. "I have."

"Then I guess I'll just have to think of some way to make sure you learn to lighten up," Walker told her. "We'll start at lunch."

Where they would be in full view of half the town, Daisy realized with dismay. Walker's tactics weren't likely to be subtle or unobserved. What had she been thinking when she'd suggested they meet her at Earlene's?

She knew the answer, of course. She was thinking that for the very first time in her adult life, she was going to feel as if she were out with a family of her own. Maybe it was a fool's illusion, but she wanted it to last as long as possible.

* * *

Daisy's face was far too revealing. Walker had watched the expressions shift during his teasing, but no matter how hard he tried, he couldn't seem to pinpoint exactly what was troubling her so. Clearly, he'd said something. Was it the accusation that she was being a little too sensible for Tommy's good? Was it the taunt that he was going to get her to lighten up? He hated not being able to get a fix on her the way she seemed capable of doing with him.

"Hey, Uncle Walker," Tommy said, drawing his attention.

"What?"

"Can I ask you something?"

"Sure you can. You can always ask me anything."

"What's pot?"

Walker felt his heart slam into his ribs. All thoughts of figuring out Daisy fled. If Tommy had asked him to explain the birds and bees, he couldn't have been any more disconcerted. He forced himself not to overreact, to keep his expression and his tone neutral.

"Why do you want to know about pot?"

"I heard some kids talking outside the high school."

Walker was more shocked than he should have been. He would have anticipated it in Washington, but not in Trinity Harbor. He had managed to delude himself that this place was far removed from the influence of drugs.

"What were they saying?"

"That really cool kids use it."

Walker sat on the edge of the boat and drew Tommy around to face him. "Really cool kids do *not* use it," he said adamantly. "Kids who try marijuana—that's the actual name of the drug—could really mess up their lives. For one thing, it's illegal, and you can get in a lot of trouble. For another, it can lead to using more dangerous drugs, drugs that could kill you.''

Tommy's eyes widened. ''You mean even a kid could die like Mama?''

''Exactly.'' He met Tommy's gaze directly. ''If you ever see any pot, I don't care who has it, I want you to tell me or Daisy or Tucker at once, do you understand me? That's very important, Tommy. I know that tattling on your friends isn't considered cool, and in most instances, I'd agree, but not about this. Okay?''

Tommy's head bobbed up and down.

''When you heard this at the high school, do you know if the kids had any or were they just bragging?''

''I guess they were just talking. I'm not really sure. They didn't try to give me any or anything. I don't even think they knew I was around. They don't pay much attention to younger kids like me.''

''Were these kids you know?''

''Not really. They're in high school.''

''Is this the first time you've ever heard anyone talking about pot?''

Tommy looked at the ground and scuffed the toe of his sneaker in the dirt. ''No,'' he said softly. ''But I never had anybody to ask before. Mama was really sick the last time I heard about it. And then I guess I forgot.''

''That's okay. You did the right thing by talking to me now.''

''Are those boys gonna get in trouble?'' he asked worriedly.

''If they're caught with marijuana, yes, they could get in big trouble.''

''Don't they know that?''

''They should, but it's not up to you to tell them.

You come to me or Daisy or one of her brothers next time you hear anything like this, okay?''

"Okay," Tommy said, apparently satisfied with Walker's responses. "Could I have a cookie now?"

"Sure. Bring me a couple, too."

As soon as Tommy had gone, Walker released a sigh. He needed to talk to Tucker about this and find out what the hell was going on down here. In a town this size, they should be able to keep a better watch on drugs, especially around a school. He vowed to track Daisy's brother down before the weekend was out.

And he needed to tell Daisy herself, to warn her that she was going to have to be incredibly vigilant about the kids with whom Tommy spent time. That was not a prospect he was looking forward to. She was bound to jump to the conclusion that he was criticizing her ability to keep Tommy out of trouble. He'd already discerned that she was highly sensitive on that subject, anticipating disapproval of her parenting skills at every turn. Too bad. This was a talk they needed to have.

He was still considering the best way to go about bringing up the subject when he and Tommy went to meet her at Earlene's. The restaurant was even more crowded than it had been on his last visit, this time with a mix of tourists and locals. Daisy was already in a booth, though, looking flushed from her walk and, in his opinion, more desirable than ever.

His arrival drew several speculative glances and a few whispers, something that made him feel vaguely self-conscious as he and Tommy headed for the back to join Daisy. Despite his better judgment, Walker squeezed into the booth next to her and let Tommy take the side across from them. She frowned when his thigh brushed hers and stayed there. He noticed, though, that she didn't move away. In fact, she sent a challenging glare in the direction of some of the more obvious spectators. The offenders quickly developed a sudden interest in their meals and the whispers died down.

"How was your walk?" he asked.

"Lovely," she said, turning her attention back to him. "There's a wonderful breeze today, but summer's definitely just around the corner. Did you two get a lot of work done on the boat?"

"Some," he said.

"Uncle Walker and me had a long talk," Tommy chimed in, startling Walker. "About marijuana."

Daisy choked on her sip of iced tea. "I beg your pardon."

"He says it's really, really bad," Tommy explained.

Daisy's indignant gaze clashed with Walker's. "It certainly is. How did this come up?"

As the waitress approached, Walker deliberately nudged Daisy with his elbow. "Why don't we order now? I'm starved."

"Fine," she said, eyes flashing over the postponement. "But this discussion isn't over, not by a long shot."

He chuckled at her fierce expression. "Yes, ma'am." Then he leaned down to whisper in her ear. "You must be hell on wheels in the classroom."

The corners of her mouth twitched unmistakably. "And don't you forget it."

Walker seriously doubted if he could even if he wanted to. Daisy kept surprising him in the most unexpected ways. Despite her obviously genteel Southern upbringing, the woman refused to back down from a fight. He'd be willing to bet those ancestors of hers had given the Yankees a royal fit.

12

Marijuana! What on earth was a ten-year-old boy doing asking about drugs? Daisy couldn't imagine, but she certainly intended to find out at the very first opportunity.

She had waited through an endless lunch, then waited some more while Tommy dragged Walker off to explore the shops in town. She had been tempted to go along just to see how Walker would handle the crowded aisles in the old houses that had been converted into boutiques, but had decided to let them go without her. The phrase "bull in a china shop" came to mind, when she envisioned his broad shoulders squeezing past displays of delicate Christmas ornaments. Then, again, Tommy was probably going to head straight for the toy store to see what he could persuade his uncle to buy. He'd been talking a lot lately about the train he'd seen in the window, and Walker struck Daisy as an easy mark.

Sure enough, they had come home with not only the train and track, but enough accessories to set up a village the size of Trinity Harbor. She had insisted they wait until after supper to assemble it.

"You don't think you might have gone just the tiniest bit overboard?" she asked Walker when Tommy had gone to get a screwdriver from the drawer in the kitchen.

"He liked the train."

She had also seen the spark of excitement in Walker's eyes as they'd started assembling everything in the middle of her living room floor. "Did you ever have a train when you were a boy?"

He looked up from his examination of the locomotive. "No. Why?"

She grinned. "I just wondered. You seem almost as fascinated by all this stuff as Tommy is."

"Every boy ought to have a train, that's all."

"Did your sons?"

Regret filled his eyes. "No," he said tightly.

Daisy let the matter drop. It was evident that he was making up for more than his absence from Tommy's life. He was trying to make up for years of neglecting his own sons, too. She doubted he needed her to point that out.

She sat back for the next two hours and watched as the two of them turned her living room floor into an elaborate train setup. The minute they had it running, though, she called to Tommy and tapped her watch.

"Time for bed."

He glanced toward his uncle, clearly hoping for a reprieve, but Walker shook his head. "She's right. It's getting late."

"You can read for a little while," Daisy told him. It was a habit she'd been trying to encourage. It was certainly better than having little heart-to-hearts about drugs, which was what his uncle seemed inclined to do.

Once she was satisfied that Tommy was in bed, she turned on Walker. "Let's go outside. We need to talk."

When they were settled side by side on chaise longues, she said, "I think you'd better explain to me how the topic of marijuana came up today."

"He asked me about it," Walker said quietly. "Believe me, I was as floored by his mentioning it as you are."

"How does he even know about it?"

"Apparently he overheard some kids outside the high school talking about it."

Daisy felt as if the wind had been knocked out of her. She knew there were drugs in Trinity Harbor. It seemed no place was immune these days. Tucker had even told her how to spot evidence of drug use among her students, but Tommy was still in elementary school. To think that he was being exposed to such things was obscene. Worse, it was because of her. He was at the high school because he was coming to meet her at the end of the day.

"This is all my fault. He walks over there to meet me when he gets out of school."

"Don't be ridiculous," Walker said. "Those kids are the culprits, not you."

"Did he say who they are?"

"He said he didn't know them, but he could be covering for them. I stressed that he's to tell you or me at once if anything like this comes up again."

"Do you think he will?"

"I hope so." He glanced at her. "What do you think of this Gary, who's been helping him with the boat?"

"He's new in town. I haven't met his parents. He stayed for supper the other night, but I couldn't get much out of him. He seems like a nice boy, very polite, but perhaps troubled about something. I suppose it's not easy being the new kid in town. I heard his father was retired from the military.''

"How old is he?''

"Thirteen.''

"Isn't he a little old to be hanging out with Tommy?''

"He's at the same school. Middle school and elementary kids are in the same building. They probably got to know each other on the playground.''

"Well, keep an eye on him,'' Walker said, his expression grim.

She was shocked by the implication. "You don't think a friend of Tommy's is involved with drugs, do you? Tommy said he didn't know the kids.''

"I know, but we're going to have to be alert with everyone he spends time with.''

Too restless to sit still for this troubling conversation, she began to pace back and forth on the deck, fully aware that Walker's gaze followed each step she took. That only added to her unease.

"I suppose you're going to use this as an excuse to take Tommy away from me,'' she said, pausing in front of him and ready to do battle if he tried.

Walker stared at her. "Why on earth would I do that?''

"Because I haven't protected him from such things.''

To her annoyance, a smile tugged at his lips. "And you think he'd be more protected in Washington?''

She dared to allow herself a momentary feeling of relief. "I see your point,'' she said, then picked up her pacing again with Walker's attention once again riveted on her.

"You have to speak to Tucker,'' she said eventually.

"I intend to."

She started toward the house. "Should I get him over here now?"

Walker reached up and snagged her hand, preventing her from going anywhere. "Tomorrow's soon enough." He gestured toward the chaise she'd abandoned. "Settle down. Let's just sit here and enjoy the peace and quiet. You don't know what a rare treat this is for me."

She remained standing, her hand clasped in his. Walker thought this was peaceful? Daisy was jumpy as a june bug with her hand enfolded in his. If the conversation had been disconcerting, his touch was downright provocative.

Every nerve tingled. She was fairly certain all of her senses were operating at full throttle. She could hear every leaf rustle, every bird's chirp. She could smell the last of the scented daffodils by the back steps. The river was calm tonight, but she could hear the waves lapping at the shore. She could spot every single star in the darkening sky. When one tumbled toward earth, she sighed and made a wish.

She turned, then, and caught the amusement on Walker's face. "What?"

"I was just wondering what you wished for."

She sank down on the edge of the chaise and tugged her hand free of his. She couldn't think when he was touching her like that. "How did you know I made a wish?" she asked.

"I saw the falling star, too."

"Did you make a wish?" she asked, curious to know if he was at all superstitious, at all whimsical. Most of the time she thought he took himself far too seriously. Then again, he seemed not to take her seriously at all.

"Of course," he said.

"And?"

"I wished that there would be a lot more nights like this one."

Her pulse ricocheted unsteadily. "Do you mean that?"

"I always mean what I say. I can't remember the last time I sat outside like this and just let my mind wander. I'm usually listening for the sound of bullets being fired."

"In your neighborhood?" she asked, horrified. That was where he intended to take Tommy?

"I'm exaggerating," he said. "But only a little. My neighborhood's safe enough, but I work in enough bad areas that subconsciously I'm always on alert. I never relax the way I have today. I can honestly say it's been hours since I thought about work. You have no idea how rare that is."

She knew that Tucker often took his work home with him, too. How much worse it must be for someone in law enforcement in a place like Washington. "Your work must be very difficult," she said.

"Sometimes. And sometimes it's incredibly rewarding."

"Right now, though, it must be awful," she said, her gaze resting on his face. "Frances told me about the little girl who was killed. I'm sorry."

"Me, too. They buried her today. Watching that made my heart ache," he admitted. "And it makes me furious. I'll find the slime who did it, though. I won't rest until I do."

"You really care, don't you?"

"This isn't a job to do unless you let it matter. You

have to believe in right and wrong. You have to want the bad guys behind bars.''

"It must be frustrating, though, when they don't stay there. Tucker finds that infuriating," Daisy told him.

"Oh, I have my go-arounds with the prosecutors who plea-bargain or let some bleeding heart lawyer talk them into treating a hardened kid as a juvenile, rather than as an adult. If you work the streets long enough, you know exactly which ones will be back again and which ones can maybe be saved."

He glanced over at her. "Take this kid, Rodney. He's the same age as Tommy. He saw this shooting go down the other night, but he refuses to talk. He thinks the teenagers involved are his friends, and he's determined not to squeal on them. This time he's just a witness, but next time he may decide he needs to prove himself to them. Unless his mom can get him away from there, he's doomed."

"How terrible. Will she be able to do it?"

"Doubtful. She's a struggling single mom. She works hard. She loves her kid, but Rodney spends too much time without parental supervision. Naturally he wants to belong to the gang he sees ruling the neighborhood. It's partly a way to be cool, partly self-preservation. If he's one of them, he thinks he has a better chance of staying alive."

"When the exact opposite is true," Daisy concluded.

"Precisely."

Walker's description confirmed everything bad she'd ever imagined about big city life, especially in Washington. She would never let him take Tommy there.

"You would raise Tommy in a place like that?" she demanded, practically shaking with indignation. She stood up and glowered at him. "I won't allow it. Do you hear me, Walker Ames, I will not allow it."

She had barely turned to go when Walker was on his feet, his arm firmly around her waist from behind, holding her snugly against him. She fought to ignore the riot of sensations his touch aroused.

"Slow down," he ordered. "First of all, I haven't even agreed to take Tommy. Second, if I do, he's not going to be living in the worst part of D.C. I'll get him into a good school. There are plenty of decent neighborhoods and law-abiding kids around."

She twisted around until she could face him. "Most of those kids are in private schools, I imagine. Can you afford that?"

"If I have to."

She started to say more, but he touched a finger to her lips, silencing her.

"I love it that you care so much, but I'm not the enemy," he said. He smoothed a curl away from her cheek, then let his hand linger.

Daisy felt her pulse jump. Suddenly all thoughts of Tommy and any desire to argue fled in the face of the raw desire she saw in Walker's eyes. When had any man looked at her like that, as if he had to struggle with himself to resist her? Never that she could think of.

Walker's arm was still snug around her waist. Her thighs brushed against his. Her hips seemed to sway until she was fitted more tightly against him. And then there was no mistaking the fact that he wanted her.

Her blood pounded. Heat pooled low in her belly. And a need so fierce it shocked her slammed through her. If taking Tommy in had been an act of rebellion, then this was insanity, pure and simple. But recognizing that didn't seem to temper her desire one bit. She wanted Walker. She wanted to experience the pure recklessness of seizing the moment, of feeling vibrantly alive.

When his mouth settled over hers, a little moan of pleasure escaped. It was enough to inflame him. The kiss turned demanding. His hands cupped her bottom until their bodies fit together intimately. Nothing had ever felt more right.

But it still wasn't enough. Daisy felt like screaming with the frustration of all those layers of clothes separating them.

"Hot," she murmured, reaching for buttons. His, hers, it didn't matter. She just wanted the sensation of skin against skin.

Her knuckles finally grazed Walker's bare chest. His skin burned beneath her touch. Her hands slid beneath his shirt, reveling in the crisp curls of hair, the muscles under well-toned skin, all that heat.

She heard a ragged groan, but couldn't be sure if it was his or hers.

Then, as suddenly as things had gone up in flames between them, she felt the chill of the evening breeze against her skin, felt herself being lifted and set aside, then abandoned.

Her eyes fluttered open and she stared, dazed, at the man who stood before her, raking his hand through his hair, looking sexily disheveled from her attack on his clothing.

"I'm sorry," he said, not meeting her gaze.

Since all of her clothing was still neatly in place, she couldn't imagine what he had to be sorry for. Embarrassment flooded through her. "No," she whispered. "I apologize. I...I don't know what I was thinking."

He tucked a finger under her chin, forcing her to look up. This time his gaze was direct. "You have nothing to apologize for," he said fiercely. "I'm the one who took advantage."

She gestured toward his shirt and gave a shaky laugh. "Oh, really?"

A smile started at the corners of his mouth, then faded. "Would you feel better if I mussed you up a bit, too?"

"Actually, yes," she said.

He laughed at that. "Bad idea. We got into enough trouble when I managed to keep my hands mostly to myself."

"But that's exactly the point—why did you?"

He studied her thoughtfully. "Daisy, do you really think that I didn't want you? Is that why you're so flustered?"

"I'm not flustered," she insisted. "Just confused. I don't understand why you stopped."

"Because it wouldn't be right for me to take advantage of this situation. You and I are going to be spending some time together. There's an attraction here that could get out of hand, but we don't need to act on it. I don't have anything to offer you. I live eighty miles away. Once this situation with Tommy is settled one way or another, we'll never see each other again except perhaps when one of us visits Tommy. And you're not the kind of woman who engages in a casual fling."

"How do you know what kind of woman I am?" she demanded, vaguely insulted by the assumption. Mostly because she found it darned inconvenient. A casual fling held a whole lot of appeal for her about now.

She sighed at the thought. Of course he was right.

She wasn't the kind of woman who indulged in such behavior. Propriety was as ingrained in her as breathing. That didn't mean she didn't occasionally wish it weren't so. Tonight was one of those nights, and Walker was the kind of man who made her wish she could just toss aside the values she'd always believed in.

Maddeningly, he grinned at her. "You're a schoolteacher. It's obvious from everybody I've seen you with that you command a lot of respect, and not all of that is because you're King Spencer's daughter. Your best friend is a minister, for goodness' sakes. Your brother is the sheriff."

She frowned at him. Ignoring the rest, she asked, "You're scared of my brother?"

He chuckled. "No, I'm not scared of Tucker. The only thing that scares me is the likelihood that I will hurt you and your reputation."

"Damn my reputation!" she said, though only halfheartedly. What had her sterling reputation ever brought her, except heartache and disappointment?

"You don't mean that."

"I do," she said stubbornly. "I'm sick and tired of being King Spencer's dutiful daughter, the sensible one. Just for once in my life I want to stir things up a little, do something unexpected and unconventional."

"And an out-of-towner seems like your best shot?"

She faltered at the suggestion that she might be merely using him because he wouldn't be around later, because she wouldn't have to face the consequences day after day as she did every single time she bumped into Billy at the local supermarket.

"It's not like that," she protested, but her temper had died down. "Not exactly."

"Tell me, then, what is it like?"

The heat between them, the slam-bang surge of desire had been real. She hadn't chosen it because he was someone she wouldn't have to deal with later. How could she possibly explain that to him, though, without feeling like even more of an idiot? Despite his protests, he clearly hadn't wanted her the way she had wanted him. Otherwise he would never have stopped. Men weren't that thoughtful. Men generally took whatever they were offered. Billy certainly had. He hadn't given two figs about her reputation.

She looked into Walker's eyes and saw genuine concern. That threw her. Maybe she was wrong. Maybe this was one man who did think before he acted, who cared more about her than he did about fulfilling his own momentary needs.

And *that* suddenly made him more desirable than ever.

Walker stretched out on the bed in Daisy's guest room and stared at the ceiling, his body tense, his thoughts restless. He'd done his best to warn her off, hadn't he? He'd told her that he wasn't going to start something that was destined to end badly. Hell, he'd barely laid a hand on her, just to prove how noble his intentions were.

And she'd stood right there looking at him as if she wanted to award him a medal of honor, preferably while he was buck naked.

Where had he gone wrong? It had probably started with the kiss. He should never have succumbed to the temptation, but she'd been so close and he'd remembered exactly how she'd tasted from the other times.

Of course, those had been a mistake, too. Apparently it was one he was doomed to repeat.

He did not get involved with women like Daisy. Despite that little show of defiance she'd put on, she was a respectable woman, from an even more respectable family. Visions of shotgun weddings danced in his head. He doubted King Spencer would care that Daisy had initiated any seduction. He'd tar and feather Walker without so much as blinking if he caught Walker compromising his daughter. And after the looks and the whispers at Earlene's earlier, Walker knew they were being watched. Gossip, which had never before concerned him, was clearly rampant, and he'd barely been in town and living under Daisy's roof for a day.

He considered Daisy's stunned reaction to the possibility that Walker might be intimidated by her father or her brother. Much as he wanted her to believe that nobody scared him, the truth was it wasn't Tucker or King who terrified Walker half as much as one curvy little schoolteacher with lush lips and a damn-the-consequences attitude. The woman was dangerous. He had a sinking sensation that she would be glad to know that was how he saw her. Daisy Spencer was looking for trouble, big-time, though he seriously doubted she could handle it if it found her.

"I'm not going to provide it," Walker said aloud. "No way."

He repeated that to himself several times on his way to the kitchen in the morning. It was still echoing in his head when she turned from the stove and greeted him with one of those smiles that could have melted the entire Arctic ice cap.

"Good morning," she said cheerfully.

She looked rested, he thought, feeling thoroughly

disgruntled. Obviously nothing had kept her awake all night.

"Morning," he said, fully aware of his sour tone.

"Coffee?"

"Please."

"Cream? Sugar?"

"Black."

"I should have known," she murmured.

Walker scowled at her. "What?"

"Nothing," she responded. "What can I fix you for breakfast?"

He leaned against the counter to watch her efficient movements. She looked totally at home.

She looked too blasted desirable.

"Whatever you're having will do," he responded eventually.

"I'm having fruit and a bran muffin," she said, barely containing a grin. "I'm fixing pancakes for Tommy."

Walker knew there was a dare in there somewhere, but he was too exhausted to try to figure it out. "Pancakes," he said, then took a long swallow of coffee. It was hot and strong, just the way he liked it. A woman who made coffee like this would make some man a terrific wife.

As soon as the thought skimmed through his mind, he shuddered. Not him, though. Never him. He had the battle scars to prove he wasn't suited for marriage. Of course, he had even deeper scars to prove he wasn't suited for fatherhood, biological or otherwise, but he hadn't opted out of that possibility quite yet.

"Where's Tommy?"

"Out working on the boat," she told him. "I told him I'd call him when breakfast was ready."

"He ought to be helping."

"He did. He set the table."

Which explained why silverware and napkins had been dumped in a clump at each place, Walker concluded. Apparently Daisy considered that to be close enough. She was letting the boy get away with murder.

"If he's going to do it, he ought to do it right," Walker grumbled.

She glanced toward the table as if seeing it for the first time, then shrugged. "We don't stand on ceremony much around here."

"And that's the way you were raised?" he asked doubtfully.

"At my house, the housekeeper set the table."

"But I'll bet you were taught how to do it properly."

She met his gaze with a puzzled expression. "Walker, why are you making such a big deal out of how the table's set?"

"I just don't think you should let a child get away with doing anything less than his best. It sets a bad example. Next thing you know, he'll be bringing home mediocre grades."

"I'm not sure I see the correlation, but I'll be sure to keep a close eye on Tommy's grades," she retorted.

"How are they now?"

"Excellent, as a matter of fact. He's very bright. Ahead of his class in reading. He brought home an A on his math test on Friday. The teacher says he's settling down again. After your sister died, he had a few rough weeks. His grades suffered."

"But of course now that he's with you, everything's perfect again," Walker said.

Daisy flinched. "I never said that."

Walker saw the hurt in her eyes and stifled a curse.

"I'm sorry. Obviously, I woke up on the wrong side of the bed this morning, and I'm taking it out on you."

She regarded him knowingly. "Did you wake up that way, or did you not get any sleep at all?"

Walker frowned. "Don't even go there."

"Where?" she inquired, her expression innocent.

Because he had no intention of being drawn into that minefield, he shifted away from the counter and headed for the door. "I'll be outside with Tommy."

"Just in time to tell him breakfast's ready," she said, laughter threading through her voice.

Walker sighed, called his nephew, and turned right back around to face Daisy's amused expression.

"You're getting a kick out of this, aren't you?"

"Out of what?"

"Making me crazy."

She looked pleased with herself. "Am I?"

"It's a really bad idea, Daisy."

"So you've said."

"Because it is."

"That's your opinion."

He decided he'd better lay it on the line in plain English. "Dammit, Daisy, we are not going to have an affair and that's that."

She beamed at him. "If you say so."

"I do," he said, scowling.

"That's that, then."

Walker was pleased that he'd gotten through to her at last. But when he looked into her eyes, when he saw the amusement lurking there, he sighed heavily. He was deluding himself. This wasn't over, not by a long shot. She wasn't going to let it be.

Worse, neither was he.

13

Sunday dinner at Cedar Hill was a family tradition that Daisy and her brothers ignored at their peril. King expected attendance, and with rare exceptions—such as last weekend when things had been in turmoil over Tommy—they all complied.

Daisy was not looking forward to today's meal. When she had called to inform her father that she would be there only if Tommy and Walker were included, his grumbled acquiescence indicated things were not likely to go smoothly. Now she just had to get Walker's agreement. Given his mood, that wasn't going to go so well, either.

She wandered outside to find Tommy, still in his Sunday clothes from church, already hard at work on the boat with Walker. She winced at the streaks of dust on his dark pants but concluded that was a battle for another day. Right now, she had to conserve her energy for the struggle to get them out to Cedar Hill.

She decided the best approach would be to assume compliance. She'd discovered with her students that they responded best to high expectations. That would probably work well enough with Tommy. Walker, she feared, might be another story.

"We'll need to leave in an hour," she announced very firmly, ignoring the way Walker's T-shirt stretched tightly over the wide expanse of his chest. Why did men in T-shirts and snug jeans always look so blasted *male?* And why had she never been so fixated on that before now?

When neither Walker or Tommy responded, she asked, "Did you two hear me? I said we were leaving in an hour."

"Okay," Tommy mumbled, not even lifting his head to gaze in her direction.

Walker's head shot up as if her words had just registered. "Leave for where?" he asked suspiciously.

"Cedar Hill."

His gaze narrowed. "Why?"

"Sunday dinner."

"You go on. I'll grab something in town or make myself a sandwich here."

Tommy looked up at that. "I'll stay with Uncle Walker. A grilled cheese sandwich will be fine."

Daisy frowned at both of them. "We are all going to Cedar Hill. We're expected."

Walker scowled. "But—"

She cut Walker's protest off before he could get started. "I am not going over there by myself. There will be too many questions I have no intention of answering."

"Then don't go," Walker suggested reasonably. "You can come with me and Tommy. Or I'll even make those sandwiches right here myself. I may not be a whiz in the kitchen, but I think I can manage grilled cheese. And I saw a bag of chips on the counter."

"And Daisy made brownies this morning and more cookies," Tommy added enthusiastically. "Her brownies are the best. She brings them to church sometimes for the bake sales. My mom always bought one for me."

Daisy ignored all their flattery and played her trump card. "You can talk to Tucker," she pointed out to Walker.

"Your brother will be there?" he asked, sounding a bit more amenable.

"Of course. Both he and Bobby will be. Sunday dinner is a Spencer family tradition. Nobody gets out of it."

He nodded. "Okay, then. We'll all go."

Nicely done, she commended herself as she hid a smile and turned around to go back inside.

She was almost through the door when she realized Walker was right on her heels.

"Don't think you won that round," he whispered in her ear.

"How would you interpret what just happened?" she asked, facing him.

"Just a pragmatic decision on my part. I need to talk to Tucker. You've provided me with an opportunity to do it."

She grinned. "Clever of me, wasn't it? Face it, until I mentioned my brother, you had no intention of going anywhere near Cedar Hill with me today. Now you're coming. So I win."

He studied her intently. "Is everything between us going to turn into a contest?"

"I'd say that's up to you," she replied, casting a steady look directly into his eyes. "You could give in gracefully now."

"Give in?" he repeated, as if the words were unfamiliar.

"Or not," she said with a shrug. "I've always found a challenge to be stimulating. How about you?"

She walked off before he could respond, but she was pretty sure she heard the sound of choked laughter trailing after her. Or maybe it was just the choking sound of a man who realized he'd just lost another round in a contest of wills with a woman he'd underestimated.

Walker had sidestepped Daisy all afternoon. The woman terrified him. She was playing some sort of game and hadn't bothered to tell him the rules. He knew the end result, though. He'd wind up in her bed, and they'd both regret it for the rest of their lives.

It wasn't going to happen, he vowed solemnly. Not if he had to drag in unsuspecting family members—or even perfect strangers—to make sure they were never alone together.

"Something wrong between you and Daisy?" Tucker asked with the perceptiveness of a trained observer, or maybe of a protective big brother.

Walker had finally managed to catch the sheriff outside after the strained meal they'd all shared. Despite the excellent food, it was a wonder they didn't all have indigestion from the tension around the table. King had confined himself to casting disapproving looks toward Walker and Tommy. Bobby and Tucker had remained silent. Daisy's few attempts to start a conversation had quickly dwindled out.

"Nothing important," Walker told him. He was not going to ask Tucker to explain his sister. There were other issues that took precedence. "But I do need to ask you a couple of questions."

"About?"

"Drugs."

The word caught Tucker's undivided attention. "What about 'em?"

"How much trouble do you have with them around here?"

"No more than most places, I imagine. Do they exist? Yes. Do we know who's behind most of it? We have our ideas. Getting the proof has been trickier. Why?"

"Tommy was asking me about marijuana yesterday. He'd heard it was cool. Apparently that's the word around the high school. He overheard some of the older kids talking."

"Damn," Tucker muttered heatedly. "Did he know them?"

"He said he didn't."

"I'd better talk to him. He might remember something else. He might be able to describe them, so I can warn the principal and the teachers to be on the lookout."

"I'll get him," Walker said, heading indoors.

Unfortunately, Tucker had no better luck getting details from Tommy than Walker'd had, but he did extract a promise that Tommy would come to one of them immediately if he heard anything else.

"Can I go now?" Tommy asked.

"Sure," Tucker said. "Just remember your promise."

After Tommy had gone, Tucker muttered another expletive.

"Yeah, that's what I said when he first brought this up," Walker said. "I've seen the statistics. I've even seen that commercial that points out what percentage of drug use takes place among kids in the cities, then asks, 'Where do you think the rest is?' But driving into

Trinity Harbor for the first time last week, I've gotta say, I never once thought I'd find it here."

"The good side is that we hear about a lot of it early on. We can zero in on the dealers. Parents tend to report what they hear faster. But obviously we haven't eliminated it."

"Maybe that's not even possible," Walker said, feeling as despondent as Tucker sounded.

"Thanks for passing this along to me," Tucker said. "I'll tell my deputies to keep a closer watch on the high school, too. Did you tell Daisy?"

Walker nodded. "She was afraid I was going to blame her and take Tommy away with me."

"Are you?"

"Blaming her? Of course not."

Tucker regarded him seriously. "What about Tommy? Are you going to take him?"

"Honestly? I don't know. I haven't yet figured out what's best for him."

"You can't let it drag on this way forever. If you do and then decide Tommy belongs with you, you'll break my sister's heart."

"I know that. It's the last thing I want to do."

Tucker studied him intently, then nodded. "Okay, then. I'll trust you to do your best to see she doesn't get hurt."

"I can't guarantee that," Walker said.

"Life doesn't come with guarantees," Tucker said. "Daisy's a smart woman. I'm sure she understands that, too. Just do the best you can. That'll be enough for me."

"And for your father?" Walker asked ruefully.

Tucker grinned. "Now, there, my man, you are on

your own.''

''I was afraid of that.''

King had spent most of Sunday regretting his decision to let Daisy bring that boy and his uncle into his home. Something was up with those three and, for the life of him, he couldn't figure out what. One thing for certain, he didn't like the way Walker was looking at his daughter, as if she were a prize he wanted to take home from the State Fair.

King didn't like the way Tucker was acting around Walker, either. He supposed a couple of lawmen were bound to have a few things in common, but those two had looked thick as thieves when they'd slipped out back after dinner. Since neither one of them smoked, he had to assume they'd gone outside because they wanted to keep their conversation private.

As if all of that hadn't been annoying enough, here he was on Monday, trying to have a peaceful cup of coffee with his lifelong friends, and all they wanted to talk about was his daughter and that Yankee cop.

''Saw 'em in here myself on Saturday,'' Pete Yates said.

Pete had retired from the insurance business and obviously had way too much time on his hands, in King's opinion. ''Did you now?''

''What's up with that? Looked mighty cozy if you ask me. Had the kid with 'em, just like they were a family.''

''Watch your mouth, old man,'' King snapped. ''There's nothing going on between Daisy and that Ames fellow. His nephew's staying with her for the time being. That's it.''

''Way I heard it, the uncle's staying with her, too. You saying that's not so?'' Donnie Williams asked.

Donnie had had three wives, so his self-righteous tone grated on King's nerves.

King glowered at his companions. "He's a guest in her home. You want to make something out of that?"

"Of course not," Donnie said, backing down at once because he needed King's business at his feed and grain store. "Everybody around here knows Daisy is as fine a woman as there is."

King nodded in satisfaction. "All right, then. I don't want to hear anybody suggesting otherwise."

"Of course not," Pete said, head bobbing like one of those ridiculous toys people stuck in the windows of their cars.

"Absolutely," Donnie echoed.

King sat back, satisfied that for the moment he'd put the rumors to rest. Of course, they weren't going to stay dead long, not the way the old ladies in this town liked to talk. And the men were just as bad. He had the proof of that right in front of him.

As long as that man was showing up every weekend and Daisy was traipsing around town with him, there was going to be talk. If it reached the members of the school board, who knew what could happen? The morality of teachers could be a hot-button topic, especially around election time. King was pretty sure he could protect Daisy's job, but he didn't want to have to put his influence to the test. Something had to be done before things got that far along, and he thought he knew what.

The minute he left Earlene's, he headed for the Social Services building looking for Frances. She could put an end to this right here and now. She'd do it, too, unless she wanted to start her retirement in the very near future.

He found her behind a desk stacked high with paperwork, yammering into the phone about something that couldn't be half as important as what he had to discuss. He lowered himself into the chair opposite her, waited impatiently for her to notice him, then finally said, "Hang up the blasted phone, woman. We have things to talk about."

"Excuse me," she said quietly to whomever she'd been talking to. Her gaze lifted to clash with King's as she added pointedly, "A rather obnoxious man seems to be trying to get my attention."

"Obnoxious? Obnoxious?" King sputtered. "Who do you think you're talking to?"

"If the shoe fits," she declared. "Now, settle back, King, I'll be finished here in a minute. If you're in such an all-fired hurry that you can't wait, then ask to speak to somebody who isn't busy."

King sat back and fumed. The gall of the woman. Nobody talked to King Spencer like that. Nobody! Of course, the truth was Frances always had had a lot of sass and vinegar about her. She'd told him off the first day of kindergarten and hadn't let up since.

She'd been Frances Riley back then. There were folks around who'd thought she'd been sweet on him, but King had known better. Frances had never had eyes for anybody but Skeet Jackson. The man had turned out to be a damned fine mechanic, but he'd had a bad ticker. Died and left Frances a widow before her fiftieth birthday. They'd never had any kids of their own, which, based on the way King was feeling about his offspring these days, could have been a blessing.

He studied Frances as she deliberately dragged out her conversation just to annoy him. Still a fine-looking woman, he decided. The fact that her hair had gone white aged her some, but that didn't bother him. At their age he didn't see a lot of reason for pretending that time hadn't passed by. And, to tell the truth, he liked a female with a little meat on her bones. Who wanted to go to bed and tangle with a bunch of bony elbows and knees?

The instant he realized where his thoughts had drifted, he caught himself. What business did he have thinking about Frances that way? He was here to talk her into handling this mess with Daisy, not to ask her out to dinner at the Moose Lodge.

He was still a little flustered by those unexpectedly wayward thoughts when she finally hung up the phone and asked what she could do for him. If he'd answered with the first thing that popped into his head, she'd probably call Tucker and insist he be locked away for psychiatric evaluation. She'd be right to do it, too.

"We have to talk about Daisy," he said, when he could finally clamp down on his wild ideas. There were years of bad blood between the Rileys and the Spencers over which family had gotten to Trinity Harbor first. He certainly wasn't going to be the one to try to bridge that gap.

"Why?" Frances asked, being deliberately obtuse.

"That boy doesn't belong with her."

Frances regarded him with mild interest. "Is that so?"

"Don't patronize me. You know it and I know it."

"I don't know any such thing. Daisy is a perfectly fit foster parent. And she wants him there."

"Do you know what people are saying about her?"

"No, but I imagine you're going to tell me," she said with a resigned expression. "Though I never thought I'd live to see the day when King Spencer went around spreading idle gossip about a member of his own family.''

"I'm not spreading it,'' he retorted. "I'm telling you so you'll do something to stop it.''

"You, of all people, ought to know you can't stop people from talking.''

"You can if you don't give them anything to talk about.''

"What exactly has Daisy done that's so wrong?''

He scowled at her. "Do I really have to spell it out for you?''

"Since I don't get it, then, yes, you do.''

He frowned at that. "You don't think she's doing anything wrong?''

"Frankly, no.''

"That man is living with her,'' he said. "She's a single woman, and that man, that *stranger,* has moved in with her.''

Frances chuckled. "So, that's what's really got your goat. You don't like Walker Ames. Why? Is it something personal or is it just because he's from Washington?''

King shuddered at the reminder. "Isn't that reason enough?''

"From all I hear, he's an outstanding policeman. It's an honorable profession. Your own son is a sheriff. Is there something wrong with that?''

"Of course not.''

"Could it be the fact that Walker is a very desirable, very sexy, very available man?''

"Frances!'' King couldn't have been more shocked if she'd uttered a profanity.

"Well, he is. I'm fifty-nine. I'm not blind or dead.''

"Ladies don't discuss such things.''

Her burst of laughter mocked him.

"Well, they don't," he blustered.

"And I suppose fine gentlemen such as yourself don't sit down at Earlene's and ogle the summer tourists in their shorts and tight T-shirts, commenting on the likelihood of silicone implants."

"Absolutely not," he said, wondering if God would strike him dead on the spot for the blatant lie.

"King Spencer, you are such a liar," Frances scolded. "Shame on you. That's the only reason you men go in there. It's certainly not for Earlene's coffee. She hasn't brewed a decent pot in twenty years."

Unfortunately, she was right about that, King conceded. Not that he intended to admit it aloud.

"We're getting off the subject here," he said instead. "What are you going to do about saving my daughter's reputation?"

"Nothing," she said mildly.

"Nothing?"

"That's what I said. Maybe if you defended Daisy, instead of running around behind her back acting as if she's doing something wrong, her reputation wouldn't be in danger in the first place. People around here take their cues from you, though I can't imagine why."

"Spencers have always set a good example," he said proudly.

"Which is exactly what Daisy's doing. She's doing a good deed, King. She took in a little boy who had no one. She's giving him the love he needs so desperately after losing his mama. And she's providing a home for him until things can be worked out between him and an uncle he didn't even know he had. You tell me where the shame is in that."

Put that way, King didn't have a response. He still

didn't like it, but it didn't sound so bad when Frances described what Daisy was doing.

"If she gets hurt, I'm holding you responsible," he said as he rose to his feet.

"I'll keep that in mind," she said, clearly unintimidated.

He made his way to the door of her office, then turned back. "You busy tomorrow night?"

Her gaze shot up. "What?"

"Are you deaf, woman?" he snapped, already regretting his impulse. "I asked if you were busy tomorrow."

"No. Why?"

"I've heard you like to play bingo. Never understood it myself, but I'd be willing to take you."

He saw her lips twitch, but she managed to keep a straight face, which kept him from bolting out of there without waiting to see if she said yes or no.

"How could I possibly refuse such a gracious invitation?" she said. "The game's in Colonial Beach at the Rescue Squad."

"Long way to go for a game," he grumbled.

She did laugh then. "King, it's little wonder you never married again after Mary Margaret died. No other woman would put up with you."

"Don't go getting any ideas about changing me," he said.

"Of course not," she said at once. "Only a fool would try to mess with a cantankerous personality that it's taken fifty-nine years to shape."

"You got that right," King said. He was outside in his truck by the time he realized the woman had insulted him. Worse, he had left without accomplishing a blessed thing to get Daisy's life straightened out.

* * *

"Daddy's doing what?" Daisy asked, staring at Anna-Louise in shock when they met for pizza on Monday night.

"You heard me," the pastor said. "He's taking Frances to play bingo in Colonial Beach tomorrow night."

Since Anna-Louise was hardly likely to lie about something as mind-boggling as that—or about anything else, for that matter—Daisy supposed she had no choice but to believe her.

"Where did you hear that?"

"From Frances herself. I think she's in shock."

"She must be, if she said yes. I thought those two hated each other."

Anna-Louise grinned. "Hate is often just the flip side of love. All that passion roiling around inside."

Daisy frowned at her. "Should you be talking about passion?"

"Absolutely," Richard said, slipping into the booth beside his wife and giving her a very thorough kiss. "She's a minister, not a saint. More importantly, she is my incredibly sexy wife."

"I don't want to know this," Daisy said. "I never once even thought about what sort of love life Pastor Duncan had."

"He was seventy-five when he retired and looked like a cherub," Richard pointed out.

Daisy nodded. "Exactly. Can we please change the subject? Maybe talk about walking the straight and narrow?"

Richard regarded her with evident fascination. "Why? Are you thinking of venturing off that path? With Walker, perhaps?"

Anna-Louise poked her elbow sharply into his ribs.

"Hey," he protested. "I like the guy, even if he did run off with my wife the first time we met."

"Did we come here for pizza or did we come here to gossip?" Anna-Louise asked, frowning at her husband.

"I don't gossip," Richard said, clearly offended. "I report facts."

"Well, none of this is suitable for next week's edition," Daisy said, looking across the Italian restaurant to see what Tommy was up to. He'd joined friends at the video machines the minute they'd arrived. As near as she could tell, they were all around his age, so there was little likelihood that these were the culprits involved in the discussion of drugs.

"How are things going with Tommy?" Anna-Louise asked, her gaze following Daisy's.

"Well enough. He's got a real case of hero worship on Walker."

"And how is his uncle taking that?" Anna-Louise asked.

"I'm not sure he's even aware of it. Sometimes I catch him looking at Tommy as if he can't quite believe that he's his nephew. They'll be doing really well together, and then it's like this wall goes up between them."

"Walker's doing?" Anna-Louise guessed.

Daisy nodded. "I think he's afraid to get close. I get the feeling he was never all that close to his parents. He cared about Beth, but he couldn't stop her from running off with Tommy's father. His wife left him and took his kids. I think he feels himself starting to care about Tommy, and then he shuts down because nobody in his life's had much staying power. Of course, he blames himself for that."

"Typical," Anna-Louise said. "If he's lost a lot of people he cared about, he's not going to risk himself by getting close to Tommy." She looked pointedly at Daisy. "Or anyone else."

"What are you implying?" Daisy asked, wondering how Anna-Louise could possibly have picked up on any vibes between her and Walker.

"Nothing. It's just that I've met the man. He's very attractive. Since you're my friend, I thought it appropriate to issue a fair warning."

"Okay, then. Message received," Daisy said. "I don't have any illusions about Walker."

"I hope not," Anna-Louise said, regarding her worriedly. "This situation is volatile enough as it is."

Daisy frowned at her. "Why? Because for once in my life I might take a chance and put my heart on the line?"

"With Tommy or Walker?" Anna-Louise asked.

Daisy avoided a direct answer. "Look, just because I've tried to help a little boy who needs someone in his life doesn't mean I'm going to throw caution to the wind in general. Besides, aren't you the one who's always preaching that anything worthwhile in life is worth risking a little pain?"

"I've heard you say that," Richard agreed.

"Throwing my own words back in my face, how rotten is that?" Anna-Louise protested. "Okay, I won't say another word. You do whatever you need to do, whatever you think is right, whatever you think will make you happy."

"And you won't say 'I told you so' when it all falls apart, right?" Daisy said, grinning.

"I never agreed to that," Anna-Louise said. "To quote my handsome husband, I'm a minister, not a saint."

But despite the teasing, Daisy knew perfectly well that Anna-Louise would be the first one there to support her if her life ended up spinning wildly out of control, even if it was her own doing.

14

Saturday morning, with Walker's likely arrival still hours away, Daisy sat on the back deck with a cup of tea and studied her yard. She'd been so busy the last couple of weeks that she hadn't had time to plan her garden, and it was past time to get started. Her rose bushes needed pruning and fertilizing, and the beds that usually held neat rows of pale pink and white impatiens should be mulched. The warm weather was holding well enough now for the flowers to be set out. And the honeysuckle was twining around places it had no business going, which meant she needed to start her annual war against that before it took over everything.

Normally she loved this time of year. She liked digging in the warm, dark, rich soil, feeling the sun on her shoulders. She even liked the way her muscles ached after working outdoors all day with pruning shears, a hoe and a trowel. And that battle with the honeysuckle was a test of wills she enjoyed winning.

Today, though, as she considered doing the same old predictable thing, it didn't hold the usual appeal. Why shouldn't she scatter wildflower seeds instead? Or maybe mix bright red and orange zinnias with purple cosmos? Let the honeysuckle run amok? Why shouldn't she shock everyone with a garden that was as wild and untamed as her emotions?

"Why not?" she asked aloud.

Filled with determination, she marched into the house, shouting for Tommy as she rinsed her cup and left it on the counter to dry. Even that was a tiny act of rebellion. Usually she insisted dishes be dried and put away after every use. A tidy kitchen was a symbol of respectability. Housekeeper after housekeeper at Cedar Hill had drilled that into her.

Of course, given the way Walker was dominating her thoughts these days, she concluded that her days of respectability were numbered. Hopefully, anyway.

"What's up?" Tommy asked, regarding her with a puzzled expression as he wandered into the kitchen.

"We're going shopping."

Alarm flared in his eyes, and his expression turned stormy. "But Uncle Walker will be here soon."

"He has a key, and I'm sure he wouldn't mind having a little time to himself to unwind."

"But he's coming to see me," Tommy protested.

"And he *will* see you," she said. "When we get back." She shooed him toward the door. "Let's go. The sooner we leave, the sooner we'll be home."

Dragging his feet, his expression sullen, Tommy followed her to the car. "I don't see why we have to go somewhere now," he grumbled as she backed out of the driveway. "Why can't I stay here and wait?"

"Because I can use your help," she said flatly.

Tommy studied her intently, then asked, "Are you mad about something?"

"No," she said. "As a matter of fact, I intend to have a very good day. I can't wait to get to the nursery."

"Nursery? We're going to see a bunch of babies?" he asked, clearly shocked.

"Not babies," Daisy corrected. "Flowers."

He stared at her with predictable male horror. "That's even worse. Why would you want to go look at a bunch of dumb old flowers?"

"Because I'm going to plant them and you're going to help."

"No way," he said, retreating to the far side of the car as if he feared contamination by the very idea.

"You'll like it."

"No, I won't," he said. "That's sissy stuff."

"Don't be ridiculous. My father has a garden. Do you think he's a sissy?"

"I'll bet his garden has tomatoes and corn and stuff, not flowers."

"Okay, you've got a point, but growing things teaches us important lessons about life."

"What kind of lessons?" Tommy asked doubtfully.

"About responsibility and nurturing, for starters."

"Why do I need to know about that?"

"Because you do. Everyone does."

"I'll bet Uncle Walker never planted flowers, and he's responsible."

Daisy wasn't about to explain that his uncle's nurturing skills could probably use a little work, though they weren't in as bad a shape as he liked to pretend.

"You'll have to ask him about that," she said finally, as she pulled into the driveway of a well-stocked nursery where she'd been buying her plants for years. The owner, Marcy Mann, spotted her and headed her way, a grin on her already tanned and well-lined face. Whatever the world's concerns about the damaging effects of the sun on the skin, Marcy had dismissed them years ago.

"I was wondering when you were going to get in

here," she said. "You're late this year." She smiled at Tommy. "And this must be the young man I've been hearing so much about. Are you going to help Daisy with her garden this year?"

"Not if I can help it," Tommy muttered.

"As you can see, he's not overwhelmed by the prospect," Daisy told her friend.

"Let's go in the hothouse. I have some beautiful impatiens plants set aside for you."

"No," Daisy said. "I think I'm going for something different this year."

The older woman regarded her with amazement. "Such as?"

"I want wild. I want colorful. I want splashy."

Marcy's laughter rang out. "About time," she concurred eagerly. "Let's see what I can come up with. You have no idea how long I've wanted to see you do something new with your garden. You have all that room and that spectacular view. It needed some color to shake things up."

With Tommy reluctantly trailing along behind, she led Daisy up and down rows and rows of seedlings, picking out the most vibrant colors and the most unusual specimens.

"Tommy, you load those into the back of Daisy's car," Marcy said when they had a cart completely filled. Then she led Daisy into the small shed that served as her office.

"Here's what you're going to want to do with those," she said, taking out a sheet of paper and starting to sketch. She drew in every type of flower they'd chosen and neatly labeled it. "You can't go wrong if you follow this. Just promise to invite me over to see the results. I'd say by mid-June, it's going to look spectacular."

"I can't wait," Daisy told her.

"So, what brought this on?" Marcy asked as she rang up the sale.

"Boredom," Daisy admitted. "I've been in a rut."

"So you're breaking out in a big way," Marcy concluded. "Taking in Tommy, a new man and a new garden."

Daisy wasn't surprised that Marcy had heard all the rumors. Even though she lived on a farm miles from town, everyone in Trinity Harbor showed up here sooner or later to get plants or supplies for their flower and vegetable gardens. And Marcy had the questioning skills of a sly, well-seasoned prosecutor. People told her things before they even realized she'd been digging for revealing information.

"Nice try," Daisy said with admiration for the sneaky skill with which she'd tried to ferret out information about Walker. "No comment."

Marcy regarded her with an innocent expression. "I have no idea what you mean. I was just making a simple observation."

"Were you really?"

"Of course. You know I would never pry into your personal life, even if not knowing is killing me," she said pointedly.

Daisy hugged her. "Thanks."

Marcy looked disappointed. "That's it?"

"That's it."

"Well, damn. How am I going to explain that I had the source right here and she slipped out of my hands?"

"Who would you need to explain anything to?" Daisy asked.

"My customers, naturally. There are people who count on me to know the latest. And once they catch a glimpse of your new garden, they're going to know you've been here. I'll probably be overrun with the curious before the end of the weekend."

"Send them to me," Daisy advised. "I'll tell them the same thing I told you."

"Which is precisely nothing."

"Exactly. Now let me get out of here, before Tommy decides he's going to walk back to town or, worse, drive himself."

"At ten?"

"What can I say? He's unpredictable. I don't like to take chances."

In the car, she glanced over at Tommy, who was studiously ignoring her. "Okay, what's wrong?"

"Uncle Walker only comes for a little while, and we're missing it. It's not fair."

"We'll be home in twenty minutes. He probably won't even be there yet."

But, of course, he was, probably just to make her look like the bad guy because she'd stolen a few minutes of their time together.

She didn't like the way the sight of him stretched out on a chaise longue on her deck made her heart race. Nor did she like the way heat rose to her cheeks when his gaze met hers. He stood slowly and ambled toward them.

"Where have you guys been?"

"Daisy made us go to the dumb old nursery and buy a bunch of flowers," Tommy said, practically quivering with disgusted outrage.

"Where are they?" Walker asked.

"Still in the car," she said.

"Then let's get 'em," he said to Tommy, then looked at her. "Where do you want them?"

"I put 'em all in the car," Tommy said. "I don't see why I should have to take 'em out."

"Because it's the gentlemanly thing to do," Walker told him. "Now let's get a move on."

"I want to work on the boat," Tommy said, his expression mulish.

"Not until these flowers are wherever Daisy wants them," Walker replied evenly.

Tommy flopped down in a chair. "I'm not doing it," he said defiantly.

Daisy saw the day disintegrating into a contest of wills that no one would win. That wasn't what she wanted for Tommy. But before she could step in, Walker scowled at his nephew.

"Then you can go to your room," he said firmly.

Tommy stared at him, tears of betrayal shining in his eyes. "That's not fair."

"Neither is refusing to help someone who's been very kind to you. Think about that while you're up there. Now *go*."

Tommy cast a desperate look toward Daisy, clearly hoping for a reprieve, but she didn't dare contradict Walker's order. When she said nothing, Tommy stomped off, slamming the door to the house behind him.

"I'm sorry about that," Walker said. "He has no right to treat you that way."

"He was just upset because he thought I was ruining the little bit of time he has with you," Daisy said.

"That's no excuse."

"You know something? You sound suspiciously like a parent."

Walker looked taken aback. Then, slowly, a smile tilted the corners of his mouth. "How about that? Will wonders never cease?"

"The instincts have been there all along," Daisy told him.

"If you say so," he said, clearly uncomfortable with prolonging the topic of his parenting skills. "Let's get those flowers. Do you want them back here?"

"That'll be perfect."

With Tommy banished to his room, Walker pitched in to help Daisy with her garden. She had to admit it went much faster with him preparing the soil and raking the mulch over it, while she set out the new plants based on the rough design Marcy had created for her.

By lunchtime, the sun was bright and hot. She was filthy and thirsty. But her garden was taking shape in the most amazing way. She loved the change already, with its wild mix of varieties and clashing colors.

"I recommend a hot shower and lunch at the marina," she said as they stood side by side surveying their work. "I'm sure Tommy has gotten the message by now."

She glanced up and realized Walker's gaze was locked on her. "What? Do I have a smudge on my nose or something?"

"No, you just never cease to amaze me. If anyone had asked, I would have sworn there was no way in hell you would ever look like this."

"Like what?"

"A dirty little street urchin." He rubbed his thumb along her cheek, his gaze intent as if he found whatever streak of dirt was there to be fascinating.

Daisy's heart leapt into her throat. "Is that a good thing?" she asked, her voice choked.

"Umm-hmm," he murmured distractedly, then met her gaze. "Makes me wonder what other surprises I should expect."

"Nothing very exciting, I'm sad to say."

"I don't believe that. Something tells me you are a very unpredictable woman."

"Me? Hardly."

But even as she spoke, she realized that the denial was more halfhearted than it might have been a few weeks ago. Daisy had a hunch if Walker—and Tommy, of course—hung around, the predictability of her life could change dramatically. She had never been a big proponent of change. Like her father, she had always thought things were just fine when they were steady and reliable. Now, suddenly, she wanted to seize every chance she got to break out of old patterns. She craved excitement.

And the most exciting thing to come along in years and years was standing right in front of her...six-feet-one-inch of pure testosterone. Unfortunately, with the strides he was making in parenting, he also seemed more and more likely to be the person who was going to take Tommy away from her.

Walker gazed at Daisy over the top of his menu. Her hair curled damply around her face, and he had the oddest desire to brush the errant tendrils away, to maybe let his fingers linger against the soft, flushed skin of her cheek. Only Tommy's still-sullen presence kept him from doing it.

The kid continued to pout over being banished to his

room. Nor was he especially happy that they were wasting time over lunch at the marina.

"Go and look for Bobby," Daisy finally said with a touch of exasperation. "Ask him if he'll take you to see some of the yachts. A few of the owners might be around, and they could let you come on board."

Finally, a flicker of excitement rose in the boy's eyes. "Would he do that?"

"If he's not too busy in the kitchen, I'm sure he would," Daisy said. "And ask him if he'd like to join us for lunch."

Still struggling not to show too much enthusiasm, Tommy shrugged. "I guess I can do that."

He walked slowly between the tables on the outside deck before breaking into a run.

"Clever tactic," Walker said approvingly.

"He loves boats. I thought it might distract him."

"I was thinking of the way you managed to get me all to yourself again," he teased, just to see the color rise in her cheeks.

"I did nothing of the kind," she said, bristling.

"Here we are, all alone," he pointed out. "Worked like a charm."

"You're impossible." She frowned.

"Pretty much," he agreed. He glanced around at the sea of unoccupied tables. "It's awfully quiet here today."

"It's still early in the season," she said, sounding vaguely defensive. "Besides, with the sun out and the temperature finally in the low eighties, the people who are around are probably working in their yards or out on their boats. I imagine this place will be busy enough at dinner."

"I wasn't criticizing," Walker said.

Daisy sighed. "I know. It's just that you sounded a lot like Daddy. He never has anything good to say about this place. He hates the fact that Bobby's here, instead of taking over his herd of Black Angus. It would be bad enough if it were just a marina, but his son—his namesake—actually cooks."

Walker chuckled. "Yeah, I can see where that might grate on a man like King."

"Mind you, it doesn't stop him from bringing his friends here so he can boast that he's buying them the best crab dinner in the Northern Neck. He just doesn't like admitting that it's his son who's preparing it."

"Does his attitude bother your brother?"

"Not much. Bobby has a very strong sense of who he is and what he wants in life. Ironically, he got that from Daddy. He says once he owns most of the waterfront property in town and puts this place on the map, Daddy will be bragging to everyone that *he* was the one who encouraged him."

"But you don't believe it, do you?" Walker guessed, reading the doubt in her expression.

"No. I think Daddy's going to hate that even more. He's a huge believer in the status quo. He doesn't see any reason to change Trinity Harbor from the sleepy little town it's always been."

"And what do you think?"

"If you'd asked me a month ago, I'd have been on Daddy's side. Now, I think shaking things up around here has a lot of merit."

"Good for you, Sis," Bobby said, leaning down to drop a kiss on her forehead as he set their tall glasses of iced tea in front of them.

"You're waiting tables now, too?" she asked.

"I told Steve I'd do it, since I was heading this way

anyway. He's got your crab cake sandwiches and Tommy's burger ordered. They should be ready in a minute. I'm trying out a new assistant in the kitchen. You can help me decide if his food passes muster.''

"What did you do with Tommy?" Walker asked. "Throw him off a dock?"

"Nothing that drastic," Bobby assured him. "I left him over on the first row of slips checking out this speedboat. I've never seen anything that souped up. Must go one-forty. It's top of the line, too. Had to cost a fortune."

He avoided looking at Walker when he said it, but Walker's antennae shot up, anyway. "Why would anybody around here need a boat that goes that fast? Are there races down here?"

"Not out of Trinity Harbor," Bobby said. "There are some down in the Chesapeake."

"Mind if I go with you to take a look?" he asked. He felt Daisy's puzzled gaze on him and forced a grin. "Nothing to worry about. You know how we guys are about speed."

"I suppose," she said doubtfully.

Walker followed Bobby over to the slips, admiring some of the yachts that were docked side by side, each more impressive than the one before. Cabin cruisers, fancy fiberglass fishing boats with swimming platforms off the back and built-in bars trimmed in teak. People had obviously invested thousands of dollars in their weekend toys. There were no dilapidated wooden craft at Bobby's marina.

When they reached the speedboat, he saw at once what Bobby had meant. Long and sleek and designed for speed, this piece of machinery wasn't owned by some casual boater. It belonged to someone who raced.

The question was, were they racing in perfectly legal boating competitions, or had it been souped up to outrun the authorities? He had a nagging feeling that Bobby had wanted him to take an interest in it for just that reason.

"Think anybody would mind if I took a look around?" he asked, already hopping down into the boat.

Bobby regarded him with unease. "I don't know, Walker. This guy's new. He might not take kindly to anyone poking around on his boat."

"He's not a local, then?"

"No."

"Name?"

"Craig Remington."

"From?"

"D.C., I think. The boat's registered in Maryland, though."

Good, Walker thought. Both were things he could check out more thoroughly once he was back home. "Single guy? Family man?" he asked.

"My age," Bobby said. "Late twenties, I'd say— maybe thirty. I didn't ask if he was married. What's up, Walker? Why so many questions?"

Walker evaded the inquiry and remarked, "Too young to have this much money tied up in a boat, don't you think?"

"Hey, playboys have their cash invested in all sorts of things. You should see the men who cruise in here on the weekends with their gold chains and their trophy women. I doubt if any of them waste a lot of time trying to catch fish, despite the top-of-the-line equipment they have on board. Maybe this guy made a killing with tech stocks."

Walker felt Tommy tug on his sleeve and realized the boy had followed him onto the boat.

"How come you care so much about this boat?" he demanded.

"Just curious," he said, but he doubted Bobby bought the reply. Tommy seemed to accept it at face value, though.

A superficial glance around the boat didn't reveal anything out of the ordinary, and he could tell from Bobby's expression that there was no way he was going to permit a more thorough search. Walker couldn't blame him. It wasn't as if he were here in an official capacity, much less armed with a warrant.

He scooped Tommy up and set him back on the dock, then stepped up after him. They were just in time to hear Daisy call, "Food's here, guys."

"I'm starved," Tommy announced, and darted off at once.

Walker hung back. "Look, I don't want to put you in the middle, but keep an eye on this guy, okay? If you get so much as an inkling that he's into anything suspicious, talk to your brother."

"Drugs, you mean," Bobby said flatly, his expression dejected.

"Exactly."

Bobby rubbed a hand across his face. "That's the last thing I need around here. I'd been hoping I was wrong."

Walker regarded him with surprise. "This was the boat we saw on the river a couple of weeks ago, wasn't it? The one that had you looking as if you'd just sucked on a lemon. You were already worried about it."

"I was trying not to be," Bobby said. "In fact, I was hoping the guy would decide this part of the world was just too slow for him and take off. He hasn't given me any reason to throw him out.''

"You can always dream," Walker said. "In the meantime, the next time the guy shows up, if I'm in the vicinity, give me a call. I'd like to have a chat with him."

"What if he's legit?"

"Then talking to some guy who's crazy about boats won't bother him a bit, will it?"

"I suppose not," Bobby agreed with obvious reluctance.

"Hey, cheer up. If this guy is into something heavy, you don't want his business anyway. He'll bring you down with him."

Bobby sighed. "And send Daddy into orbit. Calling you is definitely the least of all the possible evils."

"Remember that," Walker said just as Daisy called out to them to hurry up before their food got cold. "Now let me get to that crab cake. With all this snooping around, I've worked up an appetite."

When they got to the table, Tommy was chattering a mile a minute about the fancy boat. Daisy's gaze shifted from the boy to Walker.

"Sounds impressive," she observed, a question mark in her eyes.

"Definitely not your run-of-the-mill pleasure craft," Walker said.

Daisy's lips clamped together in a disapproving line, but she said nothing more until she was alone with him later at the house. "If you think that boat is used for drug smuggling, you have to tell Tucker. Bobby can't get caught up in something like that, even peripherally. He has too much at stake. He's invested everything in the marina and his real estate deals. If people start thinking he's mixed up in something shady, it will destroy him. Once a person's reputation is tarnished in Trinity Harbor, it pretty much stays tarnished forever.''

"Bobby's reputation is not going to be ruined."

She studied him with a worried expression. "You would tell me if you thought he was in any danger, wouldn't you?"

"He's not in any danger," Walker said flatly. At least not right now. "Bobby understands the situation."

"Does he? He's out of his depth in something like this. He's too trusting. Tucker's the suspicious one."

"Stop worrying, Daisy. The thought of drugs might not have crossed Bobby's mind before today, but it has now. I made sure of that."

"I hope you're right," she said with a sigh.

Truthfully, Walker prayed he was, too. He didn't like the idea that Bobby—and by extension Daisy and Tommy—might get caught up in something ugly. For the first time in years, the protective streak that had made him become a police officer in the first place had been redirected into something very personal.

15

As if Saturday hadn't been stressful enough, Daisy found herself sitting tensely on the edge of a chair in her own living room on Sunday as a surprisingly flustered Frances presided over what she called "a little update get-together."

Though Walker was lounging in a chair with his usual relaxed posture, Daisy wasn't one bit fooled. She could read his tension in the tiny lines around his mouth, see it in the way his fingers beat a silent rhythm on the arm of the chair.

Only Anna Louise looked thoroughly calm and composed, as usual. Daisy could have hated her friend for that. Didn't the pastor have any idea what was at stake? Daisy was fairly certain that King was behind this. He'd probably been pressuring Frances ever since their bingo date to get Tommy—and thereby Walker—out of Daisy's house.

Frances addressed Daisy. "Why don't you tell me how things have been going? Tommy's teacher says he's settled down again at school."

"He has," Daisy said. "And he's been wonderful here at the house. He does whatever I tell him." She saw no need to mention the little incident with the flowers the day before. Every kid rebelled about something once in a while. "I think he's adjusting quite nicely."

Frances nodded, though Daisy thought she looked vaguely dismayed by the report.

"Walker, is that your impression as well?" Frances asked.

"Seems to me the kid's doing just fine," he said with a hooded glance at Daisy.

"Are you any closer to deciding what you want to do once school is out?"

Daisy's breath caught in her throat as she waited for Walker's answer. She hadn't dared to broach this subject herself, because she was too terrified of what his answer might be. Besides, it was too soon to be making that decision. School wouldn't be out for weeks and weeks. Okay, only three weeks, but that was still plenty of time. There was no need to rush.

"I think a decision like that is premature," she blurted out before he could say anything.

"I agree," Walker said, looking relieved. "When is school out? Not till mid-June, right? Why get Tommy all stirred up now?"

"I'm not suggesting we tell Tommy," Frances said. "I was just trying to get a fix on where your head is. I've already investigated the custody ruling in your divorce case to be sure there's nothing in that that would preclude you from taking custody of Tommy."

"You *what?*" Walker shouted, halfway out of his chair.

His heated reaction startled Daisy, but Frances merely stared him down.

"It's my job, Detective. The point is, there is nothing in the record that would disqualify you. So, have you considered what arrangements you might have to make? Have you looked into schools in Washington? A baby-sitter? Anything like that?''

Walker sank back into the chair, a frown creasing his brow. That deer-caught-in-the-headlights look was back.

Daisy jumped in again. "I'm sure Walker will do whatever's necessary when the time comes." She stared at him pointedly. "*If* it comes."

"That's right," he said, his expression glum.

Frances looked rattled. "Walker, this isn't something to be put off. The next time we meet, I expect you to have a plan, unless, of course, you've decided by then that you don't want custody of Tommy at all."

"I didn't say that, dammit." He scowled and looked at the others. "Did anyone hear me say that?"

"I certainly didn't," Anna-Louise said. "Frances, I think we can all agree that Tommy is happy right now, and that's what counts. Let's not anticipate problems or upset the status quo until it's absolutely necessary. I'm sure Walker and Daisy will be able to agree on what's best for Tommy when the time comes, and will work together to make any transition as smooth as possible." Her penetrating gaze shifted from Daisy to Walker and back again. "Isn't that right?"

"Of course," Walker said at once.

"Yes," Daisy muttered with considerably less enthusiasm.

Anna-Louise gave a nod of satisfaction. "Good. Then I suggest we all get out to Cedar Hill before Tommy, King and the other men eat all the fried chicken. You know what voracious appetites they have. Frances, are you coming?"

To Daisy's astonishment, the social worker actually

blushed. "King invited me," she said with an almost apologetic look at Daisy.

"Then I'll see you there," Daisy said with ingrained politeness. Seeing her father and Frances together was going to take some getting used to. She knew that her father had had women friends over the years, but he hadn't paraded them in front of the family. That meant there was something different about his relationship with Frances. She wasn't sure she wanted to know exactly what that difference was.

"Walker and I will be along in a few minutes," she added to buy herself some time to gather her composure before she witnessed firsthand whatever was going on between King and the social worker. She had this sick sensation in the pit of her stomach that it was some sort of unholy alliance brought on by her father's desire to get Tommy and Walker out of her life and out of town. If so, she was very much afraid Frances was destined to be hurt.

The minute Anna-Louise and Frances had gone, Walker shot to his feet and began to pace. "What is that woman's problem? Why does every single decision have to be made right this second?"

"It doesn't," Daisy said, calm now that the others were gone and the status quo was still in place. In fact, she thought delay was a very good thing. It gave her more time to convince Walker that Tommy's best interests would be served by letting him stay right here with her. "She can't bully either one of us. I'm sure she only tried today because my father was putting pressure on her."

"Yeah, I got that," Walker said. "Are the two of them some kind of an item?"

"I honestly don't know what to make of it. If they

are, it's very recent. They've only had one date that I know of," Daisy said. "I just hope he isn't using her because he wants her to do his dirty work and get Tommy out of here."

"Would he do something that underhanded?"

"In a heartbeat," Daisy said with regret. "In the world according to King Spencer, the end always justifies the means. He doesn't like anyone questioning his authority, and, lately, I've not only questioned it, I've trampled all over it."

"Does being at odds with your father bother you?"

"Not as much as it would have a few months ago." She shrugged. "I guess I'm finally growing up. Since I'm thirty, I'd say it's about time."

Walker paused in front of her, his gaze intense. "You look plenty grown-up to me," he said in that low, sexy voice that disconcerted her and made her yearn for all sorts of wicked things.

"Really?"

A grin spread across his face. "Really," he confirmed. "You have no idea how attractive you are, do you?"

"There's no right way to answer that. If I say no, it'll sound like I'm being coy and fishing for compliments. If I say yes, you'll think I'm conceited."

Walker laughed. "You are the least conceited woman I've ever met. I don't think you need to worry about that possibility. As for being coy, so what? I'm willing to throw a few compliments your way if it'll keep that color in your cheeks and that sparkle in your eyes."

"Walker Ames, are you flirting with me?"

"No way," he denied vehemently. "Flirting can get a man in trouble, especially with an innocent woman."

"Innocent?" she repeated, appalled. "You don't think I'm a thirty-year-old virgin, do you? Because you'd be wrong. I'm experienced. Well, somewhat, anyway."

"Actually that particular thought hadn't crossed my mind," he said, looking thoroughly disconcerted. "And to tell you the truth, I wish to hell you hadn't planted that particular image in my brain."

"Why not?" she asked, genuinely curious about how she'd managed to so completely fluster a man like Walker, who had certainly lived a far more sophisticated life than she had ever dreamed of.

"Because it makes the fact that I want to take you straight upstairs to bed on a Sunday afternoon when we're expected for dinner seem almost obscene."

Daisy went absolutely still. "Now? You want me now, this second?"

Walker's gaze met hers and he sighed heavily. "Hell, yes," he said emphatically, then added just as forcefully, "But I'm not going to do anything about it." His gaze locked with hers. "And neither are you."

Maybe not *now,* Daisy thought, then grinned. Then again, who knew what she might decide to do later? Her life was definitely taking some interesting and most unexpected turns lately.

Walker was looking forward to some serious crime. He needed to get his head straightened out.

He needed to get Daisy Spencer, with her sweet innocence and sexy eyes, out of it.

Admitting to her that he wanted her on Sunday had been a very big mistake. A *huge* mistake. The kind he never allowed himself to make. He'd realized it the instant he saw that gleam of fascination light up her eyes. He'd spotted trouble brewing right then.

That was why he'd steered the hell away from her at Cedar Hill and headed for D.C. right after dinner, even though the heavy meal had put him half-asleep. He'd had to stop for coffee three times en route to avoid killing himself on the way home.

He was at the station at the crack of dawn on Monday, doing paperwork and praying for some big case to come his way. Or preferably a break in Keisha's murder. Despite all the pressure from his mother and Walker, Rodney hadn't cracked. Nailing a suspect in the drive-by killing was proving as elusive and frustrating as ever.

Because Daisy was still managing to disrupt his powers of concentration, he was relieved when he saw Andy arrive and head for his office. He grabbed a cup of coffee and followed him in.

"You look like hell," his boss observed.

"Thanks. You don't look so hot yourself. Bad weekend?"

"Gail decided we needed to paint the house. Every muscle in my body aches, and I got no sleep because of the blasted paint fumes. I'm telling you, next weekend I'm getting out of town."

His expression brightened. "Maybe I'll bring her down to Trinity Harbor so we can meet this nephew of yours. That'll distract her. I'll give her a charge card and a wad of cash, and I can finally get some rest."

Walker wasn't at all sure how he felt about having Andy anywhere near Trinity Harbor. The man might be his best friend, but he could be a nag. He considered himself to be Walker's moral compass.

As for Gail, he sure as shooting didn't want her anywhere near Daisy. She'd been after him for years to get married again. He'd finally persuaded her to lay off. One look at Daisy might rekindle her determination.

"You're not saying anything," Andy noted.

"It's just that things down there are pretty complicated," he hedged.

"Maybe I could help you uncomplicate them."

"I doubt it." He scowled. "And don't look at me like that."

"Like what?"

"As if I were a problem you were just itching to solve."

"Maybe I'm just itching to avoid painting again. There are four rooms left."

Walker couldn't restrain a grin. "Feeling a little henpecked, are you?"

"You know Gail when she gets a notion into her head."

"I do indeed," Walker said with heartfelt sympathy. "Of course, weren't you the one who mentioned Gail's desire to move to Trinity Harbor? Coming down for the weekend could get her batteries all charged up over that idea again."

"It's still better than painting," Andy insisted.

It crossed Walker's mind that he could use Andy's take on that boat at Bobby's marina and the likelihood that it was being used for something illegal. "Okay, come to Trinity Harbor. I'll even spring for dinner."

"At the marina?" Andy asked eagerly. "Best crabs around."

"So the chef likes to brag," Walker agreed. "And the marina suits me just fine."

Andy nodded happily. "I'll call Gail right now.

Maybe it'll keep her from making a trip to the hardware store for more paint.''

"You can always dream," Walker told him.

Frankly, he wouldn't bet money that Gail wouldn't have Andy painting every evening this week to get the job done before they left. That was what happened when a man let a woman into his life. It put an end to any peace and quiet.

Daisy's image popped right back into his head. He acknowledged it with a sigh. That was exactly what he meant, no peace and quiet at all.

When Tommy didn't show up in her classroom after school on Wednesday to ride home with her, Daisy was more annoyed than alarmed. Boys Tommy's age tended to get distracted. He was probably still over at the elementary school with his friends. Somebody had probably started a ball game, and Tommy had joined in without giving her another thought.

She consoled herself with that idea all the way over to the school. But when she found the school yard empty and the doors to the school locked, she began to panic. Relieved that she'd followed Tucker's advice and bought a cell phone even though she'd considered the idea insane at the time, she found it in the bottom of her purse and called her brother.

"I can't find Tommy," she told him, even as she pounded on the door of the school in case one of the teachers or the principal was still inside.

"Where are you?" Tucker asked at once.

"At the elementary school. He never showed up to ride home with me, so I came over here. He's not here either, and the school's locked up.''

"I'll be there in five minutes. Keep knocking in case anyone's around."

Daisy pounded until her knuckles hurt, but no one came to the door. She was near tears when Tucker arrived in his sheriff's cruiser, lights flashing.

"Where could he have gone?" she asked. "Why would he run away from me? I thought he was happy living with me."

"He is. Don't go jumping to conclusions. He's probably off somewhere with his friends. He might even have decided to walk home. Did you call the house?"

"No," she said, then punched in the number on her cell phone. When it went on ringing and ringing, she shook her head. "Nothing."

"Okay, then, let's take a drive around. You come with me," Tucker said.

"We can cover more ground if we both drive."

"You're in no condition to be behind the wheel," he argued. "You're too upset. Besides, two pairs of eyes in the same car are better than one."

Tucker drove to the park first to see if any of the kids were playing ball or even hanging out. There were a couple of dozen around, but none of them had seen Tommy since school let out.

"He might have gone with Gary," one boy said.

"Who's Gary?" Tucker asked.

"He's a friend of Tommy's," Daisy replied, relieved that he might be with someone she knew. "An older boy, about thirteen, I think. New in town. He came to supper recently. I'm sure that's it. Tommy must be with Gary."

After they'd gotten back into Tucker's car, he regarded her soberly. "You don't suppose this Gary was one of the boys talking about marijuana, do you?"

"Of course not. Tommy said he didn't know those boys, and besides they went to high school."

"He could have been lying to protect his friend."

"Tommy wouldn't do that," she said fiercely.

"You obviously have more faith in him than I do," Tucker said grimly.

"I refuse to believe this is about drugs. Walker talked to him. He knows he's not to do anything like that. He's supposed to come to one of us. Walker was very firm with him on that point."

"But Walker's not here, is he?"

"No, but Tommy already idolizes him. He wouldn't go against his uncle's wishes, not when he's so desperate for Walker's approval. I just know he wouldn't. And you're condemning this Gary without even meeting him."

Tucker merely sighed.

Daisy glowered at him. "I'm telling you, this isn't about drugs," she insisted, as another idea occurred to her. "Go to the marina."

Her brother slanted a puzzled look at her. "You think he's gone to see Bobby?"

"No, I think he's gone to see the boats. He's talked about Gary's dad having a fishing boat—maybe they went over to visit it. Or he might have wanted to show Gary that fancy boat he saw the other day."

Tucker nodded and turned the car in the direction of the marina. It only took ten minutes to get there, but they were the longest ten minutes of Daisy's life. Tommy had to be on the docks. He just had to be, because if he wasn't, if he didn't turn up safe and sound very soon, she was going to have to call Walker. That was the last thing she wanted to do.

The minute Tucker slowed to a stop, she was out of

the car and running. Tommy had talked of little besides that speedboat he and Walker had seen last weekend. Surely that's where he was and she knew exactly where it was docked.

Stumbling a little on the gravel in the parking lot, she caught herself and ran on, Tucker hard on her heels, warning her to slow down before she broke her neck or fell in the river. Panting, she reached the slip where the boat had been, only to find it empty. A sob crept up the back of her throat.

"It's not here," she whispered brokenly.

"What?"

"The boat, the one Tommy thought was so awesome."

"The one Walker thinks could be used for running drugs," Tucker guessed. "Bobby shared that little tidbit with me."

Daisy muttered a very unladylike expletive as she made the same connection. "Who does this boat belong to?" she asked. "Nobody mentioned that to me."

"A guy named Craig Remington. Bobby says he's in his late twenties."

Relief flooded through her. "Then that can't be it. Gary's last name is Finch. His dad's retired from the military. I'm sure that's what Tommy said."

"Let's go talk to Bobby," Tucker said. When Daisy didn't immediately follow, he regarded her intently. "You okay, Sis?"

"No. I won't be okay until I see Tommy and can prove to you that he is not getting involved with a gang of drug dealers." She frowned at him. "You've wanted to believe the worst about him from the very beginning."

"I wasn't wrong about the jewelry, was I?" he reminded her mildly.

"You know why he took it," she snapped. "And he gave it back."

"The point is that he took it in the first place."

"So now you've labeled him as a criminal for life? Great! Whatever happened to second chances? Whatever happened to giving a kid the benefit of the doubt?"

"Whatever happened to your common sense?" Tucker shot back. "You don't need this crap, Daisy. And I intend to tell Walker exactly that when he shows up this weekend. Tommy is his responsibility. It's time he accepted it and took over."

She stood toe to toe with her brother, oblivious to his powerful build, and practically shook with outrage. "You do that, Tucker Spencer, and I will never speak to you again. Never!"

He blinked at that, but to her regret, he didn't back down.

"If it will keep you from getting your heart broken by this boy, then it's a risk I'll have to take."

"The only person who's breaking my heart is you," she shouted at him. "When did you become such a cold, hard-hearted jerk? Did it come with the badge?"

"Hey, hey, hey, what's going on out here?" Bobby asked, running down the dock. "I could hear the two of you all the way inside."

"Just a little disagreement," Tucker said mildly.

Daisy scowled at him. "If you believe that, then you really are an insensitive idiot."

Bobby stared at both of them in shock. "Sis, what's going on? You're the peacekeeper in the family, the one who's always mending fences."

"I've changed," she said tersely.

"Maybe you'd better go back to the beginning," Bobby said. "Obviously, I've missed something."

"Tommy's disappeared," Daisy told him. "And instead of being worried sick about him, our brother has concluded that he's become a member of a crime family."

"What?" Bobby said, regarding Tucker with astonishment. "Are you nuts?"

Tucker sighed heavily and ran his hand over his close-cropped hair. "I never said he was part of a crime family. Daisy's exaggerating. I said it was possible he was getting mixed up with the wrong people. Even Walker was worried about that."

"The only thing anybody ought to be worrying about right now is where he is," Daisy said impatiently.

"Well, I can answer that one," Bobby said. "He went out on Paul Finch's boat with Paul and his son, Gary." He looked at Daisy. "He swore to me he had your permission."

"Well, he didn't," she said succinctly.

"I'm sorry, Daisy. I would have stopped him, if I'd known."

Tucker shook his head. "So what do you know about this Finch?"

Bobby glanced at Daisy, then said calmly, "He just retired from the marines. He and his wife bought the old Milstead place. He's got a nice twenty-seven-foot fishing boat he keeps here. He took the boys out for a ride." He cast another apologetic look at Daisy. "I swear I never gave it a second thought. I knew you knew Gary, that he'd been over at the house helping Tommy with his boat."

Daisy sank down on one of the pilings with a sigh. "Thank God. When are they due back?"

"Paul said they'd be back by sunset, unless the fish weren't biting at all. Could be sooner. Why don't you two come inside and have something to drink, maybe stop scowling at each other?"

"I'm still furious with him," Daisy said, refusing to look at Tucker.

"Okay, okay, I apologize," Tucker said.

She studied his face for signs of genuine contrition, then finally nodded. "I accept."

"That doesn't mean I'm going to stop worrying about you," Tucker added.

Bobby chuckled and threw an arm around their brother's shoulders. "Tucker, you never did know when to leave well enough alone."

"Well, I'm not," Tucker grumbled.

Daisy stood on tiptoe and kissed his cheek. "I know and I love you for it, but in this case you're being as mule-headed as Daddy."

Tucker gave an exaggerated shudder. "You've made your point."

Daisy grinned. "I thought that might do it." She linked her arm through his. "Now let's go inside and see if we can persuade the chef to fix us a couple of crab cakes while we wait for Tommy."

"And while we're at it, we can think of a suitable punishment," Tucker said with a little too much enthusiasm.

"Anything that involves a jail cell is overkill," Daisy warned.

Tucker scowled. "Not in my book."

"Which is why you're not the decision-maker here," she told him.

"Something tells me Walker might side with me on this," her brother said.

She was very much afraid he could be right. "Then that's a very good reason not to mention this little incident to Walker, don't you think?"

Tucker looked as if he might argue, but Bobby shot him a warning look that had Tucker falling silent. Daisy beamed at them. "Isn't family unity a wonderful thing?"

"Wonderful," Bobby agreed. "Tucker?"

"Personally, I think it sucks." He turned a speculative look on Bobby. "But a couple of your crab cakes with a side of fries and some coleslaw could definitely change my mind."

"Couldn't that be considered attempting to bribe an officer of the law?" Daisy inquired sweetly.

"Nope," Tucker said, "I'm officially off-duty. Besides, you'd better hope it works, because in my book that kid is still in serious trouble for scaring you half to death."

"In that case, bring on those crab cakes, Bobby."

By the time the fishing boat came back in, they were all feeling considerably more mellow. Even so, Tommy took one look at Daisy and groaned.

"I'm in trouble, huh?"

"You bet," she said. She surveyed Paul Finch, took note of the square jaw, the military crew cut and the guilty expression. "You must be Mr. Finch."

"That's Major, ma'am. Sorry if you were worried about Tommy. I thought he'd cleared this with you." He scowled at his son. "You assured me he had."

Daisy took pity on the boy, who looked panicked by

his father's criticism. "Don't blame Gary. Apparently that was a widely held view," she said dryly.

"It won't happen again," Gary's father promised. "I'll call you myself."

"I'd appreciate that." She glanced at Tucker. "Shall we go?"

Suddenly a grin spread across his face. "By all means."

When they walked into the parking lot and headed for the sheriff's cruiser, Tommy's gait slowed. Daisy noted with satisfaction that his eyes widened with the first little inkling of alarm.

"You're arresting me?" he asked, his voice squeaking.

"Have you done anything wrong?" Daisy asked mildly.

Tommy's frantic gaze met hers. "I forgot to tell you where I was going," he said at once. "I'm sorry. I'm really, really sorry."

"And you lied to Bobby, didn't you?" she prodded.

"I'll tell him I'm sorry, too," he promised.

"And to Major Finch?"

Tommy nodded, his expression glum.

Daisy glanced at Tucker. "What do you think? Probation this time?"

"Personally I like the idea of grounding better."

Daisy studied Tommy thoughtfully, then nodded. "I think you're right. This was a serious offense."

"For how long?" Tommy asked, his shoulders slumped dejectedly.

"For the rest of the week," Tucker said.

"Till when?"

"Sunday."

"But Uncle Walker's coming Saturday," he protested, then fell silent. "I really messed up bad, didn't I?"

"You did," Daisy agreed. "You scared me, Tommy."

He stared at her in shock. "You were scared?"

"Very."

"Then you should ground me," he said, his expression resigned. Then hope flared in his eyes. "How about just till Saturday, though?"

"It's not much of a punishment if it doesn't take away something that really matters," Daisy told him.

"Yeah, I guess."

Daisy couldn't bear to see the look of dejection on his face. She thought he'd learned his lesson well enough to permit a slight bending of the rules. "But I imagine a person who's grounded could still go into the yard," she said eventually.

Excitement crept into his eyes. "And work on the boat?"

She nodded, then was shocked when Tommy threw his arms around her in a fierce hug.

"I love you," he declared.

Tears stinging in her eyes, Daisy hugged him back and whispered, "I love you, too, sweetie."

She didn't dare risk a look at Tucker at that moment, because she knew what she'd find—at best, brotherly concern, at worst, outright fear. And somewhere deep inside where she didn't want to acknowledge it, she knew he was right to be worried. She was in way, way over her head with this child.

And with his uncle.

16

"Hi, Uncle Walker. I'm grounded," Tommy announced on Saturday the minute Walker stepped inside the house.

Walker's gaze shot to Daisy. She hadn't mentioned anything about this on the phone. In fact, she had indicated that everything in Trinity Harbor was "just fine, excellent, in fact," when he had called on Friday to let her know what time to expect him. This must be part of her increasingly evident pattern of not wanting him to use any problems against her. As if he would, he thought irritably. He was grateful she'd stepped in. No matter how things turned out, he always would be.

"Oh?" he said mildly, frowning at her. "Anybody want to tell me what this is about?"

"Nothing serious," Daisy said, clearly lying through her teeth. She wouldn't even look him in the eye when she said it.

Walker turned to Tommy. "What about you? Anything you'd care to say?"

Tommy must have finally sensed the tension in the room, because he turned to Daisy guiltily. "Did I say something wrong?"

She sighed. "No. You told the truth. I was just hoping not to worry your uncle with this."

"I'm not worried," Walker said. "But I am getting annoyed."

"We can discuss this later," Daisy said.

"I think now would be better. Tommy, go to your room."

"But I don't have to stay in my room," he protested. "I can go outside."

"I told you to go to your room," Walker thundered, then rubbed his hand over his eyes. "I'm sorry I yelled. Would you please just do as I ask, so Daisy and I can talk about this?"

Tommy whirled and left, his expression mutinous.

"You certainly handled that well," Daisy said, apparently concluding that a good offense was the best defense.

"My behavior is not the issue here."

"It is with me. I'm not interested in discussing anything with a bully."

Walker bit back an expletive, but only because he knew it wouldn't help matters. Once Daisy got her back up, he'd never get a straight answer out of her.

"Okay, fine. You want polite, I can do polite. Let me pour myself a cup of coffee and we can sit down. Then you can fill me in on what's been going on this week."

While Daisy stared at him and fumed, he took his time pouring the coffee, setting the cup on the table, then graciously pulling a chair out for her. "Care to join me?"

"Not especially."

He shrugged. "Suit yourself. So, what kind of mischief did Tommy get into that warranted grounding?"

"It doesn't matter. I handled it," she said, still standing, her shoulders tense and her chin set stubbornly.

"Handled what?"

She regarded him with evident exasperation. "Oh, for goodness' sakes, you'd think a child never misbehaved, the way you're carrying on."

"I'm sure this child misbehaves quite a lot. I also think you're a real softie. For you to ground him, what he did must have been way, way out of line. I'm thinking busting a whole lot of windows. Maybe shoplifting. Or sneaking out in the middle of the night to take up residence in Madge Jessup's toolshed again."

"Don't be ridiculous. He wouldn't do any of those things," she said irritably.

"Then enlighten me."

She glowered at him for a full minute, then sighed heavily. "Okay, if you insist—here it is. He took off without telling me where he was going and went fishing with a friend and the friend's father, and he lied to Bobby and to Major Finch and said he had my permission."

The words came out in such a rush, Walker had trouble following them. When he finally sorted them out and made sense of what she was saying, he stared at her incredulously. "That's it? He went fishing? Not that I want to minimize the fact that he did it without your permission, but you had me worried he'd committed a felony."

"He wouldn't do that," she snapped impatiently. "Isn't it enough that I was scared to death? I had no idea where he was, and then Tucker was convinced the kid he was with must be the drug supplier you've been so worked up about and everything sort of spun out of control after that."

"Of course you're right. What he did was wrong,

but I was imagining some sort of calamity,'' he said, raking a hand through his hair.

"Because you always assume the worst,'' she accused.

"I do not.'' He regarded her evenly. "And in this instance, you were the one assuming the worst, weren't you?''

"Actually, it was Tucker, but I've straightened that out. He won't be so quick to misjudge Tommy in the future,'' she said grimly.

He had a feeling there was a story there, but he let it pass. "Okay, then, I have just one question. Why didn't you tell me Tommy had done something wrong, so we could have handled it together?''

She scowled. "I told you that I handled it. You weren't here.''

He picked the portable phone up off the table and held it under her nose. "Is this thing broken?''

She gave him a sour look. "No.''

"Then next time call.''

She lifted two fingers in a mocking salute. "Yes, sir.''

Walker sighed. "We have a more serious problem here, don't we?''

"I have no idea what you mean.''

"You were afraid to tell me what he'd been up to, weren't you? You wanted me to believe that everything was just hunky-dory.''

Alarm flickered in hers eyes. "Don't be absurd. Why would I be afraid?''

"Because you've somehow gotten the crazy notion that I'll use it against you to justify taking Tommy away.''

The color drained out of her cheeks, and she finally

sat in the chair he'd pulled out for her earlier. "Will you?" she asked worriedly.

The vulnerability he read in her expression cut straight through him. Now he knew exactly why Tucker and her father were so worried. Daisy was already emotionally involved with his nephew, more emotionally involved than a temporary foster parent should be, in a way and to a degree that he didn't fully understand.

"Let me ask you something," he said, rather than giving her a direct answer. "How do you see this turning out? When the school year ends in a few weeks, what do you see happening?"

She swallowed hard and met his gaze with tear-filled eyes. "I don't know," she whispered.

His heart ached for her. "You want him to stay here with you, don't you? This whole time you've just been giving lip service to the idea of Tommy and me getting closer, of him coming to live with me."

"That's not true. I want the two of you to have a relationship." Her chin rose defiantly. "But I could be a good mother to him. These things that have happened, they don't mean I wouldn't be a good mother."

"Of course not," Walker agreed.

He reached across the table and took her icy hand in his. She was trembling. For the first time in a very long time, he felt completely and utterly helpless. He could handle the worst kind of crime scene, but a terrified woman who felt her fate was in his hands left him shaken. He didn't want people depending on him, not Tommy, not Daisy.

"Maybe that's the way it will go," he said at last. "Maybe you are exactly what Tommy needs. Lord knows, I never felt qualified to be a parent."

"You'd be an excellent father," she said fiercely, even though it was against her own best interests.

He smiled at her instinctive sense of fair play. "I wish I could tell you how this is going to end up, but I can't. I don't know what's best. I really don't. I never expected to be confronted with a situation like this. And after my ex-wife took off on me about what a lousy father I was, the prospect of taking on Tommy scared the hell out of me."

"But you're so good with him," she said.

He gave her a half smile. "Yeah, you've done your best to make me see that. I'm almost convinced."

"How ironic," she said.

Walker smiled. "Isn't it?" He rubbed his thumb over her knuckles, suddenly all too aware of how silky smooth her skin was, how it was heating under his touch. "If Tommy does wind up with me, though, I promise you this, you will continue to be a part of his life."

A tear spilled down her cheek. She swiped at it impatiently. She closed her eyes and took a deep breath. "How can I be, if he's in Washington?"

"We'll make it happen."

"It won't be enough," she said sadly. "Not nearly enough."

Walker tried to put himself in her shoes and knew she was right. Seeing his own kids on scattered holidays and summer visits wasn't enough, either. He'd told himself he didn't deserve more, didn't even want more, but it wasn't true. He missed them every single day. He just hadn't allowed himself to admit it, because to do so would be too painful.

He was still sitting there, Daisy's hand in his, contemplating the sorry state of his life and the potential damage he could do to hers by claiming Tommy, when the doorbell rang.

Daisy guiltily jerked her hand away and stood up, clearly flustered. "I can't imagine who that could be."

"I can," Walker said grimly. "I meant to tell you when I first got here. My boss and his wife are spending the weekend in Trinity Harbor. I suspect this is their first stop. Gail is very eager to get a look at Tommy."

And you, he added to himself, well aware that potential disaster loomed just outside the front door. "Maybe we could ignore it," he suggested hopefully.

"Is your boss the kind who gives up and goes away?" she asked, regarding him curiously.

"Unfortunately, no," Walker admitted. "And his wife's worse."

"I heard that," the very woman in question said, appearing at the open kitchen door.

"Sorry, Walker. I couldn't stop her," Andy said ruefully. "You know Gail."

"I do, indeed. Okay, you might as well come on in," he said with lukewarm enthusiasm.

"Walker," Daisy chastised, clearly recovered from her shock. "That is no way to treat your friends."

"Who said they were friends?" he grumbled.

Andy chuckled. Gail came in and planted a loud kiss on Walker's cheek.

"You don't scare me," she told him, then turned to Daisy and studied her with interest. "You must be Daisy. I'm Gail. And my husband is Andy. Ignore everything Walker says about us. We're actually very nice people."

"Is there anybody you can get to testify to that?" Walker asked, aware that Daisy was looking a little shell-shocked by Gail's natural exuberance. Gail, with her flame-red hair and go-for-broke personality, had that effect on people. Smart friends just allowed themselves to be caught up in the whirlwind, rather than fighting it. From time to time, Andy still tended to look a little dazed by her unpredictable ways.

"It's very nice to meet you," Daisy said, her characteristic Southern hospitality kicking in. "May I offer you some coffee or some tea? And I baked this morning. There's a pecan coffee cake."

"You didn't offer me any," Walker said, vaguely miffed.

"We had other things to discuss," she said. "I got sidetracked. Besides, you usually sniff out the baked goods the minute you walk in the door. I never get a chance to offer."

Gail watched the two of them with fascination. Too much fascination, in Walker's opinion. He turned to Andy. "I thought you were going to give her cash and credit cards and turn her loose."

"I tried. For once, she had something other than shopping on her mind."

"Shopping?" Daisy's expression lit up. "I never get to hit all the little shops in town. I could take you. I have some birthday presents I need to pick up."

The thought of Daisy alone with the matchmaking queen of Washington made Walker queasy, but he couldn't see any way to prevent it without sounding totally paranoid.

"In a minute," Gail said. "First, I want to meet this mysterious nephew of Walker's. Then you guys can do your thing for the rest of the day, and Daisy and I will go and buy out the shops."

Walker considered trying to send Tommy with the

women, just to keep them from getting too chatty. He could just imagine Daisy's reaction to that, especially since he didn't dare intervene in the boy's deserved grounding. No, he and Andy were doomed to staying right here with his grounded nephew.

"I'll get him," Daisy offered, already halfway out of the kitchen. "You stay and chat with your friends."

"My, my, my," Gail said, the instant they were alone. "Andy didn't mentioned that Daisy was gorgeous."

"Neither did Walker," Andy pointed out. "We haven't been sitting around the precinct discussing her."

Gail rolled her eyes. "As if I believe that."

"It's true," Andy said defensively. "Walker never said a word about her, at least not about her looks."

"And I wouldn't expect him to go running to you, even if I had," Walker said. "Some things I tell your husband are confidential. Sacred guy stuff."

Gail chuckled. "If you believe that, you don't know me very well. I can get almost anything out of him, if I want to know badly enough."

Walker regarded his friend with exaggerated pity. "Good to know. Remind me never to tell you anything remotely personal again."

"What can I say? I'm putty in her hands," Andy said with an unapologetic shrug. "And she always knows when I'm hiding something. Always."

"Well, fortunately, there are no secrets here," Walker said firmly, his gaze on Gail. "None."

"If you say so," she said, her expression smug.

"Don't go there," he warned.

"Where?" she asked innocently.

"Wherever you were heading in that devious mind of yours."

There was no time to explore the subject further, because Daisy reappeared with Tommy in tow. He was wearing a clean shirt, pressed jeans and new sneakers. His hair had been slicked back. Walker hardly recognized him. Obviously Daisy intended that he make a good impression. She looked to Walker to make the introductions.

"Andy, Gail, this is my nephew, Tommy Flanagan." To his surprise Tommy stepped forward and shook Andy's hand. More of Daisy's coaching, no doubt. He even held out his hand to Gail, who ignored it and swept him into a warm hug.

"Oh, you darling child, I've been dying to meet you ever since I heard about you. You are so lucky to have an uncle like Walker. He is truly one of the good guys."

Walker was startled by the praise. He and Gail usually maintained a sort of love-hate relationship in public, though privately they got along well enough. In fact, he was actually rather fond of her, but he tried never to let her know it, because it was tough enough to keep her out of his personal life when he kept her at arm's length.

"Tommy, maybe you would like to go shopping with Daisy and me," Gail suggested.

"Afraid not," Walker said, before Tommy could jump on the invitation. "He's staying right here with Andy and me."

"I'm grounded," Tommy announced, clearly not viewing it in quite the shameful terms Daisy had probably intended. "I messed up, and Daisy grounded me for the whole rest of the week, starting on Thursday. I can go outside, but I can't leave the yard.''

"I see," Andy said with some amusement. "Does that mean you can still work on that boat I've been hearing so much about?"

Tommy's expression brightened. "Yeah. Do you want to help?" he asked hopefully.

"I've been looking forward to it," Andy said.

"Then why don't I get us a couple of cans of beer and we can get started?" Walker suggested, heading for the refrigerator. "Tommy, you want a soda?"

"Sure. And some cookies."

"Of course," Walker said. "You know where they are."

Tommy grabbed a handful, then offered some to Andy. "They're really, really good."

"That they are," Walker agreed.

"No, thanks. Not just now," Andy said, studying Walker curiously. He bent down and gave his wife a distracted kiss. "Have fun shopping."

"Will do. I'm sure Daisy and I have lots and lots to talk about."

Her words filled Walker with a sense of doom. He had a feeling he was in more trouble now than he had been since the first day he set foot in Trinity Harbor. Andy's chuckle only confirmed it.

"You are in way over your head, my friend," Andy muttered as they went outside, Tommy racing on ahead.

"If I wasn't before, I am now," Walker agreed despondently. "And I have you to thank. Couldn't you have taken Gail to Ocean City or Rehoboth Beach? Any place but Trinity Harbor?"

"Are you kidding me? She would have divorced me

if I'd tried. This trip was preordained from the second she found out about Tommy." He grinned. "Discovering Daisy was just the icing on the cake. I have to admit, after watching the way the two of you interact, you have me wondering what's going on, too."

"*Nothing* is going on," Walker said emphatically. "Nothing!"

Andy regarded him sympathetically. "Yeah, right. I said the same thing right after I met Gail, remember?"

Sadly, he did. "It's not the same," he insisted.

"We'll see."

"Oh, wipe that smug look off your face," Walker grumbled.

"Can't do it," Andy said, his grin spreading. "I've been waiting too long for this."

"Nothing is going on," Walker repeated. But he had a hunch no matter how often he said it, it wasn't going to change a blasted thing. Clearly, judging from Andy's amusement, it hadn't convinced him. Walker was beginning to have a hard time buying it himself.

Daisy should have known that Gail's eagerness to get out of the house had very little to do with her desire to shop. In fact, within seconds of arriving in downtown Trinity Harbor, she had steered Daisy into Earlene's as if she'd been going there for years. She guided Daisy straight for the most private booth in the place. Not that any of them were all that private, given the penchant for eavesdropping shared by Earlene and her customers.

When they had thick, old-fashioned chocolate milk shakes in front of them, Gail regarded her intently. "Okay, now, tell me everything."

"Everything about what?" Daisy asked, her brain

scrambling in search of a way to avoid this conversation.

"You and Walker, of course."

"I hardly know the man."

"Sometimes it doesn't take long to know all you need to know," Gail remarked sagely.

Daisy swallowed hard. This was so embarrassing. She was being cross-examined by a woman she barely knew about things she hadn't even wanted to think about herself. No wonder Walker had looked so aghast when Daisy had offered to go shopping with Gail. He had known exactly what she was in for. Had she? Was that why she had suggested coming along, because she wanted to get a fix on Walker from someone who'd known him longer?

"Why don't you tell me about him?" she suggested, turning the tables. "You've known him far longer than I have."

"Nice move," Gail said approvingly. "Very clever."

"Apparently not," Daisy said dryly. "You haven't answered me."

"Okay, let's cut to the chase. Are you interested in Walker or not?"

"He's Tommy's uncle. Of course I care what kind of man he is."

Gail rolled her eyes. "Please. This isn't about Tommy."

"It *is*," Daisy insisted.

"Then you're as blind as that foolish woman who left him. Walker is an incredible man. He's handsome as sin. Honorable. Funny. He'd be a great catch for any woman. Are you telling me you haven't noticed any of that?"

Daisy flushed under her penetrating gaze. "Okay, I've noticed he's handsome."

"Now we're getting somewhere," Gail said enthusiastically. "I was beginning to worry about you."

"It really isn't about me and Walker, though," Daisy said one more time. "We've been thrown together because of his nephew and because of what happened to Walker's sister."

"Relationships have been started with far less. You already have a bond, that wonderful little boy."

Daisy chuckled at Gail's ability to see only what suited her purposes. "Should I point out the long list of things we don't have in common?"

Gail waved off the suggestion. "Being opposites just adds spice. Look at Andy and me. He's thoughtful and quiet—me, I often leap before I look, and I never shut up. I was divorced and had two kids when we met. Andy never wanted children, but he couldn't have been a better father to them. Now that they're in college, I think he misses them even more than I do."

"Do you work?"

"Actually, I'm looking for something to keep me from going crazy now that the kids are away from home. If it had been up to me, they would have gone to Georgetown or George Washington and lived at home, but, no, one of them's at Stanford and one's at the UCLA. They couldn't get much farther away."

"They're great schools, though. You must be proud of them."

"I am, but I would have been just as proud if they'd stayed closer to home."

Daisy sympathized. She imagined she would be despondent if Tommy left after only a few weeks. Having a child leave after being underfoot for eighteen years must be incredibly difficult.

"So, what would you like to do?" she asked.

"A business of some kind." Gail's expression turned wistful. "If I could talk Andy into moving to a place like this, I'd open a little shop in a heartbeat."

"Any particular type of shop? An art studio? Crafts? Antiques? A bookstore, maybe? We could really use a good bookstore," Daisy said, suddenly wistful herself. "The racks at the supermarket only carry bestsellers."

"A bookstore and coffee shop, maybe," Gail said, gaining enthusiasm. "Oh, that would be perfect. I'd love it. I wonder if there's anyplace available."

"Are you serious?" Daisy asked, surprised that she wanted to go that far in pursuing her dream. "Do you really want to take a look at property? Or was that just an impulsive, off-the-cuff remark?"

"When you know me better, you'll understand that most of what I do is impulsive," Gail said. She looked seriously tempted by the prospect of checking out real estate.

"Andy would kill me," she said, then grinned. "Let's do it. He knew the risks when he brought me down here this weekend. I've been talking about this for ages, ever since we came here the first time five years ago. Maybe it's time I force the issue. It'll serve him right for dreaming up this trip just to get out of painting our house."

"It's not like you'd have to sign a lease just to look," Daisy said, getting into the spirit of the hunt as she led the way down the block to the closest real estate office.

"Exactly," Gail agreed.

But an hour later, when they walked through a cottage that had fallen into disrepair, there was no mistaking the glint of excitement in Gail's eyes. "It's perfect," she murmured. "Just perfect."

Daisy stared around them at the broken railings on the porch, the shattered windows and the years and years of dust and cobwebs that had accumulated inside. "Perfect?" she echoed doubtfully. "Sorry. I don't see it."

"Use your imagination. Just think what these floors would look like once they've been sanded and polished. And there are lots of little nooks and crannies inside for cozy reading areas and a coffee bar. The porch could have little tables on it overlooking the yard."

Daisy studied the overgrown bushes and tangled weeds that had all but obscured the dandelion-infested lawn. "Obviously, you have a better imagination than I do."

Will Bryson clearly sensed that Daisy was trying to put a damper on his prospective client's enthusiasm. As laid-back as anyone in Trinity Harbor usually, he suddenly became a whirlwind of facts and figures and potential repair costs. Daisy was pretty sure he was underestimating by several thousand dollars, if not tens of thousands.

"So, you want to make an offer?" he concluded, when he'd just about run out of breath.

"Give me an hour," Gail said, eyeing the house with longing. "I'll call you."

"You're not serious," Daisy said when they were back in her car. "I never thought you'd take it this far."

"Well, I am. This is exactly what I've wanted to do,

and now's the perfect time," Gail said. "Let's get back to your place. I need to see my husband."

"You're not going to take him over there, are you?" Daisy asked, trying to envision what Andy's reaction would be to that dilapidated horror. She didn't know him well enough to guess.

"Heavens, no," Gail said, then winked. "I'm taking him straight back to our motel room. *Then* we'll go take a look at the house."

Daisy regarded her with new respect. When it came to persuasion, obviously this was someone who could give her a few lessons. "Good luck."

"Oh, sweetie, luck won't have anything to do with it," Gail said.

Daisy wondered if there was any chance that she would ever, ever have that kind of confidence. She thought of the way Walker could rattle her with a look, and sighed. Not a chance.

17

The whole darn town was falling into the hands of Yankees! King listened in disgust as Will bragged about his big sale over the weekend to a crazy woman from Washington, who intended to open a bookstore and coffee shop in the old Kincaid cottage.

"Who the hell needs a coffee shop in Trinity Harbor?" King grumbled. "What's wrong with Earlene's?"

His friends rolled their eyes.

"Earlene does a lot of things well, but brewing a decent cup of coffee isn't one of them," Pete said, shuddering as he took another sip. "Tastes like battery acid."

"How would you know what battery acid tastes like?" King retorted, regarding Pete with disgust. "I don't care what you say. This coffee shop business sounds like a lot of yuppified nonsense to me. Next thing you know somebody'll come along and open one of them fancy boutiques with clothes by some foreigner. Give me a plain old T-shirt and jeans from a Wal-Mart store. That's good enough for me. So's Earlene's coffee."

"Notice you didn't say anything about the bookstore part," Pete said.

"Probably because the only thing King reads are cattle futures and feed and grain reports," Will commented.

At the mention of feed and grain, Donnie's face perked up. The man had a single-track mind, in King's opinion. If it didn't have to do with oats and hay or females, Donnie didn't have much use for it.

"Ain't nothing wrong with reading about feed and grain," Donnie said, jumping to King's defense.

"It's not exactly intellectual," Pete countered.

"I wonder if she'll have a magazine section," Donnie said, his expression hopeful.

"If she does, I'll bet she won't carry *Playboy,* so you can forget about it," Pete said.

King scowled at the lot of them. Somehow the conversation had gotten off-track. The point was this shop was going to be run by a Yankee.

"Let's get back to that book business," he said. "I'll have you know I read a great book about Robert E. Lee just last week. Now there was a fine gentleman. Came from right up the road. Understood about roots and history, too."

His friends groaned. "Don't you think it's time to stop fighting that war, King? It's over. The Yankees won," Pete said.

"Not around here, they didn't. I've still got my land, don't I? No Yankee ever set foot on it, and none will."

"I thought that Walker fella was over there just the other day," Will said.

"That doesn't count," King said. "I have to keep an eye on him, don't I?"

"I thought Daisy was the one doing that," Pete said, with a guffaw that had King seeing red.

That man had caused him more trouble lately, but darned if he could see any way to get Walker Ames out of town for good. Frances kept putting him off. Daisy flat-out ignored him. Anna-Louise gave him a sermon, instead of taking action. And Tucker insisted that the man hadn't broken a single law.

Maybe it was time King just laid it all on the line and told Walker Ames he needed to take his nephew and go before he ruined Daisy's reputation and broke her heart to boot. Man to man, that was the way to get things done.

He considered calling him right this second, but thought better of it. A conversation like this needed to happen face-to-face. You could tell a lot by looking straight into a man's eyes, and he wanted Walker to know he was dead serious about this.

Saturday would do. He'd be waiting for Walker when he got to Daisy's. He'd need to find some way to get her and the boy out of the house, but that shouldn't be too difficult unless she figured out what he was up to. Then there would probably be hell to pay, but it was a risk King was willing to take. After all, it was his duty to protect his daughter, even if she couldn't see that she needed protecting.

There had already been a few rumblings from the parents in town that she was setting a poor example by letting a strange man live with her. Once those rumblings got to that weasel of a principal, things were likely to get blown out of all proportion. King doubted the man would have the backbone to stand up for Daisy.

King knew he would have to spend a little time thinking about the best approach, the one likely to guarantee the best results. Persuasion was a tricky business, but King had had a lot of practice.

And if persuasion failed, there was always his trusty

old shotgun. There wasn't a man alive who couldn't be made to see reason when he was staring down the barrel of a shotgun.

To his astonishment, Walker found himself beginning to enjoy his weekly visits to Trinity Harbor. Okay, the truth was, what he really enjoyed was flustering Daisy. The woman was an intriguing mix of pure innocence and wicked temptation. He was beginning to wonder if he could manage to drag this arrangement out all summer long. Maybe longer.

And now that Gail had somehow persuaded Andy to buy a property so she could open a shop once she talked him into retiring, he had even more reason to stick around. He'd give anything to know how that had come about, but Andy was tight-lipped on the subject. In fact, Walker thought he looked a little shell-shocked, just the way Walker sometimes felt around Daisy.

So far, Andy had insisted that he had no intention of retiring, but he'd had no intention of buying property in Trinity Harbor either, as far as Walker knew. Now here he was, saddled with a place that looked as if a stiff wind might topple it to the ground. It was a high price to pay to get out of painting those remaining rooms of his house in D.C. He'd be plastering and painting and hammering from now till doomsday to get this new place in shape. Maybe that's what Andy was counting on, not having it ready for another ten years or so, but keeping Gail pacified in the meantime.

If keeping an eye on Gail's pet project promised to be fascinating, then getting to know his nephew better had its own rewards. Tommy had a smart mouth, but overall he was a good kid. After a few weeks of initial distrust, he was slowly accepting that Walker was going to be a part of his life. Not that he didn't test his uncle every chance he got, but so far Walker had been up to the challenge. They'd even gotten through that grounding last weekend.

As a result, Walker was almost convinced that his ex-wife had gotten it all wrong about him being a lousy father. Maybe she'd just never given him a chance to get it right, whereas Daisy seemed to expect him to live up to his responsibilities and never doubted that he would.

Still, more and more lately, Walker thought about how he was going to manage with Tommy in D.C. Frances had been pestering him for a game plan and he'd had none to offer. He didn't have a nine-to-five job. The kid couldn't be left on his own. It was plain that Tommy needed supervision. Okay, a lot of supervision. And, truthfully, Walker didn't like the thought of taking Tommy away from a town where he was safe and happy and putting him in a city where too many kids had to grow up too fast just to survive. The prospect was troubling him more than he wanted to admit. There was one obvious solution, but he'd been resisting it. He was a big city cop. He'd go nuts in a week in Trinity Harbor.

Yet he'd left D.C. well before dawn to get down here early. He'd decompressed on the drive and arrived feeling better than he had in a long time. He'd actually reached the house before either Daisy or Tommy were stirring. He'd made a pot of coffee and taken a cup onto the back deck.

He breathed in the fresh air and sighed. The grass was still covered with dew, and there was a mist hanging over the river. Any minute now the sun would come creeping up to turn the sky and the river a shocking shade of orange. The transition reminded him a lot of Daisy, all peaceful and quiet and prim one second and all fiery sensuality the next.

He groaned at the image. What was happening to him? He was turning all mushy and poetic. That's what happened when a man spent too much time around a woman who wasn't his type.

He heard the French door to the deck open, but he didn't glance up. He'd discovered that his first glimpse of Daisy in the morning was always a shock to his system.

"You look like a man with a lot on his mind," she commented, standing above him and studying him intently.

She looked sleepy and tousled in her rumpled T-shirt and an old pair of shorts. Her face had been scrubbed clean, so that the dusting of freckles on her nose was apparent. Her feet were bare, and she'd painted her toenails a shocking red. Walker couldn't seem to take his eyes off of them.

She gestured toward his empty cup. "You drink too much caffeine, by the way."

How she knew was beyond him. Why she thought it was any of her business was also beyond him. But for once the thought of challenging her held no appeal. "Probably," he agreed.

Daisy stared at him. "What? No witty retort? No advice to mind my own business? I'm shocked, Detective."

The taunt stirred the desire that had been simmering all morning. Before he could stop to think about the wisdom of his intentions, he snagged her wrist and brought her tumbling into his lap. He slanted his mouth across those kissable, sassy lips of hers just as she began to utter a halfhearted protest.

It began as just another way to torment her, a way to silence her, but it quickly took on a whole different dimension. Any protest died on her lips. Her mouth opened to his tongue. Her hands began to wander, tugging impatiently at his shirt until she could slide them against bare skin. Her legs tangled with his. Her hips fit snugly against his, not shying away from his arousal.

Who would have thought it? Certainly when he'd first met her, he'd never have suspected that prim little Daisy was capable of such seething passion. Over the last few weeks, he'd experienced more than a few of her surprises, though. Even so, she was still capable of shocking him.

His heart was racing and his blood was sizzling by the time he managed to clear his head and ease her away.

"What was that?" she murmured, looking dazed and a little lost.

"A big mistake," he said, bounding off the chaise and heading for the steps that led to the driveway.

He walked away before he could change his mind. It was getting harder and harder to stay sensible around her. She wasn't doing a blasted thing to help, either. She didn't resist, didn't even murmur more than a token protest. In fact, he had the distinct impression that she would have eagerly complied if he had gotten even more carried away.

He was still shaken when he walked through the door to the local diner. The very last person he wanted to run into was Tucker Spencer, but that was exactly who slid into the booth opposite him and surveyed him with the practiced eye of a cop.

"Everything okay, Walker?"

Since he could hardly tell the man that he had just come within a hairsbreadth of seducing his sister, he muttered a noncommittal response, turned a relieved gaze on the teenaged waitress and ordered a cup of coffee.

"Regular or decaf?"

Thinking of what had set him off in the first place, he said with a hint of defiance, "Regular. And make it strong."

"A mistake," Daisy muttered after Walker had gone. She touched her still-sensitive lips. "He calls that kiss a mistake? Well, who started it, I'd like to know? Not me. Did I just throw myself at him? No, indeed. I was standing there minding my own business when he grabbed me. *He* grabbed *me*," she repeated to reassure herself of precisely where the blame lay.

"Who're you talking to?" Tommy asked, walking into the kitchen in his pajamas, sleepily rubbing his eyes.

"No one."

"But—"

"What do you want for breakfast?" she demanded testily.

Tommy regarded her warily. "It's Saturday. We always have pancakes on Saturday."

Daisy shook herself. "Of course we do. I don't know where my head is this morning." She got the mix and a bowl out of the cupboard and made the batter, stirring it a little more forcefully than necessary.

"Where's Uncle Walker? Is he here yet?"

She started to respond that she didn't give a rat's behind where the man was, but she couldn't very well say that to Tommy. Besides, it wasn't true. She wanted very badly to know where he was, so she could avoid him. She didn't want to see the man again until she had her temper and her raging hormones back under control. Mid-July would be nice. Next December would be even better.

Unfortunately, Tommy had signed up for baseball during the week with their blessing. He had a practice game this afternoon, and she and Walker had both promised to be there. Short of death, there was no excuse for not keeping her word. Walker could do whatever the heck he pleased.

"He's been here, but he went out," she told Tommy finally as she poured batter onto a sizzling griddle.

"How come?"

"You'll have to ask him that."

Tommy's gaze narrowed worriedly. "You didn't have a fight, did you?"

"Your uncle and I have no reason to fight," Daisy said stiffly, flipping the pancakes. "But it's not my job to keep track of his comings and goings."

"Geez, I just asked," Tommy grumbled. "It's not like it's a big deal or something."

Daisy sighed and set his food in front of him. "No, of course not. I suppose I just got out of bed on the wrong side this morning."

"Maybe you should go back and get out on the other side."

Daisy grinned. "Maybe I should," she agreed, but deep inside she knew it wouldn't help. Unless, of course, Walker happened to be in that bed when she got there. Now *that* might improve her mood considerably.

Or not, she thought irritably.

"Got any of those pancakes left for an old man?"

Her head snapped around at the sound of her father's voice. This was all she needed. She knew better than to think that he'd just dropped by for breakfast.

"Why are you here?" she asked suspiciously even as she poured more batter onto the griddle.

"Is that any way to greet your father?" King grumbled.

"Sorry, Daddy," she said, and went over to give him a kiss on his cheek.

"She's having a bad morning," Tommy offered as he stuffed the last bite of pancakes into his mouth. "She got up on the wrong side of the bed."

Her father regarded her curiously. "Is that so? Any particular reason?"

"Nope. Just one of those days," she said, but she could tell that he wasn't buying it.

"I guess I'll go work on the boat till Uncle Walker comes back," Tommy said, pushing his chair back from the table.

"No," Daisy said hurriedly. She did not want to be left alone with her father. Whatever his mission was this morning, she wanted no part of it. "You haven't finished your breakfast."

Tommy gazed at her, looking puzzled. "Yes, I have. See, my plate's all clean. If I eat any more, I'll pop."

"Let the boy go," King said as he poured maple syrup all over his pancakes. "It'll give you and me a chance to catch up."

Which, of course, was precisely what she was afraid of.

Tommy seized on King's permission to take off and was about to hit the door at a full run, when Daisy reminded him to go upstairs and change out of his pajamas. It took him all of five minutes before he clattered back down, tore through the door, then let it slam behind him.

Her father shook his head. "Doesn't that boy know better than that?" he complained.

"Tucker and Bobby never did. Must be a male gene," Daisy commented, pouring herself a large glass of orange juice and settling nervously across from her father.

"You slammed your share of doors, too, young lady. Never did understand why."

Daisy grinned. "It was the only way to make a point without getting into more trouble for sassing you."

"When did you ever get into trouble with me? You could always wind me right around your little finger. Besides, until lately, you never gave me a minute's worry."

"You don't have anything to worry about now, either," she told him.

"Of course I do. You're crazy about that boy, and it's going to break your heart when he leaves. Then there's his uncle." King shook his head. "People over at Earlene's were talking about him again just this week, wondering what he's doing here and how long he's going to keep hanging around you."

Daisy regarded him skeptically. "*People* were wondering this?" she repeated. "Or was it you, Daddy? You and Pete and Donnie and Will and all the other old gossips you hang around with?"

"Other people asked," he insisted. "I didn't know what to tell them."

"Try telling them to mind their own business."

"Wouldn't do any good. People talk. Always have,

always will. Only way to stop it is not to do anything that'll attract their attention."

Daisy stood up and started slamming dishes into the sink and filling it with sudsy water. "So you've said. I am *not* having this conversation again," she said emphatically.

"Then I'll have it with Walker. When's he getting here?"

"He's been here already."

"Then where is he? Why has he left the boy with you? I thought the whole point of these weekend visits was for the two of them to spend time together."

"He didn't just go off and abandon him here. Tommy lives here, Daddy. I wish you'd accept that."

"Mighty cozy arrangement from Walker's perspective. You've got all the responsibility. What's he got? He shows up, says howdy and takes off again."

Daisy bit her tongue. She was not going to explain that Walker had taken off because he regretted the fact that they'd shared a kiss so steamy that it would have fogged up all the windows if they'd been indoors.

"Leave it alone," she said tersely.

"Blast it all, girl, how can I do that? You're my daughter. The man's taking advantage of you."

"I'm not complaining, so why should you?"

"Your thinking's gone all daft because of the boy. If you'd married Billy Inscoe..."

Daisy whirled on him. "I wouldn't have had Billy Inscoe if he'd come with a million-dollar check and a bow tied around his neck. And even though you refuse to admit it, you know he was the one who walked out on me, not the other way around, so don't go acting as if he were some prize catch that I stupidly threw back in the river."

"Okay, okay, settle down. I shouldn't have brought up Billy," King admitted. "The man didn't have the character I thought he did."

"Amen to that."

"But he could have changed," King said stubbornly. "He was from around here. I've known his mama and his daddy for years."

"In other words, even a lousy, low-down skunk of a Southern man is better than a Yankee."

"Damn straight," King said. "Every relationship has its share of bumps in the road. If you'd wanted him back—"

"I didn't want him back," she said with an amazing display of patience. This conversation was her own fault for never having explained the whole story to her father. Maybe that would have put the subject of Billy to rest once and for all.

"That's nothing but your pride talking."

Daisy would have laughed if she hadn't been so outraged. He actually believed what he was saying. "Daddy, you are my father and I love you, but you are crazy as a loon."

He stared at her indignantly. "Is that any way to talk to your father?"

"It is when you deserve it. Give it up. Billy Inscoe was scum. And, just so you know, there is nothing going on between Walker and me that you need to concern yourself with."

"Maybe not yet," he said, his tone dire. "But you can't predict what kind of liberties a man like that will take."

Thanks to an all-too-recent experience, Daisy had a pretty good idea. In fact, Walker's unfortunate rein on his hormones was what had pretty much ruined her morning. Now her father seemed determined to destroy the rest of the day.

She reached for a dish towel and dried her hands. "Daddy, I've got things to do. You can stay here and keep an eye on Tommy. If I'm not back by noon, take him to the park. He has a baseball game at twelve-thirty."

"You're leaving me here to baby-sit?"

"I'm sure you can handle it. Just try to steer away from talking about the war. Tommy's expressed a lot of interest lately in Ulysses S. Grant. I don't want to discourage him."

She managed to hide her smile until she got outside. She could still hear her father's indignant curses echoing through the house.

"Sorry, Tommy," she murmured, stopping to give him a hug.

He stared at her, startled. "For what?"

"Leaving you here with a crazy man."

His eyes widened. "You mean your dad?"

She glanced toward the house. "That is exactly who I mean. Don't be surprised if he comes out here and starts lecturing you about Robert E. Lee and the army of the Confederacy."

"Why would he do that?"

"I might have given him the idea that you were partial to the Yankees."

"Why?"

"Because he was annoying me," she explained, then kissed his cheek. "It was better than bopping him over the head with a cast-iron skillet."

Tommy stared at her. "Grown-ups," he muttered with heartfelt derision. "I sure am glad I'm still a kid."

"Me, too," she said.

"Who's gonna take me to my game?"

"If neither your uncle nor I are back, my father will take you."

"But you're coming, right?"

"Absolutely. I wouldn't miss it."

"And Uncle Walker knows where it is?"

"He knows," she assured him. "We'll be there."

"Okay, bye." He turned back to the boat.

Daisy marveled at how simple it was to make a boy happy. If only her own needs were as easily met. She wasn't even sure anymore that she could adequately explain what they were.

18

It took most of the morning before Walker cooled off enough to risk going back to Daisy's. Discovering that she'd taken off and left King baby-sitting Tommy didn't do a thing to improve his mood. Not that there was anything at all wrong with King taking care of Tommy. It was just that Walker recognized that look in the old man's eyes and regretted that he'd come home before King was long gone.

"Been wanting to talk to you," King said, herding him onto the deck and away from Tommy's hearing.

"About?"

"What do you think?" King retorted with a scowl. "This situation, that's what."

For one wild second, Walker had the terrifying thought that maybe Daisy had told him about what had happened that morning, about what had happened on a few other occasions. Or maybe even about what Walker had wanted to happen, what he'd been thinking about for weeks now, which was getting Daisy into his bed. The blasted woman knew it, too. Had she tattled to her father, told him Walker had inappropriate designs on her?

Hardly, Walker thought. Daisy wouldn't breathe a word of that to her father. She had to know that would fire King up and make him insist on getting Walker and Tommy out of that house. Walker didn't understand a lot of what was going on lately, but he did know that Daisy didn't want Tommy to leave under any circumstances. She wouldn't do or say anything that might precipitate that. What she felt about Walker beyond an undeniable physical reaction was a little less clear.

He considered all of that in a split second, then decided he'd better proceed with caution until he understood exactly what was on King's mind.

"Maybe you'd better spell things out for me," he said slowly to King. "What situation?"

"You staying here under my daughter's roof all the time. Hanging around town with her. Making eyes at her in public. People are talking."

Making eyes at her? If only King knew. "I'm sure Daisy can handle a little idle gossip."

"Well, of course she can. But she shouldn't *have to,* if you see what I mean. It's time to put a stop to it before things get out of hand. This isn't D.C., where anything goes. We have certain standards here in Trinity Harbor, especially where our schoolteachers are concerned."

Walker warned himself not to get into a fight with King that would accomplish nothing. Telling him that this was Daisy's decision to make would only exasperate him. He suspected that Daisy had already told him that, anyway, assuming King had dared to approach her, rather than simply sneaking behind her back to address his concerns to Walker.

"What would you suggest?" he asked mildly, determined to behave as if he were ready to listen to anything reasonable King wanted to propose.

"Well, since asking you to move out and go back

to Washington would just upset my daughter, I have another proposition," King said, a calculating glint in his eyes. "Marry her."

If King had suggested that Walker submit to tarring and feathering, he couldn't have been more stunned. "Excuse me?" he said, his blood running cold. "You want me to marry Daisy?" Didn't that fly in the face of everything he'd been told about King violently objecting to any and all Yankees?

"What's wrong with you, son? Are you deaf?"

"I just couldn't believe what I was hearing. You don't even like me. You hate Tommy living here. Why would you want me to marry your daughter and turn this into a permanent arrangement?"

"Because we have a situation," King repeated. He shook his head. "I thought I was making all this pretty clear. Maybe you're not as smart as I thought."

Suddenly King's strategy sank in. "You sneaky old fox," Walker said admiringly.

King regarded him with a disgruntled expression. "I don't know what you're talking about."

"You thought the idea of some sort of quickie wedding being forced down my throat would terrify me so badly, I'd be out of town before nightfall, didn't you?"

"No, no, you've got it all wrong. I think marriage is a perfect solution," King said, clearly not ready to give up the game. The man was probably a crack poker player. Not even an eyelash twitched to give away the blatant lie.

"Okay," Walker said, calling his bluff. "Should I get Anna-Louise over here?"

For the first time alarm flickered in King's eyes. "Why would you want her over here?"

"To talk about when the church is available, of course."

King regarded him evenly for several long minutes, then sighed heavily. "Dammit, Walker, you don't scare easy, do you?"

"Afraid not," he said. "But I have to admit, it was a darned fine bluff."

"I don't suppose we have to tell Daisy about this little talk, do we?"

Walker allowed himself a little time to enjoy King's obvious discomfort, then shook his head. "I won't say a word."

"That's that, then," King said with a sigh of relief.

"Not quite," Walker said. "I think maybe we ought to agree to let Daisy handle this so-called situation from now on. You might be surprised to know that your daughter's a pretty tough cookie. I don't think you need to worry so much about her."

"Tough cookie or not, a father never stops worrying. You take on that boy, you'll see what I mean."

It was Walker's turn to sigh. "I imagine you're right." In fact, he suspected Tommy could get into more trouble than Daisy and her brothers combined ever dreamed of. Sadly, most of the time he had no idea at all how much trouble his own boys managed to get into. Laurie's calls tended to focus on the timeliness of his support payments, not the behavior of his sons. Maybe it was about time he insisted on changing that.

Walker saw precious little of Daisy over the rest of the weekend. Even at Tommy's ball game, she managed to steer clear of him. He went back to D.C. on Sunday night feeling oddly disgruntled, as if he'd left something important unspoken. Or maybe left something important behind. He spent a restless night trying to figure out which it might be.

When he got to the station Monday morning, he was tired and cranky and in no mood to deal with finding Rodney sitting at his desk scattering peanut butter cracker crumbs all over the place.

"What are you doing here?" he asked irritably.

"You don't want me here, I can go," Rodney said a little too eagerly.

Walker studied him. Underneath the bravado the kid looked scared, but determined. Walker looked into his eyes. "If you've got something to say to me, Rodney, I'll listen. Have you got something to say?"

"I'm here, ain't I? It's not for the food."

"Mind telling me what made you change your mind about talking?"

"We was coming home from church yesterday and something happened," he said, looking as if he might be near tears.

"What happened?" Walker asked quietly.

"These guys, the same ones who shot Keisha, they drove up next to us."

"And?"

"They said some stuff."

"What kind of stuff?"

"Just stuff."

"Did they threaten you? Or your mom?"

Rodney shrugged. "Not exactly. I mean, my mom didn't get what they were saying or anything, but I knew. And when she wasn't looking, one of 'em pointed his finger, just like a gun, straight at her." Tears spilled down his cheeks. "I don't want nothing to happen to my mom, okay?" he said, his lower lip trembling.

Walker nodded. ''Then let's do what we can to make sure it doesn't.''

Walker nodded and reached for a tape recorder. Rodney stared at it uneasily.

''Why you got that thing?''

''To record your statement.''

''Oh, no. I ain't making no statement, not so you can play if for anybody to hear.''

''I thought you said that was why you were here.''

''I'm here to tell *you* what I know. Nobody else.''

Walker sighed. This was tricky territory. Unless Rodney were willing to testify in court, they were probably spinning their wheels bringing in the people responsible for Keisha's death. Then, again, anything that would positively ID the creeps would be a start. Walker would just have to do some fancy footwork to get them to admit to the crime or to start fingering each other.

''Okay,'' he said finally. ''This is just between you and me. What did you see that day?''

''You know Jermaine?''

''Keisha's uncle?''

''That's the dude. He's old, twenty-five at least, and he hangs with some real bad people. They doin' drugs all the time.''

''You've seen them?''

Rodney nodded. ''They don't notice I'm around, 'cause I'm just a kid.''

''Okay, what else?''

''They was hangin' that day, when a car—one of them old classic convertibles, you know what I mean?''

Walker nodded.

''It was bright red. Man, it was something,'' he said with awe. ''Anyway, it came flying 'round the corner on two wheels. I thought that thing was gonna flip over, but instead, I saw this guy lean out and holler at Jermaine. Pointed a gun right at him, but Jermaine, he fast. He took off running. The guy shot just as Jermaine passed Keisha. The bullet…'' His voice trailed off and huge tears tracked down his cheeks as he confronted a memory he'd been determinedly blocking out for weeks now.

Walker put his hand on Rodney's shoulder. ''It's okay, son. It's okay.''

''I didn't know the guy,'' he said, staring up at Walker with watery eyes. ''I swear I didn't. That's why I didn't think it would matter if I didn't tell.''

''But Jermaine knows,'' Walker said grimly. ''And I think I know who can get him to talk if *I* can't get through to him.'' Keisha's mom would tear that man from limb to limb for putting her baby in jeopardy and for keeping silent about the guilty party. And Walker wouldn't be the least bit inclined to stop her.

''Nobody's gonna know I told you, right?'' Rodney asked, his perpetually worried expression etching deep lines on his ten-year-old face.

''They won't hear it from me,'' Walker promised. ''But you might want to lay low for a bit, just the same. In fact, I think I'll talk to your mom about sending you away to camp for the summer. How would you like that?''

Rodney's eyes lit up. ''A real camp, with cabins and horses and swimming and stuff?''

''Absolutely,'' Walker said. ''You stay right here, and I'll make the arrangements.'' He wanted Rodney out of town before he picked up Jermaine.

''What's happening with the kid?'' Andy asked when Walker came into his office. ''Did he finally give you something?''

Walker filled his boss in on everything Rodney had said and his own idea for getting him away from Washington for the summer. There was a camping program for inner city kids. It was usually for a shorter term, but he was pretty sure his boss could pull some strings.

"If there's no budget for it, I'll cover it," he added. "I don't want Rodney anywhere near here when things start to happen. Plus I think he needs a chance to see that there's more to the world than what goes on in his neighborhood."

"Done," Andy said. "You call his mom. I'll call the camp and get one of the plainclothes detectives to drive him out there. Once he's safe, I'll let you know, and you can bring in Jermaine and get this case moving."

It took three round-the-clock days to wrap things up. Jermaine was a tough nut to crack, but once he had to look Keisha's mom in the eye, it was all over. He named names so fast, the words were spilling over each other.

"I'm sorry. I'm sorry," he kept saying, his voice choked with sobs as Keisha's mom beat her fists against his chest, her own heartbroken, anguished sobs echoing through the precinct.

Walker hoped he would never hear sobs like that again in his life, but he knew he probably would. By the time they brought in the low-down sleaze who'd actually fired the shot and the men—teenagers, really— who'd been in the car with him, Walker was totally drained.

"Get out of here," Andy ordered, when the accused had been booked and charged by midmorning Thursday. "Go on down to Trinity Harbor and relax. You did great work this week."

"Then why do I feel like such a failure?"

Andy regarded him sympathetically. "Because a little girl is dead. You couldn't have prevented it, Walker. Nothing any of us could have done would have prevented it. But at least these creeps will be off the streets for a little while."

As consolation went, it wasn't much. Walker envisioned years and years of the same overwhelming sense of sadness, the knowledge that no matter how much he did, it would never be enough.

"Go," Andy said again. "Something tells me you need to spend a little time with Tommy and Daisy. Get your perspective back. A long weekend away from here will do you good."

Daisy was standing at the kitchen counter, up to her elbows in dough and flour, when she realized that Walker was standing at the back door. Her heart slipped into overdrive just as it always did.

"Where did you come from? It's only Thursday, and it's barely four o'clock. I just got home from school a half hour ago."

He stepped into the kitchen without a word. Daisy took one look at his haggard face and wiped off her hands.

"Sit," she said. "I'll get you some lemonade."

"A beer would be better."

"Start with the lemonade, then we'll discuss the beer afterward."

He scowled at her. "Do you always have to be the boss?"

"I spent a lot of time around three mule-headed men. My temperament comes naturally."

His lips curved slightly at that. "Yes, I can see how

growing up around King could do that to a person."
He nodded. "Fine. I'll take the lemonade."

She handed him the drink in a glass filled with ice,
grabbed the tray of cookies she'd just taken from the
oven and put some on a plate. Walker's smile spread
when she set those in front of him.

"Do you think food's a cure for everything?"

"No, but it's a fine start," she said.

That lost, lonely look swept across his face again.
"In this instance, I can think of something that would
help more."

"What?" she said at once.

He beckoned to her. "Come here."

Her pulse ricocheted wildly, but she didn't even hesitate. She walked up until she was standing right in
front of him.

"Closer," he said.

"Walker, I can't—"

The protest died when he tumbled her into his lap.
Before her head stopped spinning, his mouth was on
hers, hot and hungry and demanding in a way it never
had been before. There was something dark and dangerous to this kiss, something urgent. Her breath
snagged in her throat and a white-hot flame spiraled
through her.

Then his hand was on her breast and something deep
inside her melted. She could feel the liquid heat spreading low through her body, reminding her of sweet,
wicked sensations she'd all but forgotten. If he stopped
now, if he pulled away as he had in the past, she would
have to kill him, she decided.

"Where's Tommy?" he asked, his voice ragged.

"Out fishing with Bobby. They just left a few
minutes ago. They won't be home for hours."

"Thank God," he murmured fervently, then stood and aimed for the stairs on powerful legs that ate up the distance in a few strides.

Cradled against Walker's chest, Daisy prayed that he would get to his room or hers before reason kicked in and told her to start asking questions. She had no idea what had brought this on, why he was suddenly turning to her in a way he'd insisted was a lousy idea, but she didn't want him to change his mind. Right or wrong, good idea or bad, she wanted this. Needed it. She needed to feel like a desirable woman again, to know that she hadn't died just because she was all dried up and barren inside. And she wanted Walker, this man she had come to trust and admire, to be the one to prove it.

He headed straight for her room, then kicked the door closed behind him, before allowing her to slide down his body until her feet touched the floor.

"If you have any doubts about this, tell me now," he said, his fingers tender against her cheek, his eyes stormy with some dark emotion Daisy couldn't read.

"No doubts," she said at once, and reached for the bottom edge of his polo shirt and began tugging it over his head. That bare chest, with its swirl of dark hair that had been taunting her for weeks now, was totally exposed in all its masculine glory. She slid her palms over the warm skin, felt it heat, then found the dark male nipples and circled them with her nails.

The muscles in his throat worked, but he didn't try to stop her. But when she reached for the buckle on his belt, he put his hand over hers.

"Not just yet. Let's even things up a little."

He worked the buttons on her blouse free, but unlike her, he went about it slowly, patiently, taking his time easing the opening apart, then letting his gaze linger on the lacy scrap of a bra that covered her breasts. Daisy could feel her nipples swell and tighten under the intensity of his scrutiny. She desperately wanted him to touch her—with his hands, with his mouth— but all he did was stare with that amazing look of wonder and yearning in his eyes.

Finally, after what seemed like an eternity, he eased the blouse off her shoulders, then flicked the clasp of her bra with a single, practiced motion. When he scooped her breasts into his hands, then covered first one nipple and then the other with his mouth, her knees almost buckled from the incredible, dizzying sensation that swept through her.

Then suddenly slow, sweet torture turned to a frenzied stripping away of the rest of their clothes. He scooped her up, then settled onto her bed, straddling her, his eyes locked with hers. She could feel the tip of his hot, hard arousal pressing against her and her hips automatically jerked upward, trying to connect with him in the way her body was urgently demanding.

"Not just yet," he whispered again, and began a slow exploration of her body with clever fingers, and kisses that stirred the most astonishing sensations in places she'd never imagined being responsive.

Writhing and slick with sweat, she wanted him inside her, wanted him to fill her and take her the rest of the way on this restless, wondrous journey.

"Please," she whispered, her voice husky with need. "Walker, I want you. Please. Now."

"Now," he agreed at last.

When he pulled a condom out of his pocket, she bit back a cry of protest. She didn't want anything between them, not even that, especially since he was protecting her against an impossibility. But explaining that would slow things down, perhaps stop them altogether, so she said nothing.

With quick, effortless movements he slipped it on, then held himself poised above her until she thought the anticipation alone would drive her wild.

His fingers slid inside her, tormenting her, teasing, then withdrawing just when she neared the edge. And then he was really inside, stretching her, filling her. Slow, tormenting strokes. Fast, frenzied, relentless strokes. Just when her body adjusted to one rhythm, he changed until she was off-kilter and verging on out of control.

She wanted...she needed...something. Oh, sweet heaven, she thought as she reached yet another peak, then tumbled over, muscles contracting in delicious spasms, her body free-falling through time and space as Walker's own climax rocked through him.

The only sounds in the room were her ragged breaths and his, with the distant, smooth hum of the air-conditioning as a counterpoint. The musky scent of sex was everywhere, on him, on her, on the sheets. Daisy decided she might not wash them for a month, if it meant she would be able to remember the wonder of this moment.

Walker heaved a sigh, then rolled onto his back, carrying her with him until she was sprawled across his chest, her head resting under his chin. She wanted to look into his eyes, to see if they reflected the same turmoil that was bound to be in hers, but he kept her snugly trapped, his fingers tangled in her hair.

"I think you've destroyed me," he whispered eventually.

Daisy caught herself smiling.

Walker chuckled. "It's not something to be proud of. I might never move again."

His arousal stirred to life against her thigh, proving him very wrong.

"Never mind," he said, laughter threading through his voice. "My mistake."

Daisy reached for him, stroking until he was hard. "You think this is a mistake?" she teased.

"Just a surprise," he said.

"You didn't want me to pretend I didn't notice, did you?"

"Oh, no." He stretched his arms above his head. "Do whatever you'd like about it."

So she did, feeling as if something had broken free inside her, as if after years and years of doubt, she was suddenly, gloriously alive again, in touch with her sexuality in a way she'd never expected to experience.

Later, Walker opened his mouth and started what sounded like the beginnings of an apology or maybe a litany of regrets and admonitions. Daisy cut him off.

"This was what it was," she said firmly. "I will not regret it for one single second, and neither should you."

"But I can't make you any promises."

"I don't expect any."

His gaze searched hers. "Do you mean that?"

"No promises," she repeated.

She didn't even want to know what had driven him into her arms this afternoon. Whatever it was didn't matter. He had given far more than he'd taken, and she would remember that...no matter what happened between them down the road.

19

Walker had to get out of the house. Even though dark was falling and Tommy was due home any minute, he needed some fresh air, some space, to try to grapple with what had just happened between him and Daisy. It had been coming since the day they'd met, but he hadn't expected to be so shaken by it.

He hadn't expected it to matter.

He slid out of the bed, trying his best not to wake her, but she stretched and yawned, her lush body drawing him like a magnet. This time, though, he resisted and determinedly pulled on his pants and jammed his feet into his shoes.

"Where are you going?" she asked sleepily.

"Tommy will be home soon. I shouldn't be in here. I thought I'd take a run into town, maybe pick up some ice cream for later, give you a little time to get yourself composed to face him and your brother."

"Ice cream's a good idea," she said, leaving her opinion of the rest of the explanation unspoken.

Her easy acceptance of his response made him irritable. Shouldn't she be suspicious? Shouldn't she be making him feel lousy for deserting her right after they'd made love? That's how most women would react, with pouts and recriminations.

Walker sighed. Didn't he know better than anyone

that Daisy wasn't like most women? She trusted him. She wanted to believe in the good in everyone, especially him. No wonder her family worried about her. They were right to, because he had years of history to prove them right. He wasn't good enough for a woman like Daisy.

"I won't be long," he said tersely as she sat up slowly and unselfconsciously let the sheet fall away, exposing her full breasts, the rosy nipples still engorged and way too tempting. He swallowed hard and backed up a step.

He was halfway out the door when she called his name. He stopped, anticipating—maybe even hoping for—all the nagging comments she hadn't voiced before. Instead, she merely said, "Will you bring back some cherry vanilla for me?"

Walker's mood suddenly lightened. "That's it?" he teased, amazed by her all over again. "No chocolate with walnuts and marshmallow swirls? No banana with dark chocolate fudge and pecans?"

She grinned. "I know it's not exotic, but it's my favorite. I try not to keep it around, because I'll eat it all at once."

Walker smiled at that, delighted to discover that she had at least one vice, albeit a tiny one. "I'll bring a gallon," he promised, enjoying the flare of temptation in her eyes.

"Don't you dare." It was part order, part plea, as if she knew she'd never be able to resist.

"With hot fudge sauce."

She groaned. "Walker, what are you trying to do to me?"

"I wish to hell I knew," he murmured with a heartfelt sigh, then took off before she could ask any more questions he couldn't answer.

Walker liked Tucker Spencer, but the man did have an annoying habit of being around every time something happened between Walker and the man's sister. Walker always had the uncomfortable sense that Tucker could see straight into his head and knew that if he hadn't just committed some unpardonable sin with Daisy, he was about to.

Tonight Tucker was in front of the ice cream store, leaning against the bumper of his cruiser, eating a cone. Cherry vanilla, from the looks of it. Must be a family preference, Walker concluded.

"When did you get into town?" Tucker asked, finishing the ice cream, then tossing his napkin into a nearby trash receptacle with a clean shot Michael Jordan would have envied.

"Nice shot," Walker acknowledged. "I got in earlier this afternoon."

"You usually don't come till Saturday morning."

"Do you keep such close track of all tourists, or is it just *my* comings and goings you find so fascinating?" Walker asked, unable to keep a note of annoyance from creeping into his voice. The fact that he deserved Tucker's suspicion made him even more irritable.

"Just observant," Tucker responded without taking offense. "And you are staying with my sister, so maybe I do pay a little closer attention than I might otherwise. She send you out for ice cream?"

"No, I just thought I'd get out from underfoot for a while."

Tucker nodded, as if that made perfect sense. He shifted away from the car. "The town's quiet. Maybe

I'll come in and sit with you for a bit. We can have a cup of coffee before you head back.'' He studied Walker intently. ''Unless you'd rather not have the company?''

Walker couldn't see any graceful way of declining. Besides he wanted to get a fix on what had been going on around town. He still wasn't at ease about the whole drug thing. His professional instincts had kicked in. And once Tommy heard enough to start asking questions, it had become personal.

''Can't stay too long,'' he told Tucker. ''Your sister's expecting me back.''

''With a pint of cherry vanilla, I imagine.'' Tucker grinned. ''Since you're buying, maybe I'll stop by and have a little more on the way home. One paltry little scoop just gets my taste buds itching for more.''

''Why not? I imagine your brother will stick around, too. He's been out fishing with Tommy. They're due back anytime now.''

''So I heard. The kid's winning over everyone in the family.''

Walker studied him, wondering at the grim note he thought he heard in Tucker's voice. ''But not you?''

''Not me,'' Tucker admitted. ''Right after your sister died, he got into some trouble. Petty stuff mostly, but it's the kind of thing I like to keep an eye on.''

''Has there been any more trouble lately?'' Walker asked.

''No,'' Tucker conceded grudgingly. ''Daisy's been a real good influence on him. You, too, when you're around.''

Walker was pretty sure there was a criticism buried in there, but he chose to ignore it. ''Then give the kid a break,'' he advised instead. ''You've got bigger problems around here than any mischief Tommy is likely to get into."

"Drugs," Tucker deduced, his expression grim. "You're right about that. Bobby's been keeping an eye on that souped-up boat at the marina, but the owner hasn't been doing anything suspicious, at least not right under my brother's nose."

"But you are worried, aren't you?"

"There are just too blasted many places for a criminal to slip into the area by boat and remain undetected," Tucker said. "The river's Maryland's problem, but the shore's mine. There's no way I can keep an eye on everything, not as understaffed as I am and as big as this county is. The state helps some, but it's never enough."

It was a familiar refrain. They had talked about his staffing problems before. And during every one of those conversations, Walker had been nagged by an insane desire to jump in and offer to help out. He could spare some time in an unofficial capacity whenever he was in town. Still, he'd prevented the words from crossing his lips each and every time. Part-time help wasn't what Tucker needed. He needed another deputy, one with solid investigative experience.

Tonight, with the taste and feel of Daisy still fresh, Walker could tell he wasn't going to have nearly as much luck keeping silent. In fact, from the moment Tucker began his familiar litany about his difficulties in keeping enough well-trained officers on his staff, that nagging voice in Walker's head began to set up an impossible-to-ignore clamor.

What if he didn't offer to help out part-time? What if he just threw in the towel in D.C. and moved here? It would keep Tommy in the community he loved.

Daisy would be nearby to drive Walker a little bit crazy with the inexplicable, but definitely insatiable need she stirred in him. Who knew where that might lead? Maybe even marriage, if he could ever convince himself that the disastrous failure of his first marriage wasn't entirely his fault.

But could he manage to be content with such a different lifestyle? What if he got everyone's hopes up, then decided he couldn't hack it? Then, again, did he even have a choice anymore? Tommy was here and Daisy was in his blood. He had to give it his best shot.

Thoughts whirling, he drummed his fingers on the table, aware that Tucker was studying him curiously.

"Okay," the sheriff finally said. "What's on your mind? You've been jumpy ever since you sat down."

"That case I was working on," he began, trying a diversionary tactic.

"The murder of that little girl?" Tucker asked.

Walker nodded. "It's over. We've got the punks responsible behind bars. They'll stay there until the trial and, if there's any justice in the world, for a long time after."

"Congratulations! That must feel real good."

"If you can ever feel good about a thing like that," Walker said, then gave in to the mental nagging. "But it's made me start thinking."

"About?"

"Whether this might not be the right time to think about making a change."

Interest immediately flared in Tucker's eyes. "What sort of a change?"

"Are you serious about looking for help down here? Do you have the budget for another deputy?" As soon as the words were out of his mouth, he regretted them, but he couldn't seem to make himself take them back.

"If I don't, I'll find it," Tucker said at once. His gaze narrowed. "Do you mean it? You'd leave D.C. and come here?"

"It's something to consider," Walker said with undisguised reluctance. "This situation with Tommy isn't going to go away. I don't like the idea of taking him to Washington. I've thought about it from every angle, but no matter which way I look at it, I can't see ripping him away from here so soon after he lost his mother. I don't need to talk to a psychologist to know it wouldn't be good for him, not that Frances has kept her opinion to herself, either."

"I imagine not," Tucker said with a commiserating grin.

"She seems to be of two minds, that he needs to be with me, but that he'd be better off living down here. Maybe this would be the best solution. It would put me a little closer to my own kids, too. Maybe I'd get to see more of them."

"It sure as hell would be the answer for me," Tucker agreed. "But would you be satisfied? We have our share of homicides, but thankfully, it's nothing like Washington."

"All in your favor," Walker admitted candidly. "To be honest, I don't know how many more senseless deaths I can take."

"My temptation is to haul your butt up to headquarters in Montross and make you fill out the paperwork before you change your mind, but I'm not going to do it," Tucker said. "You think it over. You decide you really want to make a change, I've got a job with your name on it. I've been interviewing applicants, but not a one of them comes with your qualifications."

Tucker's gaze turned speculative. "There's something else I'd like to know, though. What role does my sister play in this sudden desire for small-town life?"

The man was too darned perceptive for his own good, Walker thought irritably. "I can't answer that," he said finally.

"Can't or won't?"

"Same difference," Walker said.

"Maybe you shouldn't consider making the move until you can," Tucker said. "I'm not blind to the fact that there's more connecting you two than Tommy. I don't know how far it's gone and I don't want to know, but her broken engagement tore her up pretty bad. Though she'd deny it with her dying breath, bumping into Billy from time to time can still knock the stuffing out of her. I don't want her getting her heart broken a second time."

Tucker's words made Walker uncomfortable. He was asking for reassurances, and Walker didn't have any to offer. "This is between you and me," he said. "Let's leave Daisy out of it."

"I don't think I can do that. She's my sister. What you decide is going to affect her, no question about it. I don't want us to start out on the wrong foot. I want things to be very clear. You do anything to hurt her and I'll run you out of town. I don't care how good a cop you are."

"Understood," Walker said, appreciating a man who put his opinions on the line. Tucker was a lot like Andy in that regard. He reached a decision he'd probably be second-guessing for years. "Let's go do that paperwork."

"Tonight?" Tucker asked, clearly taken by surprise.

"Tonight," Walker confirmed. By this time tomorrow he might come to his senses, but right this second the decision seemed inevitable and right.

Tucker didn't need to be asked twice. Apparently he felt he'd made his point and assumed Walker had gotten it. He didn't ask another question about Walker's motives, which was a good thing, because Walker had no idea if his decision was in his own best interests or even Tommy's. He had a very strong gut feeling that it had everything to do with the way Daisy had felt in his arms.

Once the decision was made, though, he signed the employment forms without the slightest hesitation. He supposed time would tell if he'd completely lost his mind.

Daisy couldn't imagine what was keeping Walker so long. She'd been uneasy ever since he'd climbed out of bed and taken off as if he had something on his mind. She hadn't wanted to examine what that something might be. If he was regretting what had happened between them, she never wanted to know it.

She sighed heavily and sipped her third cup of raspberry tea. It wasn't having the soothing effect she'd hoped for. At the sound of a car in the driveway, her heart beat a little faster, but it was Tommy's voice she heard, then Bobby's responding.

A minute later Tommy came charging inside shouting at the top of his lungs. He skidded to a stop when he saw her and plopped the ice chest he was carrying on the floor in front of her. "You know what?"

"Judging from your shouts, I'd say you had good luck fishing."

He grinned. "You bet." He opened up the ice chest and pulled out a line of medium-sized fish. "Can you believe it? I never, ever caught this many before."

"Hey, I caught some of those," Bobby complained, coming in just in time to overhear him.

"Only two," Tommy retorted. "The itty-bitty ones. Even Gary caught more than you."

"Watch it, kid. Next time I'll go alone."

"No, you won't," Tommy said confidently. "I bring you luck. You said so yourself."

Daisy grinned at the bantering. She wondered if her bachelor brother had any idea what a wonderful father he was going to be one of these days. She just hoped he wasn't so caught up with all his wheeling and dealing and his restaurant that he missed the right woman when she came along.

"I didn't know Gary was going with you guys," she said to her brother.

"He and his dad were down at the docks when we got there. Paul said he didn't mind. In fact, he looked relieved."

"Gary's so cool," Tommy said. "He knows lots of stuff. He said the fish would like shrimp better than worms and he was right. We used shrimp and Bobby used nasty old worms and we won. We caught the most."

"Well, I don't care who caught them, I say we have a big fish fry tomorrow night," Daisy said. "What do you think? Maybe the Finches would like to come. I'd like to get to know them better. Bobby, can you come to do the cooking? We might as well take advantage of having a gourmet chef in the family."

"No way. Friday's a busy night at the restaurant now that summer's here."

"Besides, Uncle Walker won't be here," Tommy protested.

"He's already here," Daisy informed him.

Tommy's expression lit up. "He is? Where? I gotta show him my fish."

"He went into town a little while ago to get ice cream. He should be back any minute."

"We drove past the ice cream store," Bobby began, then fell silent when Daisy shot him a warning look.

"Tommy, go take a shower," she said. "You smell as if you've been swimming with those fish. Put on your pj's. We'll have ice cream when your uncle gets back."

Tommy opened his mouth to grumble, but a look from Bobby had him scampering off. As soon as Tommy was out of earshot, Daisy turned to her brother.

"You didn't see Walker's car at the ice cream shop?"

"Nope. It looked pretty deserted around there when we came through town."

That same little nugget of fear that she'd felt when Walker had left earlier snuck back to torment her. "I wonder where he could be."

"Probably took a drive first," Bobby said.

"After driving all the way down here today, surely he wouldn't go for another drive."

"You want me to go look for him?"

She sighed. "No, of course not. Walker's perfectly capable of taking care of himself. I'm sure I'm worrying about nothing. He'll be here soon."

Sure enough, just as Tommy came back downstairs, Walker came strolling in with a bag filled with quarts of three different flavors of ice cream. Tucker was right on his heels.

Walker took a step toward her, set the bag on the table, started to drop a kiss on her cheek, then backed off with a quick glance at her brother. Daisy's cheeks flamed.

"Now I get it," she said quickly, hoping to cover the awkward moment with a taunt.

"Get what?" Tucker said, regarding her blankly.

"You two have been off talking crime fighting again, haven't you?"

"Something like that," her brother agreed, a mysterious grin spreading across his face. "Get the scoop, Bobby. Let's dish this ice cream up before it melts."

Bobby didn't budge. Instead, he surveyed Walker, then Daisy, his expression thoughtful.

"Bobby, get the scoop," Daisy said.

He did as she'd asked, but a knowing grin tugged at his lips. "Trying to divert attention?" he whispered as he handed it to her.

Her cheeks burned. "I have no idea what you mean."

"Oh, I think you do."

"Stop it, Bobby Spencer."

"Or what? You'll send me home without any ice cream?"

"You've got it."

"What are you two arguing about?" Tucker asked.

"Never mind," they said in unison.

"Seems like a lot of secrets swirling around in this room," Tucker said, his gaze on Walker. "Maybe somebody ought to start sharing."

"In good time," Walker said firmly.

Daisy regarded Walker and her brother with frustration. Whatever they'd been up to, she obviously wasn't going to get it out of them now.

As it turned out, it was another two hours before she had her brothers out of her hair and had Walker to herself. When he excused himself and started out of the kitchen, she halted him in his tracks.

"Not so fast, buster."

He turned slowly, lips twitching with amusement. "Something on your mind?"

"That little incident earlier, as a matter of fact."

"The one in your bedroom?" he inquired, all innocence.

Her face flushed. At this rate, she'd never need to buy blusher again. "No, *that* one I know about," she said. "I mean you and my brother. What's going on?"

"What makes you think something's going on between me and Tucker?"

"Instinct. Do you deny it?"

"No." He pulled out a chair, turned it around and straddled it. "I suppose you might as well know, since I doubt Tucker is capable of keeping a secret from you."

"Never has been before," she agreed, filled with curiosity about what the two of them had been up to. "Spill it."

"Okay, here's the deal in a nutshell. I'm moving here. I'm going to work for your brother," Walker said, knocking the wind right out of her. "We've already filled out the paperwork. That's why I was gone so long tonight."

She stared at him blankly, not daring to believe that she had heard him correctly. "You're moving here? To Trinity Harbor?"

"Yes," he said, evidently amused by her shock.

This was a turn of events she definitely hadn't considered, hadn't dared to hope for. Had tonight, the two of them making love, swayed him? Suddenly she had visions of a future with both Tommy *and* his uncle in it.

No, she told herself firmly. She was not going to go there. This move was about Tommy. Nothing else. She had to keep reminding herself of that.

She studied Walker's face, trying to read his thoughts. Usually she could get an accurate picture of what was going on in his head, but tonight his expression was inscrutable.

"Isn't this a little sudden? Why are you doing this?"

"Why not?"

"But you...I..."

"I guess you're going to be stuck with me," he said, regarding her with a knowing expression.

One night in her bed and he thought he was just going to move in, lock, stock and barrel? No way. She was willing to let the gossips have a field day with things as they were now, but having Walker as a full-time resident of her house would be intolerable, and not just because of the ensuing gossip. Having him underfoot all the time would make it impossible to ignore the way she felt about him.

A stolen night like tonight was one thing. A steady diet of stolen nights would have her emotions so tangled up, she'd be devastated when he eventually left her...which, of course, he would. Walker wasn't suited for a quiet life in Trinity Harbor. The decision to come here was all about Tommy, nothing else, and once Tommy's life was stable, Walker would take off.

"Stuck with you? I don't think so," she said very, very firmly before her conviction that this was the right decision could waver. "If you move to Trinity Harbor, you'll be getting your own place."

His gaze narrowed. "You don't seem nearly as pleased about this as I thought you'd be."

"I am," she said. "For Tommy."

"But not for yourself?"

She sighed. His move meant that he'd decided that Tommy belonged with him. It meant she would be losing the boy. Oh, he would still be here in Trinity Harbor, but he wouldn't be hers anymore. The illusion that she had a family would come crashing down around her. So, no, there was no way she could be happy about that. Not entirely.

"This isn't about me," she said, trying to keep her voice steady and the tears from spilling down her cheeks.

Walker reached for her hand. "Maybe it is."

Daisy lifted her gaze, met his eyes. "How?"

"Tonight, it meant something, Daisy. I don't know what yet. I can't make any promises. You'll just have to trust me when I say that you played a role in my decision."

She couldn't let herself count on vague promises and false hopes. And she couldn't relent and let him stay in her home, where temptation would face them every single minute of every single day.

She forced a smile. "I'm sure you'll keep me posted on what you decide."

Walker looked disconcerted by her attitude. "Then you're not interested in keeping me under your roof where you can keep an eye on me?"

"That has nothing to do with it and you know it. My father's upset enough about this as it is. You moving in would give him apoplexy, to say nothing of what would happen to what's left of my reputation." *Or her heart.*

His gaze narrowed. "You really are worried about this reputation business, aren't you? Has something happened?"

She tried to downplay it. "A few parents are complaining."

"About what? Me staying here on the weekends?"

She nodded. "They say it sets a bad example, especially for my impressionable students."

"Why didn't you say something?"

"It's not that big a deal. They'll get over it."

"Will they?" He ran his hand through his hair in an impatient gesture. "Dammit, Daisy, I thought this was just a little idle gossip. Now, from what you're telling me, it's beginning to sound like more than that."

"It's no reason to get upset. I'll handle it, but you can see why it would be best if you didn't stay here once you move to town."

"No problem," he said at once. "I'll find someplace else to stay. The hotel will do until we see how all of this goes."

"What does that mean?" she asked, reminded of her own prediction for the way all of this was likely to turn out. "You'll decide you hate it here, pack up Tommy and leave?"

"Maybe. Or I could decide I want a farm or a place on the river. Who knows?"

Daisy felt a sinking sensation in the pit of her stomach. Walker's decision to move to Trinity Harbor should have elated her. Instead, she feared it was going to cost her the very thing she'd been fighting so hard to keep—a family of her own.

She felt Walker's gaze on her. She glanced up. "What?"

"The hotel's no place for Tommy. He needs a room

of his own, a cookie jar he can raid. Can he stay here till I make that final decision?''

Her heart leapt. ''Of course.''

''As for you and me, we'll find some time to be together without stirring up any more gossip,'' he promised. ''I'm not going to be responsible for ruining your reputation.'' His gaze locked with hers. ''But I'm not going to give you up, either.''

To seal the promise, he stood, then bent down and kissed her until the room went spinning and the temperature soared.

The future might be in doubt, Daisy concluded when he'd gone off to bed—alone—but the present was very much worth fighting for.

20

It didn't take long for word to spread that Tucker had hired Walker and that he was going to be moving to Trinity Harbor. The general assumption seemed to be that he would be staying with Daisy. Denials weren't getting around nearly as quickly as the speculation.

While Walker was back in D.C. tying up loose ends on his cases and working out his two weeks notice, Daisy was left to cope with the fallout. She heard the whispers everywhere she went, but she kept her back straight and her smile in place. Eventually someone else would do something outrageous, and she'd be out of the spotlight.

The one person who'd been surprisingly silent was her father. Ever since the news had gotten out, she'd been anticipating an attempt to steamroll over her plan to keep Tommy until Walker was settled. Maybe King was too busy these days with his own love life to worry about hers. He and Frances had definitely become an item around town. They'd even gone to church together the last two Sundays.

She should have known, though, that her father's silence was way too uncharacteristic to last. When she came home from school on Thursday, he was sitting in a rocker on her front porch. Even more ominous, Anna-Louise was right beside him.

"You're late," her father grumbled.

"You didn't call to tell me you were stopping by," she shot right back, determined not to let him put her on the defensive.

"Since when does a man have to call his own daughter before dropping by?"

"Since he apparently expects her to be there at a certain time."

Anna-Louise regarded the two of them with amusement. "This is certainly getting off to a good start. King, I thought you had something you wanted to talk to Daisy about."

Daisy met her father's gaze evenly, though she was quaking inside. "Is that so?" she asked, grateful that Tommy had gone fishing with Gary again. "Anything in particular?"

"This nonsense about Walker moving in with you when he starts work down here. The rumors can't be right. You've got more sense than that."

"Walker is not moving in," she said.

King looked taken aback by her calm reply. "He's not?"

"No, we concluded it wouldn't be in my best interests since everyone's already in an uproar about us without knowing any of the facts. Tommy, however, will go right on staying here."

"Then why the devil is Walker coming, if he's not going to take responsibility for the boy?"

"He will, just not right away, not until he can get settled."

"But if his nephew's here, then he'll still be hanging around day and night," King complained.

"So what if he is? He'll be going off to his own

bed, in his own hotel room every night." *More's the pity,* she thought to herself.

"I don't like it," King groused.

"You weren't so quick to complain about all the time I spent with Billy Inscoe," she reminded him.

"You were living under my roof then. No one would have dared to suggest the two of you were up to no good. Besides, that was leading up to marriage."

Daisy lost patience. "Walker and I are trying to do what's best for Tommy and for my reputation. Our decision is made and it's final."

"I don't think you've thought this through the way you should have."

"Well, that's just too bad, isn't it?" she snapped, and stalked inside the house, leaving Anna-Louise to deal with her father's grumbling.

But after a few minutes, she began to feel guilty about leaving the pastor to handle King. She went back to the porch and met his gaze evenly.

"Daddy, this is going to work out. You'll see."

"Having Walker stay at a hotel is like trying to coax the horse back into the barn. It's too little, too late. People will still believe the worst."

"Since when do you care what anybody says?" Daisy asked. "Public opinion certainly never stopped you from doing anything you wanted to do."

"First off, I'm a man."

"Oh, brother," Daisy muttered. "Talk about your double standards."

King scowled. "Second, I don't give two cents what they say about me," he retorted impatiently. "We're talking about you. If your mother were here, she would never allow this."

"I seem to recall that you and mother lived together

your senior year in college and didn't get married until several months after that.''

"And my folks didn't like it one bit," King said unrepentantly. "Now I know how they felt. Besides, your mother and I were in Charlottesville, not right in our own backyard where our parents would have to live it down every single day."

He turned to the minister. "Anna-Louise, I backed you when the church had doubts about bringing in a woman for the job. Now I expect you to do something."

Anna-Louise rolled her gaze heavenward. "I knew that was going to come back and haunt me. What is it you think I should do?"

"Fix it. Get her to see reason. Tell her she has to get that boy out from under her roof so Walker won't have any excuses to be hanging around. Explain what happens to sinners. Give her one of those fancy sermons on morality. Maybe she'll listen to that."

Apparently satisfied that he'd made his point, he left.

Daisy sank down into the chair he'd vacated and set it to rocking. Eventually, she turned to Anna-Louise. "Is he right? Is this a mistake, too? I thought for sure not letting Walker stay here would be enough to stop the talk."

"In a perfect world, it should be."

"But you don't think it will do the trick?"

"Like your father said, it could be too late. You have to let your conscience decide what's right."

Daisy nodded. "I've done that. Keeping Tommy here, at least for the time being, is what's best for him. He's thriving. There's some stability in his life. Having his uncle nearby will only add to that. That's all that matters. If people can't understand that, if they want to make something out of Walker's visits, I can't stop them.''

"Then it sounds as if you've made your decision.''

"I have,'' Daisy said emphatically. "I'm sorry if my father and I made you uncomfortable by dragging you into this.''

"Just part of the job.'' She leveled a penetrating look at Daisy. "One thing, though. Just a warning.''

"What?''

"I know you and Walker are trying to do what's best for Tommy, but think long and hard about what's really right for him, not just short term, but for the long term as well.''

"I don't understand.''

"Right now, I suspect he's living a fantasy, thinking of the three of you as a family. What happens if it all falls apart because you and Walker aren't committed to each other?'' She studied Daisy's face. "Or have I missed something?''

Daisy wanted to talk about her feelings for Walker, about what had happened between them, but though she thought of Anna-Louise as her friend as well as her pastor, she couldn't bring herself to do it. She was too afraid of whatever judgment she might read in the other woman's eyes.

"No, we're not committed to each other,'' she said softly, leaving it at that.

"Do you think that could change?''

"Honestly? I don't know,'' Daisy said. More troubling, though, was how desperately she wanted it to.

She thought of little else all night long, weighing her own feelings against what was right for Tommy, what was convenient for Walker and the risks Anna-Louise had been right to raise.

She still hadn't made a decision when she arrived at school and was immediately called into the principal's office. Evan Washburn, a gray little man who had been a brilliant teacher but was out of his element in his new capacity, sat behind his desk, his fingertips touching as if he'd been playing that childhood game about a church and steeple. Or maybe he was just praying for guidance, since he'd never been any good at administrative details or confrontation.

He waved to Daisy to shut the door, then waited until she was seated.

"It has come to my attention—" he cleared his throat, color flaming in his cheeks "—that there is a man living with you."

So, it had come down to this, after all. How ironic, when she and Walker had already concluded that it was time for him to stay elsewhere. She covered her dismay with indignation. "Excuse me? Why would that be any business of yours?"

"There are a few people—several in fact—who have called to express some dismay that a woman entrusted with schoolchildren would be carrying on in such a way. I don't have to remind you that you are a role model, and such behavior is hardly suitable when dealing with impressionable teenagers."

"Perhaps what those teenagers ought to understand is that it is important for all of us to step in and help out when someone needs assistance. Tommy Flanagan needed a home. I provided it. There's no more to it than that."

"And that's all there is to it?" he asked, plainly skeptical.

"Are you asking me if Walker Ames and I are having sex?'' Daisy asked bluntly, determined to get the real issue out in the open.

Evan squirmed uncomfortably, clearly hating the situation into which he'd been thrust. Little wonder that he'd been so vehemently opposed to having sex education in school. He blushed at the mention of the word.

"Absolutely not," he insisted, looking horrified.

"Good, because it wouldn't be any of your business if we were." She stood up. "If that's all, I have a class to teach."

"Yes, yes, of course."

She turned back at the door. "Evan, if anyone else calls, why don't you refer them directly to me?"

"Yes, I'll be glad to," he said, clearly relieved. "Let's see to it that this doesn't get out of hand. I'm sure things will die down by fall and it won't be an issue at all."

"I'm sure," Daisy said wryly.

Outside his office, she drew in a deep breath. Though Evan hadn't said anything directly about her job being at stake, the implication had been there. This whole mess was getting out of hand. She doubted that King was behind the calls to Evan, which meant he'd been right that there were people in the community who thought what she was doing—no matter how well-intentioned—was wrong. Sending Walker to a hotel had clearly been too little, too late to save the day. Or else that particular word just hadn't spread yet.

She couldn't let that matter, though. This was the right thing to do. She was convinced of it. She had only to think of how well Tommy was doing to reassure herself that she had no other choice. Her relationship with Walker, whatever it was, wasn't an issue at all.

Except to her. And somehow, some way, she would manage to keep it in perspective and live with the fact that she was likely to spend the next several months all hot and bothered without doing a blessed thing about it. Because if keeping Walker out of her house and out of her bed was what it took to make the talk die down, then that's what she would have to do. Not that she thought for a second that people wouldn't believe whatever they wanted, no matter how much distance she put between herself and Walker.

"What's wrong?" Walker asked when he called that night.

It still threw her that he could read her so well. Few men had ever taken the trouble to even try.

"Not a thing," she insisted brightly. "How are things going up there? How did Andy take your news?"

"His biggest complaint is that, thanks to me, it's going to be harder than ever to keep Gail from wanting to move down there right away to open that store. He's not ready to retire, which is what he says I'm doing."

"Is that the way *you* think of it?" she asked, dismayed because she knew he would never be happy if it was.

"Absolutely not. There are a lot of positive aspects to this. Maybe I'll finally be someplace where I can really make a difference."

"You will, especially for Tucker."

"Leave it to you to see this as a way to keep your brother from working so hard."

"Well, it's true. He's incredibly dedicated and I admire that, but he needs to get a life. He needs to meet someone and have a family. Neither he nor Bobby is getting any younger.''

"This from their big sister," he teased.

"Okay, the same could be said for me, but I'm content with my life. It's the one I've chosen."

"Is it, Daisy? Is it the way you would have wanted it to be?"

"Of course," she insisted. "Why would you think otherwise?"

"Because anyone with so much love to give should have a family of her own."

She sighed, wishing that were as easy as he made it sound. "Some things just aren't meant to be. Now, enough of that, when will you be here?"

"Not till next week."

"Then let me get Tommy. I know he'll want to talk to you. He's so excited that you're going to be here all the time."

"And you, Daisy? Are you excited?"

She didn't know how to answer that. There was the honest answer—a resounding yes. Or the safer reply—that she was thrilled for Tommy's sake.

"Nothing to say to that?" he asked, picking up on her hesitation.

"It's...complicated," she said.

"Meaning?"

She forced a laugh. "That it's too complicated to get into now. I'll get Tommy."

"Daisy, wait."

"What?"

"Don't think I didn't notice that you never answered me."

"About?"

"What's wrong? Something is. I can hear it in your voice."

"It's nothing for you to worry about," she insisted. "I've already handled it."

"And you don't want to tell me whatever it is you had to handle?" he asked, clearly as exasperated as the last time she'd tried to keep a secret from him.

"No."

"I'm a pretty good investigator. I'll find out."

"Poking around in things that are none of your concern won't win you any points, Detective."

"I'll win my points the old-fashioned way."

"How's that?"

"Charm."

Daisy chuckled. "Awfully sure of yourself, aren't you?"

She was surprised when he sighed.

"No, Daisy. Lately, I'm not sure of anything at all."

She was still thinking about that response when Tommy hung up the phone a few minutes later and turned to her, his expression excited.

"It's gonna be really neat to have Uncle Walker here all the time, isn't it?"

"You bet," Daisy agreed.

"It'll be like having a real family again." His face clouded over. "I mean, not like having my mom exactly. I know I can't ever get her back, but this is almost as good, having you and Uncle Walker."

Daisy's heart ached for what he had lost, and what he had never known, a father's love. "I'm glad you're happy here," she said softly.

Tommy met her gaze with an earnest look. "Do you think maybe you and Uncle Walker might get married?"

She shouldn't have been startled by the question, but she was. It was exactly what Anna-Louise had warned her about.

"Oh, sweetie, I don't think so."

"Why not? He likes you. I can tell. And you like him at least a little bit, don't you?"

"Of course, but it's more complicated than that." There was that word again. It seemed to sum up her life lately.

"Well, I hope you do," Tommy said, his face set stubbornly. "The kids at school say I'm nothing but a lousy orphan, that I don't have anybody who really loves me."

Daisy was horrified. "That's absurd. I don't ever want to hear anyone say something like that. You have a lot of people who love you."

"It's not the same," Tommy said, his shoulders slumped wearily. "I'm going to bed."

Long after he'd gone, she stared after him. Darkness gathered, but she stayed where she was. Giving Tommy a make-believe family wasn't the answer, just as Anna-Louise had said. He needed to belong to a real family. Walker was his biological family, so that was where it had to begin. And it was up to Walker to provide him with a mother. As long as she was in the middle of things, that would never happen. It would be too easy to allow things to drift along, because they were convenient and comfortable and because they all got along well enough.

Tommy had to have more than that, and it was up to her to set things in motion.

She was waiting for Walker when he arrived with his things the following week. She met him on the porch and blocked his way inside.

"This isn't going to work," she said bluntly.

"What isn't?"

"Keeping Tommy here. You can stay tonight, but in the morning I want you and Tommy to find your own place."

Walker dragged her over to a chair, then gestured toward it. "Sit," he ordered in a tone that normally would have had her refusing. "Tell me what this is all about. You're not making any sense. I thought this was all settled. I thought you were happy about keeping Tommy with you a little longer."

"It's a bad idea."

"Why?" His gaze narrowed. "This has something to do with whatever was upsetting you last week, doesn't it?"

She wasn't going to explain that Tommy wanted them to marry. She wasn't sure she could do it without letting Walker see how badly she wanted that, too.

"Why doesn't matter. It's my decision and it's final." Her gaze locked with his and her chin set stubbornly.

She could tell there was a storm brewing in Walker's eyes, but he finally gave a curt nod.

"Your decision," he said tightly. "Maybe I'll just stay at the hotel tonight, so I won't be underfoot while you explain this to Tommy. Or have you told him already?"

She hadn't. She wasn't sure she could bear to. "I haven't said anything. I thought…" She swallowed hard. "I thought we could tell him together."

Walker shook his head. "I don't think so, because I

don't know what the hell is going on. This is your show, Daisy. You'll have to do your own dirty work.''

With that, he whirled around and stomped off the porch, leaving her once again in darkness, her thoughts troubled, her heart aching. She honestly didn't know what was right anymore. If this was it, though, then why did she feel so blasted lousy?

Walker had no idea what had gotten into Daisy. Nor had he liked the way his stomach had started churning when she'd gazed up at him with those big violet eyes shimmering with tears and told him to go and take Tommy with him.

He'd wanted to argue with her. Hell, he'd flat-out wanted to plead, but pride wouldn't let him. But he sure as heck intended to find out what had put this particular bee into her bonnet.

Instead of checking into the hotel, he headed straight for the parsonage so he could talk to Anna-Louise and Richard. Between them, they were bound to have answers. Tucker certainly hadn't had any clue about this turn of events, or he would have said something when Walker had seen him earlier.

He found Anna-Louise and Richard sitting in back of the cozy little parsonage enjoying the breeze off the river and tall glasses of lemonade. The steeple of the white church next door cast a shadow across the yard.

Walker waited impatiently while Anna-Louise fixed a glass for him, then told them what had just happened at Daisy's.

"She what?" Anna-Louise asked, her expression shocked.

"You don't have any idea why she would do this?" Walker asked.

"None at all. She told her father to butt out of it when he objected. She all but told me the same thing. Her mind was made up. This is a complete turnaround."

"I think I might have an idea," Richard said slowly.

Walker and Anna-Louise stared at him. "You do?" they said simultaneously.

"I got a couple of letters at the paper."

"About?" Walker said, an uneasy feeling in the pit of his stomach.

"A local teacher—unnamed, of course—who was setting a poor example for her students by having a man all but living with her. They indicated that they'd gone to the principal several weeks ago and nothing had happened, so they were calling on the school board to take some action."

Walker muttered an expletive, then cast an apologetic look toward Anna-Louise. "Sorry."

"Don't be. That was my sentiment exactly. How could they? There is not a finer teacher or a better example to her students in this county," she said indignantly.

"And the ridiculous part is that I'm not moving in," Walker said. "We'd already decided against that."

"But with Tommy there, you'll still be in and out," Anna-Louise said. "It's a fine distinction, and some people won't consider it at all."

"So that could explain why she wants Tommy gone, too," Walker concluded. "Can she be fired over this?"

"Possibly, if these people can get enough others worked into a frenzy," Richard said. "The school board would at least have to take a look at the complaint."

"Are you printing the letters?" Anna-Louise asked, looking as if she were ready to do battle if he said yes.

Richard shook his head. "They were anonymous. I only print letters with signatures."

"Thank goodness," Walker said, relieved that the man's journalistic integrity and friendship weren't going to butt heads.

Anna-Louise's expression turned thoughtful. "I know this is terrible, but I don't think this is behind Daisy's decision not to let Tommy stay. She's never been one to back away from a fight, particularly when it's something she feels passionately about, and that's exactly how she felt about having Tommy there. This kind of pressure would only make her mad."

"Then what else could it be?" Walker wondered aloud. Unfortunately, before they could discuss it further, his brand-new beeper, provided by Tucker less than two hours earlier, went off.

"I've got to go. Apparently my new boss has something on his mind, too. Or maybe, if things have gone completely haywire, he's going to tell me he's not even my new boss anymore."

"Don't kid yourself. Tucker's not going to fire you," Richard said with certainty. "He's too ecstatic to have someone with your background on the force. I've got a whole piece on it running in this week's paper. He's singing your praises as if you're single-handedly going to save this county from crime."

Walker groaned. "I hope you tempered his comments some. I'm not a superhero."

"Don't tell Tucker that," Richard said. "He's a happy man."

When Walker reached the station in Montross, Tucker was waiting along with Bobby. For one fleeting instant, Walker had the sinking feeling that they were there to ambush him about whatever they thought he'd done to Daisy.

"We've got trouble," Tucker announced, his tone somber.

Bobby nodded, looking just as glum.

"What's up?"

"Tucker's had me keeping my ears open around the marina. There's been some talk the last day or so," Bobby began. "Mostly kids, so I don't know how reliable it is, but I think there might be a drug deal going down."

"When?" Walker asked, glancing from one man to the other.

It was Tucker who responded. "Sometime this week."

Walker muttered a whole string of expletives. And he'd thought coming to Trinity Harbor was going to simplify his life.

21

When Daisy still hadn't heard from Walker on Saturday morning, she sent Tommy off to baseball practice, then headed for Earlene's to meet Anna-Louise. She'd been surprised by the pastor's call the night before. Usually Anna-Louise reserved Saturday mornings for her run with Richard. Maybe she'd just been looking for an excuse to get out of it this week. Her enthusiasm for jogging had definitely dwindled lately.

She found Anna-Louise already ensconced in a booth, sipping a cup of coffee, her eyes red, her complexion pale. She looked as if she'd thrown her clothes on in a hurry.

"Are you okay?" Daisy asked worriedly. "You look terrible."

"Just what every woman wants to hear first thing in the morning," Anna-Louise retorted. "Remember this. It's the way women our age look when they don't get any sleep."

"You were up all night?"

"Most of it. Jane Miller was taken to the hospital in Fredericksburg last night. They think it was a heart attack."

"But she's only fifty."

"I know, but she has a terrible family history, and

you know she doesn't take care of herself. She lives on junk food and caffeine and cigarettes.''

"How is her husband?"

"Keith was devastated. He kept blaming himself for not insisting that she follow her doctor's orders, at least about the smoking. Of course, he said that while he was puffing away. No wonder she hadn't quit. At any rate, I sat with him while they tried to get her stabilized. It took most of the night, but they think she'll pull through.''

"Thank heavens," Daisy said. "No wonder you're exhausted. You should have called. We didn't have to do this today.''

"Yes, we did," Anna-Louise said.

Daisy hadn't thought it possible for her friend to look any more somber, but she did. "Why?" she asked, suddenly uneasy.

"Because I heard something last night, something you need to know. It's too important to wait.''

"What did you hear?"

"That there are people trying to get you fired," Anna-Louise said bluntly. "I know it's absurd, that the school board would never fire you, but these people could certainly stir things up and make your life pretty uncomfortable.''

Daisy wasn't nearly as shocked as Anna-Louise had been. "How did you hear about this?" she asked.

"They've been sending letters to Richard. Fortunately, they were sent anonymously, so he's refusing to print them. If someone signs a name, though, I imagine he'll feel obligated to publish them.''

Daisy sighed. "It's gone that far, then.''

Anna-Louise regarded her with a shocked expression. "You knew about this?"

"I knew there had been complaints some time ago. I knew Evan had gotten calls at school. He and I talked. I thought it was settled."

"Apparently not. They were anticipating that Evan would take action. When he didn't, they wrote their letters to the paper. They're not going to let it drop."

"Dammit all!" Daisy said without apology.

"And there's more," Anna-Louise said without commenting on Daisy's language. "Richard told Walker when he stopped by last night. He's furious. At first he thought that might be why you told him Tommy couldn't stay, but after we'd talked a bit, I think we all concluded something else must be going on. Whatever it is, you need to explain it to him before he goes charging off to take on your enemies."

Daisy wasn't sure what stunned her more, that Walker had dropped in on Anna-Louise for a little heart-to-heart after he'd left her house, that he'd told her about Daisy's decision or that he was ready to do battle with the town in her behalf.

"That's ridiculous," she told Anna-Louise indignantly. "As if I would ever let a bunch of busybodies dictate anything to me!"

"That's what I said." Anna-Louise took another sip of her coffee, then beckoned for more. When Earlene had gone, she asked, "So why did you change your mind about letting Walker move in?"

"Actually it was something you said about Tommy starting to think of us as a family. Then he asked me the other night if Walker and I might get married. I realized you were right. It's not fair to get his hopes up."

"No," Anna-Louise agreed. "But are you so sure that you'd be giving him false hope? Watching Walker last night, I got the feeling that there's a lot more going on between the two of you than you've said. He was genuinely upset, both about what you'd decided and about the threat to your career.''

"He was upset at having his plans thwarted," Daisy said flatly.

Anna-Louise regarded her intently. "You don't honestly believe that, do you?"

Daisy sighed. "Okay, I'll be as honest as I can be. I care about him, probably way too much. And maybe he even cares about me. But with all of this other stuff going on, how can we possibly spend enough time together to figure out if we have a future? That being the case, I have to think about Tommy. As much as I might hate it, his future is with his uncle. I've come to accept that after seeing them together these last weeks. Walker will be a good father. That's the certainty. The rest, well, who knows how it will turn out?"

"Then tell Walker exactly where your head is before he goes on a rampage. Right now he's ready to hunt down the people who are writing letters and making phone calls and tear them apart."

"Frankly, when it comes to that, I'd like to help him," Daisy admitted candidly. When she saw Anna-Louise's lips twitch, even as she tried to maintain a solemn expression, Daisy grinned. "Okay, I know I'm supposed to turn the other cheek or whatever, but it just infuriates me that they're talking about something they know nothing about."

"I know. Me, too. Not that I'd counsel anything except understanding and forgiveness, of course. Maybe I'll make that tomorrow's sermon. That should make the busybodies squirm."

"And I'll sit in the back so I can see who's doing the most squirming," Daisy said dryly.

Anna-Louise chuckled, then sighed. "I think God might frown on me using the pulpit in quite that way."

"He might," Daisy agreed.

"You know, sometimes setting a good example is the pits."

"Believe me, I know," Daisy agreed.

"Yes, I imagine you do." Anna-Louise glanced toward the door, then suddenly began to gather up her jacket and purse. She dropped a few dollars on the table. "See you."

"What on earth?" Daisy asked, just as a shadow fell over the table.

She glanced up into Walker's troubled eyes. She noticed he didn't look a whole lot better than Anna-Louise. For the first time since she'd met him, his cheeks were unshaven. The faint stubble made him look even more masculine than usual. She had the oddest urge to reach up and run her fingers over his face. If only she had the right to, if only half the town weren't apparently watching for her to do just that or more to confirm their worst suspicions about the nature of the relationship.

"I was on my way out," Anna-Louise said. "You two have things to talk about."

"We do, indeed," Walker said, sliding into the spot she'd vacated.

Under the table his knees brushed Daisy's, but he made no effort to shift away. Neither did she. What had ever made her think she could simply will herself not to respond to this man?

Once Anna-Louise had gone and Walker had

downed half a cup of coffee in one swallow, he carefully set the cup aside and met her gaze.

"Why didn't you tell me?"

Daisy didn't pretend not to understand. "Because, as I *did* tell you, I handled it."

"If you'd handled it any better, you would have been out of work," he complained. "That could still happen, couldn't it?"

"It won't. People in this town don't go up against King Spencer. And if push comes to shove, my father will back me. He'll defend my choices because that's what Spencers do. We stick together."

"Even though he wants me gone, too?"

"He wants my happiness more," she said simply. "At the moment, he just can't imagine how a rebellious boy and a Yankee could possibly bring me anything but pain."

"He might have a point. Look what we've done so far."

"You haven't done anything. I'm the one who made the decision to take Tommy in. I'm the one who invited you to stay when you came down for visits. And I thought it would be best if Tommy stayed on till you got settled."

"But now you don't? Why? Is it because of the complaints?"

"Absolutely not," she said fiercely.

"What then?"

"Can't you just accept that it's best for Tommy to be with you, starting now?"

"I could if it made any sense. Explain it to me."

Daisy really didn't want to get into Tommy's expectations with Walker. She didn't want him to think for a second that marriage was in any way on her mind. Which it wasn't. At least not all the time.

"He just needs to learn that you're the one he should count on, not me."

Walker's gaze searched hers in a way that had her stomach churning, but he finally nodded. "Okay, then. Have you told him yet?"

She shook her head.

"Then you're going to have to do better than that," he said. "He won't buy evasions any more than I do."

"I don't see why I have to explain myself. It's my decision, my house."

"Can your decision be reversed?"

"No."

"Not even temporarily?"

Something in his voice alerted her that his asking wasn't simply a matter of trying to find a convenient place for Tommy to stay, a way to cajole her into changing her mind. "Why? What's happened?" she asked at once.

"I'm going to be tied up at night for the next few days. I don't want Tommy in a strange place all alone."

Uneasiness stole over her. "This has something to do with work?"

Walker nodded. "Thanks to Bobby, we have a lead on a drug deal. It's supposed to go down soon. When it does, it will probably be at night. Tucker wants me doing surveillance out on the river."

She didn't even hesitate. "Then of course Tommy can stay with me until this is over," she said readily.

He clasped her hand in his. "Thank you."

Daisy jerked her hand back. "Don't do that."

"Do what?" His gaze darkened. "Don't touch you?"

"Yes."

"Why?"

Because she wanted it too much, because the instant he did, she remembered every exhilarating detail of making love with him. "Because I asked you not to," she said, her voice barely above a whisper.

"But it's not what you want, is it, Daisy?"

"Walker, please."

This time he sighed. "You're right. I'm not being fair. This is exactly the kind of thing that will keep people talking."

"Yes, it is," she said, grateful for once for the gossip. It was the perfect excuse to keep him at a distance. He'd seen for himself now that very little in Trinity Harbor could be kept private.

"Walker, is this surveillance you're going to do dangerous?" she asked, thinking not just of him or even herself, but of Tommy.

"Tommy's not going to lose me, if that's what you're worried about," he said, then added quietly, but emphatically, "Neither are you."

Daisy had a feeling she was going to cling to those words in the days and weeks to come, because behind them she thought she heard a promise that went far deeper than the immediate situation in which they found themselves.

Was it at all possible that she'd gotten it wrong, that Walker's move here wasn't just about Tommy, after all? Was it possible that he'd begun to care for her, too?

Walker had known better than to believe that he'd left drug-related crimes behind when he quit his job in

D.C. He just hadn't expected to become immersed in a smuggling case so soon after his arrival in Trinity Harbor. He'd thought his suspicions and Tucker's were a long way from turning into a solid, all-consuming investigation. Now, several sleepless days and nights into it, he had concluded that police work could be twenty-four/seven no matter where a cop lived.

The timing sucked. This situation with Daisy needed more attention than he could afford to give it right now. He'd hoped to spend his first weeks in town trying to analyze the way he felt about her, trying to make sense of the fact that for the first time in years he was linking a woman and the future in the same thought. Instead, he barely had a minute to himself.

Tommy's presence was complication enough. He knew he couldn't get his nephew's hopes up about all of them becoming a family only to dash them if he decided he'd made a mistake, that he wasn't capable of the forever kind of relationship, after all.

Add to that the pressure of all the gossip, the expectations of Daisy's family and the threats to her job, then throw in the drug case, and his life was just about totally out of hand. All he needed now was his ex-wife calling and suggesting she bring the boys up for a visit. She'd been stunned—and clearly intrigued—when he'd told her about his decision to leave Washington. She'd been totally flabbergasted when he told her about Tommy and his intention to raise him.

"And how do you think your sons are going to feel about that?" she'd demanded.

"I think that depends a whole lot on what they're told," he'd replied, implying that she wasn't to use it as another way to point out what a lousy father he was to them. "Tommy isn't replacing them in any way. Are we clear on that?"

"If you say so. I'm sure they'll want to meet this mysterious cousin for themselves."

"They can do that as soon as I'm settled," he'd assured her, but knowing her, she would haul them up here sooner, probably at the worst possible moment.

Well, for now, there was nothing he could do about that. In fact, work was the one thing he felt confident about these days. Stakeouts he understood. Not that he'd ever done one on the water, but the principles were the same. Stay out of sight, keep his eyes open and wait. Boring as hell, but amazingly productive... eventually.

Before he'd left D.C., he'd studied some of the material available on drug cases along the Potomac River and Chesapeake Bay. He'd seen the reports about boats slipping into out-of-the-way, less-heavily-policed coves along the river to deliver to distributors who would carry the illegal substances up and down the East Coast. Trinity Harbor was ripe for such activity.

Unfortunately, he suspected there were too many inlets and coves for his surveillance to be effective. He was going to have to concentrate on the marina itself, since Bobby was convinced that at least one of the boats involved was docked there, the same boat Walker had initially suspected of being too fast for a mere pleasure boat. Even though the owner's record looked clean, it didn't mean he was innocent. It could mean only that he'd never been caught. Or that he'd changed his name.

Just to be sure, the other night Walker had managed to get a set of prints from Craig Remington when he'd bought him a drink at the marina. He'd sent those up to Andy and asked him to have them run through the computer to see if a match turned up.

"You're not wasting any time getting into the thick of things, are you?" Andy asked, sounding amused when Walker called to follow up on the prints. "Are you sure you didn't create this case just to give yourself something to do?"

"Actually, I dreamed it up to lure you down here. I'm in cahoots with your wife. She really, really wants to get that store up and running."

Andy groaned. "You don't need to tell me. She's been bugging me to death about it. So what's the deal? Is something going down or is Tucker overreacting?"

"There are definitely drugs around. And Bobby overheard some kids out on the dock bragging that they were going to be able to lay their hands on all the pot they wanted pretty soon."

"And you think this Remington guy could be involved?"

"He's got the kind of boat a drug smuggler would love to own. It can outrun anything the authorities have."

"How did he seem when you talked to him? Nervous?"

"Not at all," Walker admitted. "He was as friendly as everyone else around town."

"Maybe I'll come down next weekend and you can lay it all out for me. Might help you to talk it over."

Walker chuckled. "I have plenty of people I can talk it over with right here. In fact, Tucker is the talkingest man I've ever met. He dissects everything. Listening to him wears me out. Not that I wouldn't be glad to have another perspective, if you're headed this way anyway."

"Oh, I am," Andy said, sounding resigned. "Gail's itching to get to work on that house she bought last time we were down. The garage is already filling up with mysterious boxes and the kitchen table is littered with catalogs. I haven't checked the bank account, but I'm pretty sure I'm heading for the poorhouse. She seems to think she's going to open a business there by Fourth of July weekend. Apparently I get to commute if I want to see my wife at all after that."

"It's gone that far?"

"Oh, yeah. Gail might seem flighty and impulsive to the casual observer, but once she gets a notion into her head, there's no stopping her. She's so organized, it makes me regret she's not a cop. I could use someone down here who pays that much attention to details and paperwork."

"I think that particular ship has sailed, pal. In fact, it sounds as if your own days as a cop are numbered."

"Could be."

"And?"

"I'm actually getting used to the idea. I've been at this thirty years. Maybe that's long enough. That doesn't mean I don't need a little mental stimulation, and you're the one I'm counting on to supply it. Because if I don't find a way to hide out with you, I'm going to be spending every weekend from now until she gets this place open painting and plastering and fixing a roof. And if that's what I'm doing, guess who's going to be working right beside me," he said ominously.

"I actually like to paint," Walker said. "It's good, mindless work that allows me to think about whatever case I'm working on. Many a case has been solved while I have a paintbrush in hand."

"Not me," Andy said fervently. "The fumes cloud my brain. But you have my permission to spend all the time you want with my wife helping her out with her little project. I suspect you might have trouble convincing Tucker that you're working on his case for him at the same time, though."

Walker laughed. "I imagine you're right about that. See you this weekend."

"I'd like to say I'm looking forward to it, but I can't," Andy said. "In the meantime, if I get anything on these prints, I'll let you know."

"You know, Andy, maybe you should stop fighting this. You're the one who said it—Trinity Harbor is not a bad place to be," Walker reminded him.

"You're honestly not bored yet?"

Walker thought not of his current case, but of Daisy. "No," he admitted. "Granted I haven't been here full-time that long, but I'm definitely not bored."

In fact, the most positive aspect of this smuggling investigation was that it had given him such a reasonable excuse to delay moving Tommy out of Daisy's house. Granted she had managed to make sure that she and Walker seldom crossed paths, but one of these nights, soon, he was going to fix that. The anticipation of their next intimate encounter kept him going. Whatever was going on between them wasn't over, not by a long shot.

In fact, in recent days he had concluded that delayed gratification had its benefits. He'd never wanted a woman as badly as he wanted Daisy. He'd never had one get under his skin and into his head the way she had.

Walking into the house after she'd just taken off, he was greeted by the scent of her perfume. The still-steamy bathroom filled his mind with amazingly erotic images of her soaking in the tub, bubbles up to her chin, foaming over the tips of her breasts.

The signs of her presence were everywhere, overshadowing Tommy's careless scattering of schoolbooks, jackets and toys. Walker had discovered that Daisy's neat-as-a-pin image—the only one she had allowed him to see up till now—was a fraud.

Now that he was dropping in whenever he could catch a quick break, it turned out that she was the one who left a trail of provocative silk in her wake, a kicked-off pair of heels inside the front door, an open jar of lavender-scented hand lotion on the kitchen counter. The house was a minefield of sensual images that made getting to sleep back at the hotel all but impossible.

If his days were restless and uncomfortable, the nights were worse. The air had turned balmy, heavy with humidity and the hum of crickets and the mournful sound of doves. Being on the calm, moonlit water was just a little too romantic. It made him wish he were out there with Daisy, gazing at the stars, talking about anything and everything, maybe making love on deck.

The fantasy made his body hard, but the cold reality was that he was out there all alone in a borrowed boat with only a pair of night-vision binoculars and his gun for company.

And at the rate things were going, he didn't see that changing any time soon.

22

"**I** thought you were going to get that man out of your house," Evan said, practically quivering with indignation as he faced Daisy across his desk. "Look at this, just look."

In his hand was an inch-thick stack of letters and pink message slips. "I spend all my time lately talking to parents."

"Isn't that your job?" Daisy asked flippantly.

The principal scowled. "This is not a joking matter. Your career is on the line. Don't you get that yet? I have tried to protect you."

"Oh, really?"

"I did. When the president of the school board called me, I told him we had talked and that you understood that this behavior would not be tolerated."

Up until now Daisy had managed to keep a tight rein on her temper, but she was rapidly losing her grip on it.

"What behavior would that be?" she demanded, concluding that it would be a waste of her breath to explain that Walker was not actually living with her. "We're not back to S-E-X, are we?"

Evan's cheeks flamed. "I warned you—"

"I know, that this is not a joking matter. Trust me, I am taking it very seriously. In fact, I am thinking of suing the lot of you for slander." She stood up, then leaned down until she was in his face. "And now, if you'll excuse me, I have a final exam to give."

"You can't walk out on me," he protested. "We're having a conversation."

"Not anymore."

By the time she reached her classroom, her fury had subsided, only to be replaced by a sense of inevitability. She gazed around at the displays she and her students had worked so hard to create about the American Revolution and the Civil War, at the exam questions she had written earlier on the blackboard. The smell of dusty chalk assailed her, filling her with an odd sense of nostalgia. The bell rang, followed by the explosion of students into the corridors, shouting as they raced for their next classes or to their lockers for a forgotten paper.

She could lose all of this, she thought, because of the small-mindedness of people she'd considered her friends, people who didn't know all the facts and chose to believe the worst.

But even if it had been true, even if she and Walker were having a torrid, passionate fling, what possible difference could it make as to whether she was qualified to do her job? She would fight any attempt to oust her, she decided, fight for her right to a personal life, fight for the happiness she'd experienced these past few weeks, even if it was only meant to be fleeting.

One day, when the drug case was solved, Walker would take Tommy away from her. They would become their own little family with her as a friendly outsider, someone who'd once done them a kindness. She would be alone again, but she wouldn't trade the time until then for anything, not even for the job she loved.

Given her mood, the last thing she wanted to do that night was entertain, but she had invited the Finches over. It had taken several weeks to work out a date, but she had been determined to get to know Tommy's friend and his parents better.

When the three of them arrived right on the dot of six, she plastered a smile on her face and went to greet them. Tommy already had the front door open.

"Come on, Gary. We can work on the boat." He glanced at Daisy. "Dinner's not going to be ready for a long time, right?"

"A half hour," Daisy said. "And try not to get too filthy, please." She turned back to greet Paul and his wife. "I'm so glad you could come. I should have had you over long before now since Tommy and Gary are such good friends."

Maribeth Finch looked vaguely uncomfortable. In fact, Daisy thought she might be ill. Her complexion was pale, her eyes a little too bright.

"We don't have a lot of time for socializing," Paul said, his voice oddly tight.

"Then I'm doubly glad you could come tonight. Let me get you something to drink."

Though she'd had a lot of experience entertaining King's friends over the years, nothing had prepared her for the stiffness of Maribeth's responses and Paul's gruff demeanor. She was relieved when he wandered outside to take a look at the boat the boys were working on.

Daisy smiled at Maribeth. "How do you like living in Trinity Harbor so far? I hope you've had a chance to make some friends."

"Not really," Maribeth said. "There's just so much to do after a move."

"I'm sure as a military wife, you've had more than your share of experience with that," Daisy said. "It will probably be good to stay in one place."

"Yes, I'm sure it will be," she said, though she sounded as if she weren't a bit certain of that.

Something was off here, Daisy concluded. She couldn't put her finger on it, but it went beyond her inability to spark the right conversational note. Maribeth seemed nervous, and Paul wasn't at all the friendly, outgoing man who'd greeted her that night at the marina when he had inadvertently taken Tommy fishing without her permission. Even under those tense circumstances, he had been more pleasant than he was as a guest in her home.

Dinner didn't go any more smoothly. Other than Daisy and the boys, no one made any attempt at small talk. When Maribeth pleaded a headache right after dessert, Daisy wasn't the least bit surprised. And only Gary looked dismayed.

"Can Gary spend the night?" Tommy asked.

Gary shot a hopeful look toward his father, but Paul was already shaking his head. "Not tonight."

Before Tommy could protest, Daisy rested a hand on his shoulder to silence him. "Another time, then."

As soon as they'd gone, Tommy looked up at her, his expression puzzled. "How come everybody was acting so weird tonight?"

"I wish I knew," she said. Her instincts told her something was very wrong within the Finch family, and while it might be none of her business, if Gary continued to be Tommy's best friend, she would keep a close eye on their activities. She was glad they were working on the boat over here—the thought of Tommy going over to the Finches to play with Gary made her feel decidedly uneasy.

King was hot and sweaty and foul-tempered. He'd just lost one of his best bulls. Seemed like nothing was going the way he'd intended lately. And finding Anna-Louise and Frances on his doorstep was not designed to reassure him that the day was going to get any better before sundown.

"What do you two want?" he growled, leading the way inside and heading straight for his office. He wanted a drink and, by golly, he intended to have one, whether the two of them were offended or not. He poured a splash of whiskey into a glass, then downed it, before looking at them. Truth be told, the two women looked more worried than offended. "Oh, sit down, why don't you? I'm not turning into a drunk yet."

"Never thought you were," Frances said. "Would you mind if I went into the kitchen and made some iced tea? It was hot as blazes waiting on your front porch."

He waved her off, then frowned at Anna-Louise. "Something's on your mind, I imagine."

She grinned at him. "What was your first clue?"

"You know, for a woman of the cloth, you have a mighty sassy mouth."

She laughed at that. "I pride myself on it."

"Thought pride was a sin."

"I try not to indulge too often. Can you say the same?"

"Woman, if there's something on your mind, just get to it. I'm soaking wet and filthy and I need a shower. Plus, it's already past dinnertime and my stomach's rumbling. I'm in no mood for word games.''

"As soon as Frances gets back, we'll be brief.''

"Can't talk unless there's two of you ganging up on me? Must be something you know I'm not going to like.''

"You aren't,'' she agreed.

"Then spit it out. Don't keep me in suspense.''

"Okay, then. Have it your way. The school board's going after Daisy's job.''

King stared at her as if she'd suddenly started speaking in tongues. "You explain to me how the devil they think they can get away with that.''

"Despite your influence, they do have the power to hire and fire.''

"On what grounds?''

"Exactly what you feared. They say she is setting a poor example,'' Anna-Louise said, watching him closely.

King frowned at her scrutiny. "And you think I might agree with 'em about that, don't you? That's what you and Frances are over here all worked up about. You want to know if I'm going to back my own daughter or join the idiots who want to tar and feather her, is that it?''

"You have been pretty vocal about your objections to her inviting Walker into her home and about Tommy staying on there,'' Frances said as she returned with a pitcher of iced tea and three glasses. She poured the beverage and pointedly sat a glass in front of King, then removed the whiskey glass.

"I was vocal because this is exactly what I thought might happen. If I told her once, I told her a thousand times that she was courting disaster.''

"And now you get to say you told her so," Frances said. "That's definitely the kind of help she needs."

"Oh, blast it all, woman, I don't intend to tell her that—or them, either. Do either of you know Dave Higgins's phone number? By the time I'm through with him, the school board will think again about messing with King Spencer's daughter."

Frances handed him a slip of paper, a smug smile firmly in place. "I told you he'd take care of this," she said to Anna-Louise.

King frowned at the pastor. "You doubted it?"

"You can be a stubborn cuss," she pointed out. "I wasn't entirely sure you weren't behind it."

"Don't think too much of me, do you?"

"You have your good points," she said politely, then added, "and your bad ones."

"Not when it comes to family," he said fiercely. "Spencers stick together, and that's that. No matter what I might think of Walker myself, I wouldn't set out to hurt Daisy. She's my own flesh and blood, for goodness' sakes."

He snatched up the phone and dialed the school board president, who also owned the local John Deere Machinery dealership. King spent a lot of money with the man and brought other customers his way as well. He could just as easily take that business elsewhere, and Higgins knew it. He could tell it the second he heard the false joviality in the man's voice.

"Let's cut to the chase," King told him. "You take on my daughter, you take on me. Daisy doesn't need that job of yours, not half as much as you need her. She's the best teacher in the district, and you know it."

"Of course she is," Dave said. "If it were just about her teaching—"

King interrupted him. "Would you mind telling me what it is about if not her teaching?"

The question drew silence, just as he'd anticipated. The man was not about to start leveling charges about Daisy's morality, not to her father.

"I thought you might see it my way," King said with a huff. "Do I have your word that this ends here and now?"

"I can't promise you that," Dave said. "The board—"

"Does what you tell 'em to do."

"Not on this," he said with what could have been real regret. "You know I admire Daisy, King, but she's been flaunting her relationship with this man all over town. People are up in arms."

"What people, I'd like to know? One or two people who've always had it in for the Spencers, I imagine."

"I'm not about to name names, but enough have come to me and the others that the board has to ask questions. Frankly, I'm amazed that Social Services hasn't taken that child away from her. You using your influence with Frances to stop that?"

King sputtered, filled with indignation, then got control of his temper. It wouldn't help the situation. "You ask your questions," he said slowly and evenly. "Then I've got a few of my own that I intend to ask. We'll start with your affair with that woman over in Kinsale."

"I never..." Dave said.

He sounded shaken, which was exactly the way King wanted him. "You were over there every Saturday night, weren't you? Till all hours?" He went on, "And there's the time Maureen went off to Atlanta with that fellow from Richmond."

"That was her cousin," the man said, on the defensive all of a sudden now that the tables had been turned. "King, you know that."

"Do I? Appearances can be mighty deceiving, can't they? Think about that before you start slinging mud on my daughter's reputation, okay? Think long and hard about it." He slammed the phone down with satisfaction. "That ought to do it."

He caught Frances and Anna-Louise exchanging a look. "What?" he asked.

"Was Dave Higgins really having an affair?" Frances asked, her expression shocked.

King chuckled. "Who would have him? Even his own wife took off."

"But you said—"

"I said that things could look a certain way without being true. Now will you two go on and get out of here? I have things to do."

"What things?" Anna-Louise asked suspiciously.

"I'm going to go hire me a moving van and get that boy out of that house before there's a ruckus I can't solve."

"Daisy's going to object," Anna-Louise warned.

"You think I don't know that? That's how this mess came to be in the first place. This time I'm not asking or suggesting. I'm going to make it happen."

"With Walker on these night-time stakeouts, Tommy can't be left alone," Frances warned. "I'd have to step in."

"Oh, for Pete's sake, I'm not going to put him on the street," King snapped. "I'll move him and Walker in here." He shook his head. "Never thought I'd see the day I'd have a damn Yankee sleeping under this roof."

Frances suddenly began to chuckle and couldn't stop. "Oh, King," she murmured between guffaws.

He and Anna-Louise stared at her. Frances wasn't a woman prone to giggles.

"What?" Anna-Louise asked eventually.

"Walker's no more Yankee than you or I," Frances said. "He was born in Richmond. I have it right in my report. Talk about appearances being deceiving. I guess this one's on you." She erupted into laughter once again.

King took the ribbing in stride, but his thoughts turned speculative. If Walker wasn't a Yankee after all, then maybe he'd been handling this all wrong. There wasn't a Southern gentleman on earth who wouldn't come to a lady's rescue. He'd tried the marriage ploy on Walker once before to no avail, but that didn't mean it wasn't worth a second try, not with Daisy's reputation—her entire life's work—so plainly on the line.

He sat back down. "Forget the moving van," he announced.

"Oh?" Anna-Louise asked, regarding him with suspicion.

"I think maybe it's time Walker and I had another talk." He dialed the sheriff's office, only to be told that Walker was out of contact for the rest of the night.

"Then have him call me first thing in the morning," he told the dispatcher. "Tell him it's urgent and that I expect him here for breakfast. Eight sharp."

He leaned back and regarded the two women with satisfaction. "How about I take you two ladies out for a nice crab dinner at the marina? I'm feeling real good, all of a sudden."

"Yes, I can see that," Anna-Louise said. "What

worries me is why? What do you have up your sleeve, King?''

"Nothing for you to trouble yourself about," he assured her.

"Maybe I'd better say a little prayer, just the same," she said, her tone wry.

"You do whatever you want. I've got things under control," he replied. In fact, things just might be taking a real turn for the better.

"How come Uncle Walker's going fishing every night?" Tommy asked Daisy after Walker's brief visit. She hadn't had time to tell him anything at all about the dinner with Gary's family because he'd had to leave for another night on the river.

These quick, drop-in visits had been the pattern for a while now. Sometimes, when Walker could spare the time, they ate dinner, then Walker took off for work. She and Walker had agreed not to tell Tommy the full story about his surveillance since Tommy had a tendency to blab whatever he knew indiscriminately to his friends.

"Now that he's out of the city, I think he's just enjoying having some time to himself," Daisy said evasively.

"Why can't I go with him?"

"Maybe one of these days he'll take you," she said. "In the meantime, be glad he's on this kind of a schedule. He has more time during the day to coach your baseball team. It'll be great having him around during the day this summer, won't it?"

"Yeah," Tommy said, after giving the idea some consideration. "That's pretty cool. I never had a dad to do stuff like this before." He regarded her worriedly. "Uncle Walker's almost like a dad, isn't he?"

"Absolutely."

At the time Tommy had seemed satisfied by her answers. But later that night when she stopped in Tommy's room to check on him on her way to bed, she realized she'd been lulled into a false sense of complacency. He was missing. She knew without a doubt where he had gone, and it made her blood run cold.

She was shaking like a leaf as she dialed Tucker, rousted him out of bed and explained what had happened. "He asked too many questions tonight. I just know he snuck on that boat. You have to get word to Walker."

"Calm down, Sis. Walker's been out there night after night and nothing's happened. There's no reason to think tonight will be any different. I'll call Bobby, and we'll take his boat out to meet them and make sure everything's okay."

"I'm coming with you," she announced. "I'll meet you at the marina."

When she showed up with her shotgun in tow, Tucker looked as if he might explode. "Put that damn thing back in the car. You are not bringing it along."

"Tucker Spencer, I've been shooting every bit as long as you have. I have terrific aim."

"Damn Daddy for ever teaching you," he muttered. "Blast it, Daisy, you've been aiming at bottles on fenceposts, not human targets!"

"Then let's hope there are no human targets out there," she said, taking Bobby's outstretched hand and stepping onto his boat without another glance at Tucker.

"What's going on?" King demanded, arriving out

of the blue and surveying the scene. "Why are you all getting ready to go out on a boat at this ungodly hour? And why does Daisy have a shotgun, for Pete's sake?"

"I forgot to mention that Daddy was here when you called," Bobby said. "Dining with Frances and Anna-Louise, as a matter of fact, and looking awfully damned smug. I tried to avoid him on my way out here, but obviously his eyes are sharper than I'd thought."

"Great, just great," Tucker muttered. "Go back to your dinner, Daddy. Everything's under control."

Her father shot a look in her direction. "Yes, I can see that. The last person who told me things were under control almost lost her damned job."

"And before the night's out, I could end up throwing her in jail," Tucker declared ominously.

"For what?" Daisy demanded, tired of being discussed as if she weren't present or as if she weren't perfectly capable of running her own blasted life.

"Interfering with a police investigation, carrying a loaded weapon. I don't know, I'll work on the charges. I'll make them stick, too."

"Daddy will love that, won't you, Daddy?"

"Will somebody please just tell me what in tarnation is going on?" King said. "Right now, I've got my whole family down here making a spectacle of themselves. If Richard gets wind of this, it'll be in this week's paper."

"How would Richard find out?" Daisy asked reasonably.

"I did mention that Anna-Louise was dining with Daddy, didn't I? I'm sure I did," Bobby said, sounding more and more amused.

Daisy scowled at him, then turned back to her father. "Okay, here's the deal in a nutshell. Walker's on a drug stakeout. We think Tommy snuck onto the boat to be with him. Now do you see why we can't just stand around here talking?''

Her father stared hard at Tucker. ''Is this true? There are drugs in Trinity Harbor? Why wasn't I told about this?''

Daisy lost patience. ''Could we dissect this later? Please, let's just get out there before something happens to Tommy.'' She faced Tucker. ''Did you reach Walker?''

''I did. And Tommy is with him. He found him hiding below deck. I think he was about to blister his nephew's butt.''

''If he doesn't, I might,'' Daisy said grimly. She'd never been so terrified in her life.

At least that's what she thought until she heard the sound of shots ringing out across the river. That was when she started to pray.

23

Between the fog rising off the river and the well-deserved lecture he was giving Tommy on his irresponsible behavior, Walker didn't notice the suspicious boat easing past on his port side until it was less than a hundred yards away.

"Tommy, go below now!" he ordered tersely, focusing his binoculars on the deck of the expensive fiberglass fishing boat. Thankfully the boy scrambled to do as he was told without a lot of questions.

There were two men he didn't recognize on deck, neither of whom seemed to be holding fishing rods or showing the slightest interest in the crab pots bobbing on the water. Midnight was not a likely hour for a pleasure cruise or even a fishing trip. It was an hour when someone on the water could very well be up to no good.

He steered his boat closer, hoping for a clearer view. When only a few yards separated them, he called out, ordering them to drop anchor and prepare to be boarded. That was when the first shot came zinging straight at him, catching him in the arm. He hit the deck, reached for his rifle and took aim at the other boat's motor, hoping to disable it. He already knew that Tucker was en route. If he could keep these jokers from running, he'd have backup in no time.

Unfortunately, drawn by the sound of gunfire, Tommy slipped onto the deck, shouting hysterically. "What's happening?" he cried, sliding on the slippery deck in his haste to get to Walker.

"Go back down!" Walker shouted, trying to get between his nephew and the shooters.

"What's happening? Are you shot?" Tommy asked, eyes wide as he noticed the blood soaking Walker's shirtsleeve.

Walker had never experienced such terror in his life. He hunkered down and gazed steadily into the boy's eyes, all too aware that he was putting his back directly into the line of fire.

"Listen to me," he pleaded, expecting to hear the pop of another bullet at any second, anticipating the pain of it slamming through flesh. "Calm down. I want you to go back down below and stay there until I say you can come up again. Tucker will be here any minute, and everything is going to be just fine."

"But—"

"Just do it, Tommy. Please. Right now. This is no time to argue with me."

"But you're hurt," he protested, his voice catching on a sob. "I don't want you to die like Mommy did. Please, Uncle Walker." He dragged at Walker's arm. "Come with me. You've got to. Please."

"I am not going to die."

"How do you know? They shot you. People die when they get shot, like that little girl."

Walker stared at him in shock. "How did you know about Keisha?"

"I heard you and Daisy talking. She was shot and she's dead, so you could die, too. Please don't make me go away. Please, just come with me."

Walker heard the sound of the engine revving up on the other boat and cursed the missed opportunity. He had a split second to make a decision, a split second in which to choose duty over Tommy.

But he had heard the unmistakable hysteria in Tommy's voice, seen the panic in his eyes. Given the choice between catching a couple of two-bit drug traffickers and consoling a little boy who'd already been through way too much, there was no choice at all.

"Come here," he said, opening his arms to his nephew as the sound of the other boat's engine slipped away into the fog.

Shuddering with sobs, Tommy collapsed in his arms, clinging to Walker with all his might.

"It's okay, son. I'm going to be fine. The wound's not serious. The bullet barely scraped me."

"But you're bleeding," Tommy protested.

"It doesn't matter. We're going to be just fine," Walker reassured him.

For the first time since he'd learned of Tommy's existence, he actually believed it.

Of course, that was before Daisy arrived, took one look at the blood on both of them now and, after ascertaining that the blood was all Walker's and that his injury wasn't life-threatening, proceeded to deliver a fire-and-brimstone sermon that would have rivaled anything Anna-Louise could conjure up for Sunday morning.

"I'm sorry," Tommy whispered.

He might as well have saved his breath. The apology didn't make a dent in Daisy's tirade. She had more to say. A lot more, apparently.

Walker knew from experience there was no way to shut her up except to kiss her, which he did…quite thoroughly, if he did say so himself. Left him feeling downright faint, but maybe that had something to do with the loss of blood.

Daisy shoved and wriggled and opened her mouth to protest from time to time, but Walker was persistent. Eventually, it was as if all the starch drained out of her and she melted against him, pliable and willing and maybe even a little bit frantic. Walker was pretty sure he'd never been kissed with such a wild range of emotions in his life.

When they eventually came up for air—much too soon, to his way of thinking—four wide-eyed males were staring at them. He didn't like the stormy look in her brothers' eyes one bit. Even more worrisome was the speculative glint in King's eyes.

"Are you and Daisy gonna get married?" Tommy asked, his expression hopeful.

"It was a kiss, Tommy. It didn't mean a thing," Daisy said emphatically, pushing away from Walker and dusting herself off as if she could wipe away what had happened as if it were nothing more than a sandy nuisance.

Walker studied her pink cheeks and dazed eyes. "Didn't it?" he asked mildly.

"Looked pretty official to me," King observed. "Like sealing a deal."

"Oh, stay out of it, Daddy," Daisy snapped.

Walker felt something ease inside him as the idea of marrying Daisy took a firmer grip than it had in past days. Things had been working out okay since he'd arrived in town. His feelings for Daisy had grown, not diminished. Why not just take a deep breath and go for it? For a man who prided himself on logical, careful thinking in his work, he'd been making a lot of impulsive personal decisions lately. What was one more? Especially one that felt as right as this one did.

He met Daisy's turbulent gaze and saw that despite the firm denials she'd uttered, she looked slightly nonplused by the entire discussion. He thought that was a good thing. She was always more agreeable when he caught her off-guard.

"Now that we've been found out by your family, I think maybe we'll have to," Walker said, his steady gaze on King, Tucker and Bobby. Then he turned to Daisy. "What about it?"

She stared at him with a shocked expression that quickly turned to indignation. "Is that your idea of a proposal, Walker Ames?" she demanded.

"What's wrong? Not civilized enough for you?" he taunted, knowing he was going about this all wrong, but counting on family pressure to accomplish what he hadn't.

"Not by a long shot," she said, scrambling away from him and back onto her brother's boat before Walker could think to stop her.

He glanced at Tucker and Bobby and saw that they were both grinning from ear to ear. King seemed mighty pleased with himself. He gave Tommy's shoulder a quick, approving squeeze, as if to thank him for getting the ball rolling with his innocently asked question.

"Looks as if you have your work cut out for you," Bobby noted. As he followed Daisy back to the other boat, he called over his shoulder, "Come on, Daddy. Let's leave this in Tucker's capable hands." His grin spread. "See you guys back at the marina."

Walker watched the sheriff warily. "You're not going back with them?"

"Oh, no," his boss said quietly. "Seems like there are a few things you and I need to talk about."

"Think I'll stick around and put in my two cents, as well," King said, waving a dismissal at Bobby and settling into a deck chair.

"I'm not leaving, Uncle Walker," Tommy declared, his expression mulish.

Walker couldn't deny his nephew the right to stay, but the other two were a damned nuisance. "Am I the only one who noticed that there are two suspects out here on the river who are getting away, while we talk over what should be a personal matter?" Walker said, hoping to divert them.

"Long gone," Tucker said, then asked with little more than mild curiosity, "Did you get a decent look at them?"

"Not really. I did see the boat, though. It wasn't the one we've been watching. This was a trawler, though I didn't see much evidence that the men on board were interested in fishing."

Tucker nodded. "Then we'll get a description out when we get back to the office. In the meantime, let's talk about just how serious you are about marrying my sister."

"Good question," King said appreciatively. "Well, Walker, what do you have to say for yourself?"

Before responding, Walker glanced at Tommy, who was half in his lap, seemingly sound asleep. Satisfied, he tried to make his point to Daisy's father and brother clear. "I say that you two are not the ones I intend to have this conversation with."

"Was it an impulse, one you're already regretting?" Tucker asked pointedly.

"I told you, I am not having this conversation."

"Dammit, boy, you owe her," King said. "Damned near cost her her job. If it weren't for me, she'd be out on the street right this minute."

Walker stared at him. "What are you talking about? Has something more happened?"

"Had a talk with the school board president just tonight. He and the board were ready to fire her, till I made them see reason."

"Bullied them, in other words," Tucker said.

"Damned straight I did. She's my daughter. What would you have me do? Sit back and let them ruin her life? I don't give two figs if Daisy never sets foot in the classroom again, but *she* does. She loves teaching, loves those kids. The woman ought to have a whole passel of them at home."

He glared at Walker. "When it comes to the school board, my influence will only go so far. An engagement ring—or better yet, a wedding ring—on her finger would do the rest."

Walker thought about that, thought about Tucker's earlier question about whether his proposal had been nothing but an impulse, one he regretted. There was no denying the words had come out of his mouth before he'd had a chance to consider them, but he hadn't wanted to take them back. Not for a single second. He hadn't felt relieved when she'd thrown the proposal right back in his face. He'd felt let down.

"Can I say something?" Tommy piped up, startling all of them.

Walker gazed down at the boy who was curled snugly against his side.

"Everyone else has an opinion. I might as well hear yours, too," he told him.

"I think you should send her flowers. Lots and lots

of flowers. Girls like that," he said confidently. "And candy. Mommy used to get all teary when I'd give her a box of candy, even when it was kinda squished."

"And maybe a gallon of cherry vanilla ice cream, now and then," Tucker chimed in.

Walker rolled his eyes. "I'm getting courting advice from a ten-year-old and a bachelor with no prospects in sight." He gazed at King. "You have any advice you'd like to share?"

King's expression turned thoughtful before he finally nodded. "I might at that. I've got her mama's diamond ring at home. It was my mother's before that. Women like a sentimental touch like that."

Walker stared at him in shock. "You'd give me that ring to offer Daisy?"

"It's hers by right and, yes, if it'll get the job done, I'll give it to you."

Walker was more touched by the evidence of King's unspoken approval than he had been by anything in a long time. He knew it wasn't given lightly. "Thank you," he said quietly.

"Nothing to thank me for," King said gruffly. "For some reason you make her happy. That's all I want for any of my kids." He grinned. "Doesn't hurt that I found out you're not a Yankee, after all. Why did you let me think you were?"

"You were enjoying it so much, why ruin your fun?" Walker said. "Besides, you wouldn't have been all that impressed by my Southern bloodlines, either."

"No man born in Richmond, capital of the Confederacy, can be all bad."

"Don't be so sure," Walker retorted, thinking of the father who'd abandoned them before Tommy's mother had been out of diapers. Trent Ames might have been

Southern, but he was no gentleman. He was scum to the core.

"Okay," Tucker said, starting the boat's engine. "Now that Daisy's future has been settled—"

"With everyone except Daisy," Walker pointed out, not nearly as confident of the outcome as they apparently were.

"You'll get the job done," King reassured him. "But it might do to use a little more finesse the next time you pop the question."

"Let's just get back to shore so Walker can have that arm looked at by the doctor and the two of us can sit down and go over what he learned about our suspects tonight," Tucker said. "I'd like to try to salvage something from this, so the night's not a total loss."

Walker felt Tommy's tug on his shirt. He looked down into the boy's sleepy eyes.

"Is Daisy going to be my mom?"

"I'm going to do my best to see that she is," Walker promised.

"Will it be okay if I still miss my real mom?"

Tears stung Walker's eyes. "It will always be okay to miss your mother. I miss her, too."

"She was the best, huh?"

Walker thought of the bright-eyed, beautiful, rebellious girl he'd loved, but hadn't been able to protect. "She was the best," he echoed.

"Marry him, indeed," Daisy blustered all the way back to the Trinity Harbor marina. "Is the man crazy?"

Bobby, to his credit, didn't utter a word until they were back at the dock, probably because he knew she would have tried to toss him overboard if he'd opened his mouth. She was livid enough to do it. Anger that deep was no doubt accompanied by a powerful adrenaline rush. She almost regretted Bobby's discretion, because she was itching for a fight, longing to do something physically violent. Shredding a handful of marina cocktail napkins that she'd grabbed to staunch Walker's bleeding wasn't getting the job done.

"Daisy, maybe this is none of my business," Bobby began cautiously as he tied up his boat at the dock.

"It's not."

"But you're crazy in love with the guy," he continued determinedly.

"I am not."

"Of course you are."

"I think I know my own mind, Bobby Spencer."

"I see the way you look at him. Just as important, I see the way *he* looks at *you*, like he's a little dazed and bewildered. Couldn't you maybe give the guy a break? He's struggling here. He'd just been shot, for goodness' sakes. The proposal was well-intentioned, even if it wasn't all dressed up in pretty words. In fact, I'd say you could trust something spoken under these circumstances a whole lot more than if he'd planned it all out."

"Maybe," she conceded. Sometimes the truth was blurted out in moments of stress.

"Think about it," Bobby urged. "You don't want to throw this opportunity away."

"What is that supposed to mean? Are you suggesting this might be my last chance to catch a man?" she demanded irritably.

He regarded her with the patient expression that men tended to get when they were at their most patronizing.

"Of course not," he chided in a tolerant tone. "I'm suggesting that you're inclined to cut off your nose to spite your face, to manufacture reasons not to do something you badly want to do.''

"When I want counseling regarding my love life, I'll get it from someone who doesn't cook for a living.''

Bobby flinched at the scathing description of his gourmet skills, but he stood his ground. "I may be a chef, but I'm also your brother. Nobody understands you the way I do, the way Tucker does. I know that the only thing you've wanted your whole life long is to have a family. Goodness knows, you tried your best to mother the two of us, even though you were barely a year older than Tuck and two years older than me. Seems to me you have a darned fine family right under your nose, if only you're not too stubborn and full of pride to admit it.''

She frowned, not daring to believe that Walker's lukewarm proposal could have been based on genuine emotion rather than duty. "I hate it when you throw logic back in my face.''

"Then forget the logic and listen to your heart. You want to marry him. I know you do. You love him, pure and simple. Don't throw that away. Not many people in this world are willing to tangle with a Spencer for the long haul. We're a daunting bunch.''

She studied his face intently. "Has somebody turned you down?''

"Not lately.''

She thought back to the one love of Bobby's life, at least the only one she knew about. "You're talking about Ann-Marie, aren't you?''

"That's ancient history, and I wasn't really in love with her,'' he denied a little too heatedly.

"Could have fooled me and everybody else in Trinity Harbor. I thought you were destined to be together."

"Well, destiny took a wrong turn and she married somebody else. No big deal."

Daisy wasn't buying it. It had been a big deal. In fact, she suspected that was why Bobby was so consumed with buying up half the town and getting a five-star rating for his restaurant. He wanted to prove that he was the better man, and he wanted to do it in a way that would be visible to Ann-Marie and her husband, who also happened to be Bobby's one-time best friend and biggest rival.

"You work too hard," she told him.

He scowled. "How did we get from you and Walker to my work habits?"

"You need to meet somebody new."

"New people come through the door of the restaurant every single day. Boaters dock at the marina, too. I live my life among strangers."

"But how many of them do you actually meet? You need a social life. When was the last time you had a real date?"

"Not that long ago," he said defensively.

"When?" she persisted.

"I went to the VFW dance with Marge Lefkowicz."

Marge was the hostess at Bobby's restaurant and a long-time friend, not a potential lover. "Correct me if I'm wrong," Daisy said, "but wasn't that last fall, and didn't you go as a favor to try to make her boyfriend jealous?"

"Damn but you have a long memory."

"It serves me well at times like this." She regarded him thoughtfully. "Maybe I'll start looking around for the right woman for you."

"Don't you dare," Bobby said, his expression horrified. "I will handle my own love life as I see fit."

"Then stay out of my relationship with Walker."

"I thought you said you didn't have one or want one."

"Oh, go suck an egg," she snapped, and scrambled out of his boat and onto the dock. Sometimes having brothers was almost as big a trial as being King Spencer's daughter.

24

Walker carried the now-sleeping Tommy into Daisy's house, trying not to notice how badly his arm ached. He'd refused the pain pills the doctor had offered, and he suspected he was going to come to regret it.

He glanced around with some trepidation as he entered the brightly lit kitchen, waiting for Daisy to launch into another full-scale attack. He was too exhausted to cope with that right now. In fact, about the only thing that appealed to him was the thought of a steaming hot shower and crawling into bed—hers, if he had his way. Not very likely, he conceded, given the way she'd stormed off earlier.

So far, so good, he thought as he crept through the kitchen and headed for the stairs. He got Tommy into his room and into bed, then went looking for a bottle of aspirin in the bathroom medicine cabinet. Nothing, not so much as a children's strength ibuprofen. He muttered a curse, then stepped into the hall and right into Daisy's path.

"Looking for these?" she inquired mildly, holding up a bottle of extrastrength painkillers in one hand and peroxide in the other.

"As a matter of fact, I am," he said, studying her warily. There was a gleam in her eyes he didn't like one bit. He held out his hand for the supplies.

"Oh, no," she said, shooing him toward his room. "I intend to take a look at that wound." Her chin shot up. "And if I don't like what I see, I'm calling the doctor."

"I've already been seen by a doctor, thank you very much."

Her gaze narrowed. "Let me see."

He displayed the bandage, amused by her obvious disappointment. "You were really looking forward to dousing me with that peroxide, weren't you?"

"As a matter of fact, I was."

"Not feeling particularly compassionate?"

"Nope."

He searched her face for a clue about what was really going on in that complicated mind of hers. "I didn't intentionally put Tommy in danger, you know."

Shock spread across her face. "Of course you didn't. I know that. If anything, it was my fault for allowing him to sneak out of the house."

Walker sighed. "Nevertheless, I thought you might be thinking of using what happened tonight to go running off to Frances and stake your own claim for custody."

"Don't be absurd. I hate it when people use children as a pawn in their own fights. Tommy's your nephew, and it's clear that you love him and that you're ready to be a father to him. I've accepted that."

"A boy needs a mother, too," he said cautiously.

Her hand shook as she handed him the aspirin and a glass of water. "I'm not discussing that with you."

"I think you got the wrong impression earlier."

"You have no idea what impression I got," she retorted. "I'm not marrying you, Walker Ames, and that's that."

She turned her attention to the kitchen counter, which she began scrubbing with a vengeance. Walker snagged her hand, noting the alarm that flared in her eyes.

"This thing between us isn't over just because you say so," he said softly.

"There is nothing between us," she stated firmly, though she wasn't able to control the patches of color that rose in her cheeks.

"I say there is." He ran the pad of his thumb along her jaw and saw that telltale color heighten. "And it's just getting started."

She took a determined step away from him. "Talking won't make it so, Walker." She picked up that sponge and attacked the counter again, then started snatching dishes out of the dishwasher and slamming them back into the cupboards with so much force, he was surprised they didn't shatter.

"How was the dinner with the Finches?" he asked, hoping the neutral topic would settle her down. They hadn't had time to talk about it earlier when he'd stopped by for a quick visit with Tommy before going out on the river.

She stilled. Her expression turned thoughtful as she faced him. "Weird, as a matter of fact. She's uptight, and he's not very friendly. Frankly, I'm surprised they even accepted the invitation."

"Maybe they did it for Gary's sake."

"Maybe. Tommy invited Gary to spend the night, but his father refused to give him permission. Gary looked as if that was what he'd expected. I've never seen a boy his age look so...I don't know...defeated, I guess."

Walker regretted that he hadn't been there to pick

up on the vibes for himself. ''Abuse?'' he asked, thinking out loud.

Daisy looked stricken. ''I never thought of that. I've read about the way abuse victims behave sometimes, but I've never seen it. Maybe that's it. Or maybe Paul Finch is just a strict disciplinarian.''

''Maybe,'' Walker agreed, but he vowed to spend a little more time with Gary and his dad to see if he could get a sense of what was going on there.

''You look exhausted,'' Daisy said. ''Why don't you go on up to your old room and get some sleep?''

''You want me to stay here? Isn't that a bad idea under the circumstances?''

''It's for one night, and if anybody wants to make something of it, I'll remind them you were shot tonight and somebody had to look after you.''

''Does that mean you're going to come upstairs and play nurse?'' he inquired, grinning at her.

She frowned at the teasing. ''Don't count on it, Detective.''

He made his way to the stairs, then turned back to find her staring after him. ''You might be surprised to discover what I'm counting on, Daisy Spencer.''

''He's driving me crazy,'' Daisy announced to Anna-Louise the next afternoon when she dropped by the parsonage on her way home from work. She needed some of her friend's calming chamomile tea and sensible advice.

''What else is new?'' Anna-Louise inquired, her eyes flashing with amusement.

''Even with everything that's going on, I let him stay at the house last night,'' she admitted. ''I couldn't stand the thought of sending him away with an injured arm.''

"Of course not.''

"That has to be the last time, though.''

"I'm sure he doesn't expect to keep staying there. He understands what's at stake. If he doesn't, I'm sure King and your brothers will be happy to remind him.''

"I don't think they'll help,'' Daisy said ruefully. "They seem to have gotten the insane idea that he's right, that I should marry him.''

"It would solve a number of problems,'' Anna-Louise pointed out.

"Now there's a romantic prospect. Marry the man because it'll put an end to a few pesky little problems.'' Daisy scowled. "Whose side are you on?''

"Yours, of course. And being on the brink of being fired is hardly a 'pesky little problem.' You have to start taking it seriously, Daisy. Your principal certainly isn't being any help. And King's intimidation tactics can only go so far. I hate to think what would happen if Richard got wind of that.'' She shuddered.

"Got wind of what?'' her journalist husband inquired, suddenly appearing in the kitchen.

"Nothing,'' Anna-Louise said. "Anything you hear in this room, in this house, out of my mouth, ever, is confidential. Not for publication. Not for attribution.''

He grinned. "I get your drift,'' he said as he bent down to kiss her.

Anna-Louise nodded. "Just wanted to be sure.''

"So what did King do?'' he asked.

"You were eavesdropping,'' Anna-Louise accused.

"I was coming into my own kitchen to get a glass of iced tea. This isn't the sacred confessional,'' he protested.

"Our church doesn't have confessionals. Sometimes my kitchen serves the same purpose. Remember that."

"Duly noted," he said as he poured his tea. "What did King do?"

Anna-Louise regarded her husband with a frown, then turned to Daisy. "Sometimes living with a journalist isn't easy. They're annoyingly persistent."

"About King?" Richard prodded.

"Oh, for heaven's sakes," Daisy said. "Just tell him. He won't publish it. I trust him."

"Thank you," Richard said. "It's a terrible thing when a wife doubts her own husband's integrity."

"I don't doubt it. I just don't care to test it by putting too much temptation in your path." Her gaze narrowed. "If I do tell you, will you also promise not to go running around to other sources to try to confirm it by some other means that leaves me out of it? Trinity Harbor is not Washington. It is not one of those wartorn countries you covered."

She glanced at Daisy and explained, "Once a bigshot investigative reporter, always an investigative reporter. A whiff of scandal brings out his training and his competitive spirit. He can't help it."

Richard's eyes lit up. "This secret is that good?" He began edging to the door. "Maybe I'll just start making a few calls."

"Freeze," Anna-Louise ordered. "Don't you dare."

He grinned. "Okay." He pulled out a chair and sat down. "What's the scoop?"

It was Daisy who finally spilled the beans. "Daddy used his clout to get the school board to get off my case," she explained. Richard was going to find out the story one way or another. It might as well be from her.

Besides, she did trust him. Richard had proved himself to be an honorable journalist since coming to town. Though he didn't back down from controversy, he didn't print stories just to stir things up so he could see how the dust settled. In fact, maybe she could use all of this to get him solidly into her corner if it came to a showdown with the board.

"No surprise there," Richard said. "Wouldn't have expected him to do anything else."

"No indignation about public officials caving in to the demands of a wealthy citizen?" Anna-Louise asked, clearly taken aback by his response.

"Seems to me they're caving in to the demands of common sense," Richard retorted. "This whole thing is a tempest in a teapot. Teachers are human beings. They are entitled to a private life. As long as they're not breaking any laws, what business is it of mine or anyone else's?"

"Sounds like a good editorial to me," Anna-Louise said approvingly.

"And maybe a Sunday sermon?" he asked.

"Could be," she agreed, her expression thoughtful.

Daisy felt tears clogging the back of her throat. She had come here for moral support, not public backing. "You don't have to do that."

"This whole thing has gotten wildly out of hand. I think we do need to stand up and be counted," Anna-Louise said slowly, then gave her a pointed look. "Which is not to say that I don't think you ought to consider Walker's proposal."

"Walker proposed?" Richard asked, eyebrows raised. "And you said no?"

"Emphatically," Daisy said.

Richard shook his head. "If I live to be a hundred,

I will never understand women." He stood up, kissed his wife soundly and added, "Except you, of course."

She grinned. "Of course."

After he'd gone, Daisy regarded Anna-Louise wistfully. "I want what the two of you have."

"We didn't have it when we met," Anna-Louise told her. "It took time. There were a good many disagreements along the way, but we worked at it."

"And you love each other."

"So do you and Walker," the minister pointed out. "There's not a doubt in my mind about that."

"I wish I were as sure as you are."

"Sometimes believing in love is like believing in God. You just have to take it on faith."

Daisy thought long and hard about that over the next few days. Did she have enough faith in Walker's professed feelings—or her own for that matter—to take the gigantic leap into marriage? What if he changed his mind once he found out about her infertility? That was a topic that needed to be put on the table before things went any further. She wanted to believe it wouldn't matter, but she didn't know that.

And until she did, there was no way she would commit to him forever, not even to save her job or to keep Tommy in her life.

"How are you doing courting Daisy?" Tucker inquired as he and Walker sat in the sheriff's office late one Friday evening.

They'd been discussing the drug case ad nauseam, but to no avail. Obviously Tucker thought a change of topic was warranted. Walker would have preferred a shift to baseball, but he knew Daisy's brother wouldn't let him get away with that.

"I'm spending my nights here with you, down at the marina or out on the river," Walker grumbled. "How do you think I'm doing?"

There was a sharp knock on the door, followed by the appearance of Andy Thorensen. His Friday night visits had become a regular thing in recent weeks. Walker greeted his appearance with relief, even though Andy didn't look much happier than Walker felt at the moment.

"I left my wife with Daisy. They're talking window treatments for the store," Andy said with a shudder. "Can the two of you save me?"

"We were talking about courting," Tucker said.

Andy groaned. "Doesn't anybody talk about crime anymore?"

Walker chuckled. "I, for one, would be glad to talk about crime."

Andy turned to him eagerly. "How's the drug case going?"

For the next hour they shared information, speculation and theories. Walker was thoroughly frustrated by their inability to locate the boat from which the shots had been fired at him that night. The trouble was, he hadn't seen any of the registration numbers, or even if there had been any. The boat hadn't been distinctive in any way. There were probably a hundred or more on the local inlets and creeks that were almost exactly like it, trawlers used by weekenders for fishing.

"Have you tried the process of elimination?" Andy asked. "Making a list of every registered boat you see, then looking into the owner's background."

"It would take forever," Tucker said succinctly.

"Aren't you spinning your wheels now? You might as well be doing something."

"And that's a daytime job," Walker said thoughtfully. "It could free up my evenings, at least until we think there's another deal about to go down. I like it."

"Wouldn't free up your weekend, though," Tucker pointed out. "Most of these boats will be on the water tomorrow and Sunday."

"I haven't got anything better to do this weekend," Walker said, then glanced at Andy. "You?"

"If it will keep me away from hanging curtains, I'll do it. Besides, I've been dying to get a little fishing in while I'm down here."

"We could even bring Tommy along," Walker said. "His being there will be great cover. We'll just be a bunch of guys on the water enjoying ourselves."

Tucker shook his head. "Just don't enjoy yourselves so much that you forget to take notes."

When they got back to the house to let Daisy, Gail and Tommy in on their plans for a fishing excursion, Walker thought he noted a brief flicker of disappointment in Daisy's eyes. That was promising. Maybe absence really did make the heart grow fonder. Maybe he wouldn't have to figure out this courting business, after all.

Then he saw the way her arm protectively circled Tommy's shoulders, saw her mouth set stubbornly, and realized that her disappointment was about something else entirely. She was upset that he hadn't remembered his promise to keep Tommy as far away from his police work as possible. Obviously she'd figured out that this fishing trip wasn't exactly as innocent as he and Andy had described.

Sensing something, Tommy glanced up at her worriedly. "Is something wrong?"

"No, your uncle and I just need to have a little talk," she said.

"You're going to let me go fishing, though, aren't you?"

"We'll see," she said.

"But it's the first time we've gotten to go in forever and ever," Tommy protested. "You gotta let me."

"Maybe we should leave," Gail said, latching on to Andy's elbow and steering him toward the front door. "See you tomorrow, Daisy. Maybe I'll see you, too, Tommy. We can really use a guy's help."

"I ain't hanging no curtains," he said. "You can forget that."

Daisy frowned at him. "Don't be rude."

Walker was on the kid's side on this one, but he wasn't about to say it aloud. Daisy clearly had enough issues on her agenda as it was.

"Tommy, you go on up to bed," he said instead. "Daisy and I will work this out."

"I'm going fishing with you," Tommy said flatly.

"We'll see," Walker said. "Now go to bed."

When Tommy started to stomp out of the room, Walker added, "Say good-night to Daisy."

"Yeah, whatever," the boy mumbled, back turned.

"Tommy!"

He turned around then and said a more polite good-night, but his eyes were stormy. Walker sighed as he left.

"I'm sorry," he apologized to Daisy. "I should have talked this over with you first."

"Yes, you should have," she said, eyes flashing. "Don't think for one minute that I believe this is about catching a few fish for dinner. If it were, I'd have no objections, but you and Andy are up to something, aren't you? Some sort of police business?''

Walker saw no point in denying it. If he did, she would just go to her brother for an explanation, and Tucker would tell her the unvarnished truth. That would only raise the temperature of the hot water Walker was already in.

''Yes, but I swear to you there is no danger involved. We really are just going out to fish.''

''And observe who else is out fishing, as well, I imagine.''

He was only slightly startled by her perceptiveness. After all, she was smart and her brother was the sheriff. ''Yes.''

''Then I'm coming, too.''

''No way.''

''If it's safe for Tommy, it's safe for me. And people will be even less suspicious if you have me along, won't they? And four pairs of eyes are better than three.''

He had several arguments he could mount, including whatever help she'd promised Gail for Saturday, but he sensed it would be a waste of breath trying them on her. ''I'm not going to talk you out of this, am I?''

''No,'' she said cheerfully. ''It's been ages since I've been fishing. I used to be quite good at it.''

Walker didn't doubt it. She probably used stubbornness and charm to talk the damned fish into the boat.

''Come here,'' he urged eventually.

''Why?''

''Come on, Daisy. Have a little faith.''

''You're not the first person to use that line on me lately.''

His gaze narrowed. "I hope you're talking about Anna-Louise."

"Who else?" she said, then studied him intently. "You were thinking it might be another man, weren't you?"

"It crossed my mind," he admitted.

"And that would bother you?"

"While you and I have all these unresolved issues? Yes, it would bother the hell out of me to think you were having intimate little tête-à-têtes with another man."

"Interesting," she said, looking pleased.

He gave her a lazy grin. "Interesting enough to get you over here?"

"Maybe," she said, but she took a step closer, then another, until he could reach out and tumble her into his lap.

Walker resisted the urge to cover her breast with his hand or to cover her mouth with his own. It was enough that she was here, in his arms, and for once not protesting one thing or another, just gazing up at him with those eyes the color of violets covered with dew, all soft and sparkly and filled with anticipation.

"What am I going to do about you?" he murmured, mostly to himself.

"What do you want to do?"

"Right this minute, I'm fighting the temptation to make love to you."

She reached up and laid a hand against his cheek, then sighed. "Don't fight too hard," she whispered. "Please."

Startled, Walker stared for a minute, but as the words sank in, as her hand drifted to the buttons on his shirt, he got the message loud and clear.

"Drive me crazy, why don't you, Daisy Spencer?"

"I'm trying my best," she said with a fervor that brought a smile to his lips.

"I've missed you," she added quietly.

"I've been right here."

"No," she said impatiently, sliding his shirt away so she could drop clever little kisses across his chest. "You've been at work or down at the hotel on your best behavior."

"I thought that's what you wanted. I thought that was what we agreed to. No affair, especially with the stakes so high."

"I've changed my mind."

"Why?"

"You have a willing woman in your arms, and you want to know why?" she asked, staring at him incredulously.

"As a matter of fact, I do. It's not that I'm not thrilled, because I am. But something's going on here that I don't understand."

"You think too much," she declared, just before her mouth closed over his.

"Probably so," Walker murmured, right before he stopped thinking at all.

"Do you want children? I mean, more children?" Daisy asked out of the blue as they sat at the kitchen table in the morning.

She had already baked brownies and packed a picnic for their fishing trip. Apparently she hadn't slept all that well. Walker had the uneasy feeling that the topic of kids was what had kept her awake.

Fortunately Tommy had gone outside a few minutes earlier, because Walker was stunned into silence. This was definitely not a topic he wanted to discuss in his nephew's presence.

"What brought that on?" he asked cautiously. "Last night? We used protection." It had been a last-minute thing, but his brain had finally kicked in in the nick of time.

"There was no need," Daisy said flatly.

"Of course there was. I'm not going to be irresponsible where you're concerned."

Suddenly tears welled up in her eyes, tears he had no idea how to interpret. "What?" he said. "What did I say?"

"It wouldn't be irresponsible," she whispered so low that he could barely hear her.

"Dammit, Daisy, it is my responsibility—"

"I can't have children," she told him, her eyes shimmering as tears spilled down her cheeks.

If she had landed a solid punch squarely in his gut, Walker couldn't have been more stunned.

Or more devastated. For her, though. Only for her. Daisy deserved a houseful of kids. If ever he had run across mother material, she was it. She had proved that with Tommy.

Oh, God, that was it. That was why she had fought so fiercely for his nephew, why she had viewed him with such distrust. Tommy was more than just a boy who needed a home to her. He was her chance at being a mother.

Dealing with Daisy was a minefield under the best of conditions, but Walker had a feeling he was tiptoeing through live ammunition right this second and that whatever he said was going to decide not only Daisy's future, but his own.

He wanted to ask her how she knew, if she was

certain, but there was time for that. Now he simply took her hand in his. With his other hand, he wiped away her tears.

"I'm sorry. I know how devastating that must seem to you."

"You know that years ago I was engaged."

"Yes, you mentioned it. Does this have something to do with why you didn't get married?"

She nodded. "He didn't take the news well. He broke the engagement when he found out we could never have children of our own. Nobody knows that except for Anna-Louise. Daddy, Tucker and Bobby were furious with him for dumping me, but I wonder if they would have felt the same way if they'd known the truth."

"Of course they would. The man was a fool."

She managed a rueful smile that broke his heart.

"Yes, he was, but I could understand it in a way. I wanted to have babies, my own babies. But after a while, I realized I just wanted children, that it didn't matter if I gave birth to them. There are so many children in the world who don't have a home, who don't have a chance."

"Like Tommy," he said.

She nodded. "Like Tommy."

"I'm not going to take him away from you," Walker reassured her. "I want to share him with you. I want us to raise him together. I want us to get married. I have all the children I need."

As soon as the words crossed his lips, as soon as he saw the devastated look in her eyes, he knew it was the worst possible thing he could have said. How insensitive could he possibly be? He had just reminded her that he had something she wanted desperately, something she could never have—not just a blood relationship with Tommy, but biological sons of his own, sons he probably didn't pay nearly enough attention to, to her way of thinking. In speaking so rashly, he had put his own needs before hers, not out of cruelty but out of total, male-mentality insensitivity.

Suddenly he realized that he *had* taken his boys for granted. With stunning clarity, he admitted to himself how badly he missed having them in his life. He'd been in denial because the pain of losing them had been too much to bear, because he'd been filled with guilt over the breakup of his marriage.

He resolved then and there not only to fight to get them back into his own life, but to bring them into Daisy's.

He framed her face in his hands, looked deep into her eyes. "You will have the family you deserve," he promised her. "One way or another, you will have all the children in your life you could ever want."

She gave him a watery smile then. "You can't go out and catch them like fish," she told him.

"You caught Tommy, didn't you?"

Her eyes brightened. "In a manner of speaking."

"And now you've reeled me in."

"Have I?"

He kissed her thoroughly. "Do you still doubt it?" he asked eventually.

"That was fairly convincing," she conceded.

"Remind me when we get home tonight, and I'll see if I can do any better."

"An interesting prospect," she said. "I'll look forward to it."

But Walker noticed as she said it that there were still shadows in her eyes. He also realized that they'd been there all along. He just hadn't recognized the barely concealed sorrow for what it was, because she worked so hard to maintain her cheerful, optimistic facade.

Now that he knew the truth, he had to wonder if there was anything he could ever say or do that would chase those shadows away entirely. Or was this the kind of heartache that never completely disappeared?

25

The fishing trip was about as productive as every other attempt Walker had made to snag the drug suspects. He had a long list of boat registrations, absolutely none of which matched up to anybody who seemed anything less than squeaky clean.

"Maybe we're going about this all wrong," he suggested to Tucker a week later. "Maybe we need to be keeping an eye on the school, see if somebody's hanging around there who shouldn't be."

"It's worth a shot," Tucker agreed. "Take an unmarked car and park near the playground. If anybody's dealing drugs to the kids, it'll be after school. They'll want the area to be busy with adults coming and going. I doubt they'd try it during recess or phys ed, when the teachers are the only grown-ups around."

Walker nodded. "I'll get over there this afternoon. I think I'll take my own car, since any car you have might be familiar, even if it is unmarked."

"Works for me. Did Andy ever turn up anything on that guy with the supersonic boat?"

"Nothing. Craig Remington seems to have made his money legitimately in the tech industry, some dot-com start-up. Took his bundle, retired early and started collecting expensive toys."

"I don't care how legit he looks, it still makes me

suspicious, a guy his age spending all his time down here. Don't get me wrong. I love Trinity Harbor, but it's not exactly a hot spot with young adults.''

Walker grinned. ''It will be if Bobby has his way. Wait till he gets that boardwalk development he's been talking about.''

Tucker shuddered. ''And you think we have problems now? I dread the day the crowds start rolling in.''

''At least you won't be bored.''

''I'm not bored now.'' He studied Walker intently. ''Are you?''

Walker wondered if he could ever be bored with a woman like Daisy around. He certainly wouldn't mind having a few uninterrupted weeks to find out. Maybe, if he could get this case wrapped up before the end of her summer vacation, the three of them could take a trip or something. Maybe he'd even see about his sons joining them. Of course, maybe his first priority ought to be a honeymoon just for the two of them.

The fact that he was even considering such a thing startled him. Not once in all the years he'd been with Laurie had he been anxious to take off on a vacation. He'd even cut short their honeymoon, because he'd been too consumed with work. Was that because he was a workaholic, or because the luster on his marriage had worn off practically before the end of the ceremony? He had a funny feeling it was the latter. Getting married had been Laurie's idea, and he'd gone along with it because it had seemed like a natural progression of their relationship, but there had been plenty of warning flags, both in terms of her unreasonable expectations and his own lack of interest in changing to meet them.

He was still pondering that a few days later as he

pulled up beneath the shade of a spreading oak tree just across from the elementary school for his fourth stake-out. He'd switched cars with Daisy today, just for a change, but so far everything looked routine. Not a single suspicious person had been lurking in the vicinity. And no one seemed to be paying any attention at all to his presence.

A handful of school buses were lined up in the driveway. The drivers had congregated in the first one to smoke and chat. Other than that the block was quiet.

A few minutes later, mothers started pulling up to wait for their children. A crossing guard took up his position at the corner down the block.

And suddenly, out of the blue, a teenaged boy wandered down the street from the direction of the high school, his gait nonchalant, maybe a little cocky. He was wearing the teen uniform—baggy jeans slung low on hips so narrow it seemed impossible that they held the pants up at all, a bulky jacket and expensive sneakers. He looked old enough to be from the high school, rather than a seventh grader attending this school.

Could be a big brother sent to walk his little brother or sister home, but Walker didn't think so. There was just something about the way his gaze furtively studied the area, the way he stayed far away from the buses and the mothers.

He heard the distant sound of the bell echoing through the school, and the afternoon quiet was shattered as children rushed from every door. Some headed for the buses, a few sought out their moms, and others—mostly the older ones, sixth and seventh-graders—gathered in clusters.

And then two of the older boys drifted away from the others and approached the teen Walker had been watching. There was a lot of bravado and posturing and high fives, all innocent enough. And then, just when he was about to dismiss it as one more false alarm, he saw one of the younger boys slip something to the teen in an obvious exchange.

He took a closer look and realized with dismay that the younger kid, the one handing over what could very well be drugs, was Gary Finch, Tommy's thirteen-year-old friend.

"Damn," he muttered, opening his door just as a sheriff's car, fully marked, came screeching around the corner and slammed to a stop beside him.

The deputy was out and at Walker's side before he could react.

"Out," he ordered. "Keep your hands where I can see them."

Walker stared at him incredulously, then darted a look back at the corner to see that all three boys had disappeared, scared off by the deputy's arrival. He slammed his palm against the steering wheel in frustration.

"You idiot," he barked.

The deputy stared at him in shock, then took a step back. "Walker, isn't it?"

"It is," he said wryly. "And you have just blown a stakeout that was about to pay off big-time. What the hell were you thinking?"

"Dispatch got a call from a mom that some guy had been hanging around here every day this week. She didn't recognize him and thought it was suspicious, that he might be some sort of a pervert." The kid winced as he said it. "Sorry. We had to check it out."

"Yes, of course, you did," Walker conceded with a heavy sigh.

The blond, fresh-faced deputy looked around. "Was something really going down?"

"It looked that way. At least I recognized one of the kids involved. It's the best lead we've had so far."

"I can explain to Tucker," he offered.

"Not necessary. You were just doing your job."

"If I'd known you were in here—"

"You still would have had to check it out," Walker told him. "Forget about it. Things happen."

That night he stopped off in Tommy's room while he was doing homework. "We need to talk," he said, sitting down on the bed.

His nephew stared at him worriedly. "Did I do something wrong?"

"No, absolutely not, but I need to ask you something and I want you to tell me the truth, even though it might get somebody into trouble, okay? It's important."

Tommy's eyes widened, but he nodded.

"When you told me about overhearing some kids talking about pot a while back, was Gary one of them?"

Tommy squirmed, his expression miserable.

"Tell me the truth," Walker repeated.

"I don't want him to get in trouble. They were just talking. They weren't doing anything wrong."

Walker sighed. That was confirmation enough. "Until further notice, you are to stay away from Gary, understood? No visits to his house or to his dad's boat, okay? And not a word to him about this conversation."

"But he's my best friend. He's gonna want to know why," Tommy protested.

"Tell him you're grounded, which you will be if you don't do exactly as I ask."

"This stinks," Tommy declared.

"Yeah, it stinks," Walker said, but he doubted they were talking about the same thing.

The next day Walker laid out his suspicions for Tucker.

"Not enough for a search warrant," Tucker concluded.

"No," Walker agreed. "We could bring the boy in for questioning, though."

Tucker shook his head. "Not unless you catch him making another deal and actually see the drugs. For all you know, what he was passing out yesterday were cigarettes. I don't want to think about what a lawyer would say if we dragged a thirteen-year-old in here on such flimsy evidence."

Walker knew he was right, but he was frustrated. While they were proceeding carefully and by the book, Gary could be getting some other kid hooked on pot. And where was he getting it, if not from his father? Perhaps the mother was even part of this, as well.

"Since my cover's blown at the school, put somebody else in there," he suggested finally. "I'll go back out on the river and keep an eye out for Finch's boat from the marina, and I'll see if he happens to have anything else docked at home. If he's into this big time, it won't be long before he tries to smuggle more drugs into the area."

"Have you told Daisy about your suspicions?" Tucker asked.

"No, just that I didn't want Tommy anywhere near Gary for a while."

Tucker grinned. "Which means she's figured it out on her own by now."

"Probably," Walker agreed.

"Just in case, I'll stop by and fill her in while you're on duty tonight."

"Put in a good word for me while you're at it," Walker suggested. "I think she might be wavering on the marriage thing."

"Asking a woman's brother to do your courting for you," Tucker said with a shake of his head. "How pitiful is that?"

"I'd do it myself if you weren't working me to death. Explain that to her, too."

"And have her on my case? No way," Tucker said fervently. "But I will tout your virtues as an honorable, hardworking deputy. In fact, I'll make you sound so noble, she'll probably start a petition to have you awarded a medal."

"I don't want a medal. I just want the woman to marry me."

"Then you'll have to get this case wrapped up so you'll have time to ask her, won't you?"

"You have a unique way of providing incentives for your officers, don't you?"

"So far you're the only one I've tried it on. Now get out of here and nail this bastard."

Walker hoped it was going to be as simple as Tucker made it sound. Since the man had had even him fooled for weeks now, it didn't seem likely.

Daisy might have taught history, not math, but she could still add two and two. Based as much on what Walker hadn't said as what he had, she gathered that he suspected Gary and Paul Finch both of being involved in some sort of drug operation. Paul, maybe, she conceded, but the boy? Never.

There was one person, though, who might be as quick to defend Gary as she was: Maribeth Finch.

With Tommy safely at the marina in Bobby's care and no evidence of the Finch boat in its slip, she went to pay a call on the woman. She knew she had to go about this very, very carefully or risk Walker's wrath. He was not likely to be overjoyed that she'd inserted herself smack into the middle of his investigation.

The Finches lived on a cove a few miles outside of town. The lot was heavily wooded, the weeds out of control and the house in need of repairs, but there was a shiny new sports-utility vehicle in the driveway. Daisy rang the doorbell and waited. It took several tries before she heard the sound of footsteps inside, then a hesitation before the door opened a crack. She plastered a smile on her face.

"Maribeth, I hope I'm not disturbing you. Please forgive me for dropping by unannounced, but I had a little time before I pick up Tommy and I thought maybe we could get better acquainted."

"I...I don't know," Maribeth said, her gaze darting around nervously. "Paul's not here."

"All the better. You're the one I wanted to chat with."

The woman looked startled, as if no one had taken an interest in her in years. "Why?"

"Because you're Gary's mother, of course. And you're new in town." Defying every ingrained social grace she possessed, she pushed her way past Maribeth and stepped into the foyer, then gaped. It looked as if the boxes from their move had never even been unpacked...or as if they might be leaving again.

"I see you're still settling in," she said brightly. "Can I help?"

"Oh, no," Maribeth said. "Actually…" Her voice trailed off.

"You aren't moving again already, are you?"

Suddenly tears welled up in the other woman's eyes. She nodded. "Tomorrow, in fact."

"I had no idea. Why? You just got here and Paul is retired, isn't he? Aren't you happy here?"

Maribeth rushed from the foyer, disappearing into what turned out to be the living room. Like the entry, it, too, was filled with packed boxes. Maribeth stood at the sliding glass doors that looked out onto the cove, her shoulders shaking. Daisy joined her, tempted to offer solace, but fearful that it wouldn't be welcomed.

"Is there anything I can do?" she asked quietly.

Maribeth shook her head. "Everything's such a mess."

"Do you want to talk about it?"

"I can't."

Daisy sensed if she put the cards on the table, Maribeth would open up now, so she took the plunge. "Paul's smuggling marijuana, isn't he? Is Gary dealing it?"

Maribeth turned a horrified gaze on her. "No, absolutely not. Gary would never touch the stuff. He's seen how it's ruined our lives. His father…"

"Tell me," Daisy encouraged.

"I can't," she repeated. "I can't talk to you, of all people. Your brother's the sheriff. If Paul ever found out, he'd kill me."

Daisy's blood ran cold. She feared Maribeth meant that quite literally.

"Maybe *you* should talk to Tucker," she said. "He could protect you and Gary."

Her expression despondent, Maribeth shook her head. "It's too late for that."

Not knowing what else to do, Daisy gave her a hug. "If you ever need anything, anything at all, you can call me."

Maribeth nodded, but her gaze drifted back to the peaceful scene outside.

Her heart heavy, Daisy drove away. At the marina, she asked Bobby if she could use the phone in his office. "I need to call Walker and Tucker."

But to her frustration, both men were out of contact. "Find them, dammit. I have some information they need to know," she told the dispatcher.

"Where are you?"

"At the marina, but I'm heading home."

"The minute either one of them checks in, I'll have them call," the dispatcher promised.

Daisy could only pray it wouldn't be too late.

Walker had expected the night to go the same way every other night had gone, which was why he was so thoroughly stunned when he spotted a boat slipping away from the dock behind Finch's house shortly after midnight.

"Well, I'll be damned," Walker murmured as he followed him upstream to an isolated inlet.

Tailing him by boat wasn't nearly as easy as following a suspect in D.C. traffic. For one thing it was pitch black out, with not even a sliver of the moon to light the sky. For another the air was eerily still, the night quiet except for the lazy sound of crickets and the calls of birds. Finch's boat was the only significant sound, and matching the timing of his motor to the other man's was tricky. If Finch cut the engine unexpectedly, the sound of Walker's boat would be unmistakable.

Totally attuned to the two boats, Walker suddenly realized he was also hearing the quieter chug-chug-chug of another motor. He cut his engine a fraction of a second before the two boats set their own engines on idle. Voices called softly back and forth, and Walker's adrenaline kicked into gear.

Using his radio, he called for backup on land and by water.

"I think you can seal off this inlet in case they get away from me," he told the dispatcher. "But whatever you do, don't send anyone in here, and no sirens on land."

"Give us fifteen minutes, twenty tops," the dispatcher said. "We'll be in place."

Listening carefully, praying that the transfer of drugs going on would take some time, he waited, using oars to paddle closer. He repeatedly checked his watch, illuminating the dial for no more than a second. Five minutes passed, then ten, and finally fifteen.

"That's it," he heard someone say.

"I'm not doing this again," a familiar voice—Paul Finch—replied. "My kid almost got picked up by the cops the other day. They were staking out the school. I knew this new cop was trouble. I tried to keep Gary away from his nephew, but I couldn't. Everything's gotten out of hand."

"You'll do it until we say you can stop."

Walker eased alongside, aimed his gun straight at the man who'd spoken and said, "How about we stop it right now?"

He caught movement out of the corner of his eye and spotted Finch trying to ease toward the bow of his boat. "Stay where you are, Paul. I don't want to have to shoot you. A boy needs his dad, even if he is a lousy one."

"You don't understand," Paul said, his voice distraught.

"Explain it to me."

"I don't think now's the time," he said wryly.

"How did you get involved in this?"

"You're not going to let it go, are you?"

Walker intended to keep him talking and the other men within the aim of his gun for as long as he possibly could. "No," he told Paul. "Did you need money?"

"Hell, no. It was never about the money. It was about not letting them ruin my life, about not getting dishonorably discharged from the marines."

Walker glanced away from the other men and caught a glimpse of Paul's anguished face. "They were blackmailing you?"

He gave a brief nod. "I made a foolish mistake a couple of years ago. I got caught at a party that got out of hand. There were drugs there. And a woman. There were pictures, pictures that would have destroyed everything that mattered to me. I thought I could do this once or twice and it would be over."

"Blackmail is never over," Walker said. "It's time to come clean and put these creeps away."

Paul shook his head. "I'd rather you just shoot me," he said.

Before Walker could guess his intentions, Paul dove overboard. It was just enough of a distraction to turn the other two men brazen. Their engine revved up and the boat took off. Walker didn't hesitate. He fired, wounding first the man at the controls, then his accomplice. The boat began to spin wildly.

Suddenly there was a horrifying scream, the engine sputtered and shut down.

Walker closed his eyes. He knew what that scream meant, knew that Paul Finch had gotten his wish, that he'd been wounded by the other boat's propeller and surely would die before help could get there. He studied the murky waters but there was no sign of Finch.

He radioed for assistance even as he climbed aboard the other boat to handcuff the two suspects. After assuring himself that their injuries weren't life-threatening, he checked out the boat and found just what he'd expected—sealed, waterproof packages of marijuana, enough to destroy the lives of countless kids. An image of Gary Finch flashed in his mind, a freckle-faced kid whose dad had gotten mixed up with drug smugglers to protect his reputation, only to have it destroyed in the end anyway.

Daisy told Tucker everything she'd found out from Maribeth Finch.

"What the hell were you thinking going over there?" Tucker demanded.

"That I could help, if not you, then Gary. That boy is no drug dealer. If anything, he's been a victim of whatever's going on, too."

"Dammit, Daisy, maybe you should have taken up law instead of teaching. You'd have made a powerful ally in court."

"Only for the truly innocent, I'm afraid. Does any of this help?"

"Walker already has his eye on Finch. If what you say about them planning to leave town tomorrow is true, then we should know something soon. In the meantime, there are a few things *you* should know.''

"Such as?"

Daisy listened to Tucker's totally unnecessary explanation about Walker's absences in silence.

"He's doing his job. Why apologize to me?" she asked her brother.

"Because he asked me to." He grinned. "Actually, he asked me to put in a good word for him while I was at it."

"I wish you and Bobby and Daddy would stop trying to sell Walker to me. I'm convinced. I love him. I'm not so sure what his feelings are toward me yet." She paused and thought of their lovemaking a few nights earlier, of their conversation about children and the future. A smile tugged at her lips. "But I'm hopeful."

"Really?" Tucker said eagerly. "Wedding bells, the whole nine yards?"

"Maybe." She regarded her brother worriedly. "How do you think Daddy will take that, me marrying a Yankee?"

Tucker chuckled. "I don't think you need to worry about that."

"He's reconciled to it?"

"Actually, he's pleased as punch, mostly with himself. In fact, I think he'll take full credit for bringing you two together."

"What?"

"A word of advice? Let him have his little illusions. It'll keep the peace." He stood up. "I've got to get out of here. I'm late."

"You have a date?"

"Work," he said.

"Tucker—"

"Don't start with me." When he reached the door, he turned back. "By the way, if you were considering Walker's Yankee heritage to be part of your rebellion, I think you're up a creek. The man's as Southern as we are."

Daisy stared. "Well, I'll be. And Daddy knows?"

"Oh, yeah, but the truth is, I think he would have come around anyway. Walker's a hard guy to resist."

Yes, Daisy thought when she was alone again. Walker was definitely a hard man to resist.

Tucker was right. It was time to lay her cards on the table, time to take a risk and let Walker finally persuade her to marry him.

Of course, maybe she didn't have to rush into it. Maybe she could sit back and enjoy Walker's attempts to woo her for a few more weeks. He was getting rather good at it. Downright inspired at times. He seemed to be doing everything he could to prove that his foolish ex-wife had been wrong when she'd told him he was lousy husband material.

And as Tucker had explained earlier, now was not the time to distract him. He was doing everything he could to break up that drug-trafficking ring to make up for letting the first two suspects get away. Daisy's heart was in her throat from the time he left her house every night until he called first thing the next morning.

That decided, she went to bed after Tucker's departure, but she couldn't seem to fall asleep. When she still hadn't heard from Walker by dawn, her nerves were on edge and her heart was beating a mile a minute. She did her best to remain calm, but she was churning inside. She couldn't seem to locate Tucker, either.

When she called Bobby at the marina, he told her the boat hadn't come back in yet.

"Well, what are you doing about it?" she demanded.

"Me? It's a police matter."

"Okay, then what is the sheriff's department doing about it? Is anybody out looking for them? Never mind. I'm on my way."

She dropped Tommy off at school, called her principal and informed him he'd need to find a substitute, then headed for the marina at full speed. Her foot on the accelerator never even wavered when first one and then another sheriff's deputy took up the chase behind her, lights flashing and sirens wailing. The more, the merrier. Maybe one of the dolts chasing her could be redirected to the river to save Walker and her brother.

She skidded to a halt in the marina parking lot and bolted for the dock, aware that the two sheriff's cars were screeching into the lot right behind her. Not until she was halfway down the dock toward Bobby's boat did the first deputy catch up with her.

She whirled around to give him a piece of her mind, only to find herself staring straight into Walker's blazing eyes.

"Going somewhere, darlin'?"

She grabbed a fistful of his shirt and tried to shake him, no easy task given the difference in their sizes. "You scared me to death," she said. "Where have you been?"

"Chasing a lunatic driver through town," he said, grinning. "I guess you were worried about me?"

"Worried? *Worried?* I was *terrified.*" A tear slipped

down her cheek, followed by another and another, until they fell in a torrent.

"I'm sorry. We caught the drug traffickers last night. I was in Montross doing paperwork."

"But the boat?" she said, gesturing toward the empty slip. "It never came back."

"Docked in Colonial Beach. It was the closest place to bring them in." His expression sobered. "Bad news, though. Paul Finch is dead."

"Oh, no. Do Maribeth and Gary know?"

"Tucker's with them now. We can go over there, if you like."

"In a minute," she said, then smacked him in the chest. "Walker Ames, don't you ever do that to me again."

"Do what?"

"Not check in when you're supposed to."

"I can think of one way to make sure you know where I am at least most of the time."

"How?"

"Marry me."

This time when he suggested it, Daisy didn't care about pretty words or a romantic setting. They'd already wasted too much time to her way of thinking. "Marry me," spoken on the dock in broad daylight, would do just fine.

After all, she had a lifetime to teach him all the pretty words. It was enough for now just to know that he wouldn't have asked at all if he wasn't prepared to give her all his love.

"How soon?" she demanded.

He grinned. "In a rush, are you? I thought you Southern women liked to move at a slower pace."

"Not anymore," she said, dragging his head down until their lips touched.

By the time the kiss ended, their audience had drifted away.

"We must have embarrassed them," she said unrepentantly.

"Or they went off to find their own women," Walker said. "Being around love will do that to a man."

She framed his face in her hands and looked straight into his eyes. "You do love me, don't you?"

"More than I'd ever thought possible. And you?"

"You're everything I ever longed for."

"Not quite everything," he said, his expression serious. "I intend to give you that family, too, Daisy. We're going to have it all."

To her way of thinking, she already did.

Epilogue

Things had worked out all around in King's opinion. For a former big city cop, Walker Ames was fitting in pretty well in Trinity Harbor. And it was plain to see that he was in love with Daisy. That's all King had ever wanted, to see his daughter settled down and happy with a family of her own.

King sat proudly in the front row of the church, Frances by his side, as his daughter said the vows she had written herself. She mentioned love, honor and cherish, but he noted that she'd steered clear of mentioning anything about obeying her husband. King figured that meant Walker was in for a roller-coaster ride. Daisy did have her stubborn streak. Got it from her mother.

He didn't realized he'd murmured that last aloud until he heard a muffled hoot from Frances. He glanced over and saw the twinkle in her eyes.

"What?" he demanded.

"If Daisy inherited a lick of stubbornness from her mama, then she obviously got a double dose. You're as mule-headed as they come," Frances whispered.

King winked at her. He'd heard the unmistakable note of affection in her voice. Frances was a pistol. Had a lot of spunk for a woman her age, more than he'd ever imagined when he'd invited her out for bingo. She didn't hesitate to tell him her opinions and, goodness knows, she had a million of them. Remained to be seen how well he could live with that over the long haul, but right now it was mighty satisfying to have some lively company in the evenings.

He turned his gaze to Walker and noted that the man had the same dazed expression on his face that King had seen in the mirror on his own wedding day nearly thirty-five years ago.

And Tommy, his hair slicked back and all dressed up in a tuxedo, didn't look a thing in the world like the ruffian Daisy had taken in all those months ago. The boy had promise. King was going to be proud to call him his grandson.

In the pew across the way were Walker's own sons, two handsome little devils who couldn't sit still. King had had them out at Cedar Hill with him for a few days now, along with their mama, who wasn't doing much to hide her displeasure at this turn of events. At least she'd brought the boys up here, instead of keeping them away from their own daddy's wedding. And Daisy had taken to Walker's sons as if they were another blessing from God. She was a little more cautious about Walker's ex-wife.

King took a peek at Maribeth Finch and her boy, Gary, sitting across the aisle as well. The woman finally had a little color in her cheeks, now that all that drug business was settled. Losing her husband had been hard on her, but she was getting her life back on track, and that boy of hers was spending his fair share of time out at Cedar Hill with Tommy. King thought Gary had come through the tragedy with amazing resilience for a boy his age. Daisy and Walker had taken the pair of them under their wings, so King didn't doubt the Finches would eventually do just fine.

To his disgust, Daisy had insisted on inviting the whole blasted school board to the wedding. To his mind, every one of them should have been tarred and feathered, but maybe this was best—proof positive that they'd been a bunch of ninnies for worrying about Daisy's behavior. They wouldn't dare raise a fuss now that she was about to be a properly married woman.

King realized his attention had drifted when he heard Anna-Louise say, "I now pronounce you husband and wife."

So, he thought with satisfaction, the deed was done.

Eyes shining as brightly as King had ever seen them, Daisy tilted her head up for Walker's kiss. It was a doozy. King had to concede that the man knew how to milk a moment. He heard Frances sigh beside him and glanced down into her misty eyes.

"Don't go getting any ideas, woman," he warned.

"As if I would," she shot back. "Not with you the only prospect."

He grinned and planted a thorough kiss on her sweet mouth, just to remind her to mind her manners.

The organ music began to swell, and the bridal party started down the aisle. Daisy looked as if she were floating on air, but she paused just long enough to give King a quick peck on the cheek.

"Thank you, Daddy."

"You just be happy, darling girl. That's all the thanks I need."

"She will be," Walker promised. "I'll see to it."

"Hey, let's hurry this up," Tucker protested. "I'm ready for that fancy cake Bobby made. Eight tiers with a different filling in each one."

King winced. He would never in a million years understand why a man who could run a respectable cattle operation would choose instead to cook for a bunch of strangers. Not that it wasn't honorable work and not that Bobby hadn't made a surprising success of it, but the kitchen—no matter how big and fancy it was—was no place for a man.

He needed to do something about that, King decided as he followed his family from the church into the crisp fall afternoon. In fact, he thought maybe he'd make Bobby's situation his next project. Buoyed by the success of his meddling in Daisy's life, King felt certain he could have his eldest son married by this time next year. Might even be able to get him *raising* beef instead of *cooking* it, if he played his cards right.

Frances regarded him with sudden suspicion. "I know that look. What are you up to, King Spencer?"

"Nothing for you to worry about," he said, giving her hand a squeeze even as he surveyed the crowd to see if he could spot any likely marriage material for his son. Too old or too young, he concluded after checking out every female.

Well, it didn't matter. He'd find someone suitable. After all, he'd found Walker Ames for Daisy, hadn't he? Okay, maybe he hadn't *found* him exactly, but he'd recognized the man's potential right off. Well…maybe not *right* off, but soon enough. They were married, weren't they?

"King, over here," Walker called. "They want a family picture."

King considered squeezing himself between the bride and groom, but Walker had a pretty tight grip on Daisy's hand. King settled for his place next to his daughter. Tucker and Bobby were lined up next to him, and all the boys were down in front. His heart filled with pride.

"Best-looking family in the whole county," he declared. He glanced at Walker. "Welcome to it, Son. Took you long enough to take a hint."

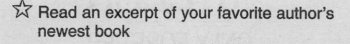

From bestselling author

JoANN ROSS

Alexandra Lyons has always been spirited and independent. But everything she believes about herself is thrown into question when she meets Eleanor Lord. The powerful matriarch is convinced that Alexandra is Anna Lord, her long-lost granddaughter and heir to a family dynasty.

Has Alexandra's life been a lie? Is she really Anna Lord—or the victim of an even darker hoax? The truth lies buried in the past, in a dark explosion of jealousy, betrayal and murder, and remains as deadly now as it was nearly thirty years ago.

LEGACY of LIES

On sale July 2001 wherever paperbacks are sold!

MIRA®

Visit us at www.mirabooks.com

MJR821

SHERRYL WOODS

| 66600 | ANGEL MINE | ___ $5.99 U.S. ___ $6.99 CAN. |
| 66542 | AFTER TEX | ___ $5.99 U.S. ___ $6.99 CAN. |

(limited quantities available)

TOTAL AMOUNT $_____
POSTAGE & HANDLING $_____
($1.00 for 1 book, 50¢ for each additional)
APPLICABLE TAXES* $_____
TOTAL PAYABLE $_____
(check or money order—please do not send cash)

To order, complete this form and send it, along with a check or money order for the total above, payable to MIRA Books®, to: **In the U.S.**: 3010 Walden Avenue, P.O. Box 9077, Buffalo, NY 14269-9077; **In Canada**: P.O. Box 636, Fort Erie, Ontario, L2A 5X3.

Name:_____
Address:_____ City:_____
State/Prov.:_____ Zip/Postal Code:_____
Account Number (if applicable):_____
075 CSAS

*New York residents remit applicable sales taxes.
Canadian residents remit applicable GST and provincial taxes.

MIRA®